SECOND FRONT

SECOND FRONT

THE ALLIED INVASION OF FRANCE:
AN ALTERNATIVE HISTORY

ALEXANDER M. GRACE, SR.

CASEMATE
Philadelphia & Oxford

Published in the United States of America and Great Britain in 2014 by
CASEMATE PUBLISHERS
908 Darby Road, Havertown, PA 19083
and
10 Hythe Bridge Street, Oxford, OX1 2EW

ISBN 978-1-61200-216-3
Digital Edition: ISBN 978-1-61200-217-0

Cataloging-in-publication data is available from the Library of Congress and
the British Library.

10 9 8 7 6 5 4 3 2 1

Printed and bound in the United States of America.

For a complete list of Casemate titles please contact:

CASEMATE PUBLISHERS (US)
Telephone (610) 853-9131, Fax (610) 853-9146
E-mail: casemate@casematepublishing.com

CASEMATE PUBLISHERS (UK)
Telephone (01865) 241249, Fax (01865) 794449
E-mail: casemate-uk@casematepublishing.co.uk

CONTENTS

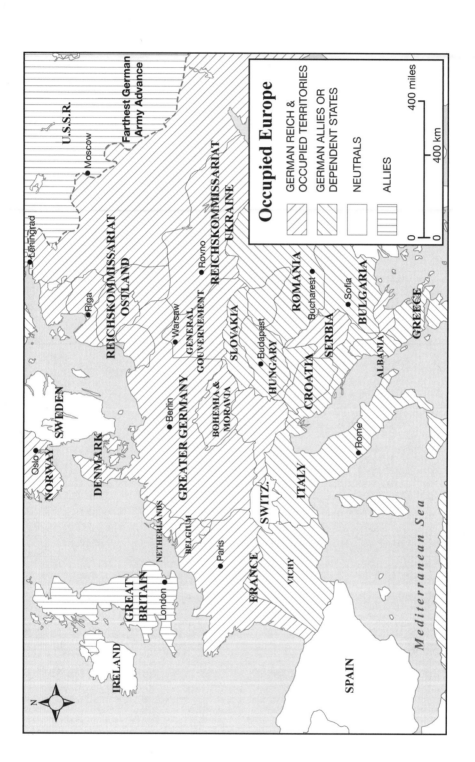

Occupied Europe

GERMAN REICH &
OCCUPIED TERRITORIES

GERMAN ALLIES OR
DEPENDENT STATES

NEUTRALS

ALLIES

0   400 km
0   400 miles

N

U.S.S.R.

Farthest German
Army Advance

Moscow

Leningrad

REICHSKOMMISSARIAT
OSTLAND

Riga

REICHSKOMMISSARIAT
UKRAINE

Rovno

Warsaw

GENERAL
GOUVERNEMENT

SLOVAKIA

ROMANIA

Bucharest

Budapest

HUNGARY

BULGARIA

Sofia

SERBIA

CROATIA

ALBANIA

GREECE

NORWAY

Oslo

SWEDEN

DENMARK

Berlin

GREATER GERMANY

BOHEMIA &
MORAVIA

SWITZ.

ITALY

Rome

NETHERLANDS

BELGIUM

Paris

FRANCE

VICHY

GREAT
BRITAIN

London

IRELAND

SPAIN

Mediterranean Sea

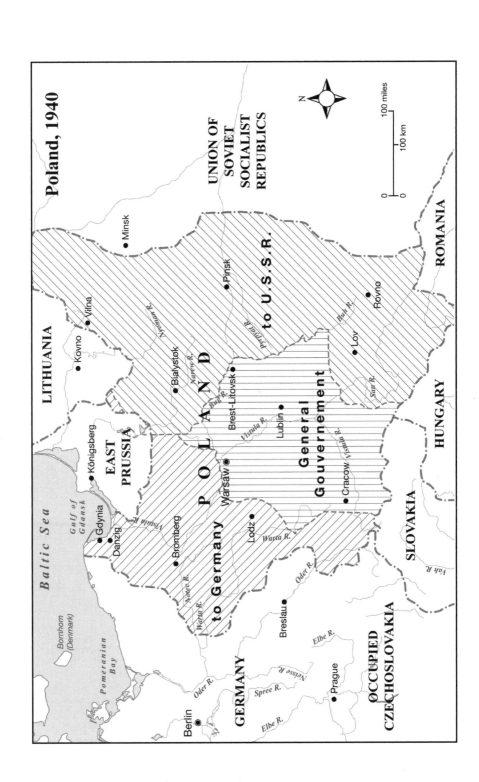

Poland, 1940

France, 1942

N

Dunkerque

Lille

Military administration of Belgium and Northern France

North-East Line

Luxembourg: annexed to the Reich in 1942

Coastal military zone 'Atlantic Wall'

Brest

Paris

OCCUPIED ZONE

German military occupation from November 1942: Northern Zone

Montoire

Territories annexed to the Reich

Strasbourg

Closed Zone Zone of German Settlement Return of refugees prohibited

Demarcation Line

Vichy
(de facto seat of government)

Lyon

Demilitarised zone (50 km)

FREE ZONE

from November 1942: Southern Zone

Bordeaux

Grenoble

Italian occupation zone

Italian occupation (Nov 1942)

Menton
(Italian occupied)

Nice

Marseille

Toulon

Corsica

Italian occupation (Nov 1942)

Ajaccio

0   100 miles

0   100 km

PROLOGUE

I F THE LINES at the movie theaters at the time of this writing are any indication, by the time this book appears in print, virtually every person in the world will have seen the motion picture *Saving Private Ryan* at least once. Apart from being just plain good cinema, this exceptional film has served the purpose of reminding the generations born since World War II just how much sacrifice our fathers and grandfathers made to defeat what was arguably the most evil regime to darken the face of the earth. The film essentially drops the viewer, as if in a glass bell, onto one corner of "Bloody Omaha" beach during the Normandy invasion, and for an intense half hour one gets a disturbing, even traumatizing, taste of the death and destruction faced by the American soldiers on that thin stretch of sand and gravel.

Beyond the scope of the film was the similar suffering of Allied soldiers in the campaigns leading up to and following D-Day. Over five hundred Allied soldiers died just clearing Vichy French troops from Algeria and Morocco in 1942, and many more fell in the fierce fighting at Salerno and in the beleaguered coastal pocket at Anzio the following year. While the Americans landing at "Utah" beach during D-Day faced far less resistance, and the British and Canadians farther to the east found the shore defenses in their sector virtually deserted, there followed weeks of desperate assaults on the heavily fortified town of Caen by the British and the agonizing advance of the Americans through the bocage country that spread throughout Normandy. Even after the breakout from the Normandy beachhead, the Allied advance across France and into Germany was crippled by the shortage of supplies brought on by the lack of a major port, with those captured from the Germans having been so thoroughly sabotaged as to require tons of munitions and thousands of reinforcements to continue to make their way ashore across the original landing beaches months after the invasion.

It is the theme of this book that none of this need have happened. Of course, a simple change in strategy would not have brought the war to a screeching halt, and many of those who died in Normandy would ultimately have died at another time and in a different place as the German Wehrmacht was painfully brought to its knees. It is my contention, however, that postponing the creation of a second front until mid-1944 and then making its centerpiece an opposed amphibious assault on the most heavily fortified portion of *Festung Europa* handed the Germans far too many advantages and greatly increased the cost of the ultimate Allied victory.

In late 1942 the Petain regime at Vichy was taking seriously Allied overtures for a French reentry to the war, but the French put up some strict and thoroughly justifiable conditions. Germany already held one million French prisoners of war as hostages within the Reich and occupied half of metropolitan France, with the unoccupied portion lying defenseless before them. Thus the French made it clear that they would not incur German wrath without at least a reasonable hope of enough Allied support to give them a fighting chance at surviving the initial German onslaught and then of reconquering their country. The most the Allies had been willing to commit was a handful of divisions to take control of French North Africa. Vichy correctly assumed that the Germans would react by seizing the rest of France, and the energetic French resistance to the Allies was prompted by the vain hope that Nazi rule would be ameliorated if at least it could be proven that the French had not simply handed over the strategically valuable territory to the Allies.

The British had opposed any talk of an early second front for some very valid reasons, the primary one being their unwillingness to see the untried American Army given its baptism of fire on the continent in the face of the full might of the battle- hardened Wehrmacht. Apart from the likely bloodbath itself, the British feared that a major defeat would dishearten the American people and cripple the war effort once and for all. Given the poor performance by the Americans in their first encounter with the Germans at Kasserine Pass, this assumption might not have been too far off the mark, although it is not generally recognized that the American forces quickly recovered from their setback and soon had the Germans on the run. It could also be argued that the American forces actually outdid the more experienced British in the Sicily campaign only a few months later.

In any event, just suppose that a deal could have ben cut with Vichy at the end of 1942. Instead of crawling ashore over the bodies of their comrades, the Allied soldiers would have poured, dry shod, onto the piers at Marseille, Toulon, and half a dozen lesser ports, ready to race inland to set up their defenses. The Germans would have reacted quickly and violently, of course, but their troops would have had to cover hundreds of kilometers of hostile territory, harassed by the Allied Air Forces, thousands of maquisards, regular French troops, and Allied paratroopers. Then, when the clash came, it would have been a meeting engagement, with both sides on an equal footing, rather than the Allies trying to batter their way through defenses on which the Germans had had years to work. It should also be remembered that this was at the height of the Battle of Stalingrad, with every spare soldier, gun, and plane already en route to the Eastern Front, and the German OKW would have had a hard time coming up with resources to face a double blow of this magnitude.

Speaking of the Eastern Front, one of the primary factors that have been identified as causes of the Cold War was the fact that Stalin understood perfectly well that Churchill really did want the Russians and Germans to continue massacring each other for as long as possible. Stalin resented every postponement of the opening of the second front and every diversion of Allied forces to peripheral targets such as North Africa and Italy. Might a determined Allied effort substantially earlier have eased Stalin's paranoia toward the West? Maybe, maybe not, but it is an interesting possibility.

That, of course, is the essence of alternative history, the acting out of some of the great "what ifs" of the past. In this work I have done considerable research into the forces available to all belligerents in late 1942. I have also made a conscious effort to avoid 20-20 hindsight and limited the actors' knowledge to what was known at the time. The book is written in every way as if it were a history compiled after the supposed events described herein, although it is technically fiction since none of this did happen. Most of the characters are historical figures in positions they might logically have occupied had events changed course, and most of the quotes are authentic statements by the participants, albeit in other circumstances. Naturally, the farther away from the historical track we wander, the more fictional this work becomes, and this is why I have chosen to cut off the discussion shortly after the ostensible end of the war, although the temptation to keep spinning the yarn was admittedly strong.

Monday morning quarterbacking is certainly easier than coming up with solutions under the pressure of events. Still, there is a tendency for us to look back and assume that the way things evolved in history was almost inevitable, and it is sometimes a worthwhile intellectual exercise to speculate on what might have happened if a different turn had been taken. I have attempted to avoid the pitfall of "Cleopatra's Nose" thinking, that is imagining the whole course of history hinging on some minor, unforeseeable event (such as how Western civilization might have changed if Cleopatra had had a huge nose, and Caesar had not fallen in love with her, and then Caesar had not been assassinated, etc., etc.). I have taken one major decision that was before the Allied commanders and simply given the choice to a different group than the one that historically prevailed, and worked from there. Hopefully, this will prompt some thought, even debate, on the part of the readers. If so, our time will not have been wasted.

CHAPTER 1

OPENING MOVES

2200 Hours, 18 December 1942
Near Marseille

L IEUTENANT COMMANDER Gregory Palmer, USN, caressed the
railing of the destroyer *Cole* as she crept through the inky waters
of the Mediterranean, barely illuminated by the ghostly light of
a crescent moon. The *Cole,* his first command, and very possibly his last he
could not help thinking, was an old four-stacker of World War I vintage, although in her day she had once held the title of fastest ship in the world with
a record speed of over 41 knots; but that was long ago. Now she was stripped
of her torpedo tubes and much of her superstructure, and her decks were
crammed with the huddled figures of a reinforced company of Rangers in
full battle gear, barely leaving the crew room enough to man their pitifully
inadequate 3-inch guns and anti-aircraft batteries. She had been chosen for
this mission, as had the similarly venerable *Bernadou* keeping pace several
hundred yards to port, neither for her speed nor her firepower, but for her
dispensability. If everything went as planned, she would not have to fire a
shot, and if it didn't, she would probably not get the chance.

Palmer scanned the silhouette of the city of Marseille, just a deeper shade
of black than the sky behind it; with only a fitful flicker of light visible here
and there, apart from the single prominent lighthouse whose beacon he only
had to keep to his starboard. Closer to, he identified a faint green light from
a picket boat that was to mark the left side of the channel through the defensive minefields, and a similar red light beyond it to mark the right side limit.
So far, so good, he thought.

The task was simple enough. Steam into Marseille, France's largest port, and one of the biggest on the continent, and capture it. He knew that powerful shore batteries ringed the port, and a fleet of several dozen warships, from submarines up to modem battleships, was based at Toulon, just a few hours' sailing time away. Aerial reconnaissance had reported the shore batteries unmanned and the French fleet at anchor at dusk, but that was at least eight hours ago, and much could have changed in the meantime. To be sure, according to the briefings he had received from Admiral Hewitt aboard the cruiser *Augusta* prior to their run in to shore, complex high-level negotiations had been going on for weeks and had finally come to an agreement by which the Vichy French government would abandon its quasi-alliance with the Axis and rejoin the war on the side of the Allies. However, the armed forces of this same Vichy government had fought against the Allies with desperate courage at Dakar and in Syria and had blatantly given German forces right of passage through Syria in support of the pro-Axis coup in Iraq in 1941. Considering how this entire operation had been on again, off again literally for months, who was to say that Marshal Petain had not had another change of heart at the last minute?

That was the primary reason for the mission of the *Cole* and the *Bemadou*. To guard against an ambush, the two old destroyers were to penetrate into the very heart of the port of Marseille and land their assault troops to occupy at least some of the shore defenses, which the French had reportedly agreed. to turn over as a sign of good faith. Palmer would then send out a coded message to the waiting Allied fleet, hundreds of ships carrying over 100,000 American, Canadian, and Polish troops and tons of munitions and supplies, signaling them to move into the port and also to land at several points along the coast. If the message failed to be received, the landings would still go forward, only with preparatory naval bombardment, under the assumption that resistance had been met.

Palmer was to steam into the entrance of the old port and land the Ranger company on the back side of the *Cap du Pharo,* where a number of coastal defense guns were emplaced, while the *Bernadou* would land her company at the *Digue du Large,* the long mole protecting the main shipping basin and the modern port facilities. With those positions in friendly hands, General Patton would have the reassurance necessary to send in the heavily laden transports.

What concerned Palmer most of all was the attitude of the French Navy.

He had heard all along that Admiral Darlan was an enthusiastic collaborator with the Germans and had been the main sticking point in the negotiations with the Allies. More importantly, the French Navy still had an ax to grind with the British, their erstwhile allies, who had launched an air attack against the partially disarmed French fleet at Mers el Kebir in Algeria, shortly after the French surrender in June of 1940. As a naval officer, Palmer understood how important it was for Britain that France's modern battle fleet not fall intact into German or Italian hands, but the deaths of more than a thousand French sailors in the one-sided slaughter brought to mind his own reaction to news of Pearl Harbor, and the Japanese had at least not been America's allies only days before. For that reason, no British troops or ships were taking part in the initial wave of landings in France, and the Allies were avoiding the naval base of Toulon altogether until after the beachhead had been secured. Hopefully, by that time, the French fleet would not only cease to be a threat but would have joined the fight against the Axis once more.

Palmer could see the squat silhouette of the *Bemadou* angling off to the left now, while he corrected his own course to swing around the looming mass of the hill on which the lighthouse stood. A dog-eared copy of a Michelin guidebook from 1932 that he kept in his cabin told Palmer that the Chateau d'If also stood atop the hill, the very place where the Count of Monte Cristo had been imprisoned. He wondered idly whether he'd have the opportunity of visiting the dungeons as a tourist or as an inmate.

Time was of the essence, he knew. There were still some eight hours of darkness left in the long winter night, but as many troops as possible needed to get ashore before dawn. There would be air cover from the Navy fighters from the carrier *Ranger* and the escort carriers *Sangamon, Suwanee,* and *Santee,* and three squadrons of Army P-40s would fly off the *Chenango* to operate from French airfields ashore, besides whatever aircraft the French themselves could get into the air; but Palmer had no illusions that the reaction from the Luftwaffe and the Italian air force would be anything less than swift and devastating. The American and British battle fleets, hopefully reinforced by the French, should be more than a match for anything the *Regia Marina* could throw at them at sea, but, until a good number of anti-aircraft batteries could be off-loaded and set up around the port, the wallowing transports would be sitting ducks for any enemy bombers that got through.

Then he saw it, a flashing light coming from the small quay that jutted out from the base of the lighthouse hill. Palmer nodded to his signalman who flashed a reply, and the destroyer swung alongside the pier with a gentle thud, just as the engines were cut. The Rangers began to clamber over cargo nets down to the quay even before the gangways could be let down, and in less than a minute, the crowded decks had been cleared, and all that could be heard was the crunching of booted feet hustling off into the darkness. His crew still manned their weapons, with even the cooks and stewards in World War I-style tin hats, gripping old Springfield rifles and setting up Lewis guns fore and aft in case of a last-minute betrayal, warily scanning the entrance to the port and the closely spaced warehouses. Palmer, throwing caution to the winds, quickly made his way down to the main deck, wanting at least to set foot on French soil.

At the foot of the gangway he saw a solitary figure, a tall man in the dark blue overcoat and white cap of a naval officer. The man saluted.

"*Commandant Jacques Martin, de la Marine Française,*" the man said matter-of-factly.

"Lieutenant Commander Gregory Palmer, USN."

"*Bien venue en France,*" the man responded with a quivering lip before he enveloped Palmer in a warm hug.

Palmer looked up to see a green flare arch upward from the crest of the hill, and another one rose up from the position of the *Bernadou* to the north. He pulled himself away from Martin and shouted over his shoulder.

"That's it, Mr. Williams. Send 'Home for Christmas.' Bring 'em on in."

"Aye aye, sir," the answer came back.

"Do you speak any English?" Palmer asked.

The Frenchman waggled his hand from side to side. "*Un petit peu.*"

"Well, come on anyway, this will be worth seeing," Palmer said jovially, jerking his thumb and jogging down the quay with Martin in tow.

They reached the tip of the headland and stopped, Palmer pointing out to sea. A pair of destroyers could be seen clearly in the moonlight, darting into the outer roads, their searchlights sweeping from side to side. Behind them came a stately column of transports. They would be carrying the 60th Regimental Combat Team of the 9th Infantry Division, a battalion of tanks from the 66th Armored Regiment, a battalion of engineers, and several batteries of anti-aircraft artillery. They would secure the port area and prepare for the reception of the rest of the expeditionary force.

As they watched, the blacked-out port area suddenly blazed with light, spreading like a burning fuse from one end of the port to the other. Floodlights bathed the immense complex of jetties and piers in a soft yellow glow, and Palmer could see trucks positioning themselves and the tiny specks of men running back and forth. The tall derricks were swinging into action, probably for the first time in months as the war had strangled maritime trade in the Mediterranean, and he could even hear the tinny sound of a brass band wafting over the water, playing the Marseillaise.

At the same time, Palmer knew that down the coast a pair of freighters flying the Polish flag would be easing into the approaches to the massive naval base at Toulon. To avoid any possible clash with the French fleet, no Allied warships were nearby, and no troops were carried, only dozens of anti-air-craft guns and tons of ammunition with which the French could beat off any intervention by the Luftwaffe in the morning. In every port, small or large, along the coast from San Tropez in the east to Perpignan in the west, small packets of transports would be pulling up to the quays, unloading a battalion or a regiment as well as mountains of supplies, making use of every foot of dock and every crane, both to speed the unloading and to avoid offering enemy air power any single target for their bombing runs. Full-scale amphibious landings were also taking place over the beaches at Frejus, hard up on the Italian-occupied zone near Cannes, and at Agde in the west, to seal off the coastal road into either end of the lodgment area, the quickest route of enemy intervention.

Seconds ticked by, then hours, and, as the first glow of dawn began to lighten the eastern sky, Palmer could see a pair of transports, already unloaded, being guided away from the pier, making room for the next relay of ships. The Allies were back on the continent in force, with over 100,000 men in this first wave alone, and, so far, not a shot had been fired.

"This just might work after all," Palmer shouted over the growling of the waves among the rocks at his feet, clapping Martin roughly on the back.

The Frenchman just nodded, hut Palmer could see that his cheeks were streaked with tears.

0200 HOURS, 19 DECEMBER 1942
OVER THE ENGLISH CHANNEL

RAF Flight Sergeant E. P. H. Peek gripped the controls of his twin-engined Mosquito fighter-bomber firmly as the aircraft was buffeted by strong gusts of air. He was flying low, low enough that the spray from the rough water in the Channel spattered against his windscreen, and hopefully low enough that German radar would not spot them. It seemed to him, however, that such drastic measures were hardly necessary, as the Germans certainly had other things to worry about tonight.

Off to his right, Peek could see the dull red glow that lit up the undersides of the scattered clouds overhead. That would be the town of Cherbourg, its defenses, and probably much of the city itself, engulfed by flames from the waves of Wellington and Lancaster bombers that had plastered the port earlier that night. It had been the largest effort of the war for the RAF, with hundreds of planes aloft, some of them, like Peek's, rushing across the Channel for a quick strike at a target near the coast, then back home to rearm and refuel for a second run. Even obsolescent Sterlings and Hudsons had been loaded up and coaxed into the air with every aircrew that could be scratched together, including training cadres and new fish fresh out of the schools. But, instead of massive thousand-plane raids that the Air Marshals had seemed to favor since Cologne earlier that year, there would be dozens of smaller raids, none of them deep into the German heartland, but all scattered across northern France, Belgium, and the Netherlands.

It was a gross violation of the principles of air warfare, as Peek had heard the officers talking about them. They should have been focusing on crippling the enemy's capability to wage war by destroying factories, refineries, and by striking terror into the civilian population. Instead, the air force was being reduced to a form of flying artillery, striking tactical targets in direct support of a ground war.

The only benefit that Peek could see was that he wasn't facing the curtains of flak and swarms of Me-110 night fighters, since most of their targets tonight would be far short of the main defensive networks the Germans had set up to screen the borders of the Reich. But these had proven to be a minimal threat to single Mosquito bombers, painted matte black and equipped with the latest "oboe" navigational and blind bombing device. Unlike the thundering clouds of heavies that charged through the enemy flak and fighters, British by night and Americans by day, the Mosquitoes flew alone, and the Germans had yet to shoot one of them down. They were just too hard to find and presented too small a target for flak to have a high chance of hitting. Of course, a single light bomber could only cause so much damage, but, with precision aiming, they could certainly throw a spanner into the operations of a single factory, one that might not merit the attentions of several wings but one that should not be allowed to continue producing ball bearings, or machine fittings, or some other vital component of the Nazi war machine. There was also the nuisance value of demonstrating to the Germans that no city, no town, was safe from air attack. The residents of Hamburg or Berlin might have come to terms with living in a bullseye, but Peek and his colleagues had the job of making sure that no one in Germany could settle down to sleep without thinking about the quickest route to the air raid shelter first.

While the large bomber formations used pathfinder squadrons that would mark their targets with incendiary bombs and "Christmas tree" flares, the "oboe" system could only be used to guide a single aircraft to its target. The idea was that a radio transponder in England would send out a signal. A circle would then be drawn around the transponder location that would pass through the location of the target. An operator at the "oboe" site could then guide an aircraft to the target, giving course corrections if the pilot drifted off the path. Since the path was only some ten meters wide, this allowed for very accurate navigation, which was, of course, supplemented by visual observation of landmarks such as rivers. The "Gee" system could guide unlimited numbers of aircraft and was used for large formations but was not nearly as accurate at this stage in the war. Since "oboe" could only handle one aircraft, it would be used for pathfinders, who would mark targets with incendiaries for the follow-on bombers, or for single plane missions such as Peek's.

On this kind of mission, all of the responsibility and pressure was, therefore, on the pilot. Peek was terrified every time he climbed into his Mosquito, but he had learned a trick as a child, a way to win the "staring game" of turning his face into a mask of ice. It would not do to let his co-pilot or anyone else know just how nervous he was during every moment of a mission. The ultimate compliment that one of them could earn was the disbelieving testimony of a colleague that he had ice water in his veins. Consequently, Peek merely grunted in reply, glad that his flight gloves did not permit anyone to see that his knuckles must have been bone white as he grasped the steering wheel with all his might.

They passed the juncture of the Sarthe and the Loire, and Peek dropped down even lower, right into the riverbed. There would be no chance of missing the bridge at this height, although he might crash into it if he didn't see it soon enough. They roared over a small skiff in midstream, and even in the ghostly moonlight Peek clearly saw a small figure dive into the bottom of the boat.

"I'll bet that shook the cobwebs out of his head," Peek chuckled. "Teach him that the worm is not the only thing that the early bird is likely to get."

They followed the river in a gentle bend around to the northeast and, suddenly, there was the bridge, a tall double span with the squat forms of flak towers at either end. Peek jerked the steering column up and to the left, soaring over the treetops and angling to approach the bridge from the north. The only way to have a decent chance of hitting a bridge was to run along its length rather than perpendicular to it, so that bombs dropped a little short or long would still have a chance of damaging the structure. He banked hard again and lined up along the rail line that ran over the bridge, the rails dully gleaming in the moonlight, and armed his bombs for release.

The bridge was easy enough to find now, since the garrison had obviously heard the approach of the Mosquito, and now golden fingers probed the sky as searchlights swept back and forth seeking a target. Peek had had to gain altitude so that his aircraft would not be shredded by the blast of his own bombs, and this would give the enemy a chance to pick him out against the sky. But there were only seconds to go now. Peek pressed his forehead against the rim of the bombsight and turned control of the aircraft over to his co-pilot, watching the ground rush by below as streams of yellow and red tracers crisscrossed all about them. Then he released the toggle switch, and the plane bucked upward, suddenly relieved of four thousand pounds of dead weight, and, only seconds afterward, it bucked again as the shock wave of the explosion reached them.

Peek should have immediately dropped back down to treetop level to effect his escape, but he couldn't resist one last high bank over the river to study his handiwork. There would be too many targets hit tonight for his to rate a visit by a Spitfire equipped with reconnaissance cameras, and he needed to know if a second raid would be required. He could see a fire raging at one end of the bridge, possibly where a bomb had caught a vehicle in the act of crossing, but the most important result was that one span of the bridge could be clearly seen slumped into the churning water of the river. No enemy troops would be using this bridge for some time. Peek smiled even as a burst of flak peppered the side of his fuselage, and smoke began to pour from his starboard engine.

He grimly grasped the controls once more and began the long process of nursing his injured ship back home.

0230 Hours, 19 December 1942
Cornwall, England

Colonel William C. Bentley, Jr., commander of the 2nd Battalion, 509th Airborne Infantry was jerked out of an exhausted sleep as the engines of the C-47 roared to life, and the heavily laden machine began to lumber over the airstrip in Cornwall, picking up speed. The rush of cold air through the open doorway was a relief after hours of sitting, crammed into the cargo bay of the plane along with twenty-two other paratroopers, waiting for word that the operation was "go." The plane had been filled with the stench of sweat, aviation fuel, and the results of at least one of the men having a nervous stomach, so even the frigid draft was welcome. He craned his neck and could see out the door, row upon row of C-47s and C-46s, everything that could be made airworthy, as they taxied into position for take-off.

This would not be the kind of invasion that Bentley had envisioned, or for which his troops had been training for months. They would not be dropping into France after all but would land and disembark on supposedly friendly airfields, like a batch of damned passengers, Bentley thought disgustedly. While this meant that the paratroopers would not have to be burdened with the weight of two chutes each, this was small comfort to Bentley, since the extra cargo capacity was made up now with bundles of ammunition, demolitions equipment, and fuel cans, all of which would explode if given half a chance. And heading out across the length of occupied France in an unarmed plane loaded with pyrotechnics and *no* chute was distinctly not what Bentley had signed up for.

He knew that the Luftwaffe would, theoretically, be kept busy by the largest air operation in history, with hundreds of bombers and fighters fanning out to hit airfields and troop concentration areas all across Northern France and to blast a path through Nazi anti-aircraft positions all the way through to the target. Dozens of other fighters would be accompanying the troopships to take up position at new fields inside France, but it still all seemed like a lot of trouble to go to just to place himself and his men right in the path of the expected onrushing tide of the Wehrmacht. It would be their job to buy time, alongside the ragtag French "Armistice Army," for the ground pounders to get ashore and establish a beachhead in the south.

The plan was to land the hastily organized American 82nd Airborne Division, to which the 509th was attached, and the British 1st Airborne in a rough ring comprising about half of unoccupied France. The two divisions were reinforced with engineer, anti tank, and light artillery units to a total of well over 20,000 men, the largest airborne operation in history, but their role would be in a multitude of isolated, individual actions, scattered over hundreds of miles. The paratroopers would help the French set up roadblocks in the rough terrain shielding the Mediterranean coast and to drop dozens of bridges over the rivers which crisscrossed the area in order to slow up the advance of German troops from the north and the Italians from the east. The British would be centered in the gap between the Pyrenees and the Massif Central around Carcassonne, blocking off access to the lodgment area from the west, and the 82nd would be concentrated in the narrowest point in the broad Rhone River valley near Valence-surRhone, the most obvious avenue of invasion for the Germans coming from the north, with detachments positioned at key road junctions throughout the Massif Central and the French Alps. Between the 82nd and the French, it was hoped that they could put up enough resistance to force the Germans to halt and deploy and maybe make an assault river crossing or two, which would, ideally take enough time for advanced elements of the 2nd Armored Division to race north from Marseille and back them up.

Unfortunately, the French Army had virtually no armor or artillery, the very things that airborne forces also traditionally lacked, and the very things most necessary to give the defenders some chance in a stand-up fight against the German panzers. When the plan had first been laid out to the paratroopers some weeks ago, this situation had prompted Major General Matthew B. Ridgway, the newly-promoted commander of the 82nd, to comment that it appeared the paratroopers were not just being asked to die, but to take long enough doing it that a line could be established behind them.

The plan also called for the paratroopers to fall back if necessary in the face of overwhelming enemy pressure. The problem with this, Bentley knew, was that, while airborne forces possessed great *strategic* mobility, being able to deploy from England to the center of France in a matter of hours, once they were on the ground, they reverted to their role as the straightest of "straight leg" infantry, with virtually no motorized support. Although much of their initial line from Le Puy-en-Velay in the west to Grenoble in the east, some ninety miles or more, was protected by the fast-moving Isere River, if the German panzers ever broke through at any point, the paras would never be able to move quickly enough to avoid being surrounded and cut off.

These thoughts, as well as memories of home, crowded Bentley's mind during the bumpy flight across the Channel. The aircraft were flying low in an effort to avoid detection by enemy radar, and, between dozes, he thought he could see the occasional lights of a town passing by in the darkness below. He squinted at his watch and estimated that, if they stuck to their flight path, they should be landing just before dawn. There would be just time enough to unload and get the precious C-47s refueled and aloft again, and hopefully well on their way home before the Luftwaffe got wind of what was afoot and chewed them to pieces on the ground. Ideally, those aircraft that survived the return flight would then be available to ferry in reinforcements and supplies, although Bentley had little hope of such flights getting through a second time. They would be lucky if they made this one trip, having taken the Germans by surprise, but it would be too much to ask to expect a repeat performance. No, if there were going to be salvation for the airborne, it would be coming up the road from the south.

The C-47 heeled over in a stomach-wrenching turn as the pilot lined up on the landing strip, and Bentley gripped his M-1 carbine tightly. He had heard from the pilot that there had been reports over the radio that a flight of British troop carriers had run into fighters near Bordeaux and had lost some planes, but their own group had arrived on target unscathed. It now only remained to land on a grass strip, lit only by the headlamps of trucks lined up on either side, and Bentley could see a number of his men nervously crossing themselves or cupping folded hands to their chins in prayer. There was a risk in any night landing, especially with no control tower for guidance, no one to keep the dozens of arriving planes from plowing into each other, but even so, they had it lucky. Some of the men and most of the heavier equipment, the 75mm howitzers and anti-tank guns, would be landing in the large Waco or Horsa gliders towed by C-47s. Any irregularity in the ground could send one of the big planes cartwheeling end over end, smashing everyone and everything aboard in seconds.

Then, with a sudden bounce, they were down. Bentley levered himself upright in the doorway, watching the grassy field pass by more and more slowly. He leaned out the door and could see the shape of a small car bouncing along ahead of the plane, a red filtered flashlight waving wildly out one window as it guided the pilot to a parking area at the edge of a grove of trees.

As soon as the aircraft pirouetted to a stop, Bentley was out the door, banging on the side of the fuselage with his rifle butt and shouting for the men to grab their gear and head out. They stumbled off under impossibly heavy loads of supplies and ammunition to where each company commander was rallying his men. Considering the chaos around him now, with the roar of airplane engines layered over that of the shouts of hundreds of men and the rattle of their equipment, the semi-darkness, and the unfamiliar terrain, Bentley could only imagine the confusion a night drop into hostile territory might bring, platoons scattered over miles of ground, many of them injured by the fall or tangled in trees, with enemy troops hunting them down all the while. Perhaps he could wait to experience that sort of thrill after all. He took one final glance in the cargo bay of the aircraft, then gave the "thumbs up" signal to the crew chief. The man smiled broadly and reached out to shake Bentley's hand even as the co-pilot tossed down the hose of a tanker from the wing, where they had hand-pumped a few precious gallons of fuel for the return flight, and the plane began to taxi for take-off. Bentley hustled to get out of the way of the tail and then jogged over to a well-lit cluster of farmhouses where the division command post was being set up.

There were already half a dozen battalion commanders gathered around a long table set up in a barn. The table was covered with maps, and General Ridgway, looking too young for Bentley's peace of mind, stood at one end in a hushed conversation with his deputy commander and what appeared to be a senior French officer. Bentley had heard voices shouting in something other than English out on the airfield, and he had assumed that the trucks out there had been driven by Frenchmen, but this was his first clear sight of their new allies. The officer looked to be in his early fifties and wore a neatly trimmed moustache, one of those stiff, round kepi hats, and a dress uniform bedecked with medals. The Americans looked like a mob of janitors in their baggy green fatigues by comparison, and they hadn't even been in combat yet.

Ridgway looked up and crooked a finger in Bentley's direction.

"Bill, get over here," he growled over the din which still filtered in from outside as more planes came and went. He pressed the map flat with the palms of his hands and jabbed a finger at a spot he had circled in red. "Things have already started to go to Hell in a hand basket. The better part of two companies of the 325th Glider Infantry didn't make it. Got misdirected somehow and ran low on fuel. Had to turn back. That leaves our left flank way too weak."

He pointed to the town of St. Etienne on the upper Loire River.

"I'm going to have the bulk of the 325th hold the crossing at Le Puy-en-Velay after they drop the bridge there, but there won't be enough of them to hold Yssingeaux as well. If the Germans make it to St. Etienne, they can either drive straight south to the Rhone to work downriver on the right bank, or they can go east to do an end run and get in behind the 325th *and* swing down here and turn our whole line. The ground's pretty rough up there, so they're going to be limited to the roads, but we've got to stop them."

"But what about the heavy stuff the 325th was bringing to stop the panzers? All my men have are bazookas and some 60mm mortars."

"What little they've got, they'll need. The good news is that Colonel d'Ormeson here," he gestured to the Frenchman who gave a crisp open palmed salute which Bentley returned casually, "says that their 92nd Infantry Regiment, more like one of our battalions really, and a battery of 75mm guns will be arriving at St. Etienne about now to back you up. They even have a couple of armored cars and an old tank or two that they had squirreled away in an old mine shaft for just such an occasion."

"Our tanks are hardly the last word in technology," the Frenchman added in heavily accented English. "We have a couple of H-35s armed with machine guns and a Somua. At least they look like tanks, and our 75s, firing over open sights, are quite capable of dealing with a tank, *if* there are not too many of them."

"Glad to have you on the team, Colonel," Bentley grinned. "But," he continued, turning back to Ridgway, "we're here at Valence, and this place must be forty miles away. I'd sure like to be there well before the Germans start to show up, but it looks like an awful long walk."

"The French also stashed a number of trucks and some gas. If you get your men mounted up PDQ, you can be up into the hills and trees before full daylight and in position before noon. The French will be blowing every bridge in the northern part of the Vichy zone about now, and the air force is plastering all the railroad marshalling yards and rolling stock they can find, so, even if the Germans move fast, we might have as much as a couple of days before we even see one of their coal scuttle helmets down here."

"Let's hope so, General," Bentley sighed. "Let's hope so."

0300 Hours, 19 December 1942
Paris, France

It was nearly dawn on the 13th of December, but Admiral Wilhelm Franz Canaris, Director of the Abwehr, the German military intelligence service, was still poring over the stacks of agent reports which littered the desk of the office he had commandeered in the Gestapo headquarters on the *Place de Ia Concorde* in Paris. As was always the case with important intelligence discoveries, the information was of varying quality, limited detail, and often from questionable sources. To make matters worse, much of it was contradictory, and it would be vital for Canaris to sort through this muddle in order to present as clear a picture as possible to the Führer and the High Command. The only thing of which Canaris could be absolutely certain was that something big was happening, and decisive action would have to be taken soon if the Reich was not to face disaster.

For weeks Canaris had been receiving reports from his network of spies in England and the United States of hurried mobilization of troops, the gathering of supplies, intensified amphibious training for infantry units, and a heightened level of security surrounding all military installations. That implied a major operation, but did not in itself indicate either timing or the target. Then he had received word that thousands of troops, mostly American, but also British, Polish, and Free French, had been loaded onto transports in England, the east coast of the United States, and in Egypt.

Those men could not be kept at sea indefinitely, although they could simply be transferred from one area to another, and could even be disembarked at their ports of origin, but that hardly seemed likely with Montgomery in the midst of a continuing, if lethargic pursuit of Rommel in North Africa after the British victory at El Alamein. This was no time for pulling front line troops out of action for simple training.

Then reports had started to come in from the garrisons along the Channel coast. Small-scale enemy commando raids were at an all-time high, attempting to destroy the coastal defense guns, blow up beach obstacles, or simply to gather intelligence about the still-weak fortifications going up all the way from Amsterdam to Brest.

There were frequent shellings by British naval craft, and daily overflights by swarms of enemy reconnaissance aircraft, focusing on the Cotentin Peninsula in Normandy and on the Pas de Calais, the closest point of occupied France to England and the most likely for a cross Channel invasion. While the Führer was certain that any Allied offensive in the West would come at Calais, some of the freer thinkers on the general staff favored Normandy as an invasion site, precisely because Calais was already the most heavily fortified and the most obvious point of attack. The Allies had, after all, virtually total control of the seas now that the U-boats of Admiral Dönitz had been crippled in the Atlantic by improved enemy anti-submarine tactics, and they were hardly limited to making a mere 20-mile jump.

But there were also disturbing reports coming from the extensive German network of informers within both the Vichy government and the resistance movement throughout France. These reports spoke of surreptitious meetings between senior French officials and the Americans, focusing on France possibly reentering the war on the Allied side. In themselves, such talks did not disturb Canaris unduly. Rumors of this sort had been rife since France's surrender in 1940. What caught Canaris' attention was the wide range of sources, from right-wing French Army officers to Gaullist rebels to Communist resistance fighters, and the consistency of their conclusion that some sort of arrangement had been made between Vichy and the West.

Canaris had passed along these concerns to his superiors, but the Führer had tended to discount them. Hitler was convinced of his personal domination over key Vichy figures, notably Prime Minister Pierre Laval. Hitler had argued, or simply declared, since the Führer did not deign to argue with underlings, that he had the ultimate trump card over Vichy in the form of more than a million French prisoners of war still being held in Germany, to say nothing of Paris and half their national territory and population. Time and again the French had knuckled under to increasingly onerous and demeaning demands from Germany for the provision of raw materials, industrial goods, and what amounted to slave labor under the STO, *Service de Travaille Obligatoire*. As leverage, the Führer had either offered up the possibility of a release of prisoners or threatened to worsen their conditions. Hitler had also found it effective to threaten to install a *gauleiter,* or German military governor, for all of France, as he had done in Poland, thus ending the fiction of Vichy independence, and this had always struck home with Marshal Petain whenever it had proved necessary to turn the old warhorse away from a dangerous course of action. No, the Führer could not be persuaded that his Vichy puppets would ever turn against him.

Canaris ultimately tended to agree with Hitler on this, even though he could not help but question the loyalty of a state which Germany continually humiliated. His faith lay instead with Admiral Jean François Darlan. As commander of the French Navy, Darlan had little cause to love the Allies, especially the British, after the massacre of French seamen at Mers-el-Kébir and the violent seizure of all French ships that found themselves in British ports at the time of France's surrender. Like many French sailors, Darlan had seen the British action not as one of desperation by the one power left facing the. armed might of victorious Germany, but one of arch betrayal Britain had left the French to do all of the fighting on land, then turned and stabbed her in the back just the way the Soviets had turned on the Poles. The attacks on Dakar and the French mandate in Lebanon and Syria had only reinforced this view. The British did not care what price France might have to pay as long as Britain had something to gain. Therefore, Darlan would never accede to any new alliance in which Britain was the senior partner, while the Americans, with no combat experience and relatively few troops yet available, could hardly aspire to leadership of the coalition at this point. And the French could not afford to bet everything, their very existence, on anything less than a certainty. If they threw in their lot with the Allies, and the Germans were then able to defeat a half-hearted effort to establish a foothold on the continent, France would be at Hitler's mercy, and mercy was a commodity in very short supply in the Reich these days.

That had been the dilemma of German intelligence over the past several weeks, but now, in the last few hours, alarming reports had begun to arrive of actual Allied landings. There had been sightings of large enemy convoys passing Gibraltar, entering the Mediterranean, but these could have been new shipments of supplies for Montgomery's army in Egypt, like the 300 American tanks that had been delivered in one fell swoop the previous summer. Then a new report had arrived via radio from a clandestine transmitter in England. The informant there had confirmed the identity of the deceased colonel, right down to the date of his disappearance during a flight from England to Gibraltar, his post of assignment, even a good physical description. There had also been a subsequent report from Spain, in answer to a series of pointed questions he had personally drafted for Stohrer. An examination by a forensic pathologist had confirmed, as nearly as possible, that the deceased colonel had apparently died of exposure, probably after having survived the crash landing only to perish in the cold waters off the Bay of Biscay. Even his pockets had been searched and had produced a convincing pile of litter, all that remained of a human life, a pair of theater ticket stubs, an unpaid telephone bill, photographs of the colonel with his family, and a half-written letter to the lady who was now his widow, hardly the stuff of a fabrication by British intelligence. The key element was that chained to the colonel's wrist was a briefcase containing detailed plans for a cross-Channel invasion at Calais.

Now, taken with the evidence of the naval bombardment of the Channel coast, and reported enemy landings there, it was apparent that any action by the enemy in the Mediterranean was meant only as a diversion to the main act in the north. The captured plans were genuine, and the Germans now had a unique opportunity to make their own preparations in the sure knowledge of the enemy's intentions.

Canaris packed up his papers and dashed down the broad marble stairs of the building and across the cobblestone street to the headquarters of Field Marshall Gerd von Rundstedt, Commander-in-Chief West, which was located in the former French Ministry of the Navy. Even though he would not be out of sight of the heavily armed guards of the two headquarters buildings, Canaris took a long look up and down the street before rushing across. He was not concerned with traffic, which was light at the best of times in a city starved for gasoline, and non-existent at this pre-dawn hour. But there was no guarantee that a Gaullist or Communist assassin might not have been waiting for just such a chance to decapitate the German intelligence service, even at the cost of his own life.

There was no wild-eyed terrorist on the comer, however, and Canaris barged past the Wehrmacht guards. He was not surprised to find the field marshal awake, poring over maps of France and the Mediterranean while a swarm of junior and senior staff officers buzzed about him, carrying messages, talking on telephones, and arguing quietly in the corners of the room. The interview took only a few minutes, since Canaris had been keeping Rundstedt apprised of his efforts to validate the Spanish lead for some time. In any event, the visit was mostly a courtesy, since the ultimate decision on releasing the armored reserves would have to be made by the Führer himself.

The one thing that he did obtain from von Rundstedt was approval to go ahead with Operation RAVEN. Since it was apparent that the Allies were doing something big whether it proved to be in the north of France, the south, in North Africa, or a combination of the three, RAVEN would enhance Germany's strategic position. What was more, it would have to be carried out in the next few hours, or the window of opportunity would close for good.

Von Rundstedt growled at a young captain who quickly called for Canaris' car to take him to the small Storch aircraft that awaited him at the airfield at Le Bourl northeast of the city. Before noon he would be in the Wolfschanze, the Wolf's Lair, Hitler's secret headquarters in East Prussia from which the entire war in Russia was being directed. They would now know where to move the panzer reserve now and would throw the attackers back into the sea just as easily as they had at Dieppe that past summer. If this landing was on as large a scale as it appeared, a resounding defeat for the Allies now might secure the coast from a new threat of invasion for years to come. This had been the best day's work Canaris had done in a long while. Although the intelligence chief had begun to have serious doubts about whether the war could be won, ever since the failure of the Wehrmacht to take Moscow a year before, and although he had begun to pull together a small circle of officers with a view to removing Hitler from power and ultimately achieving a negotiated settlement with the Allies, Canaris had taken no overt steps as yet. If a major victory could be gained now, he would just swallow his pride and continue to bask in the sun of Nazi glory.

It only remained that Admiral Darlan live up to his often-repeated promises to defend French territory from all comers. The Wehrmacht would take care of the landings in the north. Let Vichy's French Army in Morocco and Algeria, and its navy, both of which had been left in much better fighting trim than the forces in metropolitan France, take on the burden of fighting any Allied incursions there. Win or lose, the bloodshed would stand to poison France's relations with the Western Allies to the point that Petain might finally take the plunge and formally join the Axis as an active participant. Let the Allies have a few hundred miles of sand populated by camels and Arabs. Canaris would take the French fleet in exchange any day.

Canaris had every reason to believe that a French alliance was in the offing. Following the French surrender in June 1940, the British Mediterranean Fleet had presented itself off the Algerian port of Mers-el-Kébir where the French fleet had taken refuge. As part of the ceasefire agreement with Germany, the French had removed their combat ships to the safety of North Africa but had promised to disarm and mothball them there. The British, however, were understandably concerned that, with over one million French prisoners of war as hostages, to say nothing of the population of Metropolitan France, the Germans might well alter the terms and demand surrender of the fleet to them. While the French fleet was small compared to Britain's, if combined with the Italian and German navies, it might well enable the Axis to drive the British from the Mediterranean, and possibly even force a passage for the German Army across the English Channel. This could not be left to chance.

Consequently, on orders from Churchill, the British demanded that the

French fleet either come out and continue the war alongside the British, or scuttle itself then and there. The French commanders, again thinking of the millions of hostages in German hands, could not agree to violate their peace terms and refused. The British attacked. With aircraft and naval gunfire, they pounded the partially disarmed French ships, sinking most of them and killing nearly 1,300 French sailors. Several French cruisers and destroyers managed to escape to Toulon, and the French, for their part, refused to fire back at their erstwhile allies. Needless to say, the attitude in the Petain government was hardly sympathetic to the British from this point on.

As commander-in-chief of the French Navy, and with this background, the Germans were confident that Darlan would resist any inclination to side with the Allies as rumors began to accumulate that the Anglo-Americans were planning something big for the near future. The Gaullist officers within the Vichy military were also aware of this and of Darlan's considerable influence over the actions of the aged Marshal Petain. Consequently, as part of their effort to lay the groundwork for the Allied plan, a conspiracy arose to remove Darlan from the equation.

A young naval officer, Lieutenant Michel de Rostelon, was part of Darlan's staff and had been an important source of information for the Gaullists on the inner workings of the Vichy military. He was now selected to deal with the Admiral. While physical security around Darlan was not particularly strict, it would have been highly risky for an assassin, even one with access, to simply carry in a weapon and use it. Since de Rostelon knew Darlan's daily routine, however, he devised his own plan to take the Admiral outside his offices when he left the building to go home for lunch. The brisk day made wearing an overcoat unremarkable, and de Rostelon put his on, leaving his right arm, in which he held an automatic pistol, inside the coat while that sleeve was stuffed with rags, inserting the tip of the sleeve into the coat pocket, leaving his right arm free on the inside to grasp the weapon. He stood in the shadows of a doorway across the street from the side entrance to Darlan's headquarters and waited.

Shortly before dawn, Darlan emerged, accompanied by one of his aides. Darlan was a dapper little man, clean-shaven, with a crown of white hair under his naval cap. He had more of the look of a small town mayor than the most powerful man in Vichy France. He was talking jovially with his aide about something, and the smile on his face, when he had just ordered hundreds, if not thousands, of young Frenchmen to their deaths in the interests of his own personal power, by resisting the Allied landings, simply made de Rostelon all the more resolved on his course of action. He strode across the street, heading straight toward Darlan, who was waiting for his aide to open the door of his staff car. Darlan looked up and squinted in the dim light of the street lamp, then frowned at the sight of the young officer he knew should have been several miles away on a vital mission.

De Rostelon threw open his coat and fired a long burst from his MAT submachinegun at less than five yards range. The aide, who had his back to de Rostelon was hit in the shoulder, and another bullet shattered the window on the car door as the nervous assassin struggled to control his weapon, but Darlan took half a dozen rounds full in his chest. He staggered back, a look of astonished disbelief on his face as de Rostelon fired again, bowling the admiral over into the gutter. De Rostelon let the weapon clatter to the pavement and took a step forward to see if he could help the wounded aide, but the two tall spahis standing guard at the doorway did not wait to investigate, both firing their antiquated carbines from the hip as they charged down the stairs. The unfortunate aide was hit again, this time in the leg, as he tried to crawl into the car for safety, but de Rostelon was struck several times, any one of which would likely have proved fatal.

No group took official credit for the assassination, but a subsequent search of de Rostelon's quarters turned up copies of reports he had prepared for passage to the FTP. Darlan's orders to the fleet were also recovered from the body and turned over to General Giraud, who had just been named commander-in-chief of the French Armed Forces. Giraud stored the document in his personal safe and told no one. He did, however, order trusted units of the *gendarmerie* to begin the round up of dozens of known Gaullist officers throughout Vichy territory in both metropolitan France and in North and West Africa. De Rostelon's action had not only eliminated one of Giraud's primary rivals for power, but had inadvertently given him a valuable weapon in his competition with another.

0430 HOURS, 19 DECEMBER 1942
LE MANS, FRANCE

Jean Paul Belmont had been planning to move to the unoccupied zone of France for some time. He would then find a way to cross the border into Spain, thence to Portugal, and ultimately to get to a ship headed for England where he could finally join the Free French forces of General de Gaulle. Although Belmont had been a reservist in 1940, his unit had only just been called up when the Third Republic collapsed and the surrender was signed, so he had never fought for his country as he had longed to do. Since he was young and unmarried, Belmont had no strong ties to his hometown and no relatives on whom the Germans could take out their vengeance if he fled, so there seemed little reason for him to stay. However, his control officer in the FFI, the French Forces of the Interior, the Gaullist resistance, which he had joined almost as soon as it had been formed over a year ago, had prevailed upon him time and again to remain at his post, that of mechanic in the motor pool of the 3rd Panzer Grenadier Division based in Le Mans. They had explained that the information he had been able to provide on the strength levels of this and other Wehrmacht divisions had been far more valuable than any contribution he could make as a simple rifleman in North Africa. Now, inexplicably, Belmont had been told that, in exchange for one final operational act, he would not only be allowed to leave, but the FFI would facilitate his escape to Vichy territory. When he learned what they wanted of him, it became apparent to Belmont that, once he had done the job, he would have no choice but to leave.

At the end of his normal workday, at 1800 hours the previous evening, instead of joining the gaggle of lethargic French workers shuffling out the gates of the military base, Belmont had hidden in a storeroom behind one of the garages. The German guards were always scrupulous about checking the identity papers of all workers as they came to work in case some saboteur should attempt to enter with them, but they had never paid much attention to those leaving. He had made himself as comfortable as possible, peering out the grimy window of the room in the early winter darkness as the pace of activity at the base gradually diminished and the troops retired to their barracks. He pulled a small sandwich and half-bottle of rough red wine from his rucksack and fortified himself for the night's work.

At about 2200 hours, Belmont checked to see that he had the few items he required in his bag: an awl, a mallet, a small can of putty, a bag of sugar, a roll of electrical tape, and a pair of wire shears. Then he listened at the door of the room before slipping into the cavernous garage bay.

The garage was crowded with trucks, half-tracks, tanks, and little kubelwagons undergoing routine maintenance. He needed no light to find the gas tank of each vehicle. Then he used the awl and mallet to punch a small hole near the bottom of each tank, quickly stopping the leak with a wad of putty and moving on to the next. The gas containers of the Panzer IIIs and IVs were too sturdily constructed for him to penetrate without heavier tools, and make much too much noise, so he limited himself to unscrewing the gas cap and pouring a measure of sugar into each one. In terms of damage to the vehicles, it would have been preferable to do this to the trucks and half-tracks as well, but even the all-pervasive FFI had only so much influence, and they had been lucky to have been able to procure a single kilo of sugar in these hard times. As he moved from one vehicle to another, Belmont greedily licked the stray sugar crystals from his fingers like a guilty child.

The division had over three hundred tanks and hundreds of other vehicles, so there was no way that Belmont could sabotage all of them, but he made certain to check the fender markings carefully and to hit a few vehicles from each battalion. He finished in the first garage, then moved on to another, carefully sticking to the shadows between the buildings. Most of the sentries were concentrated around the perimeter of the base and the level of alert was low, but he could never have explained his presence if he should happen to stumble across a stray officer or NCO running a late errand, and he had no illusions about the kind of treatment he would receive at the hands of the Gestapo if he were caught. He had heard stories of resistants being cooked alive, hung from meat hooks, or skinned by their German interrogators in basement dungeons. When he had done all that he could indoors, he moved through the ranks of the parked vehicles outside, crawling on his belly from one to the next.

Now, after working for over six hours, he was done. If the division were mobilized and sent on a road march, the tank engines with sugared gas would seize up within a few hours, probably ruined for good. On the trucks and half-tracks, the putty would soon work itself out of the hole, and they would all begin to pour precious gasoline out onto the highway. It was very likely that many of them would simply be refilled when they ran low, wasting more fuel, before someone noticed a leak and then noticed how many of them there were. This would require a halt and some hasty repair work, as well as an inspection of all of the other vehicles, probably out on the road where they would be vulnerable to Allied air attack. Naturally, suspicion would fall on the French mechanics drafted into the German service, but Belmont would be long gone by then. In fact, this would undoubtedly help protect his fellow workers, as the finger would inevitably point at the missing man. This eased Belmont's conscience somewhat, although there was still the distinct possibility that the Germans would take and shoot hostages when the guilty party was not found. They'd done this often enough before. He gritted his teeth and pulled the shears from his bag.

Now came the truly difficult part. There was a broad open area on each side of the perimeter fence of the base. While this was hardly a prison camp, there were watchtowers at frequent intervals equipped with spotlights, and patrols, some of them equipped with machine guns. Belmont had no intention of making this a suicide mission, although he had accepted the possibility that he might well not survive. His main concern in getting away cleanly was to avoid falling alive into German hands where he had no doubt that the Gestapo interrogators would be able to extract from him any information about his own actions that day and anything else of value about the FFI. That must be avoided at all costs.

Fortunately, unlike in a prison camp, the guards here were focused on keeping people from getting *in* not out, so their attention, assuming they were not asleep, would be toward the farthest treeline, not the interior of the base. Belmont had given this considerable thought over the past weeks, and he had identified a bit of dead ground near the base of one of the towers. He waited until the searchlights were pointed elsewhere and briskly strolled up to the fence, then dropped to the ground. He cut the lower strands of wire with the snips he had carried in his pocket and crawled through. Again, he waited until the lights swung away and dashed for a small depression about twenty yards beyond the fence and threw himself flat. Again he waited, his heart pounding in his chest, but there were no shots, no cries of alarm. He now crawled on his belly, inch by inch along the depression, every moment expecting his back to be torn open by a bullet, until he finally reached the end of the cleared ground and dragged himself under the welcome cover of some bushes. He got up on one knee and peered over the bushes. The base was ablaze with lights, and he could see crowds of men pouring out of the barracks. The shouted orders of the sergeants came to him in scraps on the wind as the soldiers hastily formed into platoons and companies.

His first thought was that his work had been discovered and that the entire division had been called out to search for him, but it soon became apparent that the perimeter guards were not part of this general alert. Men were forming human chains to load crates and jerry cans onto the vehicles, and the drivers were gunning their engines in preparation for departure. He had seen this often enough, when elements of the division moved out for field exercises, but never on this scale. No, it seemed as though the division was being mobilized and sent on a mission. This must have been why he had been ordered to act tonight, not yesterday, not tomorrow, not when he thought best, but absolutely tonight! The FFI had anticipated this move, and his action was meant to thwart it.

Belmont's breast began to swell with pride. Imagine! He had just crippled a Panzer Grenadier division all by himself! Of course, his sabotage could be fixed, and he had not reached even a third of the vehicles, but the Germans might be going into battle and would find, to their chagrin, that a large percentage of their fighting power was gone, to say nothing of their mobility. He was well aware that most of the transport for the German infantry divisions was provided by simple draft horses, just as it had been for centuries, and it was only the relatively few mechanized divisions, like this one, that gave the Wehrmacht its famed and feared armored fist. Well, it would be missing a finger this time, Belmont thought.

He stood up erect and dug in his pocket for a cigarette. He lit it, contemptuous of the guard towers now and flicked the match in the direction of the base with a sneer, just before he slapped one palm down on the inner elbow of his opposite arm and raised his fist in an angry salute. He then slung his rucksack over his shoulder and sauntered off through the forest.

0500 HOURS, 19 DECEMBER 1942
NEAR CALVI, CORSICA

Major General Pierre Koenig cupped his hand over his mouth as his stomach churned. After more than a year of fighting in the waterless wastes of the Western Desert, he was ill-equipped for riding the waves in a tossing LCI (Landing Craft, Infantry). The thought that the landings here on the northern tip of Corsica were not going anything like according to plan did little to settle his stomach. He craned his neck to peer over the gunwales of the small boat at the looming hills of the island and longed to have solid ground under his feet once more. Then everything else could be sorted out.

Koenig was in nominal command of the invasion of Corsica, the only proper amphibious assault of a hostile shore involved in the entire HAY-MAKER operation. The American and Canadian troops pouring ashore along the French Riviera and the British reinforcing the French garrisons in Tunisia would be welcomed in those places, the port facilities completely at their disposal. But Corsica had been occupied by the Italians after their cowardly entry into the war in June 1940, once the French Army had been thoroughly defeated by the Germans, and there were perhaps 80,000 Italian troops in several large concentrations around the island. Koenig had developed a measure of respect for the fighting qualities of the Italian troops he had encountered in Libya and Egypt, but those had been the elite of Mussolini's army, not the third-rate coastal defense reservists that comprised most of the occupation forces here. Still, there were a lot of them, and they did have guns.

Koenig's invasion force, in fact, barely counted half as many men as the defenders. He had his own 1st Free French Division and Leclerc's 2nd, but they suffered from the shortage of manpower that had plagued de Gaulle's gallant little army since its inception and numbered barely 20,000 men between them. They were reinforced by the American 3rd Infantry Division, lavishly equipped and augmented by several independent battalions, and the Americans had been gracious enough to place the entire force under French command—his command. They would also be supported by considerable naval firepower from all five of the destroyers in de Gaulle's tiny navy and at least one American heavy cruiser, and American carrier planes would be hitting points of resistance as soon as the sun came up. But it was going to be a near run thing, and de Gaulle had had to make a deal with the devil to improve their odds.

Koenig had attended the clandestine meeting in a bunker deep under the "rock" of Gibraltar weeks before when de Gaulle had met with some "allies" of his own. The *Union Corse* was the rough equivalent of the Italian mafia, only with even less respect for the law, a much tighter organization, and a greater reputation for violence. Koenig had been called in to join de Gaulle and several of the *capos,* as these gangster chieftains were called, well after the discussions had begun. In fact, it had been apparent that the essence of the agreement for the *capos'* support for the invasion had been reached discreetly without including Koenig or the other soldiers who entered with him. Koenig later learned that Corsican cooperation had been purchased at the expense of an agreement for their domination of the black market, smuggling, and prostitution all along the Riviera and on Corsica with minimal interference by the police, after the Liberation. Koenig thought that it was just as well that he would not have this on his conscience.

He had not been overly impressed by these men, who had been described to him as something approaching heads of state. They were all typically swarthy Mediterranean types, short and stocky, and dressed in dark suits like those worn by peasants in southern France for going to Mass or a funeral. But they had impressed him with their knowledge of everything that took place on their island, the kind of intelligence generals dream of obtaining. Exact numbers and locations of all the defending forces, right down to the names of the Italian company commanders and the addresses of their local mistresses. One of the men turned out to be a veteran fisherman (read: smuggler) who knew every inch of the coast, every whim of the tides, and could tell him just where and when landings would be practicable.

It was unfortunate, Koenig couldn't help thinking, that the inexperienced American landing craft crews hadn't been able to make full benefit of this information. Although the landing areas had been carefully selected and clandestinely surveyed, a number of the scout boats had been misplaced, sending landing craft to the wrong landfalls, and some of the boat crews had simply gone off course. Nearly half of the first wave had gone ashore miles from their intended targets, and a number of boats had piled up on easily avoidable rocks, damaged beyond repair and often dumping their loads of heavily burdened troops into the choppy waves to drown.

Koenig's boat, however, hit a firm shelf of sand, leaving him and his staff only a few yards of surf to wade through. He glanced upward at the cliffs which glowered over the narrow beach, their outlines just visible against the lightening sky. Had the enemy occupied them in force, it would have been a massacre. Unfortunately, the only really good landing beaches were on the island's eastern side, which would have entailed the invasion fleet circling the island and conducting the assault with the hostile mainland at their backs.

But the *capos* had been as good as their word, Koenig was to find, as a jeep rushed him to the command post which had been set up in the main post office in the town of Calvi overlooking the little harbor. Brothels located conveniently around the Italian barracks had offered special rates the night before, and literally hundreds of Italian officers and men had awakened this morning in a drugged stupor, bound and gagged and naked, with alluring *putains* standing guard over them with their own weapons. The crews of a number of the most menacing coastal batteries had had even less luck. They had not awakened at all, their throats having been slit during the night by Corsican guerrillas wielding the knives for which they were justly famous. Koenig thought that the Italians should have taken note that the common term for the Resistance in France, the *maquis,* came from the name for the

Corsican brush in which bandits and revolutionaries have hidden and fought for centuries. Koenig took the report from Leclerc, who had gone in with the first wave. The 225th Division, a low-grade reserve unit stationed at Calvi, stunned by the few 3-inch shells which dropped on the town, its baptism of fire, had surrendered en masse when the commander had found himself sandwiched between the French landing to the south and the Americans to the north. The 20th "Friuli" Division in Bastia, and the 44th "Cremona" in Ajaccio, both regular army units, had not folded, but they had pulled in their outposts and hunkered down within their fixed defenses. This left the invaders with complete control over nearly half of the island, almost without a shot being fired. The Italian port commander had even been kind enough to provide maps of the minefields covering the harbor at Calvi, enabling Koenig to radio the fleet to send in the follow-on forces directly to the docks and to come in and pick up the several thousand prisoners already on his hands.

0630 HOURS, 19 DECEMBER 1942
AIX-EN-PROVENCE, FRANCE

Major Creighton W. Abrams, executive officer of Combat Command A of the U.S. 1st Armored Division, sat atop the turret of his MS Stuart light tank, staring back along the tight column of tanks, half-tracks, and tank destroyers which filled the narrow street leading to the *Route Nationale 7*, the road to Avignon. He slapped his palm nervously against the armor of the turret and swore under his breath, but it was still difficult not to enjoy the moment.

The street was clogged with throngs of cheering men, women, and children, hurling bouquets of flowers at the American column that inched its way painfully forward. Girls leaped into open jeeps or scrambled up the sides of the tanks to hug and kiss the delighted GIs, while old men with rows of dusty medals pinned to their coats stood to rigid attention along the curb, saluting as tears streamed down their faces. Important men in dark suits with broad tricolor sashes appeared, Abrams assumed them to be local officials, and they kept trying to step into the roadway to stop the column and give speeches, but the vehicles kept rolling and they had to scurry aside to avoid becoming roadkill.

With men and equipment pouring off the ships in the harbor, the key thing was to get as far away from the port as quickly as possible to avoid the inevitable German air attacks that would be coming soon. The flyboys would obviously do their best to hold them off, but the Allies were jumping right into the Luftwaffe's backyard, and only a handful of aircraft could operate from the carriers, and it would be some time before the French air bases could be up and running to receive the fighter squadrons that would be stationed there.

It was also vital to drive as far inland as possible as quickly as possible. Abrams could imagine the carnage if they had had to fight their way ashore and then struggle for every yard of progress against a determined and experienced enemy. His own men were, of course, totally green, and it remained to be seen how well they would do in their baptism of fire. They key thing was that that baptism should happen as far from the coast as possible, to give them room to maneuver, even to retreat, if necessary. Every second that they could advance without enemy resistance saved American lives, and Abrams would have rather have been rolling at 30 miles per hour instead of walking pace.

Abrams had done his job, stripping his unit down to the bare essentials, just the fighting vehicles, each one crammed with as much fuel and ammo as it could carry, and he had drilled his men in the order of march until they dropped from exhaustion. He had even wangled a section of heavy wrecker trucks to haul out mired vehicles and had the drivers trained in pushing disabled vehicles out of the roadway, anything to keep up the pace. What they had never counted on was the unbridled enthusiasm of the "liberated" population.

At every village and crossroads from the outskirts of Marseille to Aix, barely fifty miles, the column had been mobbed by delirious Frenchmen and women. Abrams had been obliged to pass orders back along the line of vehicles for officers to keep an eagle eye out and to collect the bottles of wine that the people were forcing on his men at every turn. There was some grumbling at this, the assumption of the troops being that the wine was being reserved for the brass, but the last thing Abrams wanted to do was face the Wehrmacht at the head of a bunch of raw, inexperienced, and *drunk* troopers. There would be time for celebration later.

Abrams had been on the radio with CCA's commander, Lt. Col. W.M. Stokes, who had in turn been on with division command and all the way up to Patton, and they were supposedly talking with the French authorities. Now that the sun was fully up, there didn't seem much choice but to find a wooded area, possibly just north of Aix, in which the column could take cover until a cordon of police could be established along the route of march to prevent this sort of thing. Abrams knew that a stationary column would be easy meat for enemy Stukas, and, if they were surrounded by hundreds of dancing civilians, well, he didn't even want to picture such a thing.

The good news thus far was that there was no word that the Germans had crossed into Vichy territory yet, and, from his own experience at trying to get unalerted armored units onto the road, it would be some time before they could load up, fuel up, and get moving. The paratroopers would just have to hold on a little longer.

0700 Hours, 19 December 1942
Vichy, France

The town of Vichy had never been designed to be the capital of a nation, but at least it was designed for handling an influx of as much as eight times its permanent population of 25,000. Hotels abounded to house the thousands of people who came annually to "take the cure" at the town's famous thermal springs. Still, having the Ministry of Interior housed in the baccarat hall of the Grand Casino did take away something of a government's dignity.

As bustling a place as Vichy had become since its conversion to the capital of the rump of "unoccupied" France in 1940, its streets clogged with dark-suited government bureaucrats and diplomats along with generals and admirals with their braid-trimmed uniforms, it was apparent this morning that something special was taking place. A pair of black police vans inched their way across the Pont de Bellerive over the Allier River toward the center of town. Most of the traffic was trying to head south, out of the city, but every intersection was jammed with cars impatient to make it through from all directions. Finally, a policeman at the north end of the bridge, recognizing the vehicles and uniforms of the Garde Mobile, managed to halt the stream of cars and trucks long enough for the two vans to pass through. The officer in the passenger seat of the lead vehicle threw him a snappy salute as they rolled past.

The semi-circular drive in front of the Hotel du Pare, which Marshal Petain had made his residence, was filled with black Citroen sedans and army trucks. A steady stream of men hustled through the tall oak doors of the hotel carrying bundles and boxes, almost like the last day of summer vacation, except that these boxes were filled with government documents and even packets of currency belonging to the treasury. The two police vans rolled slowly past the building, attracting little attention from the handful of soldiers lounging near the entrance, their rifles slung over their shoulders.

Colonel Otto Skorzeny tugged at the rough collar of his Garde Mobile uniform and anxiously examined the cars parked closest to the building. Despite the chill outside and even a dusting of snow on the clipped hedges of the hotel grounds, it was uncomfortably warm inside the van, even though there was no heater. The combined body temperatures of eight sturdy commandos of the Brandenburger Regiment, coupled with having to wear French greatcoats on top of their camouflaged German uniforms had all of the men sweating, even apart from the tension of the moment.

Skorzeny and his assault team had landed by glider in the small hours of the morning in a field near the town of Cusset, just east of Vichy. They had quietly gathered and seized the local Garde Mobile barracks, leaving the handful of sleepy policemen bound and gagged in the basement and equipping themselves with stolen uniforms and the two vans. This had all been foreseen as part of Operation RAVEN, and Skorzeny himself had reconnoitered the various operational sites and the routes between them in the preceding weeks.

Canaris, the author of the plan, had determined that, in the event of open hostilities with the Vichy government, it was of the utmost importance to gain control of the person of Marshal Petain. Loyalty to the hero of Verdun was the mortar that held the tenuous structure of the truncated French state together. Any movement that could claim the endorsement of Petain would have the support of the vast majority of the French people, while any group that he opposed would have an uphill fight from the outset. With Petain safely in German hands, it would be possible to issue all manner of policy statements and directives in his name, and there might still be a chance to swing Vichy, with its sizable navy and its considerable army in North Africa, actively into the Axis camp.

Even without serious resistance by the undermanned and poorly equipped French "Armistice Army," it would take a brigade of bicycle infantry stationed at Tours a day or two to cover the nearly two hundred miles to Vichy. And if the troops of the 13th Military District in which Vichy was located, some 8,000 men, did put up a fight, that one German brigade might not be enough. Petain would have ample warning and time to move south, further into the zone or possibly to fly out to North Africa, despite his reluctance to do just that in 1940 or at any time since. The old man had always said that, "One cannot defend France by abandoning her," but a new German invasion might just change his mind. And an invasion there would be if a deal had, in fact, been worked out between the Allies and Vichy, as the previous night's activities seemed to indicate. What Skorzeny saw at the Hotel du Pare only confirmed Canaris' suspicions. This was clearly a government on the move, and the commandos would have to act quickly.

Skorzeny was an Austrian member of the SS who had seen action on the Eastern Front. Only a few months before he had been assigned to select and train a group of elite fighting men capable of conducting missions deep into enemy territory. He had taken his troops from the Brandenburger Regiment, a special unit formed to conduct unusual operations. This unit, dressed as Poles, had staged mock attacks on German outposts to provide a pretext for the German invasion of Poland in 1939. They had slipped ahead of the armored spearheads in the Low Countries in 1940 and in Russia in 1941, often disguised as civilians or soldiers of other nationalities, to capture bridges and other key targets intact. Now, under Skorzeny's tutelage, the men he had selected had become experts at intelligence collection and sabotage, and this would be their first major mission as a unit.

The two vans pulled up to the loading dock at the rear of the hotel near the kitchens, and fourteen "policemen" got out. A lone youthful soldier of the 8th Dragoons was standing guard near the door, stamping his feet in the cold. One of Skorzeny's men was an Alsatian who spoke native French, and Skorzeny had grandly given him the rank of *commissaire* for the occasion. The Alsatian strode purposefully toward the door, but the soldier nervously unslung his rifle and blocked the path.

"Please, sir," the soldier began. "Entrance here is forbidden. You will have to go around to the front."

"Have you seen the front, son?" the Alsatian growled. "Rats leaving the sinking ship. We're here to provide a final security check and lock up the building after the Marshal leaves. Now get out of the way and let us get on with it. I want to be on the road to Avignon myself before the Germans get here."

"I have my orders, sir," the soldier insisted, but Skorzeny pushed past the Alsatian, and deftly slid a bayonet into the sentry's throat, jerking it to one side and sending a spurt of red down the front of the guard's khaki greatcoat. They leaned the still twitching corpse in the comer of the loading dock and rushed into the building, leaving two of their men to guard the vehicles. In half an hour a seaplane would touch down on the Allier River barely two hundred meters from the hotel to pick them all up. The raiders would make better time in their vans, but, if necessary, they would abandon them and try to make the rendezvous on foot, using the Marshal as a human shield.

They bulled past the confused kitchen staff and up the service stairs, each man now openly carrying his Schmeiser submachinegun and stripping off his coat. By the time they had reached the second floor where Petain had his offices, they were a squad of German paras again.

Shouts could be heard now in the crowded lobby of the hotel and the sound of boots pounding up the stairs, but a pair of Skorzeny's men positioned themselves at the top of the broad staircase and sent half a dozen dragoons and staff officers tumbling back down with a long burst of 9mm fire. Skorzeny and the Alsatian kicked open the double doors to the Marshal's inner office, and a young French lieutenant got off a shot with his revolver from behind a littered desk, catching the Alsatian in the temple. The next man through cut the lieutenant down, and in an instant Skorzeny was poised next to the Marshal's desk, his weapon pointed at the old man's chest.

Petain looked even older than Skorzeny had expected, his moustache and the fringe of hair around his bald pate pure white, his skin almost translucent in the soft light streaming in through the tall windows. In his hand he held a large cavalry pistol, the hammer cocked, leveled at Skorzeny, the barrel as steady as a rock. Other raiders darted into the room and took up positions at the windows.

"You are my prisoner, sir," Skorzeny announced in accented French, panting heavily after his exertions. "You are to accompany me to meet with the Führer in Germany. I assure you that you will be well treated in accordance with your rank and position."

"Haven't you got enough French hostages?" the old man asked calmly.

"You are not a hostage, sir," Skorzeny retorted, as Canaris had instructed him. "It is only that the Führer has urgent matters to discuss with you. We have information that the Gaullists plan to assassinate you, and that a coup d'etat is underway against your regime at this very moment. The German Army is on the way to support you, but we must make certain of the security of your person first."

"I have served France all my life," Petain said in a voice as flat as if he were ordering a cup of coffee. "I imagine that I can do the one last thing that she requires of me."

"No!" Skorzeny screamed, lunging across the broad mahogany desk.

But the thunderous report of the pistol had already filled the room, drowning out the rattle of gunfire coming from out in the hall as more French soldiers and officers charged up the stairs, ignoring the heavy casualties. The Marshal was almost thrown out of his chair by the force of the blast, and half of his head had instantly disappeared. Skorzeny snatched the pistol from the rigid fingers and hurled it against the wall in frustration.

"Shit!" he roared, and he jerked a thumb toward the window. "We have to go *now!*"

There was a tiled roof covering a long terrace which ran under the window, and Skorzeny's men leapt from the second floor window, hit this roof to break their fall, and tumbled into the shrubbery below. Skorzeny was the last to go, pitching a stick grenade out into the hall before he too jumped.

There were only twelve of them left now after the fighting in the hotel, and Skorzeny could see the shapes of men dodging from cover to cover in the park-like grounds behind the hotel. The seaplane should be coming in any moment, looking for the flare Skorzeny must fire to signal the pick-up. They had counted on having Petain as a hostage to discourage the French from firing on the plane as it maneuvered for take-off, but it could still work. There was no time to waste.

"They've killed the Marshal!" a hoarse voice was screaming from up on the second floor, and this was followed by a flurry of firing which sent a cloud of splinters flying from the trunk of the pine behind which Skorzeny was taking cover.

"To the river!" Skorzeny rasped to his men. "We'll take the plane if it can come in. If not, we can get hold of a boat, the current will take us north to the occupied zone even if we can't get the motor started."

"What about the vans?" someone asked.

"You saw the logjam on the roads. We'll never get out of town that way. This is our only chance."

A mental image of the map of Vichy that he had studied for hours leapt into Skorzeny's head. If they could scale the wall at the bottom of the hotel gardens, they would find themselves on a major thoroughfare that led directly down to the Yacht Club on the river. He signaled to one of his men, and they began dashing from cover to cover, firing economical bursts at the soldiers who were pressing them from three sides now. Fortunately, the French were all armed with old carbines or revolvers, all single-shot, which made it hard to hit a moving target. Even so, only nine men landed on the far side of the garden wall and raced down the street toward the river.

A traffic policeman at the first intersection tried to draw his pistol, but one of the raiders cut him down, firing from the hip. They ran in a crouch, weaving between the cars and trucks that swerved drunkenly to avoid them. More soldiers were coming from the hotel, firing wildly after them. A man running next to Skorzeny gasped and threw up his hands, tumbling head over heels and coming to rest against the mailbox on the curb. Skorzeny paused to help him, but the man's chest was a mass of red, and his eyes were already glazed over.

They reached the river's edge and could see the masts of the boats in the yacht club barely a hundred yards farther on. Skorzeny fumbled with the flap on his holster and drew his flare pistol, firing the red flare skyward and quickly breaking the weapon open to reload.

But it proved unnecessary. With a roar, the seaplane swooped overhead and angled to touch down on the near edge of the river. Skorzeny and his men tossed aside their weapons and tore off their uniform jackets as they raced to dive into the water. It would be cold, Skorzeny thought. Even in summer a stream coming from the Alps was like ice, but they had no old man to load aboard now, and every second they could buy would improve their chances of escape.

The pilot eased back on his throttle but kept his propellers turning as he guided the plane closer to the shore. Suddenly, however, sparks and bits of fuselage began to fly off the craft as machinegun rounds tore into it from one end to the other. The pilot increased power and tried to position to take off, but the stream of tracers found one of the engines and black smoke now began to billow from under the cowling. Skorzeny turned to see an old armored car stopped along the quay, pouring fire into the plane from its turret gun. In another moment, the plane was engulfed in a ball of flame and broke up into pieces that. were swept away with the current.

Skorzeny's men turned to look at him, their expressions asking for orders, but there was nothing to do. The armored car was sitting in front of the entrance to the yacht club, and a skirmish line of dragoons was moving down the street to where the Germans were helplessly clustered. Skorzeny shrugged his shoulders and slowly raised his arms over his head, and his men followed his example.

A French officer strode down the hill from the hotel. Skorzeny could see that his left sleeve was soaked with blood, and his teeth were clenched against the pain. Skorzeny smirked coyly and shrugged his shoulders again. This was apparently the wrong thing to do.

"Scum!" the officer shrieked and raised his pistol.

"Wait!" Skorzeny protested, putting his hands out to protect himself. The officer and his men fired together.

CHAPTER 2

DUELING STRATEGIES

1200 HOURS, 10 JUNE 1942
WASHINGTON, D.C.

THE SUBJECT OF the opening of a second front in Europe had been raised as early as the ARCADIA conference between American President Franklin Delano Roosevelt and British Prime Minister Winston Churchill in Washington in January 1942. At that point in time, Churchill considered it vital to obtain a commitment from his new allies to an armed presence on the continent as soon as possible, and he lit a fire under the inexperienced American military leaders that proved hard, indeed impossible, to extinguish.

On balance, things that January looked substantially better for the British than they had only a few months previously. In the spring of 1941 Britain still stood alone against the consistently victorious Germans, and had been stripped of her allies one after another on the battlefield. Although the specter of an imminent German invasion across the Channel had receded, Hitler now had the industrial might of the entire continent at his disposal, and there was no reason to believe that he might not renew his plans to crush Britain once and for all at any time. But Hitler had chosen to turn east and, on 22 June 1941 invaded the Soviet Union. The initial euphoria that this apparently overly ambitious campaign caused in London was short-lived, however, as German armies tore through the Russians like a hot knife through butter, carving out huge chunks of territory, destroying mountains of weapons, and sending hundreds of thousands of Red Army soldiers into prisoner of war camps. The same could be said of the sudden entry of the United States into the war—while welcome in itself, the Japanese were soon running roughshod over the thin defenses of the East Indies, scattering the forces of the U.S., the Netherlands and the British Commonwealth with no sign of stopping.

Still, Churchill could now speak with certainty about the existence of a "grand alliance" including the two *potentially* greatest military powers in the world. The British had never been quite alone, of course, having at their backs the resources of their empire and Commonwealth comprising a significant portion of the land surface and population of the earth. But industrial power and usable military manpower were always in short supply in comparison to that available to the Axis. Even after nearly two years of preparation, the United States had little in the way of an army or air force, merely a vast mob of half-trained men, since most of America's new weapons production had gone to help arm the British, and later the Russians; but this was only a temporary problem. The Red Army had taken a horrible savaging at the hands of the Germans, but the German spearheads had been hurled back from the gates of Moscow with considerable loss, and the Russians still possessed a huge army equipped with hundreds of superb new tanks. Britain's own war seemed to be going well, with the Afrika Korps of Erwin Rommel having been driven away from Tobruk and all the way across Cyrenaica in North Africa.

The problem facing Churchill in January 1942 was that of keeping the Russians in the field until the Americans could sort themselves out and ship a massive army across the ocean to confront the Germans directly. Despite the relief for the British of the success of the Russian winter offensive, Churchill had no illusions about the power of the Wehrmacht having been broken. In fact, it was increasingly apparent that the Germans were only now just beginning to mobilize the full resources of the enlarged Reich and its subject territories for the war effort, and, when the mud of the spring finally hardened, the Russians would be facing an armed force, if anything, even more powerful than that which had driven hundreds of miles into Soviet territory the year before. Since Stalin had seen fit to strike one deal with Hitler before, over the partition of Poland, it was not beyond comprehension that he might seek to do so again if the survival of his regime were at stake.

To attempt to shore up his only ally with troops actually doing battle with the Germans, Churchill had diverted some of his own country's precious military production to the Soviet Union and had urged the Americans to do the same. However, with every tank, truck, and bullet having to run the gauntlet of Luftwaffe bombers based in Norway on the Murmansk run or having to make their tortuous way across the Pacific and thence by rail over the entire length of Asia or through the mountains of Iran, this could never hope to be more than a relative trickle.

What was needed, what the Russians demanded, and the only kind of support that they would understand and respect, was a major land offensive by the Western Allies against German territory. Since there was no magical way that armies could be created and transported instantaneously to the theater of war, what Churchill really hoped to obtain at ARCADIA was a declaration of purpose. He recognized that it had been the surprise attack by the Japanese on Pearl Harbor that had propelled the United States into the war, and although Hitler had committed a serious blunder by making his own declaration of war against the Americans, thus simplifying Roosevelt's problem of convincing his isolationist countrymen to join that fight, the American public was focused on the Pacific.

On a strategic level, however, despite Japan's rapid gains and the stunning defeats inflicted on the Allies in Malaysia and the East Indies, it was clear that the Japanese had essentially reached the end of their tether. Nearly a million Japanese troops were stuck in the quagmire of an endless land war in China, and tens of thousands more would be tied down garrisoning their new conquests in Southeast Asia, besides those still required to reduce the dogged American-Filipino resistance on Bataan for months to come. The Japanese, therefore, simply lacked the resources to take on further major objectives, such as the actual conquest of India or Australia.

Germany, on the other hand, still stood within an ace of knocking the Soviet Union out of the war and, despite Rommel's recent setbacks, of capturing the Suez Canal and driving into the Middle East. If they achieved either of these goals, it was still distinctly possible that Hitler could redraft his priorities and turn his attention to a new invasion of the British Isles.

Although there would be bureaucratic guerrilla warfare within the American military establishment, headed by the navy and by the amazingly influential and petulant General Douglas MacArthur, Churchill found his American hosts largely in agreement with his thinking on this subject. And it stood to reason. Despite its losses at Pearl Harbor and in the Dutch East Indies, the American Navy was still the country's most powerful and battle-ready arm, and it was in the Pacific that this power could most effectively be used. American naval support for convoys to Britain would be welcome, but would require only a small percentage of either current strength or future production, with the Royal Navy making up the bulk of the effort. Europe would be a theater for land and air forces of sheer mass, while the Pacific would require small, elite, amphibious units and relatively less air power. Consequently, Churchill went away with a promise from Roosevelt to devote roughly twice as much American current strength and future production to Europe as to the Pacific, and a commitment to defeat Germany first while conducting a holding action in the Far East. As it turned out, American military might, when fully mobilized, would prove capable of pursuing the defeat of both ends of the Axis at the same time, but neither Churchill nor Roosevelt were optimistic enough to count on this in early 1942.

The ARCADIA conference also saw the creation of the Combined Chiefs of Staff, an organization designed both to coordinate strategic planning between the two allies and to give the green Americans a chance to benefit from Britain's hard-earned experience gained from over two years grappling with the Axis. It is worth noting that the Soviets were not even considered for membership in this council. Churchill, in hindsight, argued that this was because the Russians had their own, unilateral front, but one might suggest that there was enough interconnectivity, in the area of Lend Lease for example, that at least a token representation might have been justified. At the time, there were also various plans afoot to send British or American ground forces, which by the end of the year would be sitting idle in England in their hundreds of thousands, to fight on the Russian Front, as individual air units actually did, which might also have made a Soviet presence on the staff worthwhile. This decision might have avoided unnecessary complications in the making of strategic plans for the Western Allies and allowed for more candid discussions without the brooding presence of the bear, but it also sewed the seeds of distrust in Moscow about the intentions of the West. In any event, the creation of the staff did greatly facilitate joint planning by the British and Americans over the coming months and years.

The situation in mid-1942 had changed significantly, however, and with it, Churchill's attitude toward a second front. The Germans were again driving deep into Soviet territory, now threatening the oil-producing region of the Caucasus, and inflicting further massive losses on the Red Army. In North Africa, Rommel had struck again, inflicting a humiliating defeat on the British at Tobruk and reaching to within one hundred miles of Alexandria itself, facing the last defensive line before the Nile Delta at El Alamein. This was hardly a very promising scenario for the Allies.

However, the overall strategic picture had improved in other ways. The drawn battle in the Coral Sea, followed by the staggering loss of Japanese aircraft carriers at Midway had, if not exactly crippled the Japanese war machine, at least signified a turn of the tide in the Pacific. The struggle against the U-boat menace in the Atlantic had also begun to lessen as the Allies developed new anti-submarine tactics for both naval and air units. And, while organized American military units had only just begun to trickle into the United Kingdom (about 36,000 men by May 1942), this figure was growing geometrically, and deliveries of equipment in the form of tanks, guns, and aircraft quickly replaced the losses suffered by the British in the Western Desert and fleshed out new units being raised at home.

It is probably at this point, therefore, that Churchill became convinced in the inevitability of the Allied victory in the war, and his focus shifted to the shape of the post-war world. With Britain having lost virtually an entire generation of young men in the First World War, she could not afford another such Pyrrhic victory and still have the manpower and resources necessary to play the role of a great power and to retain her far flung empire following the defeat of the Axis. He thus favored a strategy of nibbling at the edges of the Reich, first finishing off the tenuous German foothold in Africa which dangled at the end of a vulnerable naval supply line; they would then gobble up the Mediterranean islands and possibly enter the continent at its remotest points such as Italy, Greece, Norway, or the Balkans. This would keep the Allies close enough to the center of action to be able to move in quickly should Germany suddenly begin to collapse, but would also have the advantage of leaving it to the Red Army to confront the bulk of the Wehrmacht in a deadly battle of attrition.

The problem was that this approach did not coincide with the "American way of war," which actually courted a battle of attrition, relying on superior resources of men and materiel to grind the enemy down with a minimum of elegant maneuver. This was the style instilled in the American Army since the days of Ulysses S. Grant in the Civil War and had been drummed into the heads of cadets at West Point as the gospel ever since. The original British encouragement for planning for a cross-Channel invasion at the earliest possible date had only spurred on this thinking, and any effort by the British to deviate from it was seen by the Americans as an avoidance of responsibility.

Needless to say, Stalin, whose soldiers were still fighting for their very lives across the steppes of the Ukraine and into the outskirts of Stalingrad, viewed this "peripheral strategy" with considerable suspicion. It was not so long ago, of course, that British, French, and American soldiers had fought on Russian soil alongside the White Russians in an attempt to destroy the Bolshevik Revolution, and relations had hardly been any warmer in the years since the establishment of the Soviet government. Reports from Soviet agents of Churchill's desire that as many Germans and Russians as possible kill each other off, leaving the Western Allies to come in after and pick up the pieces, while possibly not meant in quite that blunt a form, were just too plausible for the Soviets to ignore.

This, then, was the background for the second series of meetings between Churchill and Roosevelt in the late spring of 1942. From their extensive correspondence between "a former military person" (Churchill, because of his brief stints of "war tourism" in Egypt, India, and South America around the turn of the century) and "a former naval person" (Roosevelt, because of his term as Secretary of the Navy), Roosevelt had a good idea of his counterpart's philosophy and of the nature of the requests he would be making. Consequently, in order to have the maximum of facts on hand with which to balance Churchill's legendary persuasiveness, Roosevelt quietly called a conference with one of the few military men for whom he had unlimited respect, if decidedly limited personal affection: Army Chief of Staff George C. Marshall.

Marshall had been in regular contact with the White House for some time prior to his appointment as Chief of Staff, due to his assignment as Chief of the War Plans Division during the hectic period of Roosevelt's almost clandestine efforts to build up America's defense establishment following the start of the war in Europe. Marshall had frequently gone to bat for the president before Congress, debating with diehard isolationists the need to institute a peacetime draft and to increase the paltry budgets of the army, navy, and the new army air corps, as well as to fund the shipment of arms to Britain under Lend Lease. Of course, Pearl Harbor immediately swept away Congressional opposition to a massive U.S. military build-up; however, it was still Marshall's job to determine how to accomplish it. In this role, Marshall had been alone among his military colleagues, most of whom were far senior to him in rank, in his willingness to disagree openly with Roosevelt and to call into question the president's sometimes fuzzy military reasoning. Marshall was always scrupulously polite and capable of saluting and following orders once those orders were made firm; but he would make himself heard first and let the chips fall where they may. Roosevelt and his personal advisor, Harry Hopkins, appreciated this approach, having come to learn that what they heard from General Marshall, virtually the only person the president could not quite bring himself to call by his first name, was his unvarnished, best assessment of the situation, not what he thought his superiors wanted to hear.

Marshall, of course, knew what was coming in the showdown with the British, and had chosen to bring reinforcements to the meeting. He was accompanied by the rest of the Joint Chiefs and a strong supporting cast. The group included Admiral Ernest J. King, Chief of Naval Operations, and his deputy, Admiral William D. Leahy, who had just returned from a posting as Ambassador to Vichy France; General Hap Arnold, commander of the Army Air Corps, and Brigadier General James H. Doolittle, recently returned from his spectacular bombing raid on Tokyo; General George S. Patton, arguably the nation's leading expert on mechanized warfare, and General Dwight D. Eisenhower, current chief of the War Plans Division. Roosevelt had not been expecting quite so large a group, having only Secretary of State Cordell Hull and Secretary of War Henry L. Stimson on "his team," and from the fixed looks on the faces of the military men as they filed into the Oval Office, the president knew that they had come with a prepared agenda.

Harry Hopkins wheeled Roosevelt out from behind his desk and, after some cursory introductions for some members of the delegation, they pulled up chairs and formed a rough circle around a low coffee table, while a Filipino steward in sparkling white coat and gloves laid out coffee on a sideboard.

"Gentlemen," Roosevelt began when the steward had silently slipped out of the room and firmly closed the door. "As you know, the British Prime Minister will be arriving soon, and we have reason to believe that he will have certain requests to make of us." The men nodded. "From what General Marshall learned on his recent visit to England and his meeting with the Imperial General Staff, we can assume that Mr. Churchill will ask for an American division to be sent to Egypt to bolster their line against Rommel, to fight under British command. There will, of course, also be requests for more equipment to be diverted from the fitting out of our new forces and sent directly to Britain. Unofficial rumors in London have it that Churchill will insist on dropping any thought of an invasion of the continent this year altogether in favor of seizing the French possessions in North Africa. I have called you together as an informal discussion group to get your views on this."

All of the military men instinctively turned to Marshall to begin. Marshall cleared his throat after a brief pause.

"Mr. President, as you may be aware, I served on the staff of General Pershing for five years during and after the last war, and this kind of request is nothing new from the British. General Pershing was solidly opposed then, and I think we should oppose now, the idea of using American troops as fillers in a foreign army. We need to build and deploy an *American* army under *American* command. That is the only way to look out for the interests of our men and for our national interests."

"I would have to agree with that view," Eisenhower chimed in, nodding his nearly bald head. "From our analysis of the situation in North Africa, while the British could always use a few more tanks to replace their recent losses, Rommel simply doesn't have the strength to break their current line when he's operating at the end of a supply route over a thousand miles long, and when the British already outnumber him substantially. He may have overcome the odds more than once in the past, but he isn't a miracle worker. In any case, by the time we could get a division to Egypt, the thing is going to have been decided one way or the other. And an invasion of French North Africa, while it should be easy enough to do, will still eat up men and equipment, especially landing craft, that we need to stockpile for the main show in Europe. Even against minimal resistance, landing craft tend to be lost in high numbers, and we have all too few right now. All we'll end up doing is set back our own timetable for a build-up in England for an invasion of the continent."

"But, isn't there some substance to the theory that our green troops need a period of seasoning, supported by British veterans?" Stimson asked. "After all, except for some of our most senior officers, virtually no one in the American Armed Forces has seen combat on land, and no one has seen it in over twenty years . . . with the exception of you, General Doolittle, of course," he hastily added.

"There is some truth in what you say, what the British certainly have argued," Doolittle went on, "but every army ultimately has to stand on its own. And I would have to add," he scratched his neck nervously, "there's some question whether we necessarily, well, want to learn the British way of doing business. I mean, they've been chased off the continent three times, in France, Norway, and Greece, and now we've got the surrender at Singapore and Tobruk, while our boys, in spite of having been dealt a losing hand, only just now finally gave up the ghost on Corregidor." Heads around the circle bowed briefly in an impromptu moment of silence in memory of the defenders of the little island.

Doolittle cut himself off brusquely, awaiting an explosion from the president, who was known as an ardent Anglophile, but the explosion did not come. He did catch a stern look from Marshall, who had only recently dismissed his own deputy chief of staff, General Embrick, for waxing too eloquent on the prowess of the Germans and the ineptitude of the British.

"Not to suggest, sir," Patton quickly interjected, "that the British haven't done some amazing things. They've been fighting on their own for over a year and haven't cracked. It's more to the point that there's an old maxim in the military that no army ever learns much from another army's mistakes. Sure, our men our rookies, and we're going to trip over ourselves, more than once at first, but we're going to have to learn on our own hook sooner or later."

"Besides that," Admiral King growled loudly, "if the British can't find employment for American forces in Europe this year or even next, we certainly can in the Pacific. We went along with their insistence on getting at Hitler first, but that didn't include just warehousing our troops and equipment in England indefinitely." King was famous, or infamous, for his outspoken opposition to the "Europe first" school. "That would have the added benefit of the Pacific being almost exclusively American turf, and we wouldn't have to say 'Mother, may I?' to anyone."

Roosevelt frowned, and Harry Hopkins offered an opinion, as if it had just occurred to him. "Even though you gentlemen are fighting men, not politicians, at your rank, I'm sure you realize that the president has expended a considerable amount of political capital in bringing the American people around to the idea of taking on Germany first. To change policy now is not going to be as easy as all that."

"It goes beyond just tactical considerations, Mr. President, political or military," Marshall said in a level tone. "Over the past months I've gotten a clear idea that you have some views of what the world should look like after the war, and those views are not necessarily shared by Mr. Churchill and his people. The only way we're ever going to be in a position to realize those views is if we take the lead, if we make use of the power this nation can bring to bear in our own name, not as a surrogate for the British."

Harry Hopkins smiled broadly as Roosevelt tilted his head back and took a long pull on his cigarette. He knew that Marshall had just pushed the right button. If there was one element of foreign policy that Roosevelt had inherited from his predecessor, Wilson, it was a firm belief in popular sovereignty, to include the people of the European colonial empires.

"But what can we do about all this?" Roosevelt asked. "I'm certain that you gentlemen have not come here without having given this considerable thought and weighed all of the mysterious military considerations that we civilians can only guess at. I'm sure you know that our troop presence anywhere near the fighting front is miniscule and that our bomber command is only due to conduct its first combat mission, in borrowed British planes I might add, in about two weeks. It's going to sound pretty hollow if we march into this meeting demanding decisive action when we're not in a position to bring anything to the table."

"We're not talking about launching a cross-Channel invasion this week, Mr. President," Marshall noted, wagging his finger. "But by the end of this year, we are confident that we will have two armored, one airborne, and about eight infantry divisions either in Europe or deployable directly from the States in addition to several thousand warplanes in the theater. This total will go up rapidly over the following months, and that's not counting the substantial British army in England, which we've helped arm, besides the Canadians, Poles, Free French, etc. The question is how these forces will be used. The British proposal would leave most of them sitting in England, dribbled into the Western Desert in penny packets, or diverted to a sideshow on the Barbary Coast. We have something a little different in mind."

Roosevelt blew out a luxurious cloud of smoke and gestured with his open palm. "You'll never have a more receptive audience, General."

Marshall nodded to Eisenhower, who pulled a map out of his somewhat battered leather briefcase and unfolded it on the coffee table. The map showed all of France and the western Mediterranean along with Spain and the North African coast and parts of southern England and Italy. It was covered in clear plastic on which had been marked the position of military units in red, black, and blue grease pencil.

"Now," Eisenhower began, "we have to be realistic enough to recognize that the idea of putting a ground army ashore on the Channel coast of France within the next six months is highly optimistic, maybe suicidal. Even with full British support and with our mobilization and transportation of troops going perfectly. The German defenses are considerable now and will only be stronger by then. And even if the Russians have some success on their front, the Germans can still skim a large number of divisions from the rest of Europe to concentrate against us. Still, if we could get ashore and consolidate a lodgment area, we could almost certainly pump enough troops into that area to ensure that we couldn't be thrown back into the sea. It would be that first week that would be crucial. After that we would absolutely win the race for building up our forces, *if* we could be sure of gaining control of a major port in working order, although the Germans would obviously fight to the death to prevent that and sabotage any port we even threatened."

He had been talking to the map, using his hands to describe a pocket along the Normandy coast. He paused and looked up. Roosevelt shrugged and he continued. "That's the problem. But suppose, just suppose," he emphasized, wagging his finger in the air, "that we could put, say 50,000 airborne troops in a ring around the lodgment area, lightly armed, but occupying all approaches, before the main force even hits the beach. And suppose we could destroy bridges in a broad arc around that area. Then imagine if we could somehow neutralize the beach defenses so that the landing troops could just walk ashore and have a day, maybe even several days, before the German combat units could even get at them, and have the use of a major port and half a dozen smaller ones, with even a crew of stevedores to help. And *then*, just for the exercise, suppose that I could wave my magic wand and add a quarter million trained soldiers to our resource pool, already transported for us to Europe, and over 100,000 tons of merchant shipping as well. That would significantly improve the odds, wouldn't it?" Hull sighed. "And you expect us to pitch that idea to the British, to commit resources to a pipe dream?"

"Well, Mr. Secretary," Eisenhower admitted, "that can't be done in northern France, but it might be done elsewhere."

"And where might that be?"

"Right here," he jabbed his finger at the southern coast of France.

"Vichy territory?" Roosevelt asked incredulously. "I rather had the idea that they were pretty much on the other side. They certainly didn't welcome the Allies with open arms in Dakar or Syria. In fact, they fought with some energy."

"Exactly, sir," Admiral Leahy said. "The problem for the French has been that half of their country is occupied by the Germans and a good million of their men are being held as prisoners of war, read hostages. It's my belief after nearly two years living cheek by jowl with them that they hate the Germans now even more than before; but they're not in a position to move over to our side unless they get a clear message that we're in this business for real, that we're going to make a real commitment and have a chance of winning."

"That's just what our plan is designed to give them," Eisenhower said. "If we waltz ashore in North Africa, they'll fight us tooth and nail so the Germans won't be so hard on mainland France. They may eventually let us win, but they'll make us pay for it just to show the Nazis that it was *force majeur.* Of course, if we take North Africa, the Germans will certainly move in and take the rest of France and fortify the whole place." "Well, I'm still not convinced, and I'm sure the British won't be," Roosevelt said, shaking his head. "But just for the sake of argument, let's hear your thinking on this through."

Eisenhower bent over the map again. "The French have about 50,000 men in their army in Metropolitan France. The Germans left them with obsolete weapons and almost no artillery or armor or air force, but they're trained troops, and, what's more important, they're on the spot."

"Your mythical paratroopers," Roosevelt interjected.

"Precisely. They've got about 200,000 more in North Africa, along with a couple hundred aircraft, and they're better armed, since those troops are no threat to the Germans, and their purpose is to defend the empire against us, just as in Dakar and Syria. With, say, one well-equipped Allied division and some new gear and ammunition, that would slam the back door right on Rommel's behind."

"They also still have a first rate navy," Admiral King added. "Maybe a hundred ships including some modern battleships, cruisers, and destroyers. With them in our corner, we'd have total control over the Mediterranean and could even shift some British and American naval units elsewhere."

"Now, getting back to the ground war on the continent," Eisenhower went on. "About two thirds of Vichy territory is within this strong ring of mountains, the Alps in the east and the Massif Central in the north. Between the French troops and airborne units we could put into the Rhone River Valley and along the coast, they should be able to hold off the Germans for days, while we'd have the full use of France's largest port, Marseille, the naval base at Toulon, and a whole string of smaller ports along the coast. We'd never get that kind of harbor capacity along the Channel until after the capture of everything from Brest to Antwerp, and you know that the Germans aren't going to let those fall into our hands in any usable condition."

"The lack of viable ports has been the main limiting factor in our planning for a build-up on the continent," Marshall, who had been silent thus far, volunteered. "We're assuming that we'd have to supply our armies across the beaches for weeks, if not months if we have to do a conventional amphibious invasion. If that's the case, we'll have thousands of troops sitting around in

England that we won't be able to put into the firing line simply because we won't be able to keep them supplied."

"There is also the consideration of weather," Admiral King offered. "In the Channel we'd be looking at very narrow windows of acceptable weather for transporting and landing troops, especially if we're going in over the beach. The Germans would know this, of course, and could concentrate their forces during those periods. In the Mediterranean they don't have anything like the stuff blowing in off the North Sea, ever, and we'd be coming into regular ports, so we can pick our date at our convenience, not based on weather, tides, or anything else."

"And reports from the French Resistance and overhead photography indicate that the Germans are kind of thin on the ground in France right now," Patton said emphatically. "They've got troops there, and tanks, but the tanks are old Panzer IIIs and short-barreled IVs, even old Czech junk. That would change quickly enough once we mixed it up with them, but for the first few weeks, even months, we'd be going up against their second string. The Russians have been holding off the bulk of their army, and the British have been dealing with elite troops in North Africa. For a crucial time, we'd have the best deal going."

"And think of the air war," Hap Arnold said, sweeping his hand in an arc over northern France and the Low Countries. "The Germans are building a shield of radar stations integrated with flak and fighter wings to cover the shortest routes from England to the Ruhr and Berlin, and they're extending it southwards to stretch from Switzerland to the North Sea. If, all of a sudden, we've got bombers based right in southern France, we'll be doing an end run on them from the start. We'll be able to hit all of Germany and the industrial heartland of Italy as well and spread their defenses so thin that they won't know which way to turn. We'll even be able to have fighter cover for our bombers right onto the target. Flying from England, the short-range fighters have to turn back halfway there, and the bombers go in alone. The Germans just hold their own fighters off until the bombers are alone and then let them have it. The British have tried fighter sweeps to try to sucker the Germans up to attrite their fighter forces, but they just ignore the fighters unless they can see that bombers are with them. If one of our missions is to bleed the Luftwaffe white, this is the only way to do it. Since the Germans gave up on blitzing England on a large scale, they've been able to play defense. We'll make them come out and fight us on ground of our own choosing."

Roosevelt held up his hands in mock surrender. "I get the impression, gentlemen, that you seem to think this idea has some merit. But aren't you forgetting one thing? What about the French? Even I can see that a landing in southern France against Vichy would be easier than one against the Germans in the north, but your plan seems to count on having the active support of the French. We seem to be somewhat short of that goal at the moment."

"That's the beauty part of this whole thing, Mr. President," Patton said, spreading his hands wide. "The British come here and shit all over our idea and say, 'Go for North Africa,' and we say, 'Fine!' We go ahead with our planning and training and build-up. Meanwhile, we start negotiations with the French on our own. If the French agree, all we have to do is tell the boat jockeys. . . . No offense," he added hastily, turning toward King, who rolled his eyes. "We tell them our new destination, and we're in business. If the talks fall through, well, we just go with Plan B and do North Africa after all. We'd hit North Africa with less troops and ships, and that's always easy enough to arrange."

"But what about security?" Roosevelt asked. "It would seem that, if the Germans got wind of this, all they would have to do would be to drive across the border and the game's over. We'd never be in a position to get there fast enough to help the French."

"We've got a couple of tricks up our sleeves, sir," Marshall responded. "We, and the British, have been talking to the French right along, promising this, demanding that. The Germans hear about it, but they won't do much unless and until there's solid evidence in their hands, and we'll be shoving false evidence at them so fast they'll think twice about taking action. They've got a pretty full plate right now, and won't make any new commitments until they have to. Vichy is a sweet deal for them, having almost all the benefit of a colony without the responsibility for running or defending it."

"When you put it that way," Roosevelt admitted, "I don't see how we have much to lose. So we go ahead with planning and preparation, with or without British approval, and we don't really have to make a final decision until D-Day."

"Well," Marshall cleared his throat and looked around the room. "We were of the opinion that it would be best *not* to tell the British the full extent of our plans."

Roosevelt cocked his head and frowned. "I'm not very comfortable with lying to our one good ally."

"Not lying, exactly," Marshall continued, "just not being as forthcoming as all that. We should lay out our plan to them, just as we've done here, but I'll bet a million bucks that they'll shoot it down in flames. Then we go along. We let them have tanks if they want tanks, even if we have to strip our units being formed up. If they're hungry for North Africa, we go along, although we still draw the line at committing individual American units under British command. They'll groan, but they'll accept that. We just do our planning for the big show, and we start talking to the French. After the British attack on the French Navy at Mers-el-Kébir after the armistice, it would probably be best not to have the British involved at this point anyway. If things look like they're starting to fall into place, we raise this with the British again, with more evidence on our side. If not, no harm done."

"And what if the British still refuse?" Roosevelt asked. Marshall took a deep breath. "Then we go it alone."

Roosevelt paused for a moment, looking from face to face around the room. "I don't think we can do that. When you are in an alliance, you are either in it or you are not."

"The alternative," King said, "is to hand them an ultimatum. In the words of Abraham Lincoln, if they're not going to use our army, they should let us borrow it for awhile. We'll shift over to the Pacific where we don't have to ask permission to fight the war."

"Well, let's just hope it doesn't come to that. I'm not about to drive this alliance onto the reefs in favor of a tactical advantage." Several of the officers started to speak, but Roosevelt held up his hands. "You've convinced me, in principle, that this is an idea worth pursuing, but it is just a difference in tactics, we've got to look at the big picture."

"Which brings us to the issue of why we need to take the lead here," Marshall said. "We need to recognize that the vision of this administration, the American vision, of the postwar world, is not the same as that of either the British or of any imaginable French government. They want the status quo ante bellum, big empires run from Europe. That's what they want to make the world safe for. The British agreed with forcing de Gaulle to accept an end to the French mandate in Syria and Lebanon and the formation of independent governments, not because they give a hoot about self-determination, but because they'd just as soon see France weaker. If we ever want to see India, Africa, and Southeast Asia free, we're going to have to stop playing second fiddle to the British."

"That sounds good to me," Roosevelt agreed, "but doesn't it follow that the sooner we force a decision on the continent, the *more* of a role the British are going to be playing. It's going to be some time before we even begin to match their numbers of trained and equipped manpower."

"That's just why it might be just as well that the British don't get completely on board with this French plan. In six months, yes, they'll still have more men in the field, but within a year that won't be the case anymore. In the meanwhile, the British will be busy mopping up in North Africa, which we can leave to them, and then we'll have the French thrown into the mix in a big way."

"And we can play one off against the other."

"In a manner of speaking, yes."

Roosevelt sighed and looked out the tall windows across the lawns of the White House toward the ellipse and the Potomac beyond. "Let's give it a try."

The various military men rose to leave, but Roosevelt touched Marshall's sleeve with his hand and said softly, "I'd like to have a quick word with you." Marshall nodded and sat back down as the others filed from the room, a couple of them, Admiral King and Secretary Hull in particular, casting frowning glances over their shoulders as they left.

Roosevelt cleared his throat. "I can see that there are two key assignments involved in your proposal, even before we get into the command of armies and corps and what-not. Someone is going to have to plan this, do the real nuts and bolts work to make it a reality, and someone is going to have to talk to the French. Do you have anyone in mind for those jobs?"

"Naturally, I expect to be up to my ears in the planning, but I had Eisenhower in mind for putting it all together. His staff work at III Corps during the Louisiana maneuvers was little short of brilliant, and he's already done a lot of the preliminary studies."

Roosevelt pursed his lips and nodded. "And for the diplomatic mission? Should it be a career diplomat or a soldier?"

"While you're right that it is diplomacy, the man will be dealing with military men on the other side and ninety percent of the topic under discussion will be military. A diplomat might have the personal skills, but he couldn't have the expertise in hardware and strategy that this calls for. I talked with Eisenhower about this, and he recommended General Mark Clark. He's been our liaison to the Free French for some time, so he's familiar with the players."

"I'm not sure that close ties to the Free French would necessarily stand us in good stead on this one."

"My thoughts exactly, Mr. President," Marshall agreed. "The man I have in mind is Patton."

Roosevelt raised his eyebrows. "From what I've seen and heard of General Patton, he may be a fine field commander, the kind men will follow, but I find it hard to picture him as a diplomat."

"That's true, sir, but he served in France in the last war, and fought alongside the French. That's something they'll respect. Also, he speaks excellent French, which Clark doesn't, and I think anyone who tries to do this braying the King's English and working through an interpreter is going in with two strikes against him. And he knows armor tactics. He'll be able to answer the questions the French will certainly have about what our army can do against the Germans. And, in a sense, his somewhat abrasive personality may work for us. He won't knuckle under to anyone, and he won't mince words either. If he comes back with an agreement at all, I think that it will be one that will stick."

"Then do it, General."

"Yes, sir."

The subsequent conference between Churchill and the Imperial General Staff on one side and Roosevelt with his Joint Chiefs on the other was one of the stormiest of the war. At one point, Admiral King had to be physically restrained from climbing across the table to get at a British general who had made some disparaging comment about American "amateurs," although it was noted that it was late in the evening, and Admiral King had made several visits to the sideboard arrayed with rows of liquor bottles.

As expected, the British had rejected out of hand the idea of an attempt to bring the French back into the war as active allies, but, in the face of American insistence and the frequently repeated threat to divert more resources to the Pacific Theater, they had reluctantly agreed to staff studies of the problem and discreet efforts by the Americans to establish some sort of dialogue with the Vichy regime. It was unanimously agreed, however, that General de Gaulle and the Free French should be kept completely in the dark about the proposal. In the final analysis, Churchill went away well satisfied with a promise from Roosevelt that North Africa would be the target for an invasion before the end of the year, and he was further pleased with Marshall's offer to strip over one hundred new Sherman tanks from the American 1st Armored Division, which had just received them, and to ship these immediately to the British Eighth Army in Egypt to help gear up for Montgomery's expected offensive against Rommel. Churchill was thoroughly convinced when Roosevelt, in a private chat late one evening, commented that he desperately wanted to have American troops in combat against the Germans before the 3 November 1942 elections, adding that the only chance of meeting that deadline would be to send a division or two to support Montgomery or to send them to French North Africa.

SUMMER 1942
WASHINGTON, D.C.

This tentative approval was all that Marshall and his cohorts needed, for the moment. The wheels of the second front were set in motion.

Eisenhower was not particularly pleased with his assignment. Most other brigadier generals of his class, or even younger, were being given field commands and were supervising the training of the units they would be taking into battle. Instead of that, Eisenhower was cloistered in a windowless suite of offices in the basement of the Pentagon with a small nucleus of junior officers, surrounded by stacks of reference works on logistics, cargo ship capacity and loading doctrine, hydrographic maps of the Mediterranean Basin, training logs of new combat units, and reams of intelligence reports about the Axis forces in Western Europe. For days, and then weeks, Eisenhower poured over tables and charts, interrupted only by daily briefings he would give to the Joint Chiefs and sometimes heated meetings with his counterparts from the Navy and the Air Corps.

Eisenhower was surprised that he encountered more obstacles in the form of service doctrines than he did in the physical limitations of the resources available for the operation. For example, he learned early on that shipping capacity was not nearly as limited as he had assumed, and that there was more than adequate tonnage available to transport the forces required for the initial invasion and subsequent resupply and build-up phase. The limitation was in the size of the convoys that the Navy felt it could adequately protect on the trip from the United States to the Mediterranean. The U.S. Navy had decided that a maximum of 45 slow merchantmen could be escorted in a single convoy (compared to 55 for the British) and only 25 in a fast convoy. Since port capacity in southern France and North Africa would not be a problem,

Eisenhower had to convince the Navy of the utmost importance of making a maximum effort at getting the largest quantity of men and materiel across the ocean in the first lift. Assuming that the French were going to let the Allies in without a fight, the key thing was to get as much landed as possible before the Germans could react and either recapture some of the ports or close them through bombing. It ultimately took direct intervention by Marshall, Stimson, and the President to force the Navy to agree to the larger, British-style convoys as well as to allow fast tankers to make the crossing alone and unescorted.

He ran into similar obstructionism from the Air Corps, but on purely philosophical grounds. Between the wars, a number of influential writers had prophesied that future wars could be won from the air without the involvement of the poor, bloody infantry. The theory was that, by identifying key choke points in an enemy's industrial system, such as petroleum refining or the manufacture of vital components of modern machinery, like ball bearings, and destroying these targets from the air, the enemy war machine would simply grind to a creaking halt. Meanwhile, the taste of the enemy populace for war would be diminished by the terror bombing of major cities. The British had begun this "experiment" over the preceding months, and the American flyers were eager to test their own theories of the efficacy of daylight bombing.

The role of the air force in the new operation, now code-named HAY-MAKER, was considerably different. For a large proportion of the aircraft involved, their role would be limited to tactical, not strategic bombing. They would be hitting not the enemy's industrial base, but railroad junctions, bridges, marshalling yards, road networks, and troop concentrations. In a perverted form of logic, the airmen did not want this ground offensive to succeed for the simple reason that it would deny them the chance of proving that they could have done the same thing more easily and cheaply from the air. They argued that, just as warfare had been revolutionized when the armored formations had finally broken the hidebound traditions that tied them to supporting the infantry, it would be revolutionized again if only the fliers could be allowed to break free of their bonds to the ground forces and fight their own kind of war.

Eisenhower, and Marshall acting as arbiter, had listened to impassioned pleas from Hap Arnold and one of his leading bomber commanders, General Curtis LeMay. They listened patiently and commiserated with them about the lack of understanding among civilian politicians for the true art form that was military science, and ultimately they compromised. While there would be a brief period, probably no more than a week or two, in which all air resources would be concentrated on helping to establish the lodgment in southern France, the 8th Air Force in England would then resume strategic bombardment of Germany proper, while the newly formed 12th Air Force would have its headquarters in France itself and would carry the burden of the tactical operations in support of the invasion. Most of the heavy B-17 bombers and long-range fighters like the new P-51s, would remain with 8th Air Force, while light bombers and the older P-40s would move over to the 12th for its largely defensive and close support duties. Marshall also assured Arnold and LeMay that there would be ample opportunity to demonstrate their theories of strategic air warfare in the Pacific, since no one in his right mind looked forward to mounting an invasion of the Japanese home islands.

The most serious resistance to the project, however, came from the British. The ultimate argument of both Churchill and the Imperial General Staff, represented in Washington by General Sir John Dill, was that it was not far from suicidal to place green American troops at the mercy of the scarred veterans of the Wehrmacht. The French, they said, were mere shadows of their former selves, even assuming that they could be persuaded to take up their arms again, and would crumble at the first shot. That would leave the Americans to take their first lesson in combat direct from the masters, and it would be a hard lesson indeed, as the British, Russians, French, and virtually every other nation in Europe could testify from bitter experience.

Eisenhower typically countered with an open invitation for the British to take a larger role in the (still very hypothetical) invasion with their more seasoned forces. The British would then come back with the point that, even if the British sector held, the Germans would naturally concentrate precisely on the Americans, and collapse the line from their end. Neither side was willing to give in, and planning went forward with a major rift in the alliance. The British would only commit a single division, to be landed in North Africa, airborne troops, and some air and naval support, regardless of whether the Americans chose to insist on hitting the continent or not. It was a massive game of chicken, with each side attempting to call the other's bluff. The British, however, were concerned that, although the Americans did seem to be working on a complete plan for the seizure of just French North Africa, they seemed to be devoting much too much effort to staffing out the broader Vichy France scenario, which the British had understood to be a remote contingency plan, more of a staff exercise than a realistic possibility.

During the summer, Churchill made a declaration to the effect that it would be ridiculous to undertake a military operation of the scope of an amphibious invasion of Europe without conducting a "reconnaissance in force." Many American, and even some British military leaders were appalled at his suggestion of putting a full division on the beach in northern France with a view to determining the feasibility of capturing a port in the face of the expected German resistance. His opponents argued that, in terms of reconnaissance, there was nothing the twelve thousand men of a division would be able to see that a squad of commandos or a flight of reconnaissance aircraft could not do with infinitely less risk and cost. They also insisted that the capture of a small port by a division would not necessarily mean that a force of several divisions could then capture a large port, or that failure by the former would imply failure by the latter. What was certain was that dozens or hundreds of precious landing craft would inevitably be lost; casualties would likely be high, and it would be virtually impossible to withdraw much of the raiding force once they had gotten ashore.

Churchill was insistent, however, and most of his commanders supported his views. Lord Mountbatten thought that the raid would provide excellent training for the actual invasion of Europe, whenever it might be launched. Since it was to be essentially a British, or more exactly, a Commonwealth operation, the Americans had little cause to argue, although a small force of U.S. Rangers would be included in the landing force as a token contribution. The bulk of the force would be made up of the 2nd Canadian Division, reinforced by the Rangers and two groups of British commandos and a battalion of the Calgary Tanks.

Early on the morning of 19 August 1942, the Canadians charged ashore across the esplanade at the small seaside resort of Dieppe, just east of the mouth of the River Seine. With insufficient naval gunfire and close air support, and in the face of well-organized defenses manned by the veteran 302nd Infantry Division, the outcome was not surprising. Over one thousand Canadians died in the surf or on the exposed beaches, and not a single tank made it past the high water mark. When the disastrous attack was finally called off, with some of the survivors hauled away by the few still-functioning landing craft, another two thousand Canadians were left as prisoners in the hands of the Germans.

Some British military leaders attempted to use the failure at Dieppe as evidence of the folly of attempting an invasion anywhere on the continent at this time, but the argument rang rather hollow. There were bitter comments in the halls of the Pentagon that Churchill had sacrificed the Canadians on purpose in a poorly designed operation that was bound to fail precisely to make his point, and these sentiments were echoed in Ottawa with the added comment that it was interesting that British troops had not been chosen for the honor. If such had been Churchill's thinking, and no credible evidence has ever surfaced to this effect, he badly miscalculated. Marshall used the Dieppe fiasco in his discussions with Roosevelt to emphasize the risk involved in attempting an amphibious landing against organized German resistance. If the Allies were not simply to resign themselves to sending bombers and dirty looks across the Channel, the only way to come to grips with the Nazis, Marshall insisted, was to gain a viable foothold in the only area where the Germans did not man the defenses. The only place that fit this bill was the Mediterranean coast of France.

By late September, Eisenhower's staff had fairly firm figures for the forces that would be at their disposal between then and the end of the year. A tentative kick-off date of 1 November was set, with a view toward meeting Roosevelt's purely political concern of having American troops in the battle by Election Day. It appeared that the initial expeditionary force would consist of the American 1st and 2nd Armored Divisions, the 1st, 3rd, 9th, 34th, and 36th Infantry Divisions, and a wide assortment of supporting units, including anti-tank, artillery, anti-aircraft, and engineer units. There would also be the 5th Canadian Armored and the 1st Canadian Infantry Divisions and elements of the 2nd Infantry. The American 82nd Airborne and the British 1st Airborne would be dropped well inland to help the French establish a defensive perimeter behind which the heavy ground units could organize. The British 78th Infantry Division would land at Bizerte in Tunisia, and smaller American and British units would occupy other North African ports. Naval forces would include three British and three American battleships, two British and one American carriers, plus four more small American escort carriers, and a host of cruisers, destroyers, submarines, and corvettes, covering for several dozen troop transports and merchantmen and swarms of landing craft of all sizes. There would also be several hundred naval aircraft flying cover missions, and the bulk of the British and American air forces in England would be diverted either to supporting the landings directly or indirectly while over a thousand aircraft would transfer to bases in southern France and North Africa for future operations.

About a third of the American force would be coming directly from the United States in a massive convoy, with the rest being drawn down from the forces building in England. In fact, the 29th Division would be the only sizeable American unit remaining in Britain at this time. The role of the 29th would be to generate radio traffic and other activity to convince German observers that they represented more troops than were actually present. One regimental combat team from the division would also board landing craft and stage an elaborate diversion along the coasts of Normandy to help keep the Germans guessing as long as possible as to the correct location of the impending Allied attack.

The main force of Canadian and American troops would land, hopefully unopposed, at Marseille and a number of minor ports all along the Mediterranean coast, with the Canadians holding the western flank, and the Americans responsible for the eastern and central portions. The initial convoys would also include ships loaded with weapons and vehicles sufficient to equip two French divisions up to American standards: one in Metropolitan France and one in North Africa, with the men drawn from the Vichy troops already in uniform. The rest of the Vichy forces would operate with their current equipment for the moment, until they could be rotated out of the line and re-equipped and trained with gear provided by the United States.

It should be noted that the Canadians had been chosen to join the Americans, partly because the British were still reluctant to commit too many of their own troops, even in an ostensibly hypothetical construct such as HAY-MAKER at this point, and partly because Canadian Prime Minister Mackenzie King had been alienated enough by the Dieppe fiasco to be willing to move into the American camp on this issue. Also, there was the logical assumption that some benefit should be obtained from the dearly bought lessons of Dieppe, thus the inclusion of the reconstituted 2nd Canadian Division.

Based on intelligence reports from British and American spies, the French resistance networks, aerial reconnaissance, and even analysis of the jealously guarded ULTRA intercepts of enciphered German radio transmissions, it was estimated that it would take the Germans at least twenty-four hours to react to the landings, if anything like tactical surprise was achieved. It would take another twenty-four to forty-eight hours before the leading German elements would come into contact with the initial French line of resistance, which would be pulled back well within the borders of Vichy territory. With American and British paratroopers helping in the delaying tactics, the planners expected that the lodgment area would extend the full width of the French coast and up to two hundred miles inland before the first serious ground battles took place, around D+5. By this time, the viability of the landings should have been proven, and a second wave of predominantly British troops from England would have come ashore and would form a strategic reserve.

The initial forces available to the Axis, even assuming that they stripped the defenses of northern France to a bare minimum, were estimated at perhaps three mechanized divisions, either panzer or panzer grenadier, and less than ten infantry divisions. The Italians, to the east, could contribute several more infantry divisions, but these would likely be of low quality and limited offensive capacity. Furthermore, they would necessarily be fighting their way forward through the Alps and relatively easy to contain. The Luftwaffe could be expected to pound the lodgment heavily, but German air resources would still be split between the quagmire of the Eastern Front and the need to continue to defend the Reich against strategic raids from England. The Italian Navy based at La Spezia and both German and Italian submarines also posed a threat, but this was one that both the British and Americans agreed could be handled, especially if the French contributed their own substantial navy to the struggle. By D+7, more German troops would be available, drawn from their central reserves or stripped from the Russian Front, but the Allied build-up would be continuing apace, and the planners were certain that Allied pockets were deeper than those of the Axis.

19 SEPTEMBER 1942
VICHY, FRANCE

All of the foregoing, despite its theoretical brilliance, meant nothing if the Vichy regime did not choose to cooperate, and it was under the burden of this responsibility that the Patton mission set forth. Patton was accompanied only by Colonel Vernon Walters, a young soldier of considerable intellectual achievement who spoke not only fluent French, but a number of other languages as well. They flew to Lisbon, then on to Madrid, and then proceeded by train on a four-day trip that eventually saw them arrive in Vichy in mid-September 1942. The ostensible purpose of the mission was to discuss the release of some Allied aircrews whose machines had been forced down over Vichy territory. Since American military men had come and gone through Vichy often enough since the fall of France, no effort was made to conceal their presence, and they worked directly out of the small U.S. Embassy.

Patton's first problem was to determine with whom he should talk. There was no question that Prime Minister Pierre Laval was not only hostile to the Allies in general, he positively welcomed the German occupation as an opportunity to create in the rump state left to him a totalitarian regime modeled on Nazi Germany, replacing the liberal, bourgeois republic he had found so distasteful. The aging Marshall Petain, while his agreement would ultimately be required to obtain the obedience of the bulk of the Vichy officer corps, was kept in virtual seclusion by Laval, and he would not be the man to work out the details of any accord with the Allies. Admiral François Darlan, probably the single most influential military man in the regime, was also suspect as a collaborator and had, in fact, headed the government for a time when Laval had fallen out of favor with Petain, until the Germans had coerced the French into accepting Laval back into office. Darlan would have to be included in the talks, but no one was overly sanguine about the results if he were the main interlocutor.

Patton was met in Vichy by a young American diplomat, Robert Murphy, who headed the American mission in North Africa and who had been deeply involved in intrigues with clandestine Gaullists and anti-collaborationist Vichy officers for some time. Murphy was able to introduce Patton to General Henri Giraud, a four-star general who had electrified the world by escaping from a German prisoner of war camp the previous spring. Unlike Darlan, he had no baggage of deep-seated hatred for the British, and there was no cause to question his opposition to the Germans. Furthermore, he had steered clear of the Gaullists, who were anathema to the majority of officers in the French military for having spilled French blood in Senegal and Syria, and he carried considerable prestige in the army. Patton readily agreed to include him in their talks.

Lastly, Patton was introduced to retired General Maxime Weygand. At over seventy years of age, he was more a member of Petain's generation than Giraud's, but he was tremendously fit and boasted an obvious, venomous hatred of the Germans. Until recently commander of the Vichy forces in North Africa, he had engaged in repeated talks with Murphy and other Allied delegates on the possibility of France re-entering the struggle against the Reich.

Over a period of several weeks, the talks involving Patton, Darlan, Giraud, and Weygand were held at a variety of small, out-of-the-way offices of the military bureaucracy scattered around Vichy. The town swarmed with

German agents, and rumors were periodically allowed to leak out that the French were blackmailing the Americans, demanding shiploads of grain and fuel oil in exchange for the interned fliers. Similar talks were also going on with General Francisco Franco in Madrid at the time, which lent credence to the story.

The basic outline of the issues soon became clear. The French were willing to consider both allowing the Allies into their territory in Metropolitan France and the rest of the empire as well as taking up arms at their side against Germany *if* the Allies could convince them that the resources to be committed would provide a reasonable chance of success on the battlefield.

Darlan put it succinctly: "If you come with two or three divisions, we will fight you. If you come with ten or twelve, we will join you." He pointed out the case of Greece in 1941. Mussolini had invaded without Hitler's approval, and the Greeks had soundly thrashed the attackers and even counterattacked into Italian-occupied Albania. Then the British had foolishly sent in a single division, which was no longer needed, as a sign of support to the Greeks, but this only gave the Germans a pretext and an incentive to pour in several army corps which soon crushed both the Greeks and the British and conquered the whole country. He then launched into a diatribe against the perfidious British who had cut and run as soon as the Germans attacked in 1940, who had left the French in the lurch and then cold-heartedly turned and massacred the sailors of their former ally at Mers-el-Kébir.

Patton cut Darlan short with a reminder that it was the Germans, not the British, who occupied two thirds of France and who held hundreds of thousands of Frenchmen as slave laborers inside the Reich. He suggested that Darlan might like to sort out his differences with the British at a later date, but it seemed to him that the first enemy to be dealt with should be the Germans. Weygand guffawed at the retort and thumped the much smaller Patton on the back with a force that belied his age.

Darlan, after recovering his composure, asked the pointed question of how the French could know just how much force the Allies really would commit to the campaign. Talk was cheap, he said, and divisions could be created out of thin air and never show up on the battlefield. He added that the French had nowhere to run, no boats waiting to take them back home if things went bad. They had faced the Germans alone once and had first hand knowledge of how merciful they could be. He began to wax eloquent, suggesting that, instead of swinging into the Allied camp at a time when an Allied victory was still very much in question, was perhaps less desirable that gaining better treatment from the Germans through more scrupulous compliance with their requests for raw materials and labor.

Giraud turned on Darlan bitterly and asked him how many prisoners had been released thus far, more than two years after the armistice. None, of course. He sneered as he talked about the much-publicized "relief" program where French workers volunteered for duty in Germany factories on the theory that a French soldier would be released for every worker sent. They had volunteered in hundreds, then thousands, and still more were then coerced by the Vichy government at German demand, and still no prisoners had been released. It was time, Giraud shouted now, bending his tall, lanky body nearly double so that he could pound the dusty desk with more force, that France realize that the Germans would not be satisfied until France had been destroyed and that the least they could do was die with honor, reaching for even the slightest straw that offered any hope of salvation.

Patton acknowledged the point and suggested a simple solution. When all was in readiness for the attack, General Weygand, who enjoyed the respect of every Frenchman in uniform, from the Marshal himself all the way down to the lowliest Moroccan *goumier* manning an outpost in the Rif Mountains, would be invited to inspect the invasion fleet, or expeditionary force, Patton corrected himself He could count the ships, visit the transports and see that they were filled with men, not rag dolls, and examine the tanks in the holds. Patton assured his listeners that the Allies would not go to the trouble and risk of embarking the force they had in mind, over 100,000 men in the initial wave, building up quickly to more than a quarter of a million, with more on the way, and sending that force through waters where U-boat wolf packs lurked, just to stage some kind of massive deception. The French agreed, in principle.

The negotiations then focused on personalities, specifically who would lead the French and what would become of the collaborationists. To begin with, no one present had any qualms about sacrificing Laval on the altar of Allied cooperation. Darlan went so far as to offer to send Churchill Laval's ears in a velvet box, but the group decided that his imprisonment, possibly on the island of St. Helena, for a historical touch, would be more appropriate.

They also agreed that Petain could remain as a figurehead as head of state. Patton, however, pointed out that Roosevelt and Churchill would be hard-pressed to accept an alliance with the kind of police state that Laval had set up under the Marshal's tutelage. Darlan argued that many of the laws of Petain's "national revolution" of 1940, laws restricting the press and setting up camps to train France's youth and instill a sense of patriotism, while having a certain Nazi ring to them, were not very different from those in force in the Allied countries because of the war. He agreed that the hundreds of leftist and Jewish politicians who were languishing in Vichy jails and concentration camps could be released, although he suggested that it might be best for the peace of the nation if they were quietly shipped out to Canada or elsewhere for the duration and that foreign Jewish, East European, and Spanish refugees would also be released from the camps where they were being held. Darlan pointed out that many Frenchmen held the old republic responsible for the disasters of 1940 and would not rally to a new government that only promised a return to the old, corrupt ways. Patton agreed to this, and his instructions certainly did not include making any heroic efforts on behalf of the communists who had survived, even thrived, in their new underground existence and taken control over much of the resistance network.

Then the talk shifted to the subject of de Gaulle. All three of the Frenchmen hotly denounced de Gaulle as a traitor who had spilled French blood in a personal quest for power. He had never been elected to any office and only held the official rank of brigadier general in the old French army, which did not give him any authority to speak for the French nation. Patton argued that, for all of his faults, de Gaulle was the only man with any authority who had not accepted peace with the Germans and who had stuck by the Allies, adding that, if the Allies were to abandon him now, how could their word to any ally be trusted in the future. When the Frenchmen, however reluctantly, accepted the logic of this statement, Patton went on to assure them that the Allies had no intention of dictating to the French what form of government they should have or who its leaders should be. He suggested that de Gaulle be given the command of a corps composed of his own Free French troops, or perhaps a position in the government with a weighty title and not much substance, such as Minister of War.

Giraud cautioned, "If the Germans were to cross into Vichy territory tomorrow, the army would probably fight them. If de Gaulle's troops entered it, there is no doubt that our men would fight them."

Patton thought a long time, staring at a world map in a dusty frame that adorned one wall of the cramped office in which they sat. Suddenly, he rose and pressed his nose close to the glass.

"What about this?" he asked.

The others gathered around curiously. "Corsica?" Weygand asked. "What about it?"

"As you know, de Gaulle has not been made aware of our plans," Patton explained, "but we can't freeze him out forever. Suppose we took his Free French forces, they're about two divisions' worth now, and dropped them on Corsica. It's French territory, so he'd be relatively happy, certainly closer to home than he's been in awhile, but no Vichy troops to worry about. He'd be fighting the Italians. Once he was finished there, the rest of the army would already be busy duking it out with the Germans, and maybe the act of liberating Corsica would earn the Free French a ticket back into the brotherhood. Then you could worry about a post for de Gaulle himself. His men would see that the real war was being fought on the mainland and wouldn't boycott it just to see that their chief's feelings weren't being hurt."

"This wasn't part of your original plan, General?" Weygand said, more as a statement than a question.

"Just thought it up this moment," Patton admitted with a cocky smile. "But it would be a nice back-up. An unsinkable aircraft carrier right opposite Italy's industrial heartland, and, once we have Corsica, Sardinia won't last long. With both of them in our hands, our supply lines into Marseille would be secure. It should be a low-cost victory, and the Germans will be too busy trying to push us out of southern France to risk getting troops across the water onto that island, and the Italians shouldn't be too much of a challenge," he went on, talking faster and faster. "By God, I like it more the more I think about it!"

After each session, the three French flag officers would visit Petain and explain the day's dealings. There were further demands for American arms to re-equip the French Army and arguments about shipping capacity. Darlan put these to rest by pointing out that he would be contributing (he always considered French vessels his own personal property) more than a quarter of a million tons of merchant shipping to the Allied pool. If only a third of this were dedicated to supplies for the French Army, it would meet their needs, as well as the food import requirements of the population, and still leave a major net gain for Allied shipping capacity. To facilitate the incorporation of American equipment, the French quickly agreed to organize their new divisions along American lines, although, in the event, French divisions would always be smaller and weaker than their American counterparts, the French commanders considering it more important to have more generals' billets to dole out and larger numbers of "divisions" to discuss at Allied conferences, than effective fighting power on the ground. All of these considerations were relatively minor, however, and, by the first week in October, Patton and Walters were making their tortuous way back to Washington to brief Roosevelt, Marshall, and Eisenhower.

26 SEPTEMBER 1942
WASHINGTON, D.C.

Patton had been in communication with Washington throughout the talks via encoded messages from the embassy in Vichy, although, given their own experience of having broken both the German and Japanese diplomatic codes, the Allies were understandably reluctant to entrust much in the way of detail to this medium. Consequently, there was some turmoil in Washington when Patton outlined the specifics of his agreement with the French. Cordell Hull had objected to the lack of more guarantees of a return to full democracy in France as part of the alliance package, and Patton had bluntly suggested that Hull provide him with a copy of the guarantees that had been received from the Soviets for the same thing, and he would happily work them into the deal with the French. Admiral King was very leery of letting the French know at all when the invasion was planned to take place, in case they should choose to pass this along to the Germans and lead the convoys into the largest ambush in history, and it was generally agreed that the French would be given only a general timeframe for the move—no specific dates until the armada was actually approaching the French coast. Lastly, Eisenhower was pulling his hair, or would have been if he had some, about the complications to the logistical planning involved with the addition of invading Corsica to his original blueprint. But, ultimately the agreement was ratified by Roosevelt and the Joint Chiefs.

The real challenge, everyone knew, would be in getting that sort of agreement out of the British. It had become apparent in the preceding months that Churchill had gone along with the planning sessions primarily on the assumption that the stiff-necked French would never submit to any sort of feasible plan, and he now made a number of suggested modifications which were clearly designed to sabotage it. He insisted that Tunisia, being adjacent to the area where active operations were still being conducted against the Germans, should be placed under a United Nations mandate, but Roosevelt rejected this out of hand.

The British also became suddenly very protective of the rights of General de Gaulle, after having spared no pains to handicap his efforts to organize the Free French movement and having courted the Vichy regime openly over the previous two years. French troops on British soil when France surrendered were virtually coerced into returning to their homeland instead of joining de Gaulle, and those captured when the Allies seized Syria and Lebanon had been scrupulously returned to France without de Gaulle's agents having any opportunity to try to recruit them. Churchill now demanded that de Gaulle be given command of the French Armed Forces, probably in the hope that the Vichy regime would kill the entire project in protest, but Roosevelt killed this tactic by the simple expedient of pointing out that the French just might accept, and no one wanted to face a France with de Gaulle in a position of authority. Thus, with British involvement kept to a minimum and with dire warnings from the Imperial General Staff about impending disaster ringing in their ears, the planners were allowed to go forward.

Of course, General de Gaulle's reaction, when he was finally told of the plan to send Allied troops into his home country and the agreements reached with the Vichy regime to achieve this, was probably only slightly less hostile than the German reaction was expected to be. De Gaulle had been declared an outlaw by Petain and his followers for what they saw as an irresponsible attitude, placing millions of Frenchmen at risk, men and women who did not have the luxury of escaping German occupation. He was also accused of selling out French interests to the British in exchange for the minimal support they gave the Free French movement. Still, he had stayed the course and rallied thousands -of-his countrymen to the Allied cause, both within and outside France. Now, when it seemed that the moment of victory was within view, he was to be robbed of all authority by the naive Americans who had made a pact with the devil.

An explanation of the plan for his Free French forces to command the liberation of Corsica mollified him not at all. Even when the Americans added their own 3rd Infantry Division to the invasion force, but under the command of General Koenig, he ranted that he was being shunted aside. It was only when, at a meeting of his own senior field commanders, including Koenig and Leclerc, he was told that the only apparent option, that of boycotting the entire operation and standing aside while foreigners undertook the actual liberation of French soil, would not be acceptable to his troops, that de Gaulle finally accepted the *fait accompli* and turned his considerable persuasive talents to the task of recruiting the mafia-like *Union Corse* to the cause of the liberation.

The only issue that remained to be decided was who should command the invasion force. Another sticking point with the French had initially been that Giraud had insisted on the command for himself, but Patton had pointed out that total numbers of men would not be the deciding factor, but the presence at the front of organized divisions with modern equipment. If, at the end of a few months, France had the largest force in this category, such a demand would be justified, but that was not the case now, nor would it be for some time. Since the Americans would provide the bulk of the initial force, the British had agreed that the Supreme Commander would have to be American.

Marshall was the only serious contender for the job, and he wanted it desperately. Roosevelt was extremely reluctant to lose him as chief of staff, since he had experience in handling strategy at the global level that no one else in the military possessed at that point. He also had long experience in dealing with Congress, a vital skill for the administration. However, Roosevelt recognized the entire program as Marshall's baby, and the appointment was made. Marshall would be Supreme Commander of Allied Forces, Europe. Eisenhower would move up and take over as chief of staff, while Patton would be given overall command of the ground forces for the invasion. This last position would be eliminated once it was considered that the Allies were firmly established ashore, and Patton would revert to command of the American Fifth Army, as the combined American forces would be designated once sufficient troops were ashore.

It has been argued by historians of the period that Eisenhower was seriously considered for the post of Supreme Allied Commander, based on scattered notes and memoranda from the White House that have since come to light. Naturally, it is hard to imagine how a man who was a mere brigadier general until only recently and who had never experienced combat could have been presented as being qualified for such a command. The theory relies principally on Roosevelt's reluctance to part with Marshall, for, despite the cool personal relations between the president and his chief of staff, Roosevelt had come to depend upon Marshall's intelligence and grasp of the strategic big picture. One uncorroborated source from within the White House has claimed that what swung the decision in Marshall's favor was Roosevelt's suspicion that Eisenhower was too easily impressed by the British and too likely to knuckle under to British demands in the inter-allied squabbles that would inevitably arise during the course of the campaign. Eisenhower, from his close contacts with General Dill and other British officers, had apparently taken to referring to lunch as "tiffin" and to gasoline as "petrol." Considering the fact that Eisenhower had only spent short visits in England, this kind of cultural assimilation does imply a certain malleability m Eisenhower's personality that it is perhaps just as well was never put to a test.

With all of the agreements signed and the planning completed, it only remained for Marshall to pick a date for the assault. By the second half of October, the units involved had been trained up to standard, the required shipping gathered, and the loading of thousands of tons of equipment, supplies, and munitions begun. The timing would now depend upon finding the optimal moment for the attack in relation to events on other battlefields of the war. In North Africa, Rommel's offensive into Egypt had been stopped cold by 1 September, and General Montgomery, who had recently taken command of Eighth Army, was steadily building his strength for a counteroffensive. This was scheduled to start on 23 October, and Marshall wanted to wait at least until the offensive had begun to gain ground, focusing German attention on that front, before making his own move.

Events on the Russian Front, however, promised to be even more significant. Once it had been decided to proceed with HAYMAKER, American Ambassador in Moscow, Averill Harriman, met with Stalin on 20 October and briefed him in person on the plans for the second front. While this met the demands that the Soviets had been making of the Western Allies for months, Stalin retained his usual reserve, implying that he would believe it when he saw it. The only concession of significance from the Russians came over a week later when Marshal Georgi Zhukhov suddenly called for a meeting with Harriman and outlined for him, in very vague terms, a Soviet plan for an offensive designed to cut off the German Sixth Army, along with the armies of their Romanian and Hungarian satellites, at Stalingrad. Zhukhov would only state that the Soviets had concentrated sufficient forces in the area to destroy these three armies and tear a huge hole in the German front, with a probable jump-off date of mid-November. He suggested that, if the Allies timed their own landings to occur shortly after the collapse of the Stalingrad line, they might catch German reinforcements en route to help plug the gap, too far away from France to be of use there, and not yet arrived in Russia. The indecision and likely changes in direction this would cause might well result in substantial German units not taking part in either battle but spending crucial days being shunted around railroad marshalling yards.

This idea made perfect sense to Marshall, who noted to Roosevelt that it was the first time that the Soviets had seen fit to share a significant piece of strategic information with the Western Allies. In one late-night meeting, Roosevelt briefly brought up his desire to get American troops into the fight before Election Day on 3 November. Marshall coldly replied that he would resign before committing American troops to combat ten minutes ahead of time for purely political reasons. Roosevelt did not reply and never raised the matter again. D-Day would now be postponed until at least the third week in November.

This gave rise, briefly, to a concern that Montgomery would drive Rommel's Afrika Korps so swiftly that the Germans would be tempted to seize Tunisia in order to give themselves more maneuver room and to shorten their supply lines. The Vichy French had, for some time, been allowing the Axis to ship supplies for Rommel through the port of Bizerte—and this practice was to continue right up until the Allied landings, to avoid making the Germans suspicious—but an actual Axis conquest of the territory would have thrown the Allied timetable off considerably. Fortunately, Rommel conducted such a masterful retreat and Montgomery such a leisurely pursuit from Egypt that by mid November Rommel was still holding a line at Mersa Brega in central Libya, over four hundred miles east of the Tunisian border, more or less at the point from which he had begun both his 1941 and 1942 offensives. There was, therefore, no undue pressure on the Germans to invade Tunisia to obtain maneuver room to the rear. In fact, by the time of the landings in France, Rommel would have only retreated to Buerat, another one hundred miles to the west but with several hundred miles of Libyan Desert behind him.

In the event, the Soviet offensive was postponed as Stalin and his commanders poured still more men and guns into the vast trap that would spring on the Germans at Stalingrad, and HAYMAKER was pushed back into December. As D-Day approached, and as it became increasingly clear to the British that the Americans were actually going to go through with the operation, Churchill ordered full cooperation by his staff, since a disaster in southern France could set the Allied cause back months, if not years, and any hint that his intransigence might have contributed to such a disaster could cripple the alliance forever. It was a team of British intelligence officers, therefore, who came up with the idea of "the man that never was," a carefully concocted and scrupulously supported scheme to convince the Germans that the Allied landings in southern France, about which rumors were rife throughout Europe, was a diversion at best. They went so far as to find a recently deceased man, who had died in a mountaineering accident of exposure, and preserved his body. They had then fitted the body out as a British staff officer and dropped him off the coast of Spain, on the assumption that the Spanish authorities would certainly pass the information on to the Germans, but that lack of local technical skill would reduce the chances of the enemy discovering the fraud through timely forensic evaluation. They then sequestered the actual staff officer whose identity they had used, making it look as if he had indeed perished en route to Gibraltar carrying a copy of battle plans which were now safely in German hands. These "plans" would detail an Allied intent for a massive landing at Calais, exactly where Hitler expected it. It proved to be one of the intelligence coups of the war.

The convoys bearing nearly half of the American contingent for the invasion departed directly from several American ports and followed a zigzag route across the Atlantic. The Canadians and other American units were brought down from the British Isles, and the Free French shipped out of Egypt. In a tremendous stroke of luck, the eastbound convoys were apparently not even sighted by the enemy until passing through Gibraltar, and only subjected to one unsuccessful U-boat attack. The Free French convoy from Egypt was found near Sicily by an Italian submarine which scored a single torpedo hit against a transport, but the ship managed to limp on to Corsica while the destroyer escorts drove off the attacker.

The last act came when the elderly General Weygand was taken out to sea in a fishing smack and picked up in the dark of night by a British Shortland flying boat off the port of Sète and brought into Gibraltar in total secrecy. He spent the better part of the next day overflying the huge mass of shipping and actually went aboard the flagship *Augusta* to meet the commander of the naval force, Rear Admiral H. Kent Hewitt, and General Patton for a quick lunch. He then returned to France to report to Marshal Petain that the Allied invasion force was larger than he had ever seen. In fact, it was the largest amphibious invasion force ever assembled in history.

CHAPTER 3

POUNCE!

1030 Hours, 19 December 1942
Near La Spezia, Italy

ENSIGN CECIL FIELDING eased back on the stick of his Royal Navy Albacore biplane and wished he had something a little more modem with which to face his first encounter with the enemy. The fact that the Albacore was newer than the Swordfish torpedo planes that had succeeded in crippling the German battleship *Bismarck* earlier in the war did not alter the fact that both aircraft were hopelessly obsolete and that he would not stand a ghost of a chance if he should encounter enemy fighters. His squadron commander had assured the men of his flight at the briefing in the wee hours of the morning that they did not expect much hostile fighter activity, and a squadron of Sea Hurricanes from his carrier, *Furious,* would be flying top cover for them on the mission. Still, with a huge torpedo strapped to the underside of his fuselage, his Albacore was dreadfully slow and did not even have the superior maneuverability that biplanes allegedly enjoyed over their single-winged counterparts. With only a pair of Vickers machine guns facing forward and a single Lewis gun in the rear observer's seat, Fielding felt decidedly naked in his open cockpit.

There was nothing for it, however, and Fielding followed the lead plane in his flight as it banked toward the coast, with the headland of Portovenere off to his right, flying as low as they dared, as they headed toward the Italian naval base at La Spezia. Just two years earlier, British carrier planes had struck a brilliant blow by staging a night torpedo raid on the Italian base at Taranto, crippling four battleships and a cruiser at the cost of only two aircraft. The captain of the *Furious* had cautioned the men not to expect such an easy time of it on this occasion, since neither the Italians nor anyone else had thought such an attack possible in 1940, but now they new better. But in support of the major Allied offensive that was underway, the captain had asked them to do something "fairly spectacular" by way of giving the Italian Navy a bloody nose and encouraging them to stay out of the way. That was why the attack would be coming in from the north, sweeping over the town of La Spezia itself and hitting the fleet from the landward side on the assumption that most of the base's defenses would be oriented against an attack from the sea.

From the view Fielding got when he leveled off for the run down the bay leading south from La Spezia, it appeared that the Italians would take a good deal of encouragement to sit out this campaign. A massive column of ships was under steam and proceeding majestically down the waterway toward the open sea. From hours of studying his enemy vessel recognition manual in his cramped bunk on the *Furious,* Fielding readily identified three battleships: *Roma, Vittorio Veneto,* and *Italia,* followed by several cruisers and escorted by a swarm of destroyers. His mind swam as he quickly tried to tote up the number of anti-aircraft guns in the fleet. Each battleship carried a dozen 3.5 inch guns plus 40 machine guns, times three, plus about three dozen guns for each cruiser, times about six, plus maybe twenty guns for each destroyer. He gave up the effort before even considering the guns that would also be firing from the shore just as his flight leader banked hard to port to bring the aircraft in at an angle to the enemy column to give them a broad flank shot at the huge ships. Fielding wished vainly that he had been assigned to one of the aircraft that would drop 1,500-pound mines at the entrance to the bay and then serenely return to the carrier, their job done.

In fact, flak was already bursting around him as the surprised gunners near the port belatedly spotted the British planes and sent up streams of tracers and heavier shells that bloomed in small black clouds like little mushrooms popping up after a good rain. Fielding gave thanks as he gripped the vibrating controls that the Albacore, for all its slowness and clumsiness, was a damn tough plane, rather like a bloody dinosaur with a brain the size of a walnut, and it only had one or two vital parts that would have to be hit to bring it down. Unfortunately, he reflected, *he* was one of those parts, and he found the armored seat under his backside of very limited comfort as his craft was buffeted by exploding flak that peppered the wings and fuselage like deadly hail.

The idea was to sink or damage one or two of the big ships as they tried to leave the protected harbor, possibly blocking the channel with their carcasses. If that failed, the attack from the rear might serve to drive the survivors out into the open where a pair of British submarines lay in wait for them and might force the ships to maintain speed that would make it hard for them to avoid the floating mines that had been laid in the approaches to the harbor. If they still had their hearts set on a sortie, there was an Allied squadron just east of Corsica. The Italians' formation would undoubtedly be jumbled from the attacks from above and below, and they would have to face the guns of the Royal Navy battleships *Duke of York* and *Rodney,* the battlecruiser *Renown,* and the American battleship *Massachusetts* and a pair of cruisers, plus a host of destroyers, with *Furious* providing air cover. The Allies could have launched their attack earlier, at dawn, but it had been thought best to let the Italians get word of the landings and come out from behind their torpedo nets and other fixed defenses. If they could be brought to battle out in the open, and destroyed once and for all, the Allies could divert a significant portion of their naval power out of the Mediterranean, to the Pacific for instance, but if the Italian fleet remained a "fleet in being," safe in port, a comparable Allied force would have to remain on hand to counter it.

Suddenly Fielding's observer screamed through his headset, "Fighters, eight o'clock high!"

Fielding twisted around to his left and saw the silhouettes of two small planes, probably Fiat G-50's from the base at Lucca, but he also saw half a dozen other shapes diving on them like birds of prey, the protective Sea Hurricanes. Fielding forced himself to turn forward and concentrate on his torpedo run. It was the fighters' job to deal with the bandits. He only had one shot, and had to get it right.

The ships had spotted the danger now and were putting up curtains of fire, but it was too late. Fielding roared between a pair of destroyers and lined up on the *Italia,* trying to adjust for her forward speed as he came in at a narrow angle. He released the torpedo, and the aircraft leapt upward. He turned and saw his wingman do the same just before a fiery tongue of flame reached out from one of the escorting destroyers and sliced off one of the plane's wings, sending it cartwheeling into the water. They were flying far too low for parachutes to be of any use.

Fielding pushed the throttle forward and began to climb, but he could not resist banking to see the results of the attack. A geyser of water erupted from the side of the Italia, then another, and the steel monster shuddered vis-

ibly as the milky white of her wake diminished to a mere ripple and smoke
began to pour from the stricken vessel. Just then a wave of American dive
bombers from the *Ranger* came screaming down, and more jets of water shot
up around the *Italia* as her captain tried to ease the wallowing ship into shallow
water to beach her as well as to get her out of the way of the *Via Veneto* which
was coming up fast from behind on a collision course. The Americans came
in groups of four, their 1,000-pound bombs hitting with a steady rhythm:
miss, miss, hit, miss . . . miss, hit, hit, hit. Tongues of orange flame could
now be clearly seen amid the thick black smoke, and Fielding smiled grimly.

He loitered now, viewing the battle. Enemy anti-aircraft gunners had
plenty to do firing on attacking planes and would have no time for him. *Roma*
had also taken at least one hit and was down by the head, moving slowly, and
a torpedo or bomb had broken the back of a destroyer that was already disappearing under the waves. The sea was covered with a greasy slick of oil that
was burning in places and littered with scores of tiny black dots that would
be crewmen, living and dead. Other bombers were hitting the docks and oil
storage tanks on shore, and several ships were burning at the quay. He
watched as the last of the attackers peeled off and headed back out to sea, and
Via Veneto began to make a gentle turning arc, trying to get back to the protection of the harbor with her escorts. *Italia's* decks were awash, and a fire
was apparently out of control on *Roma 's* bow. There would be no sortie by
the *Regia Marina* any time soon. It was half a loaf, Fielding had to admit, but
it was better than none.

1100 HOURS, 19 DECEMBER 1942
MARSEILLE, FRANCE

Lieutenant Commander W.E. Ellis, USN, leader of fighter squadron VGF-26
from the escort carrier *Sangamon,* had never seen such activity in any port
in the world, even what he had thought was a veritable beehive back at Norfolk as the fleet had prepared to depart the United States. As he steered his
Grumman F4F Wildcat in a lazy racetrack pattern over the port he could see
what looked like swarms of ants besieging each of the dozens of transports
and merchantmen lined up along the quay as mountains of supplies grew
along the dockside and long columns of olive drab Army trucks wound their
way through the adjoining streets and into the city. But Ellis could not afford
to pay much attention to the spectacle taking place below him.

For nearly an hour he had been listening to the frantic radio traffic of other squadrons to the north and east as they clawed at the German and Italian bomber formations that were steadily advancing toward Marseille. It had taken the Nazis some time to realize that this major port was in Allied hands, and still more to get a respectable strike organized, with their airfields throughout northern France having been pounded the night before by British Wellingtons and again at the crack of dawn by American B17s, but they were coming now, with a vengeance. Surely every pilot aloft, on both sides, knew that the Allies would never again be as vulnerable as they were right at this moment, with thousands of tons of shipping jammed into this harbor, each ship loaded to the gills with all sorts of explosive and flammable cargo, and men. If the enemy could close the port now and prevent the off-loading of the men and guns, the German panzers would be able to walk over all resistance and take the port back, crippling the American Army in the process. If not, the Allies were back in France to stay, and it would only be a matter of time until Germany would fall.

So the Germans were throwing in everything they had, but the Allies had had all night to get ready. Ellis had listened to the pilots of the Army P-40s that had flown in off the escort carrier *Chenango* as they spotted the enemy Heinkels and Junkers and dove in for the kill. Then there were the Messerschmitt Bf-109s and the Focke-Wulf 190s that, in turn, pounced on the P-40s. The American pilots were almost exclusively new to combat, from the wing commanders on down, and Ellis could hear the fear in their voices as one after another they went off the air. From the sound of it, they had thinned out the attackers some, but they were still coming, as were the Italians who had mixed it up with VGF-27 off the *Suwannee* to the east, commanded by an academy classmate, Ted Wright. They were coming in dribs and drabs, as the Germans had been able to throw them together, six here, twenty there, rather than in a coordinated attack, and that was good, but there were a lot of them.

Ellis scanned the sky around him, above, on all sides, and especially in the direction of the sun. There had been an RAF pilot on the *Sangamon,* a veteran of the Battle of Britain, who had given them a crash course (no pun intended, he had said) in German fighter tactics, and he had scrawled on the blackboard, "BEWARE OF THE HUN IN THE SUN!" and underlined it several times. But it seemed to Ellis, as he shielded his eyes against the glare, that, if the Germans did come at him from that direction, the first he'd know of it would be tracers stitching the sky in front of him. He was also not too confident of his pudgy, stubby-winged aircraft. The F4F was sturdy and had considerable firepower in its six .50 caliber machineguns mounted in the wings, but it was far slower than the German Bf-109s, even slower than the twin-engined Me-110s, and no match whatsoever for the Focke-Wulf 190s. Ellis sighed. Designing and manufacturing a new aircraft was probably out of the question now, since he could just make out the dark specks above the horizon that would be the first enemy planes.

Ellis's squadron followed his lead as he gained altitude and then headed straight at the approaching bombers, acting on the theory that the bombers had the least firepower facing forward, even though the combined convergence speed was over five hundred miles per hour, and he would only have seconds to get off his first burst. They were Ju-88s, big twin-engined jobs painted forest green, and they tried to maneuver to avoid him as Ellis pressed his trigger, watching the yellow tracers criss-cross around his target. He could clearly see pieces of the wing surfaces tear off from solid hits as he roared by, and he quickly pulled the plane into a tight loop to get on the bombers' tail.

There were no enemy fighters in view, as any escorting fighters must have been diverted by the earlier encounters with the Army P-40s farther north, so it was nothing but a turkey shoot. Of course, these particular turkeys could shoot back. They did have two machine guns in the domed crew compartment, one forward and one rear-facing, and another in the belly facing the tail, but they were nothing like the American B17s with a total of five single and four twin .50 caliber machine gun mountings covering every angle of the aircraft. Ellis and his wingman hovered just behind one lumbering Ju-88, chewing away at its tail with their guns while weaving back and forth until they were rewarded with a thick trail of white smoke coming from one engine as the bomber began a slow, painful tum toward the earth. Ellis had planned to follow it all the way down, to confirm his first kill, but a frantic call came over the radio.

"Bogies, coming in high from the north!"

Ellis turned to gain altitude again, and he saw a large twin-engined plane pouring fire into an F4F that tried to tum out of its way. This was one of the "destroyers," the Me-110s normally assigned to take out British and American bombers, and armed with two 20mm cannon and four machine guns. They were too sluggish to stand up to the nimble British Spitfires or the new American P-51s, but it occurred to Ellis that they might be one of the few German fighters with the range to reach here from bases in northern France. The F4F was burning, and Ellis could clearly see the pilot struggling with his canopy, but it would not open. Ellis bore in on the Me-110, firing as he went, in the hope of at least distracting the attacker, but then he was past them and had to dive out of the way of yet another enemy fighter.

There were just too many of them, and Ellis's wingman was gone. In fact, he could only see two or three other American planes at all, while the sky was full of German fighters now, and he could see at least a dozen Ju-88s heading toward the port. Just then, a babble of voices came over the radio, speaking something that wasn't English, and he saw at least twenty sleek fighters, all painted a dark blue and unfamiliar to him, diving on the bombers, blasting at least half of them out of the sky on their first pass. Finally, one turned broadside to him, and he could see the three vertical stripes near the tail: red, white and blue. They were the French!

The German fighters turned away from the Americans to face this new threat, and Ellis and the surviving F4Fs pursued them with a vengeance. The odds were more than even now, and he downed one more bomber and damaged another now that he didn't have to worry about the enemy fighters so much. The battle went on for what seemed like hours, although Ellis knew that it could only have been minutes. And then, all at once, the sky was empty of the enemy. He looked around and could see a couple of fighters from his squadron heading out to sea to return to the carrier, and he joined them. As he did so, a French fighter pulled up alongside him, and the pilot waved and gave an enthusiastic thumbs-up sign before banking away himself. Down below, the port of Marseille sprawled across the coastline, and several thick columns of smoke rose from the docks and from one stricken tanker which was burning fiercely out in the roadstead, and little clouds of smoke from anti-aircraft fire still dotted the sky like wildflowers in a springtime field. But the unloading was still going on. They had won, at least this first round.

2200 HOURS, 22 DECEMBER 1942
THE WOLFSCHANZE, EAST PRUSSIA

Admiral Canaris had seen Hitler in a rage before, but never like this. The "little corporal," as Canaris could not help thinking of him, was screaming hysterically, banging the large map table in the center of his command bunker with both fists, spittle flying from his lips, and the veins at his temple throbbing. If there was one thing worse for a senior German military officer than being wrong, it was being right when Hitler was in the wrong. It had become apparent by midday on the 19th to both Canaris and von Rundstedt that the naval shelling and small-scale troop landings along the Channel coast could only be a diversion, despite the "evidence" Canaris' spies had provided. Tens of thousands of Allied troops were ashore in southern France, and the ports of the entire Riviera were jammed with shipping. Still, Hitler had clung to his conception that the main Allied blow must fall in the north, and precious hours, then days, had been wasted as the limited armored reserves available had either been held in place or even been moved up toward Normandy, *away* from the real scene of battle.

New reconnaissance reports had finally dispelled all doubts, but Hitler could not stand to have his legendary infallibility questioned. *He* had been right in France in 1940 when his generals had wanted to hold back and not drive for the Channel to cut off the British and French forces in Belgium. *He* had been right in Russia during that first terrible winter when the generals had wanted to pull back all the way to Poland in the face of the Soviet offensive, and he had proven it possible for the troops to hold their line. Now he had been wrong in believing that Petain would never go over to the Allies and that they would never consider invading the continent at any point but that at which he had decreed they should come. Coming in the wake of the complete surrounding of the Sixth Army at Stalingrad, this all put the Führer in a very bad mood indeed.

Canaris never failed to be impressed at how some of the most powerful men in the world, men who had all faced death on the battlefield many times, could be cowed into silence, if not quivering terror, by the rantings of this little man. All of the key commanders were present today. There was the dark and brooding General Wilhelm Keitel, ostensible commander of the *Oberkommando der Wehrmacht* (OKW) and the mousy, balding Alfred Jodl, the OKW chief of staff, two of Hitler's "desk generals," but there was also the venerable Field Marshal von Rundstedt, commander of the forces in the West and Field Marshal Albert Kesselring, Commander-in-Chief South. The immense Reichsmarschall Goering, commander of the Luftwaffe, moped in a chair set away from the table, out of favor since his lofty promises to supply the Stalingrad garrison by air had turned to dust, and Admiral Dönitz frowned heavily as he stared at the situation map. Even the popular, almost legendary

General Erwin Rommel was present, on medical leave from North Africa, along with a bevy of colonels and junior officers, besides the ever-present SS bodyguards in their black uniforms, towering over the lesser beings in the Spartan conference room.

Hitler had repeatedly reminded all present that Canaris and each of the intelligence services had assured all and sundry that the Allies would land on the Channel coast and that the activity in the Mediterranean was a diversion. This was true enough, and Canaris could only chide himself for having been taken in by the enemy's disinformation campaign that had certainly hindered the Axis response. But Canaris could hardly point out that it had been Hitler who had continued to reject increasingly solid evidence that had come in proving where the main Allied blow indeed had fallen. Now all the generals just wanted to get the recriminations over with so that they could get on with the business of fixing the problem. Much to everyone's surprise, it was Rommel, the junior man at the table, who spoke up first as soon as Hitler had lapsed into silence.

"It would seem that our only course of action is to withdraw the Afrika Korps from Tripolitania, along with as many Italian troops as possible, and re-equip them to form the core of a major thrust at the Allied beachhead." It seemed to Canaris that Rommel was overplaying his hand as Hitler's favorite. It also seemed to him that Rommel was more hype than substance, since his own conversations with a number of field officers who had served in North Africa painted a picture of a vain, impetuous man, many of whose victories were actually the work of his subordinates who ran the army while Rommel was out cruising about the desert, while most of his defeats could be attributed directly to Rommel's own lack of conception regarding logistics.

Jodl immediately spoke up. Years on the staff had taught him to anticipate the Führer's wishes and to voice his opinions for him. "While we are all duly impressed with the withdrawal General Rommel conducted across the desert, holding the British at bay and salvaging most of his force, we should remember that wars are never won by retreats." Hitler just nodded vacantly, staring at the map before him.

"I should point out that our attempts to seize Tunisia ran into strong French resistance, and we discovered a full British division already on the ground in Bizerte," Kesselring joined in. "While it is a shame to abandon North Africa after all the sacrifices our men have made there, with Tunisia in enemy hands, there is no hope of supplying our forces in Tripolitania. And the troops we had collected in Italy for a *coup de main* in Tunisia would be much better employed in an offensive against Vichy territory on the continent."

"And we would only have to transport the men from Africa," Rommel added. "We had only thirty tanks in running order in the whole Panzer Armee Afrika when I left, and those were mostly older models. The men, however, are among the best tankers in the Wehrmacht and have long experience fighting the British. With a minimum of shipping and air transport, they can all be brought home and fitted out with the new Panther and Tiger tanks coming out of the factories and thrown right into the battle."

"I don't believe that Mussolini will be able to survive the loss of North Africa as well as that of Corsica, to say nothing of the destruction of the Italian 8th Army and the Alpine Corps north of Stalingrad," Hitler growled. "You generals simply don't understand the political side of things. The Duce is surrounded by a pack of jackals who are only waiting for his winning streak to break to start nipping at his heels." He paused and looked suspiciously around the room, and all of the generals quickly looked away. "We must do something to help defend Corsica."

Dönitz shook his head. "The Italian fleet got a drubbing at La Spezia, and they won't show their faces again. The British and Americans made them cry like school girls." This brought some gruff laughter from around the table. "And the French fleet just bombarded Genoa, sinking at least one Italian destroyer and several merchantmen. Our U-boats and some Italian submarines have had some success near Marseille, taking several American transports, but there is a heavy concentration of escorts and aircraft there, and we have also lost contact with U-235, feared sunk. I'm afraid the balance at sea has tipped decisively against us in the Mediterranean."

"But what about by air?" Hitler asked.

"We have nearly a division of German paratroopers and another of Italians on hand, but there is no way we could bring in armor or supplies by sea. They could prolong the battle, but they could not drive the Americans and French into the sea," Kesselring concluded. "Corsica is lost, but it's still not Italian territory. If we don't hit the Allies hard on the continent, where it counts, they'll be pushing along the coast into Italy proper soon enough, and then Mussolini will really have something to worry about."

There was a long pause, and Hitler turned his back on the officers, facing a situation map of the Eastern Front without seeing it. "Then let it be so. Pull as many men out of North Africa as possible, Germans first of course. You can use them and the troops earmarked for Tunisia to mount your counter-offensive."

"But that will take time, days at least," von Rundstedt objected. "I've got the 26th Panzer and the 3rd and 29th Panzer Grenadier Divisions in France now. If you'll release them from OKW reserve, my Führer, and return to us the 6th Panzer that we sent to Russia, we can drive right through the Americans now, before they dig in. They've never seen the likes of a panzer corps, and they'll run like sheep. There will be British divisions in the follow-on shipments, and they are not likely to be as skittish. We need to hit them now if we are going to have any hope of success."

Hitler smiled and shook his head as if dealing with a small child's fears of the dark. Manstein is screaming for every man he can get to face a horde of Russians *now, today,* and he's within his rights, trying to hold open a corridor so that Kleist can pull his army back from the Caucasus and punch through to rescue von Paulus in Stalingrad, so we can't cut any corners on the support we've sent east. But you seem to be forgetting the British forces still sitting in England. What do you suppose they're planning to do? I've said all along, and I'll say again, that the only logical route from London to Berlin is through the Pas de Calais. The minute you strip the north of armor, it will be like an engraved invitation to the British to storm ashore and catch you between two fires. Will you be better off then?

Von Rundstedt opened his mouth to argue, but Hitler cut him off. "Of course not. You can have the 29th Panzer and 3rd Panzer Grenadier besides the available infantry and whatever troops Kesselring has at hand and can salvage from North Africa. That much I'll give you. That should still be more than enough." He turned to Kesselring. "Corsica is a lost cause, but I want Sardinia reinforced. It's Italian soil, and we can't let the Allies have it, or Sicily either. And I want to know why the Luftwaffe hasn't closed the port of Marseille yet."

He turned toward the bloated Goering, resplendent in his sky blue uniform encrusted with medals and ribbons, but the Reichsmarschal was lost in thought, and Hitler dismissed him with a snort and a wave of the hand.

"And I want the troops formed into a new army group with Rommel in command," he added suddenly.

Rommel stood up straighter. "As my Führer wishes," he snapped, ever the ambitious subordinate.

Canaris knew that Rommel suffered from a serious, if somewhat vague, medical problem and was supposed to be undergoing several months of rest and recuperation. While whatever the condition was would undoubtedly have been aggravated by the climate and rigors of campaigning in the desert, especially given Rommel's style of tooling around in an open vehicle in search of adventure, a tough campaign in the dead of winter in the French Alps would not likely be what the doctors had in mind for him either. Canaris could not help being put in mind of Napoleon, who had abandoned his own army in Egypt when the going got tough and returned home, not to disgrace, but to more adulation, promotion, and eventually to total power. He could not help wondering whether Rommel might not harbor the same vision of himself. Canaris smirked as Hitler swept from the room, leaving an icy silence in his wake. So that was how you lost a war in one evening, he thought.

1400 HOURS, 23 DECEMBER 1942
NEAR THIERS, FRANCE

Captain Hans Essen stood on the seat of his half-track and scanned the treeline with his field glasses. The long column of tanks and vehicles of the SS Lehr Sturm (assault training) Panzer Grenadier Brigade stretched for miles behind him in a throbbing, nervous line, and he could hear the raspy calls coming in on the radio from the brigade commander demanding to know why the advance had been halted. According to his map, they were just about to enter the last hilly, forested stretch before reaching the Loire River, and, up until now the progress of the brigade had been swift and without problems since crossing into what had been Vichy territory before dawn that morning. They had captured a bridge over the Allier River intact, cutting down a detachment of French Army engineers as they attempted to wire charges to drop the span, and there had been no further sign of resistance from either regular troops or guerrillas, until now.

The roadblock was not all that serious. A trench had been dug across the narrow country road the brigade was using at a low spot of what looked like marshy ground, making it problematical for heavy armored vehicles to maneuver around it. The ground was covered with a light dusting of snow, but it was not cold enough for a solid freeze to have set in, and there would likely be mines there as well. Behind the trench a tangle of felled trees and a couple of rusty farm vehicles formed an added hindrance, and Essen could see a telltale wire that implied that the entire structure was booby-trapped.

Still, this was nothing that the combat engineers could not handle, and they were already scuttling forward, dodging from cover to cover. What concerned Essen was whether the obstruction might also be covered by fire from the woods, and he had deployed his reconnaissance troop in an arc facing the most likely ambush sites. Then, there it was.

A crackle of rifle fire echoed across the little valley, muffled by the still-falling snow, and he saw one of the engineers fall heavily as the others went to ground. The machine guns on several of the vehicles opened up, as did the 20mm gun on an armored car, raking the treeline, while a platoon of infantry in mottled gray and white camouflage smocks dismounted and rushed off to one flank. With a practiced ear, earned on the battlefields of France and Russia, Essen listened carefully. About a dozen rifles, old ones he estimated, and one machine gun was all that they were facing. It must be *maquisards,* the damned resistance fighters. Regular troops with that little firepower would have had the sense not to attract the attention of a full brigade, much less offer to fight.

Essen made a call on the radio and, within moments, mortar shells were dropping in the woods, smoke to shield his infantry and high explosives to cut up the defenders. It was like a particularly mundane training exercise, but it was taking precious time. They had to get across the Loire before the enemy could put up a meaningful defense. His brigade was acting as spearhead for a larger thrust by the 3rd Panzer Grenadier Division, which would be following shortly. They would take St. Etienne and head southwest between the Loire and the Rhone, turning the line the French were trying to set up covering Lyon and the stronger one the Americans were forming at Valence. Then they would be out of the rough country and could drive right down to Avignon and on to Marseille at the head of the still larger force the newly promoted Field Marshal Rommel was forming at Dijon to split the Allied beachhead and end the invasion once and for all. But to do all of that, he had to get on to the Loire, and this pile of trash was in his way.

The mortars stopped after a dozen rounds, and Essen could hear the staccato tapping of machine pistols in the wood, and the sound of battle gradually died out. A sergeant of the infantry appeared at the treeline and signaled that all was clear. The engineers rushed forward to the roadblock, disabled the crude traps and tumbled the logs into the trench along with enough rocks and dirt to make the road passable again. Essen was just about to wave the column forward when the staff car of Brigadier General Lars von Gomerau, commander of the brigade, screeched to a halt beside him.

Essen thrust his arm out in a Nazi salute. "The road is clear, sir, and our patrols report no other obstacles this side of Montbrison," he anticipated the general's displeasure at the delay.

"Very well, Captain," the general sniffed, obviously troubled by a head cold. "But we must teach the locals a lesson about such actions, or they will be back in half an hour shooting up our supply convoys."

"Sir?" Essen asked, knowing what the general had in mind, but dreading it. He had certainly taken part in "pacification" operations in the Ukraine that summer, but those had been Slavs, after all, a different race, while the French were essentially Aryan, if misguided in their political attitudes.

The general rolled his eyes. "You know what to do, Captain. The 3rd Panzer Grenadier is being delayed because of sabotage to its vehicles and the destruction of two railway bridges between here and Le Mans. I will not have our advance held up by this constant sniping from the hedgerows. The next village you come to, set an example. Is that clear?"

"Yes, sir," Essen snapped and gave another salute before waving an armored car into the lead.

They came to a small village, Claire-en-Bois, about two miles farther on, and Essen pulled a company of infantry out of the column. The cobblestone streets of the town were deserted and the shutters of the sturdy stone houses were closed tight, but Essen had his men kick in the doors and begin to drag people out into the little square with its obligatory *Monument aux Morts* to the dead of the last war. Essen had a moment to glance at the names engraved on plaques around the base of the monument, quite a few for such a small place, he thought.

A round little man in a dark suit seemed to be in charge and kept calling to Essen from behind a cordon of infantrymen in their coal scuttle helmets, but Essen ignored him for the moment. When it appeared that everyone, men, women, and children, had been collected, Essen walked up to the man he assumed was the mayor.

"Bandits attacked our column near your town," Essen growled in his poor French. "We killed most of them but several escaped, and we have reason to believe that this band is either from this village or has received support from here. Tell us where the bandits are headquartered and where they hide their arms, or face the consequences."

The little man sputtered apologies and claims of total innocence. He waved his arms about him to demonstrate that there were virtually no able bodied men in the village, as if this were proof of anything except the probability that the men were up in the hills with rifles. He even said something about turning over the town's only Jewish family the year before to be sent to a concentration camp and smiled weakly.

"If that is all you have to say," Essen cut him off, "then my course is clear."

Essen barked an order to a sergeant, and the soldiers used their rifle butts to herd the crowd into the small stone church. He watched the faces of his own men carefully, looking for any sign of weakness, but three of their comrades had been killed at the ambush, and no one hesitated to do what needed to be done. When the last old woman had been shoved through the doorway and the heavy oak doors pulled shut behind her, men began hauling furniture from nearby houses, smashing it, and piling it up against the doors and windows on all sides. One squad had found a two-wheeled cart loaded with hay in a barn, and this was rolled under the eaves of the church as well. A sergeant fired a burst from his Schmeisser which shattered a stained glass window, and several men began lobbing incendiary grenades through the opening while others set fire to the piles of wood and debris.

A shout of protest went up from within the church, but this quickly turned into a collective shriek of terror from scores of throats, eighty-seven by the scrupulous count of the company clerk. Essen could hear a heavy thumping, and one of the side doors of the church burst open where the trapped villagers had used a wooden pew to batter their way through. A man charged through the burning wood piled in the doorway, but a machine gun set up nearby for just this purpose cut him down. A woman followed, clutching a bundle, or perhaps a small child, to her breast, and she, too was knocked back into the flames by the force of the bullets.

The ancient wood of the floors and roof and the tapestries hanging from the walls of the church caught easily, and soon the stone walls were a mere silhouette against the bright orange blaze which engulfed the church from one end to the other. The screaming had stopped now, and Essen jerked a thumb for his men to get back aboard their vehicles. He took one last look at the town as his half-track pulled back onto the road. It was not very different from the town he had come from in Bavaria, and he knew in his heart that, if he wanted to prevent some invader doing this very thing in his town, he had to take a firm stand here. Once the French understood that, they would simply get out of the way and avoid trouble.

Just inside a stand of trees half a mile from the village, a group of men struggled silently. There were six of them altogether, and four were wrestling with the remaining two, preventing them from charging across the open ground toward the burning pyre that was the church.

"My wife is in there," one of the two hissed in a harsh whisper, " and my little boy!"

"I know that, you fool," one of the other men said, softly. "My mother was in the town too, but there is nothing we can do now but get killed ourselves."

The two that were on the ground still writhed fitfully, tears streaming down their faces.

"But do not lose this feeling, Michel," the second man continued. "Keep it within you, and use it when we get a chance to pay these pigs back in kind."

1600 HOURS, 23 DECEMBER 1942
NEAR EPERNAY, FRANCE

Captain Woody Miles resented being used as a target. He understood, of course, that a successful bombing run on the German Panzer Division reported to be heading south toward the Allied landing area could have an important effect on the coming battle, but that job was much better suited to fighter bombers, not Flying Fortresses like the one he was piloting. He knew enough about the tactics used during the air war thus far to understand that what the brass really wanted was to use his bomber group as a magnet to draw as many Luftwaffe fighters as possible out of their camouflaged, fortified revetments where they could be destroyed in a "war of attrition." The problem with attrition, as Miles had seen it at work over the several months since his arrival in England, was that it worked both ways.

The good news was that this raid would at least be within the range of friendly fighter cover, and two full squadrons of the new P-51s were riding herd on this bomber wing, which would certainly be a help. The B-17, of course, was not defenseless, bristling with guns and well armored, and the new tactics of flying in a "combat box" maximized the concentrated firepower of the formation while keeping one plane from blocking the fire of another. The "box" consisted of three flights of six bombers each. Each flight formed into two "vees" of three planes, one slightly ahead of the other. The three flights were then formed into "vees" as well, with one just behind, above, and to the right of the lead, the other below, behind, and to the left. The wing would have three such combat boxes similarly echeloned across the sky, presenting an intricate web of interlocking fire and virtually no blind spots the enemy fighters could exploit. Still, Miles could not help but feeling like an anvil on which the hammer of the P-51s hoped to pound the Luftwaffe into rubble, and he would much rather be a hammer than an anvil.

A flurry of chatter on the radio indicated that the "little friends," as the fighters were called, had spotted a large swarm of "bandits" and had pulled off to engage them. It had been learned that having the fighters hug the bomber formations too closely limited their usefulness and merely put them in the way of the guns of the bomber wing. But what if this were merely a decoy? Miles couldn't help but wonder.

A moment later he had his answer. His ship was flying lead in the far left flight of the lead combat box, and when he checked the sky off to his left, he could see enemy fighters emerging from a cloud bank flying a parallel course with the bombers, just out of range of the B-17s' guns. This was a tactic that drove Miles crazy. The fighters would pace the bombers for a time, letting the prey get a good long look without being able to do anything about it. Then they would gradually gain speed and climb out of sight, eventually turning to charge the bombers head on. Of course, the B-17 had impressive forward firepower that most bombers lacked, but the technique was still unnerving as hell. They were Bf-109s, and there were at least twenty of them. Then they entered another cloudbank and did not emerge from the other side. Oh, brother! Miles thought to himself.

When the attack came, it was terrifying. They were trying to pick off the bombers on the fringes of the formation, which unfortunately included Miles' squadron. They dove in pairs at tremendous speed, their guns blazing. There were also heavier Me-110s out there somewhere, firing new anti-aircraft rockets from beyond effective machine-gun range. The rockets were not terribly accurate but had proximity fuses which detonated near the target plane, peppering it with shrapnel, and these fighters also carried 30mm cannon that could inflict far more damage than lighter machine guns. These "destroyers," as they were called, were easy pickings for escorting fighters, but the P-51s were busy elsewhere.

The aircraft next to Miles began to lose altitude, smoke pouring from one of its engines, and he could see that the windscreen of the cockpit had been shot away. There was a chaos of voices coming over the radio, calling out enemy fighters, ordering everyone to tighten up the formation, or just cursing or praying out loud.

At last the target was coming up, a railroad marshalling yard. Through the scattered clouds, Miles could make out the tracks, but the bombardier reported over the intercom that there was no sign of large numbers of flatcars that would indicate that the enemy division was present.

"It doesn't matter," Miles shouted over the roar of the engines and the rattle of the crews' machine guns. "The tracks don't move. If they've already passed by, we can't go looking for them, and if they haven't arrived, then we'll put a cork in this bottle and make them go somewhere else. That's what we're here for."

The bombers unloaded their tons of bombs in a broad pattern which obliterated the yards and at least two small bridges over canals in the area in addition to some rolling stock that happened to be in the target area. The formation made a leisurely turn for home, still harassed by enemy fighters, although not as many as before, and Miles could just concentrate on his flying now. He was worried about his radioman and one of the waist gunners, both of whom had been hit, and he didn't know if they were alive or dead. They were being attended to, and the best he could do for them was to fly fast and straight for home.

Just north of Epernay, troops of the 26th Panzer Division were jerked awake as they lay sprawled across their gear in the passenger cars of a train that was waved to a halt by a frantic railroad man with a red flag. A moment later they were jostled again, and curses filled the cars as the train began to reverse direction. This was the third time in eight hours that their route had been changed, and they were less than one hundred miles from their point of departure. At this rate it would take weeks to reach the area of Lyon where the battle was supposed to take place.

2000 Hours, 23 December 1942
Buerat, Tripolitania

Lieutenant Jonathan Penny, leader of a squad of Special Air Service (SAS) commandos, edged closer to the nearest building of the town, but there was no sign of activity. The unit's mission had been to land by boat well west of Buerat with a view to moving inland and hitting a supply dump the German were known to have in the neighborhood. They would then commandeer transport and drive across country until they re-entered friendly lines. Penny had done this many times in the past year, and this mission seemed to be no different than the others.

But this mission had turned out to be different, at least in that the enemy had failed to show up. The commandos had come ashore and shredded their rubber boats as usual before pushing inland. They had found the supply dump where aerial reconnaissance had pinpointed it, but there were no guards. Penny and his men had examined the stacks of crates, carefully stashed in bunkers and covered with camouflage netting, and there had been tons of ammunition, food, and water, but, oddly enough, no petrol at all. Not even the Arab scavengers had been by to pick over the booty.

They had found the same thing in the town of Buerat itself, just behind the defensive line Rommel had set up to halt the British Eighth Army. Here at least there were some scattered Arab residents, and Penny had finally snatched one and had the team member who spoke a little Arabic interrogate him about the whereabouts of the Germans and Italians. All the man could say, or all the interpreter could understand was that they were gone. Many planes, the man had said, and many boats and trucks too, pointing north and west.

Penny was tempted to search the buildings that had been used as headquarters by the enemy, but he had too much experience with the ingenious booby traps left by the Germans to be tempted now. The door of a house would be wired with grenades, or maybe there would be a pressure plate in the floor just inside a window, if you avoided the door. If you survived that, the keys on a typewriter would be wired, or the straightening of a crooked picture on the wall would set off a mine. That would have to be left for the engineers in daylight.

Penny hastily detached a sergeant and a corporal to make their way back to British lines with the news, and he took the rest of the team on a trek in pursuit of Panzer Armee Afrika, a role that appealed to Penny, thinking that, at least for a moment, he and his six men had Rommel on the run all by themselves. They soon came across a light truck that had been abandoned by the side of the road, and one of his men was able to get it running, and they continued northwest toward Tripoli in high style, even though travel by truck opened up the danger of running into a minefield, but Penny's mission was reconnaissance as much as demolition, and he had no good information yet. By dawn they were in sight of the town of Horns, the last community of any size before Tripoli itself, and still no sign of the enemy other than an increasing number of abandoned vehicles, which had allowed the team to trade up in their mode of transport twice and to replenish their fuel by draining the gas tanks of the other trucks they found. This struck Penny as odd, since petrol was more precious than gold in the desert, and to leave even a drop behind, even in a headlong retreat, made no sense at all. And the border of French Tunisia was barely one hundred and fifty miles away. Where could they be retreating to?

They did not dare press on in daylight, as the first sign they would have that the Nazis had chosen to make a stand would be an "88" round in their teeth, so Penny and his men holed up for the day in a jumble of rocks not far from the road, eating rations they had salvaged along the way and watching for some sign of life from the enemy. There was none.

As dusk fell, as it did so very quickly in the desert, they pressed on, making a wide circle around Horns, a small cluster of low white buildings in which no lights were burning, and no vehicle engines could be heard, and by the next morning they were approaching the outskirts of Tripoli itself. This was a proper city, of course, and here lights were burning and plenty of early morning activity could be seen around the town, in addition to massive fires blazing down near what must have been the port area.

The patrol edged its way around the outskirts of the city, working toward the coast. They finally found a position on a small headland where a rise afforded them a view of the port area. Through his field glasses, Penny could see hundreds of small black figures clustered about the docks and several freighters tied up there amid a blaze of arc lights and the quavering light of enormous mounds of supplies that had been set afire. The decks of the boats were jammed with trucks, and the streets leading to the docks with the burned out carcasses of destroyed tanks and armored cars.

"Bugger all!" a sergeant cursed. "The bastards are getting away!"

"Not much we can do about it, mate," Penny admitted. "If the RAF or the Navy don't spot them and hit them before they get clear, the bleeding Eighth Army certainly ain't in any position to catch them."

1000 HOURS, 24 DECEMBER 1942
ROME, ITALY

King Victor Emanuel III was visibly shaken as he presided over a meeting of his Grand Council. He was pale, and his eyes were puffy as if he had either not been to bed or had been crying, possibly both. The Grand Council was not an important body of men, just a collection of elderly men of good reputation who were used to acting as the figurehead for Mussolini's ship of state, but today they had a grim, purposeful look about them as they sat around the long conference table. Also present were General Vittorio Abrosio, head of the *Commando Supremo* and Field Marshall Pietro Badoglio, former commander of the armed forces. The two men notably missing from the meeting were Mussolini, il Duce, and Field Marshal Albert Kesselring, Supreme Commander, South, for the Wehrmacht and virtual viceroy of Italy for more than a year. It was an act approaching open treachery, at least in German eyes, for the Grand Council to meet without them, but it was a risk the men present felt necessary to take.

"Well, now we know what the Ethiopians felt like," Ambrosio was saying in a low growl. "Mussolini had sworn that the enemy would never touch Italy. We knew better after the British raid on Taranto, but no one had expected anything like this, even after the attacks on La Spezia and Genoa."

"Do we know how many dead yet?" the king asked tremulously.

"At least two thousand, probably more," Ambrosio responded. "Both of the marshalling yards in Rome were hit by American B-17s flying out of southern France just after dawn. We had trains moving troops north toward the French border, and at least one was caught, fully loaded, at the center of a bombing pattern. It will take time to sort through the rubble, but I have just come from there, and I can tell you I never saw anything like it."

One of the council members spoke up. "It would seem that the Americans were very careful to avoid hitting the historical centers of the city."

Ambrosio snorted. "That just means that they can hit whatever they want. Next time they might intentionally flatten the Forum, and there's little we can do about it."

"The Germans are moving more troops into the country to help defend against the Allies, they say," Badoglio offered. "They are setting up more anti-aircraft positions around the city and in the north as well and bringing in more fighters. You can't count them out yet. The withdrawal from North Africa was probably the greatest evacuation in military history, much more than Dunkirk. Over 70,000 men and hundreds of vehicles pulled out right under Montgomery's nose."

"We noticed that *all* of the Germans were loaded first, even though most of the ships were ours," Ambrosio responded. "And they're bringing in a lot more infantry, scattering it around the whole country. That's not going to defend us against bombers. They're not sure that we're going to stick with them, and they want to be in a position to seize the country if we try to drop out."

"And *are* we going to stick with them?" the king asked as he looked long-ingly out the tall windows, now criss-crossed with tape against bomb blasts, as the city was awakening to the worst Christmas in recent memory.

"We don't have much choice at the moment, sire," Badoglio said sadly. "The Allies haven't set foot on Italian soil yet, and it would be dishonorable to seek a separate peace at this stage."

"That didn't stop the Germans in the last war," one of the councilmen argued.

"No Allied troops had reached Germany then either. They fought, and made their allies fight, until they felt it was better to stop, and then they just stopped. Why should we be any different."

Ambrosio cleared his throat. "This must not leave this room, but it is not just a question of honor. We are dealing with an unscrupulous, vicious megalomaniac in Hitler, and he has the power to crush us if we stand against him alone. We have to wait until the Allies invade in force, not just to satisfy our honor, but to be able to take advantage of the protection of their armies when we do it. If we try to withdraw from the Axis now, and the Allies are defeated in France, the Germans will come in and obliterate us just as they did to the Poles. Now is the time to begin marshalling our forces for a pos-sible showdown with the Germans while still defending our territory against the Allies."

Victor Emmanuel sighed and thought for a long moment. "I intend to ask Mussolini to consider resignation." Several of the councilmen nodded gravely.

"It will do no harm," Badoglio said. "But it will do no good either. The only way that man will give up his power is when they carry him out feet first."

"We will have to consider that possibility as well," the king said as he rose and walked slowly from the room.

CHAPTER 4

CONSOLIDATION

I N THE AMERICAN Civil War they called a man's first time in combat "seeing the elephant," in reference to the experience of country boys going to the circus for the first time. The idea was that someone could describe an elephant to you until he was blue in the face, but you couldn't really appreciate one until you had seen it for yourself. Well, Colonel William C. Bentley and the men of the 2nd Battalion, 509th Airborne Regiment, had seen the elephant, and the elephant had kicked their butts.

After a death-defying race over icy roads in dilapidated trucks and even private cars from their initial landing site, the paratroopers had reached the town of St. Etienne only to wait for days before the first German showed up. They had not wasted the time, of course, digging in alongside the French 92nd Infantry Regiment under Colonel d'Ormesson. They had chipped away at the frozen ground with farm tools and even dynamite charges, establishing a strong line of infantry fighting positions in an arc around the northern approaches to the town, anchoring their left flank on the Loire River and their right in the rough hill country to the east. The road leading south along the river from Roanne was heavily mined, and the bridge upstream near Montbrison had been blown.

They didn't have much in the way of troops, and even less in terms of heavy weapons, perhaps 1,500 Americans and 2,000 French, not counting the several hundred civilians who had shown up begging for weapons, which were not available. At least they had served to help in the digging and as scouts to watch downriver for the approach of the enemy. The paratroopers' mortars were emplaced to the rear, and half a dozen old French 75mm howitzers dug in and well camouflaged covering the road to act as direct fire anti-tank guns. A pair of sturdy Somua tanks were backing up the line, while several light tanks and a couple of armored cars were posted well forward as an outpost to engage the Germans and force them to deploy early.

Word had come in a couple of days before about the massacre of a whole village less than a hundred miles away by a unit of the German SS, and Bentley had made sure that his men heard about it. There wasn't much joking around after that, just a desire to get into the fight.

But Bentley had been concerned about how the Allied offensive was going in general. From everything he had seen, the initial landings had gone off brilliantly. There had been no betrayal by the French, for one thing, and no huge ambush of the invasion fleet by German and Italian U-boats, although he had heard that a troop transport had been torpedoed coming into Toulon with the loss of over 500 men. The bombing campaign had apparently worked well up north, which explained why the Germans were so long in coming, and there had been no sign of the Luftwaffe whatsoever at St. Etienne, which implied that they had been given the drubbing the planners had counted on. But that was where things had stopped. Marshall had thrown this great army ashore with considerable vigor, but now it seemed to be wallowing there without any clear idea of what to do next, just waiting for the Germans to deliver the first blow, whenever and wherever they chose. Bentley had never considered himself a grand strategist, but he knew that this could not be a blueprint for victory.

For one thing, there was still no armor or any other kind of reinforcement up here at the front, and Bentley had heard that there had been bitter wrangling between the American and the French generals about where to draw the line. The French wanted to hold onto Lyon, not surprisingly since it was France's second largest city and a great industrial center, but at the same time they didn't want to fight *in* Lyon and turn it into another Stalingrad. The Americans, also not surprisingly, did not feel they had the strength to cover so wide an area for their lodgment and wanted the main defensive line to start back around Valence, farther south. The same was true in the west, where the French wanted to defend Toulouse, and the Americans and Canadians insisted that the line be at a much narrower gap between the Pyrenees and the Massif Central at Carcassonne. The result was that two defensive belts had been created, with the weak French units strung out north of Lyon and west of Toulouse, hoping against hope that the Germans would not hit them too hard, and the Allies digging in miles to their rear. Bentley feared that the Germans would thus be able to defeat each in turn where the two armies together might stand at least a chance of success. And there was still no armor, nor any other kind of support coming forward to St. Etienne. The paras and the French were on their own.

He did not have too long to brood over this turn of events, however, because at dawn on Christmas day, the Germans had arrived in force. There had been some patrolling before that, and the French outposts had fallen back, but now a full Panzer Grenadier brigade had shown up, and from the camouflaged uniforms worn by the obviously experienced infantry, the French told him that these were Waffen SS, the best the Germans had to offer. The Germans were also lavishly provided with artillery, and shells began to come down all along line, terrifying the inexperienced Americans and French alike, the airbursts hitting in the trees and showering the troops below with deadly shrapnel and splinters. The Germans were equipped with a nasty little multiple mortar, called the *nebelwerfer,* which produced an effect not unlike high explosive rain. To this was added an attack by several Stuka dive bombers, with their screaming engines and direct fire from German anti-tank guns that the men dubbed "crash-booms" since, with their flat trajectory, you heard the explosion of the shell before the report of the gun itself. There was also the fire of deadly efficient snipers, and Bentley had lost half a dozen officers who had gotten a little too curious about things at the front or who thought war was like a field exercise at Fort Benning where they could walk up and down the line, invisible and invulnerable, supervising their men. But the line had been holding, at first.

Then the Germans had pulled something no one had expected. Instead of charging straight ahead down the road from Roanne as the defenders had assumed they would, there was suddenly a flurry of firing coming from the rear, and the men in their isolated foxholes began to look nervously over their shoulders, a sure sign, Bentley learned, that an infantryman is thinking about running. The Germans had slipped a brigade of bicycle infantry upriver through the woods along the far shore of the Loire and, during the night, had sent an assault party across in rubber boats to establish a bridgehead. By dawn their combat engineers had set up a narrow pontoon bridge, and half the brigade had crossed over unnoticed and was now storming the town of St.

Etienne itself, gunning down the clerks and supply troops of both the American and the French headquarters companies. At the same instant a long line of tanks, assault guns, and half tracks roared down the road, cannons and machine guns blazing, rolling right through corridors their engineers had apparently cleared in the Allied minefield during the night.

The few French tanks had gamely driven forward, taking up hull-down positions where a fold in the earth would provide added protection and still allow them to fire their turret guns. They got in a few shots, but their 47mm guns couldn't penetrate the armor of most of the newer German tanks, so they only managed to call attention to themselves, and the German gunners knocked them out, one after another.

That was plenty for the defenders. First singly, then in small groups, then by platoons, they started to run, officers and men together, through the woods to the southeast. In a matter of minutes, Bentley found himself with only the equivalent of a platoon of men left of his whole battalion. He led them in a rush toward the town in hopes of forting up in the stone houses and at least denying the Germans the use of the crucial crossroads for a short while, but he encountered Colonel d'Ormesson halfway there who informed him that the Germans were in possession of the entire town. There was nothing for it now but to join the retreat and hope to pull together the survivors into some kind of defensive line farther on.

But several hours of crashing through the ice-covered underbrush brought no relief. The weather had closed in now, and there would be no hope of friendly air support. Meanwhile, the Germans had wasted no time in St. Etienne. Bentley and d'Ormesson were moving parallel to the road south toward Annonay, and he had gathered about them slightly more than one hundred Americans and perhaps twice as many French soldiers, but they had no heavy weapons, and some of the men lacked even their rifles. From deep within the woods they could see a powerful column of armored vehicles moving along the road, and they could hear the sound of heavy firing coming from the west.

"That would be the SS attacking your glider troops at Le Puy-en-Velay in the flank," d'Ormesson said when he saw Bentley listening intently with furrowed brow. "From the markings on the vehicles moving south, it looks like a fresh Panzer Grenadier Division that has charged through the gap and will hit your main line at Valence during the night."

"Because we opened the door for them," Bentley hissed.

"The Germans kicked in the door," d'Ormesson corrected him. "'We are just the splinters. You can take some solace in the fact that you are not the first to experience this. The Germans have become quite good at this with all the practice they get."

Bentley stopped suddenly and grabbed the Frenchman by the shoulder. "Listen! If all the Germans are on the move, maybe we could sneak back to St. Etienne and retake the place. They won't be expecting that, and I'll bet there are hundreds of our men being held prisoner there right now."

D'Ormesson shook his head. "Only the mobile troops will be moving. They will have at least one infantry division following up to garrison key points like St. Etienne. Even if only one battalion of the infantry they sent in behind us stayed in place, leaving the panzer grenadiers to continue the advance, they'd outnumber us two-to-one at least. It would be of no use, and we'd end up either dead or in the prisoner pens along with the others."

"There must be something we can do," Bentley pleaded.

"We can keep moving," d'Ormesson growled. "We'll have to wait until dark and cut across this road to continue southward through the rough country. The valley of the Rhone starts just a few miles below here, and there will be no cover for movement there. With luck, we'll be able to link up with your forces at Le Puy-en-Velay, or whatever is left after the SS finishes with them. But we've got to get out of this pocket before the German infantry catches up and hunts us down like foxes."

Bentley swore and bashed his helmet against the trunk of a tree. Then he stalked over to where an American GI was taking a puff of a cigarette and snatched it out of his mouth.

"Smoking is a filthy habit, son," he said, "and it will get us all killed if the Germans see that red tip. Let's bivouac here under cover until nightfall and then try to get out of this mess."

1300 HOURS, 27 DECEMBER 1942
CARCASSONNE, FRANCE

Captain Edward Bult-Francis of the 8th Reece Regiment, 2nd Canadian Division, sat in the turret of his Greyhound armored car, watching the main highway from Toulouse. The car was tucked well back in a wood to one side of the road in a dip in the ground that would protect the body of the vehicle but leave the turret guns free to fire. Infantry were dug in all around, with machine guns and anti-tank guns emplaced to provide interlocking fields of fire. After all the desperate rushing to get men and equipment unloaded at the small port of St. Cyprien, and the race inland to occupy this position blocking the gap between the Pyrenees and the Massif Central, they had been sitting here for days without a sign of the enemy. Typical of the army, hurry up and wait.

Of course, it stood to reason that it would take the Germans some time to organize themselves, concentrate their forces, and then cover over one hundred and fifty miles from the old border between occupied France and Vichy territory. And every minute that the Allies had to prepare had been a help. Now the full Canadian I Corps was in position, 1st Division on the left, the 2nd on the right, with the 5th Armored in reserve, and the British 1st Airbourne Division up in the Massif Central to the northeast. Rumor had it that the British V Corps would be landing any day to flesh out the line and enable them to go over to the offensive and move on Toulouse.

But the Germans were coming now, sure enough. A ragged column of French infantry was moving dejectedly but quickly along the road, heading southeast toward Montpelier. The French had put up their own line miles closer to the border, hoping to hold onto Toulouse, but General Marshall, supported by both his and the British general staffs, had refused to be spread so thin. The day before yesterday they had started hearing heavy guns, and in the evening the low clouds to the northwest were lit up by the flashes of the artillery. Bult-Francis knew that those weren't French guns. They didn't have any, so it was no surprise to see the remnants of their scant regiments now straggling back toward safety. They gave the Canadians accusing glances as they shuffled by, but none of them offered to stay and fight. There were French units on both flanks, but these would soon be pulled together in the rear and given new weapons and training and formed into proper divisions for the long war ahead.

Eventually the flow of French turned into a trickle, then stopped completely, and Bult-Francis scanned the snow-covered fields to his front for the first signs of the enemy. He kept one hand on the hatch cover handle, ready to drop down inside and clang it shut when the inevitable artillery barrage should start. But he wouldn't leave this spot. Too many of his comrades were lying dead in the shallows in front of Dieppe for him not to want a chance to pay the Jerrys back in kind. Most of the losses the division had suffered had been made good by now, but the wounds, even among the units like the 8th Reece that hadn't gone ashore, were deep.

He was surprised to see, not the bursts of artillery shells, but a cluster of motorcycles with sidecars motoring down the road. Not far behind them came several half-tracks and then regular lorries full of infantry.

"Bloody cheek!" Bult-Francis snarled. "Don't fire, wait for it!" he shouted to the infantrymen around him and repeated the same into the mouthpiece of his radio for the other cars in his troop. "The bastards think they can just drive right down to the seaside do they? I'll bet anything they've outrun their artillery." Some of the infantrymen began to fidget as the Germans drew closer, shifting their weapons. "Wait for it!" he repeated.

Finally, when the lead motorcycle had reached within fifty yards of the point where the road cut through the woods, he screamed, "Fire, fire, fire!" and pulled the trigger of his own 37mm gun.

The riders were cut down as if with a scythe, and the first several vehicles burst into flame almost simultaneously. The German infantrymen who escaped from their vehicles in the middle of the open area ran back toward their lines as fast as the ankle deep snow and their heavy greatcoats would allow, but the Canadian machine-gunners dropped them one by one with economical short bursts of fire while six-pounder anti-tank guns demolished each vehicle in turn. Bult-Francis could hear the rapid "crump" of their own field guns now, lobbing shells at pre-registered sites along the road out of their view such as crossroads and culverts while a small spotter plane buzzed overhead, calling in adjustments to their aim.

Bult-Francis knew that this would not be the end of it. The Germans would be back in greater numbers and with artillery support, but the sight of the German bodies scattered in the field, like small piles of discarded clothing, gave him a deep sense of satisfaction. It didn't quite settle accounts for Dieppe, but it was a down payment.

1800 HOURS, 27 DECEMBER 1942
DIJON, FRANCE

Field Marshal Erwin Rommel could hardly believe his good fortune. When he had left North Africa, he had assumed his military career was over. The Führer was not one to forgive failure, and there was no other way to view the campaign in Egypt. To be sure, his defeat at the hands of Montgomery was due to the massive superiority in men and equipment enjoyed by the British by the fall of 1942, and it had been little short of miraculous that he had been able to lead the Panzer Armee Afrika, more than half of which was made up of under-armed, unenthusiastic Italians, over a thousand miles across the desert to the gates of Alexandria. But that carried little weight with Hitler. What he wanted was results, nothing less.

Yet here he was, having not only avoided professional ostracism like that endured by Manstein, a genius of mythic proportions who had disagreed with the Führer once too often, but having been given a field marshal's baton and one of the key commands in the field. He would now command Army Group West, covering most of France, and lead the assault against the Allied lodgment in the south. Kesselring, his former superior, had been relegated to continuing to deal with the obstreperous Italians, to fend off new attacks by the Allies in the Mediterranean and to shore up the defenses of Northern Italy.

Even his health had miraculously improved. For months he had been plagued with nagging stomach trouble, dizziness, and general malaise. While these symptoms had no doubt been aggravated by the harsh climate of North Africa and his punishing work schedule, various doctors, including the Führer's personal physician, Dr. Horster, had found little wrong with him clinically. Rommel had heard the vicious rumors, particularly those spread by his enemies at OKW, like Keitel, that this mysterious disease was an artful way for Rommel to get away from his defeated army. When Hitler had finally agreed to evacuate the Axis troops from Libya, Rommel had actually been in Germany on a "health cure" consisting mainly of imposed rest and carefully controlled diet. Now Rommel had begun to wonder if, perhaps, his critics hadn't been at least partially right. He had had no time for a "cure" and yet he had never felt more fit.

Rommel was delighted with his command, but less than impressed with the troops with which he was to exercise that command. His valiant armored warriors from the desert, the 15th and 21st Panzer Divisions, the 90th Light, and the 164th "Afrika" Divisions, plus Ramke's Parachute Brigade, were all coming to him, those who had survived the meatgrinder of El Alamein, that is, and they were being fitted out with the latest tanks and weapons in Germany at this moment, but it would be some time before they reached the front. All he had to work with was a single Panzer Division, the 26th, and a Panzer Grenadier Division, the 3rd, and the newly formed Hermann Göring Division, a collection of Luftwaffe men retooled as panzer grenadiers, who had yet to prove themselves in combat. There were a handful of infantry divisions that had been released to him and a hodge-podge of independent regiments and brigades with which to take on perhaps a dozen enemy divisions, all fresh, if mostly inexperienced. But Rommel had faced greater foes with far less.

He had sized up the situation with his typical decisiveness and determined that the key to the battle would be to defeat and humiliate the American forces in the center of the Allied line. Kesselring could hold the line of the Alps with little difficulty, and attacking the western rim of the Allied perimeter would involve hundreds of miles of travel for the reinforcements daily arriving from Germany, over rail and roads haunted by swarms of Allied fighter-bombers that the Luftwaffe had virtually given up challenging for control of the air. Rommel knew that the Americans, stiff-necked as they appeared to be, would insist on running their own front without support from the more experienced British. If he could rout them as he had done the British in the desert, before the British had learned his tricks, he could split the lodgment, capture Marseille, and drive the invaders into the sea.

The initial moves that had been ordered by von Rundstedt, which conformed nicely with Rommel's own plans, had gone very well. The LXIII Infantry Corps had smashed into the thin French line above Lyon and shattered it unceremoniously, driving the French before them as a mob of refugees, sewing consternation in the Allied ranks. Meanwhile, an armored thrust on the west side of the Rhone had knifed through the first defense line formed of French regiments and an American airborne division. It had not been expected that these lightly armed troops would be able to stand up to veteran armored forces, but the extent of the rout had been highly encouraging. The important crossroads of St. Etienne had fallen, and the panzers had then struck the flank of the Allied line, which included regular American armored and infantry units, not just paratroops, taking Valence-sur-Rhone early that morning and causing another shameful rout by both the Americans and the French. The German forces were now clear of the rough country of the Massif Central and could push along the right bank of the Rhone all the way down to the sea. The infantry could keep up the pressure on the left bank, moving on Grenoble and rolling up the Allied line along the Italian border in cooperation with pressure from Kesselring in Italy. Even the weather was cooperating, with heavy clouds and fog virtually eliminating Allied air missions and giving his reinforcements a chance to move forward without the harassment from the air that so hindered their mobility and giving the Luftwaffe time to recover from the devastating losses it had suffered over the previous week.

Also, a battalion of the new super-heavy Tiger tanks had just arrived, their first deployment in combat. Designed to counter the powerful Soviet tanks the Germans had encountered on the Eastern Front, with the Tiger's thick armor and 88mm gun, there was nothing in the Allied inventory that could stand up to it, even if the American tactics hadn't been laughably obsolete.

Rommel felt very much at home in his new headquarters in Dijon. The scenery was radically different from the endless expanses of the desert, much more like the forests and mountains of his native Swabia, and he had to keep reminding himself that his tactics would have to change as well. Fortunately, he was surrounded by Colonel Siegfried Westphal, his chief of operations, and General Alfred Gause, his chief of staff from North Africa, even his personal secretary, Corporal Alfred Bottcher. One of the first tasks he assigned his staff was to scour the parks of captured Allied equipment for another "Mammut," one of the huge eight-wheeled British armored cars he had used as his mobile command post in the desert, and then his little world would be complete.

True to form, once Rommel had gotten his headquarters staff emplaced in a small chateau on the outskirts of Dijon, he left Gause in charge and loaded up a convoy of radio vans and reconnaissance troops and headed off for the front to gauge the pace of the advance for himself. He was always amused by the bleating of his staff at how he would undoubtedly be out of communication, as had happened so often during the North African campaign. He had the utmost confidence in Westphal and Gause, however, and the orders for the division commanders should stand for some hours yet. In Rommel's way of fighting, he could hardly be expected to give further coherent orders until he had seen the ground and been with the troops in the line. In a moment, he was off in a cloud of gravel kicked up by his tires, and the little column disappeared into the enshrouding fog.

1400 HOURS, 28 DECEMBER 1942
LE TEIL, FRANCE

Patton was a man after Rommel's heart. In fact, he had been quoted once as making a toast of, "To Hell and damnation with any general ever found in his own command post!" He was an officer who preferred to lead from the front, but, more than that, he didn't want to be around while Major General

Lloyd R. Fredenhall vacated his headquarters for the II Corps at Avignon. Patton had been with Marshall in Algiers the day before and had witnessed one of the first outbursts of temper he had seen in the Allied Supreme Commander. Normally, one could gauge the level of Marshall's ire by his complexion, which turned progressively redder the angrier he got, but he almost never raised his voice. When word of the collapse of part of II Corps had come in, Marshall had turned a bright magenta, but he had also ranted and raved loudly enough to send orderlies and staff officers scurrying for cover throughout the villa where he was in the process of setting up his new headquarters. He had ordered Fredenhall, commander of the corps, sacked on the spot, even though he and Eisenhower had both been high on the man and concurred in his original appointment. The story was that Fredenhall had suffered a complete nervous breakdown and had spent the battle cowering in a concrete bunker nearly one hundred miles from the scene of action.

Patton had been incensed himself, especially after overhearing some British staff officers beginning to refer to the Americans as "our Italians" as well as having caught portions of a sarcastic song the British troops were singing entitled "How Green Was My Ally." In all frankness, Patton had longed for the field assignment that Marshall had then bestowed on him, command over all Allied land forces involved in the invasion, the perfect culmination of all his months of planning alongside Eisenhower and his frustrating visit with the French before the invasion. Eventually, the disparate divisions that now comprised the invasion force would be organized into separate armies, and Patton would probably end up with command of one of them, but for the time being the whole show would be his. Even so, he had chosen to fly directly to the front, bypassing Avignon until after Fredenhall's departure for a new and uninspiring posting in the States. The reports from the front had been fragmentary, and it was well known that the American troops had been in battle for the first time, and it was entirely possible that Fredenhall was not entirely to blame for the fiasco. On the other hand, it had been clear to Patton early on that Fredenhall had not taken *command* of his corps and had left the tactical planning to staff officers with even less experience than he had.

All that would change now. Patton had arrived shortly after dawn and had visited the command posts of the 1st and 34th Infantry and the 1st Armored Divisions and even some of the regimental commands. He had been encouraged by the way the division commanders, notably Ernest Harmon, who had replaced General Orlando Ward as commander of the 1st Armored, had taken control of the situation and were organizing their troops to return to the fight. Together they had worked out a battle plan, not to set up a defensive line, but to go on the offensive. Patton knew, partly from the super-secret intercepts of German coded communications, the ULTRA program, that, if the Allies were still vulnerable in their new lodgment, the Germans were also fighting with a scratch force thrown together without prior planning or staff organization. Now was the time to strike a blow, which would be all the more unexpected after the sharp reverse the Americans had just suffered. If they could turn the tide, it would immediately restore the shaky morale of both the Americans and the French.

It was also important to retake as much ground as possible. Patton had studied every scrap of information he could obtain about German tactics in the desert and in Russia, and he knew that, while the Germans were hard to stop on the offensive, they were even more tenacious on the defensive, and the ground they were contesting now was excellent defensive terrain which would cost the Allies dearly to capture once the Germans had had a chance to settle in.

For the moment, the Canadians in the west had rebuffed half-hearted attacks by a German infantry corps on their front and were even advancing slowly. The American 36th Division and the French were actually pushing the Italians back quickly along the coast to the east, with naval gunfire blasting anything within twenty miles of the coast whenever the Italians seemed about to make a stand; and Nice was expected to fall quickly, unless the Germans arrived to shore up the defense. And the last Italian troops on Corsica had thrown down their arms in the face of the combined offensive of the American 3rd Division and Koenig's Free French corps that swung around both sides of the island. Furthermore, Patton had been advised that the 29th Infantry Division, the last major American unit in England, was being shipped to Marseille, as were two British divisions that had been earmarked for North Africa and would no longer be needed there in light of the Axis evacuation. He could also expect that Montgomery's Eighth Army would soon be available for operations on the continent, although he doubted it would be in his area of responsibility, something of a relief in view of Monty's well-earned reputation as a prima donna who would certainly not take orders from an American graciously. In any event, he had plenty of forces on hand to deal with the German thrust down the Rhone Valley. It only remained for him to motivate the men and their officers and drive them forward. This was the moment he had been born for, Patton was certain, and he would not let it pass.

Patton was now standing up on the seat of his jeep, returning the salutes of the troops of the 1st Armored Division as they rolled along the highway past him. The barrel chested General Harmon was standing next to him, waving them on and shouting words of encouragement as well. Like Patton, Harmon liked to wear a pair of ivory-handled revolvers, although he used shoulder holsters, and some had come to the conclusion that he was a martinet, merely aping Patton's style. But Harmon was one of the most experienced armored officers in the army and had a positive love of battle that had soon dispelled any doubts his troops had had about him, as much as they had regretted the loss of the popular General Ward who was saddled with at least part of the blame for the defeat at Valence.

"The 2nd Armored is coming along right behind us," Harmon shouted over the roar of the tank engines and the high-pitched squeak of the bogie wheels. "By tomorrow we'll be in position. That'll give the Germans something to think about." "If the weather would just clear up for a couple of days," Patton said, "there isn't a doubt in my mind that we could drive the Germans all the way back to Lyon and beyond." As he watched the passing column, he spotted an open jeep hauling a 37mm anti-tank gun and crowded with GIs. He waved it over and pointed a finger at a rather elderly major sitting in the front passenger seat, a gold cross pinned to his collar.

"Chaplain," Patton bellowed, "I'm giving you a direct order that I want you to pass along to all of the other clergy with II Corps."

"Yes, sir," the priest replied.

"I want you to devote your prayers for the next twenty-four hours to obtaining clear skies for our aircraft."

The priest sputtered. "But, General, I don't know if it's right to ask the Lord to take sides like that."

Patton roared at him: "You know what kind of animals we're up against, dammit! If God isn't on our side now, what good is He? I'm holding you directly responsible for the weather, now get on with it!"

The flustered priest simply saluted, and the jeep wheeled back into the column, gears grinding.

Harmon chuckled and shook his head. "So now God's been drafted." He paused for a moment and then went on. "I guess you missed the chaos down at Marseille, but I can only imagine what an amphibious landing would have looked like against real resistance. The British were right that we couldn't have done it across the Channel where the Germans were waiting for us."

"That was the whole point of this exercise. The idea of fighting our way ashore and then trying to supply an army across the beaches until we could capture a port and get it working just turned my stomach. That's why we've got to make this work. We'll never have another chance like this. It's like a prizefight. The Russians have given the Nazis a body blow at Stalingrad and they're staggering. Now is not the time to give them six or eight months or a year to reorganize and mobilize their resources, just giving them little jabs the way Churchill wanted to do."

"Hence the code name HAYMAKER for this operation."

"Exactly. In one fell swoop we've got all of North Africa and Corsica already, and the French are fighting on our side, even if they haven't gotten their own house in order yet, and the battle is right here on the continent. The Germans are being pulled both ways, and something's got to give. They've had it all their own way so far, picking where and when to fight. Now we're taking the war to them, and we'll see how they like it.

Patton whacked Harmon on the shoulder stoutly and hopped down from the jeep. He strode over to where a truck had skidded off the road and was spinning its wheels in a patch of ice on the verge. He shouted instructions to the terrified young driver who finally got the truck into low gear and rocked it out of the hole and back onto the road. Patton waved and climbed into his own jeep and sped off up the highway.

0800 HOURS, 29 DECEMBER 1942
AJACCIO, CORSICA

The tall, angular figure of General Charles de Gaulle appeared at the open bridge of the corvette *Savorgnan de Brazza* as it pulled up to the quay amid the frantic cheers of a mob of civilians waving tricolor flags and soldiers bearing the Cross of Lorraine patch on their shoulders. The small port was already crowded with French naval vessels, crews lining their railings at attention while the foghorns of the fishing vessels and tugs made up a raucous chorus. De Gaulle was wearing a simple army officer's uniform, covered with a slicker against the chill mist that hung in the air, and his kepi with the two stars of a *general de division*.

The jetty was kept clear of the crowd by a cordon of marines, and a reception line was formed of senior officers waiting to greet him as he strode down the gangway. There was General Koenig, commander of the Free French Corps, and General Jacques Leclerc of the 2nd Free French Division, both men having adopted false names to protect their families remaining in occupied France. There was also General Alphonse Juin, who had been commander of the Vichy French armed forces in North Africa and would lead the rearmed and reorganized divisions that were currently undergoing training for commitment to the front in France itself, General Emile Bethouart, commander of the Casablanca Division, and Admiral de Laborde, commander of the French fleet, whose flagship *Strasbourg* rode at anchor in the harbor. Lastly there were Jean Moulin, de Gaulle's envoy to the French Forces of the Interior (FFI) as the resistance was known, and Gilbert Renault, better known as Colonel Remy, head of the Gaullist intelligence network in France, the *Bureau Central de Renseignements et d'Action* (BCRA), along with a host of lesser officers and local government officials. Off to one side, part of the crowd but not quite among it, was a small knot of older men in dark suits, surrounded by fit young men in short leather jackets with noticeable bulges under one armpit: the *capos* of the *Union Corse,* smiling benignly.

De Gaulle paused for a moment when he stepped off the gangway, then knelt and kissed the ground to the thunderous applause of the crowd. It had been over two years since de Gaulle had set foot on French soil, and he had very nearly not made it this time. Ostensibly as a matter of security, de Gaulle in his shabby little offices in London, had been kept in the dark about the plans for the invasion until the last possible moment, long after the negotiations between the Americans and the Vichy regime had been concluded, and his objections to dealing with the collaborationists had been met with cold indifference. The inclusion of the Free French forces in the assault on Corsica had been meant as a sop to his pride, but one he had had to accept. But now, in the nearly two weeks since the first Allied landings, the Allied Supreme Command had found one pretext after another to postpone his travel to the liberated zone. Finally, de Gaulle had had to take matters into his own hands, virtually escaping from England aboard one of the few ships in the Free French "navy" without the approval of any Allied authority, which was why he chose to arrive here, at the one place he would be assured of a warm welcome, the territory recaptured by his own troops.

Beyond the importance of the men who were present at this homecoming, it was significant that others were *not* there. General Lucian Truscott, commander of the American 3rd Infantry Division, which had assisted in the defeat of the demoralized Italian garrison of Corsica, was at his new head-quarters at Bastia, on the far side of the island, totally ignorant of de Gaulle's arrival. More importantly, General Henri Honore Giraud, recently named commander of the French Armed Forces, and a longtime opponent of de Gaulle, was also absent.

When de Gaulle had composed himself, he stalked over to the reception committee with his stiff stride and exchanged salutes and handshakes with the assembled men. It was clear from the first that he was being treated with more deference than his two stars would have required, since he was junior to virtually every other officer present. They all stood to attention for the play-ing of the "Marseillaise" by a tinny municipal band that was soon drowned out by the emotional singing of thousands of spectators. They then marched in a line abreast up the *Place Marshal Foch* to the city prefecture where they would hold their meeting.

Once the senior officers had arranged themselves around a long baize-covered conference table, General Juin began.

"The assassination of Admiral Darlan and the tragic death of Marshal Petain have considerably altered the political skyline, as it were, of France."

Remy cast a knowing glance at de Gaulle, who sat next to him, noting the distinction between the description of the two deaths. It was clear that there had been no love lost between Juin and Darlan.

"Consequently," Juin went on, "we were hoping," and he nodded to de Laborde and Bethouart in turn, "that we could come to a workable political arrangement with a minimum of fuss. Dissension in our ranks now will only serve to benefit the Nazis on the one hand and the Communists on the other. Those of us interested in a reborn, strong France will find it necessary to make certain sacrifices to achieve this goal. We must, for the moment, put behind us all past recriminations and causes for complaint. There will be ample opportunity after France is free once more for the politicians to con-duct their investigations and inquests."

De Gaulle nodded. Since de Gaulle's announcement on the BBC in June 1940 of his rejection of the armistice with the Germans and his call to the French military and people to continue to resist the invader, there had been a constant war of words between de Gaulle's followers and those of Petain, and there had been some truth on both sides. The Free French had criticized the Vichy regime for its subservience to the Nazis, permitting the Reich to rape the country of its resources and its manpower, while the apologists for Petain replied that they were surrendering the minimum cooperation possible in order to avoid even worse demands. The Vichyists, for their part, accused de Gaulle of selling out French interests to the British and Americans in return for their niggardly support in terms of arms, while de Gaulle insisted that he fought bitterly against such encroachments but that he lacked any political or military leverage with which to resist them. The conflict had gone beyond words to actual war when Free French troops had attempted and failed to capture Dakar from the Vichy garrison and then succeeded in taking the French territories in Syria and Lebanon in 1941 with the help of the British. Such charges and blood feuds would undoubtedly provide material for years of controversy, but the men in this room were apparently willing to forego that prospect for the moment.

"This is possibly the greatest turning point for France," de Gaulle announced, his large hands gripping one another on the table in front of him, "in this century, even since the Revolution. I am here to place myself and the forces under my command at the disposition of the French people. I would be unfaithful to the memory of the brave men who fought and died at Bir Hakeim if I did anything less."

Of course, de Gaulle had originally planned to do a great deal less, insisting to both the Allies and his own colleagues that all French forces be immediately placed under his command as part of the liberation, and that many Vichy officers, those who had not already been in contact with the Gaullists, or who did not instantly declare their loyalty to de Gaulle, be dismissed. When it became clear that the Allies would sooner do without de Gaulle than without the Vichy French Army, and that his followers would follow any French general who would lead them against the Germans, de Gaulle had pivoted, "turning within his own length" as Leclerc would later comment, and was now here to compromise.

Juin puffed out his chest slightly at the mention of Bir Hakeim, the glorious episode in North Africa where an outnumbered and surrounded Free French garrison had withstood days of bombardment and assault by the Afrika Korps and had then fought its way back to friendly lines. This was something in which all Frenchmen could take pride after the ignominious defeats of the 1940 blitzkrieg.

"What we have in mind," Juin explained, "is the creation of a Committee of National Liberation, which will serve as the provisional government of all

France until the Germans have been driven out and proper elections can be held, and we would like you to assume the presidency of the CNL."

"And will the rest of the Vichy administration go along with this?" Remy asked. "With the death of the Marshal," Juin went on, "and of Darlan, we have a good opportunity to put aside Petain's 'national revolution,' or at least parts of it. We attempted to arrest Laval, but it seems that when the German commandos came to kidnap Petain, another detachment was able to facilitate the escape of Laval, who is now in Paris, but that only discredited his followers even more. Giraud will be happy to retain his position as commander of the armed forces, but he will have no direct control over troops, and the presidency of the CNL will also be invested with the title of commander in-chief We will explain this as a means of putting you on an even footing with Churchill and Roosevelt, but it will also give you the authority of dismissing Giraud if he should prove to be a hindrance. My fellow officers and I speak for at least three quarters of the officer corps in all services in making you this offer."

De Gaulle thought for a long moment and then nodded and spoke to the room in general. "Our main goal must be the liberation of all national territory, followed by the destruction of Germany. Our armed forces must play as large a role in this struggle as possible if we are to have any voice in the negotiations that will ultimately bring about an end to the war and construct the peace thereafter. We must mobilize every man and devote every resource to the war effort until that is accomplished."

Juin smiled. "We have three divisions of veteran troops receiving new American equipment and undergoing training in North Africa, and two more divisions in metropolitan France. They should all be in the line within one month. At that time we can pull the remaining troops of the Armistice Army back to refit and form new divisions with them, and there are at least 50,000 men we can mobilize in Morocco and Algeria plus a like number from Corsica and the liberated zone on the mainland, which is all we can hope to arm for the time being anyway. By the end of March we should have no less than a dozen divisions at the front, two of them armored."

De Gaulle nodded and smiled. "With that kind of force and our navy, we'll be almost on an even footing with the British and Americans in front line strength on the continent."

"And General Marshall has already proven an eager recipient of the intelligence from our networks in the occupied zone," Colonel Remy added, "in addition to the contributions our FFI has been making in holding back the Germans."

"Exactly," De Gaulle continued. "They can't afford to take us for granted anymore."

"So you accept our proposal, General?" Juin asked.

De Gaulle paused for a moment, and then nodded. "I do. Now, how can we get back to the mainland? I'm frankly more than a little homesick and definitely sick of dealing with our allies as a government in exile."

"There is a cabin on the *Strasbourg* at your disposal," Admiral de Laborde announced proudly. "And no more back doors, no more sneaking about in the night. We will sail directly to Toulon, where we will not have to answer to anyone, and you can travel in state to Marseille and set up your government there."

De Gaulle drew himself up even taller, towering over the other men in the room and extended his hand to the Admiral. According to Koenig's memoirs, a tear could be seen glistening in the General's eye.

CHAPTER 5

THE LULL BEFORE THE STORM

0700 Hours, 31 December 1942
St. Etienne, France

P ERHAPS IT WAS that not even God had the nerve to refuse a direct order from General Patton. Major Creighton W. Abrams of the 1st Armored Division had heard the story about Patton's injunction to the army chaplains to pray for good flying weather, which had made the rounds of II Corps like wildfire, and sure enough, when the American offensive had opened the previous morning, only scattered high clouds had remained in the sky and the ground was firm and hard under the treads of the tanks. Doolittle's 12th Air Force, headquartered at Marseille, had sent hundreds of P-40s and Spitfires aloft to sweep the Luftwaffe back, and waves of B-25s had pounded the German lines near Valence mercilessly while the RAF and the American 8th Air Force in England continued to make the movement of any German unit toward the front a nightmare of delays, detours, and sudden destruction.

The 2nd Armored and 1st Infantry Divisions, nearly 40,000 strong with over 400 tanks, had slammed into the 3rd Panzer Grenadier Division near Privas and had sent the Germans reeling back toward Valence. While the older model tanks that equipped both the 3rd Panzer Grenadiers and the 26th Panzer, which was also committed to the battle, had been more than enough to instill "tank panic" in the lightly armed American paratroopers and the French the week before, they were no match for the powerful guns and thick armor of the Americans' new Shermans or even their obsolescent Grants. The valley of the Rhone was now littered with the burnt-out hulks of dozens of

Pzkw IIIs and IVs. Only the arrival of the newly formed Hermann Göring Panzer Grenadier Division had stabilized the German front at the outskirts of Valence by evening. However, according to the reports of prisoners taken during the battle, this division had performed so badly overall that its commander would be reduced to threatening summary executions of some of its soldiers for cowardice, and it was spent as a fighting force until it could be pulled out of the line and thoroughly reorganized.

But Patton was not finished yet. When the thrust along the west bank of the Rhone began to lose momentum, he called up his reserve division, the 9th Infantry, reinforced with two battalions of Shermans and two regiments of the Foreign Legion brought over from North Africa, and launched them across the Isère River for a drive up the east bank of the Rhone, which was thinly held by the Germans, directly toward Lyon. At the same time, the 1st Armored was sent on a broad left hook through Aubernas to Yssingeaux and then east to St. Etienne, to get behind the Germans in a mirror image of the earlier German attack. The 1st would be supported by several French regiments and the remnants of the 82nd Airborne, who were eager to redeem themselves, sweeping the rough ground to the right of the 1st Armored's advance and assigning strong detachments to guard the crossings of the Loire River on their left. With a little luck, the double envelopment of the Germans at Valence could result in the gutting of German offensive power in central France for weeks.

Abrams scanned the town from the crest of a hill. Allied bombers had hit the town recently, and smoke was curling up from several burning buildings. Combat Command B (CCB) of the 1st Armored and the divisional support units had the job of taking the town with the help of the 504th Airborne Regiment while Abrams' own CCA, which he had taken over when the original commander had been wounded during the fighting around Valence the week before, swung around the town to strike south through Annonay and into the rear of the German units still holding Valence. The taking of St. Etienne was not a job Abrams envied CCB, using armor in what promised to be a nasty street fight through the town, and intelligence informed him that the defenders were SS troops, not given to easy surrender or retreat. The only bright spot was that the Germans had swept through here so quickly the first time that they had almost certainly never imagined having to fight here again so soon and had not made use of the days since the town fell to fortify their positions.

Abrams signaled the driver of his Grant to move out along the logging trail they were using to skirt St. Etienne. He had traded in his little M5 Stuart when it became apparent in their first battle that, while the Stuart was much faster and more maneuverable than the bulky Grant, it certainly wasn't fast enough to outrun an armor piercing round, its armor almost negligible and badly angled, and its 37mm gun no more than a doorknocker useful for getting a German tanker's attention. Within an hour the column had reached the main road running south from St. Etienne to Annonay at the Rhone, and the tanks and half-tracks poured out of the woods and onto the hardtop where they picked up speed.

Soon, Abrams could hear heavy firing from up ahead where a French armored cavalry troop spearheading the advance must have run into the first resistance. Over the treetops he could see aircraft diving and dropping bombs while several columns of smoke rose skyward. A jeep came roaring back up the highway, hugging the gravel shoulder as a double column of vehicles filled the roadway. The jeep fishtailed to a stop next to Abrams' tank, and he signaled a halt.

"We've got about a battalion of enemy infantry holed up in Annonay," a dirty faced Captain hollered from the jeep over the grumbling of the tank engine. "The French are engaging them. Your orders from General Harmon are to swing right at a farm track about half a mile ahead and head due southeast across country. You have to get within gunshot of the river before nightfall and take up a defensive position there, a laager for all-round defense. It looks like we've caught the Germans flat-footed, and the General wants to keep as much of this as possible off the airwaves."

"Roger that," Abrams shouted. "How's the 9th Division doing?"

"They're closing on the river from the south, but it's heavy going. They're almost within artillery range of the bridge this road takes over the river to hook up with the main highway up to Lyon. If they close that route off, the Germans will have to fight their way north on this side of the stream, and they've already started pulling back from Valence."

"You mean they'll have to climb over us."

"Yes sir," the captain replied, "and, by the way, Major?" he shouted up as Abrams was about to slip the radio earphones over his head again to get on his way.

"What?"

"The general says that you're a colonel now. Can't have major leading a combat command into battle, he said. Congratulations, sir." He snapped a salute.

"Outstanding," Abrams smiled. "Make sure he gets that down on paper so my wife gets the survivor's benefits. I've got a feeling that the Germans aren't just going to lie down and let us roll over them."

"Too bad we're not fighting the Italians, sir," the captain agreed as he eased back into his seat, and the two vehicles parted.

Abrams pulled his battalion commanders out of the line for a quick conference, and they studied a map of the river valley area. Abrams would have two tank battalions, one of Grants and one of Stuarts, and a battalion of infantry in half-tracks plus an 18-gun battalion of 105mm howitzers also mounted on half-tracks. He also had an attached company of M-10 tank destroyers with their light armor but 76mm high velocity guns. He would put the Grants facing south toward Valence, the Stuarts and M-10s facing north toward Lyon whence any German reinforcements would be coming, and use the infantry to fill in the gaps. If it came up in time, Harmon would place the divisional artillery in a position to fire all around his perimeter, but Abrams had to assume that he'd be on his own for awhile at least.

"Looks like we're the cork in the bottle, gentlemen," Abrams concluded to his officers as they headed back toward their units.

"And you know who gets screwed," he overheard one of them grumble under his breath. He had to agree.

The sun was getting low over the Massif Central to the west, casting longer and longer shadows across the fields as Abrams surveyed the ground ahead. CCA was halted in the last heavily wooded ground, and he had slipped forward with some scouts in jeeps mounting .50 caliber machine guns. There was about two miles of gently rolling, open ground between his observation point and the river. A narrow road paralleled the river heading north, and it was crammed with German vehicles, artillery, tanks, trucks, and even horse-drawn wagons. Then his eyes hit on what he had been looking for: a broad bowl-shaped area surrounded by low knolls, about three-quarters of a mile in diameter, its outer edge less than a mile from the river road. If he could rush CCA into that depression, the knolls would serve as breastworks, and he could shift forces from one point to another to meet any enemy attacks. He rushed back to his jeep to get his orders out.

CCA came rolling out of the woods in line abreast, over one hundred vehicles with the setting sun at their backs, every gun firing wildly while the artillery and mortar batteries fired over their heads. The effect of the concentrated fire on the close-packed German column was devastating, and immediate panic resulted. The advancing line soon became ragged as the tanks would pause to fire with greater accuracy, but in a matter of minutes virtually every German vehicle in sight was a burning wreck and dozens of men had even plunged into the swift-flowing, icy waters of the Rhone in an effort to escape.

Abrams quickly called in his units to take advantage of the enemy's undoubtedly temporary confusion to occupy his defensive position. The tanks and tank destroyers took up hull-down positions around the perimeter while the artillery and mortars spaced themselves out as best they could in the center, and the infantry began furiously to dig individual fighting pits. Abrams also sent out platoon-size patrols both north and south, well equipped with bazookas and mines to provide some advance warning of the approach of the enemy. It would take some time for word to reach the nearest German headquarters that the road was cut and still more to organize a serious counterattack, but the attack could not fail to come. This was the only game in town for the Germans, so the stakes didn't matter any more.

Abrams was called to the western perimeter just before sunset by a nervous infantry captain who had spotted movement to his front. Fortunately, his men were well enough in hand that they didn't open fire immediately, for it turned out that the intruders were a force of about 100 American paratroopers from the 509th and some 200 French who had been wandering the woods since the German offensive, trying to find their way back to friendly lines through the aggressive German patrols. As haggard as the refugees looked, Abrams was glad to have them and ordered up K-rations and a supply of ammunition for them as Lt. Col. Bentley and Colonel d'Ormesson spotted their units around the perimeter, helping to flesh out the defense.

Abrams did not have long to wait. In the gathering dusk, several probes from the south, in company strength, tested the perimeter, but they were easily spotted in the light of the still-burning vehicles, and driven back with considerable loss. Abrams was concerned. He had to make a decision and had chosen to put his heavier Grants on the southern side, on the assumption that most of the available German armor was trapped at the front near Valence. But what if he was wrong? He would not know for certain, of course, until it was too late to do anything about it.

1000 HOURS, 31 DECEMBER 1942
LYON, FRANCE

In the view of General Alfred Gause and Colonel Siegfried Westphal, Rommel's chief of staff and chief of operations, 1942 was not ending on a particularly auspicious note for the Third Reich in general or for themselves in particular. The Field Marshal had roared off to the front early that morning after the American offensive had started, and they had not heard from him since. Enemy radio jamming had prevented all but the most sporadic contact with either the 3rd Panzer Grenadier or the 26nd Panzer Divisions, but they now appeared to be cut off by armored forces that had slipped in behind them. That opened the possibility that Rommel had been either killed or captured. In any event, if Rommel had had any plans for dealing with the enemy attack, he had not shared them with his staff, and it was now up to them to issue orders to divisional, and even corps commanders in his name. They were used to this sort of thing from North Africa since there the unit commanders understood the Field Marshal's eccentricities and did not bridle at taking direction from their juniors; but in France the scattered units forming the ring around the Allied lodgment were commanded by men used to a much more structured hierarchy, and precious time was being lost in useless bickering and posturing.

The biggest problem at the moment was the attitude of General Haller, commander of LXIII Corps, the only major unit at the front that was not trapped behind the Allied advance. When it had appeared that the armored fist of Rommel's offensive would sweep all before it, Haller was given pretty much a free hand in the deployment of his three infantry divisions. One was left in Lyon to deal with a popular uprising fomented by the Communist FTP, a second sent off to the southeast toward Chambery to link up with the Italians in the Alps, and the third southward to Grenoble, leaving a yawning gap between Grenoble and the Rhone. It had been into this gap, covered only by scattered infantry and recce battalions, that the right wing of the American attack had plunged. Rommel had ordered Haller's two advanced divisions to pull back and hit the Americans in the flank while the division in Lyon should move south to meet them head on, leaving mopping up operations in the city to the SS police units that were arriving along with dribbles of reinforcements. Haller had protested that Allied carpet bombing was making the roads impassable, which was plausible enough, except that Haller apparently had a view to gaining laurels for himself (which had been lacking from a decidedly marginal performance thus far in the war) by capturing Grenoble. He argued that this would create a strategic threat to the Allied lodgment that would require them to pull back their 9th Division, thus serving the same purpose. As of the moment, however, the French garrison in Grenoble had managed to hold out against Haller's attacks, and the Americans showed no sign of going to their aid when the chance of eliminating a German Panzer Corps, now designated the XIV under Fritz Bayerlein, another alumnus of the Afrika Korps, presented itself

Rommel, of course, could have compelled Haller's obedience or had him relieved on the spot, but his staff could hardly accomplish this, and Rommel was nowhere to be found. It remained to the staff to try to scrape together a breakthrough force from the units at hand. Unfortunately, there was very little at hand. The Führer still refused to release the 29th Panzer Grenadier Division from reserve at Rouen, but with virtually every railroad bridge and culvert in northern and central France destroyed by Allied bombers or partisans, troops from the north or from Germany would never arrive in time. The only units currently available were most of the newly created 1st Parachute Division and a battalion of the new Tiger heavy tanks, and it was these that Gause ordered down the road toward the pocket, knowing almost nothing about what they might encounter on the way.

1130 Hours, 31 December 1942
Near Annonay, France

Some idiot had actually smuggled a little party horn in his pack and had begun tooting it as midnight approached, to the nervous laughter of the other men. It had taken Abrams and two sergeants major several minutes to find the culprit and destroy the offending article. The moon had set now, and, even though the Germans theoretically knew where his blocking position was located, there was no point in giving them the present of precisely fixing his placement.

There had been half a dozen separate attacks on the perimeter, all from the south, since sunset, and none had made much progress. Abrams could hear the dull rumble of heavy artillery fire from down around Valence as the rest of II Corps pressed the Germans hard, and more from the east where the 9th Division was probably pounding the bridge over the Rhone, the Germans' only other escape route. Only a few more hours, he kept telling himself If the weather held, the fighter-bombers would be up at dawn and could keep any enemy relief columns off his back, but for the moment, he was all alone.

Suddenly, there was a flurry of firing from the north this time, and Abrams' stomach knotted up. It was the outpost on the road toward Givors, and he could hear the chatter of machine guns and the occasional whoosh of a bazooka. So tanks were coming this time, he thought. Then there was silence once more. He trotted over to an M-10 tank destroyer and hauled himself up on the back deck. The TD's turret had an open top, something Abrams had never understood, since it made the crew totally vulnerable to artillery bursts, but it enabled him to snatch the commander's radio headset and raise the mortar battery. He told them to stand by.

Even though his eyes were accustomed to the dark, the night was now almost completely black. The faint starlight made the broad Rhone glisten off to his right, and the disabled enemy vehicles or clumps of trees were slightly darker patches on the landscape, so he strained to hear what might be approaching. He felt it before he could hear it, a vibration in the ground, and he had to check to make sure that the tank destroyer's engine was turned off. It was. Then came the distinct and unmistakable squeal of bogie wheels.

"Give me three flares on grid reference C, now," he whispered into the radio, and he immediately heard the muffled whump as the mortar rounds left their tubes.

The scene before him was immediately bathed in harsh white light, and he covered one eye to protect some of his night vision. Seemingly frozen in the quavering light of the descending flare, he could see several huge black shapes, interspersed with smaller ones. The squeal of the treads reached a higher pitch as the massive tanks picked up speed, and the enemy infantry-men scattered. Firing broke out all along the line from rifles and machine guns, and several M-10s and Stuarts opened up on the tanks. The rounds from the little Stuarts caromed off the massive steel beasts, which was to be expected, but so did 76mm shots from the M-10s, and when the attackers returned fire, their guns bellowed like nothing Abrams had heard before.

"Shit!" the TD commander screamed. "We're dead men!"

A shell from one of the Tigers snatched the turret off a Stuart, tossing it into the air like a crumpled ball of paper. One of the behemoths had thrown a track when it passed over a mine, but even that one was still firing, and dozens of other rounds from the defenders had not so much as slowed the other attackers.

"This isn't working," Abrams shouted into the radio. "I want the Grants to pull out of line *now* and swing around to the west. Our only chance is to get a flank or rear shot at these monsters or they're going to have us for breakfast. Everyone else go for their infantry and any light vehicles you see."

For a few moments, the Tigers stopped where they were, content to pick off one defending tank after another, contemptuous of the shells which fell around them. Artillery fire from Abrams' own guns and from division was plowing the field before them now, holding up the enemy infantry, and German mortar fire was coming down within the perimeter. Apparently the Tigers were reluctant to press forward without infantry support for fear that some enterprising foot soldier would sneak up and toss a satchel charge under their bellies, but they continued to move forward at a foot pace.

Some of the defenders were starting to drift off to the rear, and Abrams ran up and down the line, grabbing men and physically shoving them back into position, and he found Bentley and d'Ormesson busy with the same task.

"Give us ten minutes!" Abrams was shouting. "Just ten minutes. Keep their infantry back, and the Tigers won't come on alone. And try to pick off the tank commanders." He knew that this was wishful thinking, but he had to give the Grants a chance to get into position.

He ran back up to the line and found the M-10 he had mounted before a burning pile of scrap metal. He climbed up on another and ordered the pull-back.

"I want the Stuarts and TDs to pull back fifty yards," he shouted into the radio. "Wait for the Tigers to come up over the hills and go for a shot in the belly as they raise up."

This was a truly desperate measure, but there was nothing else to do. The defenders would have only a couple of seconds to fire as the enemy Tigers crested the ridge. If they missed, there was no cover at all in the center of the depression, and the Tigers would roll right through them. But the enemy was too close now for his men to get away. Better at least to be gunned down here than running. Naturally, as the Tigers came up, their turrets would clear the rise first, and they could just sit there, hull-down, and blaze away all day long. But if they had their blood up, maybe they'd just charge ahead without pausing and give his men at least a chance at a shot at their thin bottom armor.

He clung on as the M-10 he rode lurched backward down the knoll and took up a position behind a low hedge. Abrams looked about him. There were plenty of fires now, along with the flares, for him to see that less than a dozen Stuarts and only a handful of M-10s survived, but a couple of the artillery's 105s had pulled into the line, their gun tubes depressed. They weren't meant to be anti-tank weapons, but a 105mm shell in your face could still get your attention. He had seen some of his men take to their heels, but when he looked about him at the gunners and infantrymen, Americans and French-men, as they sighted their weapons and waited, a tear came to his eye, and he had to brush it roughly away. This would be good company to die in.

After a long moment, the silhouette of a head, just a man's head, appeared above the crest of the knoll, and a hundred rifles and machineguns opened fire. When they stopped, the head was gone, and Abrams always wondered if the poor bastard had survived. Then the massive turret of a Tiger appeared and was also greeted by a storm of fire, but its gun roared as soon as it came clear and quickly claimed a Stuart. Others were now breasting and rise and, as Abrams had hoped, most were not pausing to fire. His own M-10 and a Stuart fired almost simultaneously at the underside of a Tiger to their front and were rewarded with watching the turret hatch of the beast blow off and hearing a number of small explosions erupting from within the tank as the ammunition inside cooked off.

But several Tigers had begun to roll down the slope and others were firing from cover. It was all over. Just then, however, one of the Tigers lurched side-ways, and thick black smoke began to pour from its engine compartment. Abrams could now make out what sounded like sharp rifle cracks amid the deeper roar of the Tigers' 88s, and he turned to see a line of Grants off to his left firing steadily into the flanks of the Tigers. What surprised him was that there were even more Grants than he had originally possessed.

The Germans lost heart quickly at this reverse and pulled back at speed, trying to turn to face the new threat. Abrams was glad to let them go as artil-lery fire followed them back up the road toward Givors. A cheer went up all along the line.

Abrams sat down heavily on the deck of the M-10, leaning against the turret, and a Grant pulled up next to him. General Harmon emerged from the turret, and Abrams tried clumsily to pull himself to his feet.

"As you were, Abrams," Harmon waved him back down. "I was monitor-ing your transmissions, so I thought you might like some company. I brought along a battalion of Grants and the recon company that weren't really needed at St. Etienne."

"Never was so glad to see anybody in my life, sir," Abrams admitted.

Together they strolled up to where one of the disabled Tigers was still burning, the charred corpse of the driver hanging halfway out the hatch.

"Jesus!" Harmon whistled. "I hope they don't have too many more surprises like this up their sleeves."

"I guess they don't have too many of these babies yet," Abrams suggested. "First time we've seen them, and I don't care if it's the last."

"All the more reason for us to get this damn war over with in a hurry," Harmon growled, and they both turned to watch as the American armor swept on toward the river.

0600 HOURS, 1 JANUARY 1943
GIVORS, FRANCE

Rommel had never been one to accept responsibility for his own mistakes, or even to give credit for the efforts of his subordinates. This trait had irritated many of the senior officers who had served under him in the desert, and may have prompted General Wilhelm von Thoma, his replacement as commander of the Afrika Korps when Rommel moved up to head Panzer Armee Afrika, actually to defect to the Allies, although it was never proven that von Thoma had voluntarily gone over and not simply been captured. In any event, Rommel had not changed his ways, and ranted and raved about the command post when he had finally returned there half an hour before.

With the counterattack by the paratroopers and the Tigers a failure, it was easy enough for Rommel to claim that he would have done things differently. General Gause knew that Rommel lacked in France a number of advantages he had enjoyed in North Africa. In the desert Rommel had possessed a brilliant intelligence unit that routinely broke Allied codes and passed vital information to him on British plans and intentions, including detailed reports from the American military attaché in Cairo on every aspect of the British war effort. He had also become intimately familiar with the terrain throughout Libya and western Egypt (and his only significant failures, the first battle of Tobruk and El Alamein, had occurred in areas which he was unfamiliar with at the time). Here he had none of those advantages and had stumbled accordingly, making assumptions about Allied dispositions and capabilities that had proven to be unfounded.

But Rommel was at his best when dealing with adversity. He ordered the 113th Infantry Division out of Lyon, where the partisan attacks had never posed a serious threat to German control of the city, and reinforced it with a scratch force of odd tank battalions, engineer and anti-aircraft units, and rushed them south along the east bank of the Rhone to strike the American 9th Division, pushing its advanced elements back. This cleared the bridge over the Rhone, which was still miraculously standing despite artillery shelling and repeated air raids. He reinforced this with a flotilla of river ferries he slipped down from Lyon and was thus able to extricate virtually all of his armored forces from the Valence pocket. So, there would be no huge bag of German prisoners for the Allies to parade as the Russians were already doing in the East.

Rommel then pulled his forces back into the loop of the Rhone south of Lyon, which would afford them some protection but would also serve as a bridgehead for a future advance. More units continued to pour into the line from Germany, and within 48 hours he could claim that at least the northern face of the Allied lodgment had been secured, enabling him to divert further reinforcements down toward the open territory west of the Massif Central and Bordeaux. Both sides then paused to lick their wounds.

1200 HOURS, 1 JANUARY 1943
MARSEILLE, FRANCE

The American military policemen and engineers working on the railroad at Marseille were incensed at the sudden closing off of one platform and a westbound line from Toulon by the local French authorities. Inquiries up the chain of command produced no new information, and the French gendarmes politely, but very firmly blocked off the area, and it appeared that, short of open combat, there was nothing that could or would be done to budge them. Major General Mark Clark, who had been passed over for the assignment of command of Fifth Army in favor of Patton, was in a perpetual bad mood in his new post as coordinator of logistics for the lodgment area, and his humor did not improve when his queries to Giraud's headquarters received only assurances of ignorance of the matter.

Even with the full use of the port of Marseille as well as Toulon and a number of minor ports along the Mediterranean coast, Allied resources were strained for bringing in the unending flood of new divisions and the mountains of supplies and munitions they consumed daily, in addition to the hundreds of tanks, trucks, guns, planes, and other equipment destined for the new French Army. The Luftwaffe had been unable to close any of the ports, but determined air raids continued every day and night, in the face of mounting losses to the growing Allied fighter and anti-aircraft defenses, and there was always at least one thick column of black, greasy smoke rising up into the sky from the dock area or from the smoldering hulk of a merchantman that had been hit in the harbor. The road and rail lines leading north from the coast had also been pounded on a regular basis, and every square foot of cargo space in the rumbling truck convoys or the limited amount of French and now American rolling stock was crucial to the war effort. The sudden removal of a line from the supply net caused a domino effect that had quartermasters from Norfolk and Plymouth to Avignon tearing at their hair. But by the time General Clark had realized that only direct intervention would resolve the situation and prepared a motorcade to take him to the Gare St. Charles, the mystery had been solved, and the crisis had passed.

Tension had been in the air in Marseille for days, and there was little celebration of the New Year in the port city. Refugees and not a few deserters from the fighting to the north and west had clogged the roads into the city, and their stories of defeat by the onrushing panzers put grim faces on the populace as they worried about the reprisals the Germans would take if the Allied armies were driven out. Those with the money or the connections were even taking the precaution of securing passage on merchant ships to escape to North Africa if that became necessary. On the morning of January 1, however, word began to spread of a major Allied victory along the Rhone, that the Germans had been driven back to Lyon, or even beyond, and that the danger was past. For a people who had been fed a steady diet of wartime propaganda for nearly three years, such rumors were taken with a large dose of salt, but the columns of refugees had thinned appreciably, and civilian truck drivers who had been conscripted into military service were being given loads with destinations farther and farther to the north, a good sign.

The arrival of the train at Gare St. Charles at noon on the 1st had thus been timed with considerable political skill. The engine was festooned with tricolor banners as it made its regal way through the working class districts on the north and east of the city, and a flatcar located just behind the engine was crammed with a military band blaring out the "Marseillaise" over the chugging of the locomotive. Called out into the street by men and women who had, until a few weeks earlier been clandestine agents of the FFI resistance, crowds began to gather along the tracks, and they cheered themselves hoarse as they recognized the tall, angular figure of de Gaulle standing atop a platform mounted on another flatcar, practically engulfed by rows of French flags and surrounded by French generals and admirals, their uniforms encrusted with gold braid and medals.

Orders had been issued from both Washington and London that de Gaulle was not to make such a procession, and it had been part of the discreet agreement with Giraud that he be kept off the mainland for the indefinite future. However, since de Gaulle had not bothered to ask anyone's permission, and since the French military had connived at his being smuggled ashore, General Clark quickly and wisely decided that attempting to obstruct his entrance into the city would be both unsuccessful and potentially dangerous.

De Gaulle gave a brief speech to the throngs that mobbed the train station, but his words were lost in the tumult of the departing and arriving trains and trucks. It hardly mattered. With a mixture of relief, pride, and joy at his mere presence among them, the French soldiers and civilians cheered him to the echo, and even the hundreds of American replacement troops (now officially called "reinforcements" for morale purposes) transiting the station joined in lustily. Then, with the gendarmes risking life and limb to form a human cordon out to the street against the pressing crowd, de Gaulle linked arms with the mayor of Marseille and a host of dark-suited, nameless civilian bureaucrats and began a march through the heart of the city to the Cathedral de la Major, with a solid phalanx of military officers, including Juin, Weygand, Koenig, and others just behind.

The sidewalks were packed with delirious spectators, and men, women, and children dangled perilously from every window and balcony along the route. A *Te Deum* was sung at the cathedral, which was located hard by the docks. Afterward, de Gaulle made an impromptu swing along the quay, warmly shaking hands with the disembarking American, Canadian, British, Moroccan, and French colonial troops. He then strolled to the *Hotel de Ville* where he began the task of setting up his government. Giraud remained behind closed doors at his headquarters.

Mark Clark later wrote that the entire spectacle was a wonderful piece of theater. "There was hardly a dry eye in the house."

The prophet had returned.

1500 HOURS, 3 JANUARY 1943
ST. ETIENNE, FRANCE

Captain Hans Essen clutched his Schmeisser machine pistol to his chest and leaned against the firm stone wall of the house he was using as his command post. The body of his company clerk was sprawled on the floor, a neat round hole in his forehead, the price of having ventured too close to a window. It had taken the Americans some time to learn the tricks of street fighting. They had started by sending columns of men up the streets, only to be ground to dust by pre-sighted machine guns, but they had learned quickly enough. Now they knocked holes in the walls of adjacent houses for more secure movement and had learned how to clear a house, room by room, using grenades and automatic weapons. He also noticed that they had appreciated the greatly superior firepower of the SS units, which often had three or four times as many automatic weapons as their US counterparts, and he had seen American soldiers sporting captured Schmeissers and even MG42 machineguns to augment their official issue. The Americans now used tanks and artillery to fire directly into difficult strongpoints, simply blowing out the ground floors of houses sheltering snipers or artillery observers, relying on the collapse of the building to deal with the problem. They had at first tried to avoid damaging "private property," but were now leveling the city block by block as they drove the SS troopers inexorably northward, obviously less sensitive about the effect of their actions on property values.

But Essen had shown them a few new wrinkles, such as using the city sewer system to slip raiding parties behind their lines, popping up in the dead of night to massacre a mortar crew or battalion staff, and then disappearing back into the rubble. The SS Lehr Sturm Brigade had orders to hold the city until a more secure defensive line could be established to the north, and other units had been fed into the battle to prevent the Americans and French from filtering around the flanks and to keep a supply line open toward Roanne. And now the time had come to move on.

This was actually one of the most difficult of military maneuvers, breaking close contact with the enemy in a coherent fashion. One had to disguise the signs that a pullout was in progress to prevent the enemy from rushing forward and catching the retreating units exposed and on the move. At the same time one had to closely coordinate the move to make sure that no company or platoon would be left behind in an environment where radios were of little use amid the obstructions of the city and where messengers had a very short life expectancy.

Essen would have much preferred to wait until dark, but reconnaissance reports indicated that the Americans were massing armor east of St. Etienne, probably for a push behind the city to the Loire, which would cut off all retreat. As a consequence, the German artillery had been dropping random patterns of smoke all along the front during the course of the day. Essen was now waiting for the thud of new rounds falling which would signal that this was his chance to move what was left of his company back. His escape route led through the large *Cret de Roc* cemetery, northeast across the rail line to the *Pare des Expositions* and on out of the city toward the new lines beyond.

He heard the first detonations and peeked quickly around the edge of a window frame. Large blooms of white smoke were appearing, mixing to form a solid wall of mist, and he noticed that the gunners were throwing in a few high explosive rounds as well, the better to keep the Americans' heads down. He jumped to his feet and blew the long silver whistle he wore around his neck, as he had done during previous barrages, but a different series of blasts this time. He leapt down to the first floor of the building through a massive hole in the floor and skidded along a pile of smashed stone and bits of furniture and out the back door. Other men were cautiously emerging from other houses, doubled over but moving fast, their uniforms covered with plaster dust that at least served to make them harder to see.

The cemetery, apart from being a little disconcerting, was actually the easiest portion of their escape route. It was a typical European graveyard, surrounded by high walls and crowded with sturdy headstones and crypts like miniature houses, all of solid marble, providing perfect cover. Bullets from snipers still pinged around the men as they slithered between the stones, but they all made it to the point where a shell had destroyed a twenty-meter stretch of the wall on the far side. Fortunately, snipers were not usually provided with radios for calling in artillery fire, and Essen hoped to be able to move quickly enough to stay ahead of any barrage the Americans might try to lay down.

The most dangerous segment was crossing the railroad tracks, which ran at a diagonal behind the cemetery. The train station, the *Gare de Chateaucreux,* was barely three hundred meters away to the southeast and had been the focus of some of the fiercest fighting of the battle, changing hands several times. It had been reoccupied by the Germans during the night, but American paratroopers were all around it, and there was nearly fifty meters of open ground to cover, with the slightly raised roadbed of the tracks themselves in the middle. There was no cover, and the loose gravel of the roadbed would slow the running men down for what might be fatal seconds. Since the station house was a lynchpin of the German defense, it would be held until the last, but the Americans were pressed up around it on three sides and would have a clear field of fire up the tracks.

Essen looked about him and saw that he only had about sixty men left of the more than one hundred and fifty with which he had originally crossed the demarcation line into Vichy territory, and many of these were sporting grimy bandages. He strung them out along a drainage ditch running parallel to the tracks, the last bit of usable cover. They would go over in one rush, lest sending men in small groups merely attract the attention of enemy gunners. He passed the word and each man braced himself in a low crouch. Then he blew his whistle.

They scrambled up the steep, yielding bank of gravel, holding their weapons high and pumping with their arms for all they were worth. Essen heard the first rattle of a machinegun, and bullets began to kick up little geysers of dirt around the men. They were at the tracks now, bounding over them and glissading down the opposite side, but he could hear an occasional gasp or groan or simply the dull thud of a body hitting the ground, and he knew that they were taking losses. With a roar, Essen pumped his weary legs harder and rushed down a narrow street between two low buildings, followed by what was left of his company. They couldn't afford to stop here, however. The enemy would be calling in artillery and mortars on this spot, and they had to get out of the kill zone as quickly as possible. Even as he thought this, the wall of a house on his side of the street exploded outward, burying one of his men under a pile of stones and shattered beams. But the barrage was mercifully short. Perhaps the Americans were running low on ammunition, but he was beyond caring. He ducked into an open garage and threw himself flat, his lungs screaming for air. He looked about him and counted, only about forty men left.

0600 Hours, 4 January 1943
Near Marseille, France

Ensign Giovanni Labastida had always had a fear of enclosed spaces, which was why he had not volunteered for the submarine service. He had dreamt of a career in the navy, but he had imagined himself standing on the flying bridge of a cruiser or destroyer, the fresh sea breeze in his face, giving orders to the sweating gun crews as they pounded distant targets. Unfortunately, he had been a particularly strong swimmer, and on the basis of this had been selected to "volunteer" for special service. While he did not have the constricting hull of a submarine around him to give rise to his fears, he had never felt so confined, and he would have welcomed something between himself and the sea besides a rubber wet suit.

He gingerly steered his human torpedo, a kind of underwater motorcycle on which two divers rode in tandem, weaving between the cables of mines anchored to the sea bed and around the contours of the torpedo nets strung across the harbor entrance. He disliked the metallic taste of the air.from the tanks on his back, and could barely make out anything in the murky water, only just illuminated by the downward tilted headlamp of his vehicle.

Even though the navy had had a signal success in December 1941 against the British fleet in Alexandria using these "weapons," certainly the lowest item on the military food chain, sinking two battleships and other vessels, this fact only caused Labastida to worry all the more. Certainly the Allies would be expecting this sort of attack, especially since the Italian surface fleet had now been crippled. Of course, there continued to be daily air raids by both the Italian and German air forces on the port and ships coming and going, and submarine captains were running suicidal risks to press home their own attacks, but the Allies seemed more than capable of absorbing the losses and continued to unload huge mountains of supplies and thousands of men for the front. Consequently, the *Regia Marina* had pulled the final trick out of its bag, Labastida and the dozen other men of his unit. They must really have been desperate, Labastida could not help thinking.

He looked up toward the surface, which was glowing with a ghostly light, from the sweeping searchlights of the warships and the brightly lit quay, since the Allies apparently were willing to risk a night bombing raid by the Luftwaffe rather than stop their frantic unloading efforts. But directly above him was an immense shadow, the hull of a ship. It would be impossible to tell from below just which ship it might be, and it was far too risky to surface for a better look, but from the narrow, predatory bow, Labastida knew it must be a warship, too big for a destroyer, so at least a cruiser or even a battleship. It would have made more sense to Labastida to target a number of fat transports, crammed with munitions, fuel, or fighting men rather than a single combatant, and it would take all of the limpet mines carried by his unit to do any real damage to a thick-skinned battleship. There was no way in the world that the crippled *Regia Marina* could regain naval superiority against the combined fleets of France, Great Britain, and the United States, even if Labastida could sink every warship in Marseille, yet his orders were clear. Obviously the admirals were more interested in prestige targets than in actually affecting the course of the war.

Labastida took out his flashlight and waggled it at the other frogmen and jerked his thumb upward. They left their torpedo craft resting on the bottom and swam upward, each man hauling a large round metal disk that they would attach with magnets to the ship's hull. There was a forty-five minute delay on the fuses, hopefully enough time for the divers to get clear, as the concussion of the blast would crush every living thing for hundreds of yards in all directions under the water.

Suddenly, Labastida heard a distinct plunk as something hit the water overhead. This was followed by another and another, and he caught a brief glimpse of a pointed object, about the length of his forearm, spiraling down slowly trailing a stream of bubbles. Bubbles, Labastida thought. They must have had lookouts on watch and spotted our bubbles, and these were mortar bombs. He only had time for the first few words of a prayer when a flash lit up the sea. The black and white underwater world suddenly turned red as the blood vessels around Labastida's eyes exploded, and then everything went black.

1100 Hours, 7 January 1943
Rome, Italy

Field Marshal Albert Kesselring tossed another lengthy message from OKW onto the stack that teetered precariously on the corner of his desk. The young major who had brought it in imagined that he could see steam still rising from the missive as the High Command berated the Field Marshal for the loss of Nice the previous day. It was the first sizeable French city actually to be liberated from the Axis in battle, and the Führer was reported to be livid. But Kesselring had been a field commander for too long to waste time worrying about things he could not change.

In the last war Kesselring had been an artillery officer and had been chosen for his brilliance to be one of the handful of key officers retained in the much-reduced Weimar army. He had then made the switch to the Luftwaffe and had been the mastermind behind the "flying artillery" that had smashed the defenses of Poland, the Low Countries, France, and finally Russia in the heyday of the blitzkrieg. He had then left the Eastern Front to take command of the Axis air forces in the Mediterranean Theater, but he had soon graduated to command of the entire war effort in the south, on land, sea, and in the air. And he had done a brilliant job. Without his superb staff work and the political muscle he exerted with the Führer, Rommel would never have had the men and the tanks to achieve his victories in the desert, and it had been Kesselring who had engineered the salvation of those troops after Rommel had left them to their fate.

He was now left with one of the most thankless tasks in the war. Africa was gone, and with it the elite troops who had gone to join Rommel's new command in France. Meanwhile, Kesselring was responsible for the bloody, hopeless counterinsurgency effort in Yugoslavia and Greece, tying up dozens of German, Italian, and Bulgarian divisions with no chance of victory. Worse yet, he had to safeguard the hundreds of miles of Italian coastline against Allied amphibious assault, and it was known that there were twenty or thirty British divisions that had not been committed to the battle yet—all of Montgomery's 8th Army in Egypt and Libya and the British forces in England, and virtually all of the substantial number of landing craft the Allies had accumulated and not used to date.

But the most urgent threat came from the American and French forces pushing eastward along the Mediterranean coast. Although the terrain was mountainous, the Axis forces could not hold any line anchored on the sea, as the huge Allied fleets could bombard the defenders with impunity anywhere within twenty miles of the shore, providing a wall of fire and steel behind which the American 36th Division had rolled into Nice in the face of crumbling Italian resistance.

Yet, even this did not occupy Kesselring's mind at the moment. It was unlikely that the Allies would attempt to advance any farther along the coast. Their progress had not been without cost thus far, and just as the Allied ships could reach inland, German and Italian artillery safely positioned in the Alps could harass supply convoys along the coastal highway from beyond the range of the naval guns. Also, the Italians had very substantial fortifications along their pre-war border, which would not be easily breached even with all the weight of shells the Allied navies could contribute.

Kesselring's key concern at the start of the second week in January was whether the Italians, who comprised the bulk of his forces, would continue in the fight, drop out of it and leave it to the Germans to defend Italy, Sicily, and Sardinia, or even switch sides completely and leave Kesselring with hundreds of thousands of hostile, if indifferently armed, soldiers in his rear. It was his task at this moment to come up with a plan for dealing with either of the last two contingencies.

Operation ALARIC had been discussed in German staff circles at least since the start of the Axis retreat from El Alamein. The panicked Italian reaction to the defeat, and the shrill charges that their units were being stripped of transport and fuel and left to their fate at the hands of the British so that the German Afrika Korps could make good its escape, had convinced Kesselring and Rommel that the alliance wouldn't stand much more stress. Kesselring had been insulted by the insinuation, since it had been impossible to save much of the infantry, German or Italian, although a rational, objective analysis would have dictated the preservation of the skilled German tankers over the lackadaisical Italian conscripts.

The concept of securing a potentially hostile Italy had to be kept secret from the Führer at first, of course. For reasons that Kesselring had trouble understanding, Hitler actually looked *up* to the strutting Mussolini as a kind of ideological forebear and his one true ally in Europe. Consequently, Jodl, Keitel, and the others of Hitler's sycophantic "desk generals" had urged Kesselring not to dare suggest to the Führer that there might be any danger to the Reich from the south. Kesselring had argued with them that, throughout the war, despite the wartime alliance and the supposedly strong personal bond between the two leaders, construction had proceeded apace on fortifications on the Italian side of the Alpine passes separating the two countries, hundreds of miles from the nearest Allied soldier, hardly an expression of good faith.

Then, at a meeting at Berchtesgaden just before Christmas, Hitler had astounded his entourage by launching into a tirade about how, while the Duce was unquestionably loyal and had surrounded himself with trustworthy fascist militants, the Italian royal family, the military, the business class, and of course, the Jews, held the real power in Italy and were decidedly hostile to the Reich. He had added that, while they were too cowardly to move openly against Germany on their own, now that Allied troops were at hand, they could mount a coup d'etat at any time against Mussolini, and it was Germany's duty to protect her ally. With a shrug Kesselring had then been able to rattle off the gist of months of staff work as if off the top of his head, and the Führer had been delighted.

Kesselring saw the key to the peninsula as control of the Alpine passes.

If the Italians changed sides suddenly, any German troops caught south of the mountains would be lost unless those routes of communication could be held open. He suggested that Germany "offer" to emplace strong anti-aircraft defenses along the passes, each of which would actually be a fortified strong-point manned with special assault teams for seizing control of the tunnels and bridges that the Italians had gone to some effort to garrison and mine. When Hitler asked what they would do if the Italians declined the "offer," Canaris suggested that false flag bombing raids could be conducted using captured British or Russian planes and bombs, and the Führer had chuckled his approval. Kesselring went on that he would keep powerful units poised to seize political and communications centers such as Rome, Milan, Venice, and Naples, and then rush in additional infantry units to garrison the rest of the country from a reserve to be built up in Austria from units withdrawn from the Eastern Front for rest and refit. He added that he would abandon Sardinia, which was untenable after the Allied capture of Corsica, but would hold Sicily as a shield for southern Italy. Meanwhile, he would push the Italian units under his overall command forward into as much combat as possible against the Allies to squeeze the maximum advantage out of them before any change of heart while allowing his German troops some respite.

The memoirs of several of the attendees of this conference, including Kesselring and Jodl, agree that Hitler was more animated by this possibility than they had seen him for some time. The news from the battlefront had been uniformly dismal for weeks, and it now appeared that, although the front had stabilized, the Allied lodgment in southern France, which measured over one hundred miles deep and three times as wide, was not about to be extinguished. In the East, things were even worse, as the diversion of armored and infantry reinforcements as well as entire wings of Luftwaffe aircraft to deal with the Soviet breakthrough around Stalingrad had robbed Manstein's counterstroke of any real punch. The defenders of Stalingrad continued to hold out, but the question was now whether the Germans could hold open the corridor at Rostov for the escape of 1st Panzer Army in the Caucasus, which was careening backward in a desperate race with the advancing Soviet columns.

But now Hitler delved into the minutiae of planning for the lightning capture of Italy like a child with a new toy at Christmas. He squabbled with Kesselring and Jodl over the disposition of SS police units in Rome and Milan, and he pored over a detailed map of the Italian peninsula, plotting the best routes for the troops advancing across the River Po to the south. His main concern was that, should Mussolini not only be deposed by the traitors he knew abounded within the Italian government but be captured by them as well, it was imperative that the Duce be rescued and safeguarded by German troops until order could be reestablished. Kesselring hardly knew whether to be grateful that the expected confrontation with the Führer over the question of Italian reliability had been avoided or whether this tiresome addition to his "staff" was even less welcome.

Hitler accepts the ovation of the Reichstag in Berlin after announcing the peaceful annexation of Austria in 1938. Little did the rest of the world know that over the next three years the Third Reich would violently extend its dominions from the Atlantic to the Volga and from North Africa to the Arctic.

General George C. Marshall, US Army. America was the last major combatant to enter the war, joining the conflict when the Japanese attacked its naval base at Pearl Harbor at the end of 1941. But when the United States finally did come in, Hitler found himself with his greatest challenge. FDR naturally wanted to keep Marshall in Washington, DC as his chief adviser, but it was difficult to argue against letting him command in the field the most important US venture of the war: the counter-invasion of Nazi-held Europe.

American industrial capacity ramped up with amazing speed once the US entered the war. Above is a look at a Douglas Aircraft plant in Long Beach, California, where women workers perfected the plexiglass nose turrets of A-20 attack aircraft.

At left we see an American shipyard readying a plethora of transport vessels, dubbed "Victory Ships."

For the New World to launch counter-invasions across both oceans, a clear superiority in sea-borne capability needed to be established. The US Navy, as seen above, was able to achieve this.

The Germans were never able to come close to the firepower the US and British could deploy on the seas, but the Germans had their own response in U-boats. Every Allied convoy had to be prepared to stave off the stealthy vessels that lurked beneath the surface.

General George Patton was named commander of the US Army that would cut through German-held territory in France, and then Germany itself. A dynamic leader, he also had advantages in terms of material supply. While the US had to fight with its left hand against Japan, the Germans had to fight with their left against the Soviet Union, a much larger and more fearsome opponent.

Infantry troops on both sides often used their armored vehicles as protection during an advance. Sometimes this instinct would backfire, as their tanks became the main focus of enemy firepower.

Generalleutnant Erwin Rommel, former commander of Germany's 7th Panzer Division during the conquest of France, and then of its Afrika Korps. When the Allies invaded France, Rommel was foremost in securing its defense. And Allied generals such as Patton, Montgomery and Marshall could never be quite sure what Rommel had up his sleeve.

The Germans had unveiled their new Tigers by early 1943. There was not a tank in any Allied arsenal capable of matching them, and it was only the Germans' inability to build enough of them that kept them from being decisive.

The Allied invasion of France began with a massive airborne assault. Though the paratroopers were never able to make strategic gains, the chaos they sowed in the enemy's rear was enough to influence the outcome, as well as gain great respect for the brave paratroopers themselves.

Here we see American troops practicing opposed beach landings prior to the invasion of France. Though some such landings indeed needed to take place, in southern France the Americans relied primarily on ports such as Marseilles and Toulon to more easily unload their troops and supplies.

An American M-8 tank rolls up Route 7 south of Montélimar, France, past the wreckage of a German convoy. About a mile to the right of his location is the village of Allan, where a short but costly battle between US M-8's and a rearguard Panther took place.

In another view from Route 7, vehicles burn in the destroyed German column caught on the road by US artillery and fighter bombers. The Germans used every sort of conveyance, including civilian buses, in their hasty withdrawal.

While Anglo-American leaders found him problematic, there was no denying the inspirational effect Charles de Gaulle had on the French populace. He is shown here, upon his triumphant return to his homeland, along with General Leclerc, commander of the French 2nd Armored Division (center), and General Koenig (right), commander of the FFI. *Memorial du Maréchal Leclerc et de la Libération de Paris, Musée Jean Moulin, Ville de Paris*

General Bernard L. Montgomery, seen here in North Africa during the period when he personally vied with Rommel. Once the invasion of France had taken place the British general constantly urged the Americans for more influence and responsibility in the campaign.

Claus Schenk Graf von Stauffenberg, who executed the plot to kill Hitler.

While the Germans fell back in France, Field Marshal Albert Kesselring guided a more successful defensive campaign in Italy.

A photo of Hitler at his Wolfschanze headquarters, just one week before von Stauffenberg (seen at left in this photo) carried out the plot to assassinate him.

The Allied invasion of France could not have occurred without establishing air superiority in advance. US "heavies," operating in daylight, knocked out rail marshalling yards, communication centers, and bridges as their first priority.

The German fighter fleet rose to the challenge, as per the Focke-Wulf 190's shown below. But once long-range Mustangs came in on the Allied side to protect the bombers, the Germans became gradually overwhelmed in the air.

The first winter battles were hard on America's main battle tank, the M-4 Sherman, as they were no match for the Tigers and Panthers that the Germans began unleashing in 1943. However, the Germans could never make enough "zoo animals" to match the vast number of Shermans, who, supported by their Tank Destroyer cousins, gradually gained superiority on the battlefield.

While tank battles gained headlines, US infantry divisions meantime relied on their artillery to hammer down their Axis infrantry counterparts, as shown below.

Part of the premise of the Allied invasion was that the French people would rise in its support. This indeed happened, as shown in this photo of an American officer and a French partisan during a street fight in a French city after the Allies' arrival.

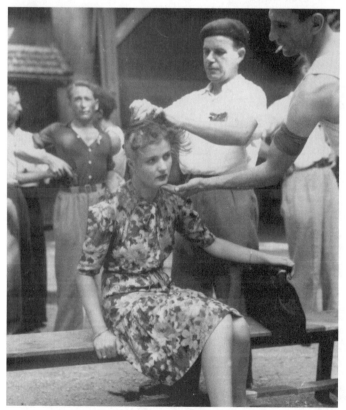

Other French citizens were punished for prior friendliness to the Germans. For females a shaved head was the usual mark of punishment for such offenses.

A U.S. anti-tank crew fires on Germans who machine-gunned their vehicle. Month after month, thousands of small-unit combats took place as the Germans did not give up their gains easily.

The Allied supply lines were fully stocked, but winter weather sometimes made it difficult to deliver chow to frontline troops across the slippery roads. In this photo we see how one delivery was eagerly welcomed by a U.S. squad.

The reports of German terror in Warsaw and other parts of Poland had much influence in Allied councils, and especially among Polish troops in exile serving with the Allies. The endgame of the war would focus much around the Allies need to rescue Europe in not just strategic terms but moral ones.

When the Germans finally surrendered it was practically wholesale in the West. In the East, however, many units continued to resist the Soviets until they or civilians could escape safely into Western hands.

CHAPTER 6
SIDESHOW

A GREAT DEAL of thought had gone into the choice of Casablanca as the site for what would in future years be referred to as a summit meeting. While London or Washington would have been much more convenient in terms of facilities for accommodating Roosevelt and Churchill as well as the French, and their respective entourages, and would have had the advantage that at least one of the parties would not have had to make a long trip involving no little measure of danger, psychological considerations took precedence. The Allied leaders wanted to express to the world a sense of forward progress, of rolling the Axis back, and North Africa, newly rejoined to the Grand Alliance, seemed to fit the bill. It was out of bomber range of Axis territory, unlike Southern France or Corsica, and was sufficiently away from the main supply lines of the campaign so that the arrival and departure of the principals and their staffs would not disrupt more important military activities.

Roosevelt, accompanied by Secretary Stimson and Generals Marshall, Eisenhower, and Doolittle, had expected a stormy session with Churchill over the course of the war in the past eight weeks. In essence, the British, due to their reluctance to support the invasion of the continent, had been relegated to a very minor role, one which did not sit very well with the Prime Minister and his key generals. That Marshall's strategy had worked out better than even he had expected would hardly ameliorate the situation when the British had been so vociferous in their opposition.

There were now seven full Allied corps in the line, three American, two French, the Canadian I Corps, and the British V Corps, from right to left, occupying a bulging arc from Nice to just south of Lyon and around to Toulouse. These were backed by two airborne divisions as a strategic reserve, hundreds of artillery pieces and warplanes in the lodgment area, and there was no danger now of the Allies being thrown back into the sea. The lines had stabilized, and both sides were in a frantic race to build up their forces; but the Allies were confident of winning this one, since German forces were still being consumed on the Eastern Front at a prodigious rate, and for the Allies this was the only game in town. There had been reverses, certainly, and substantial casualties, but nothing like those that the raid on Dieppe suggested would have awaited the Allies in a frontal assault on the Channel coast.

The primary purpose of the conference was to hash out a plan for the next step in the Allied offensive. Marshall favored pouring still more men and guns into the lodgment and forcing a breakthrough to the west of the Massif Central to sweep up the open country of central France to Paris, then "hang a right" and drive on to the heart of the Reich. Eisenhower was partial to the idea of a second amphibious invasion, this one along the western coast of France, to coincide with a push from the south that could trap as many as a dozen German divisions against the Spanish border and thus facilitate a later drive on Paris.

But the Americans realized that the only uncommitted forces were primarily British, and the decision would have to rest with them, both for their resources and by way of atoning for having gone against Churchill's wishes in launching HAYMAKER in the first place. Montgomery's 8th Army was now sitting idle in North Africa with at least a dozen veteran divisions, and even more front-line divisions were in England itself, while the American had committed all of the major units they had had available and would not be expecting even one more organized division for weeks. The French were arming fast, but their smaller divisions had limited striking power, and this was also true of the Polish corps also sitting in England.

It came as a pleasant surprise to the Americans when Churchill and his senior military officers, Admiral Andrew B. Cunningham, Allied naval commander in the Mediterranean, Field Marshal Sir Alan Brooke, Chief of the Imperial General Staff, Air Chief Marshal Sir Arthur W. Tedder, commander of the Allied air forces in the Mediterranean, Field Marshal Sir Harold Alexander, overall Allied commander for the Mediterranean Theater, and the newly-promoted Field Marshal Montgomery, all fairly gushed over the success of HAYMAKER to date. Although Eisenhower, who had experienced Montgomery's imperious nature at firsthand as a mere brigadier general earlier in the war, later wrote that the victor of El Alamein was much more guarded in his praise than the others, constantly making little hints of how *he* might have done things differently, Churchill's fulsome praise for the Allied achievement went far to ease the tension of the first meetings.

The French, on the other hand, were a case unto themselves. Both Giraud and de Gaulle insisted on being present. In fact, de Gaulle had not been formally invited to attend, but had shown up just the same, and both contenders for the leadership of France set up their own little courts in isolated villas at opposite ends of the city. There was an endless round of "entertainments" offered by the different delegations, and de Gaulle and Giraud consistently scheduled their own receptions at the same time, refusing to amend their plans and judging the "loyalty" of their allies by the size and importance of the attendees at each.

From past experience in dealing with the abrasive and demanding General de Gaulle, both the American and British leaders had a natural tendency to favor Giraud, and to bend their rules of conduct slightly in the hope that he would emerge as the ultimate leader of the French phoenix. And, for a time, Giraud did seem the most likely victor. He did not bear the stain of outright collaboration that the late Darlan had suffered, yet neither had he compromised his position with the other French military commanders through overly subservient behavior to the British since the 1940 armistice. However, Giraud was to throw away these advantages and to antagonize each of his supporters in turn.

His demands for higher rank and greater authority rubbed other senior French commanders, like Juin and Koenig, the wrong way, in contrast to de Gaulle who, however unwillingly, had accepted what appeared to be a powerless figurehead position in the interests of promoting harmony within the French camp. His constant calls for more equipment and resources for rebuilding the French army, in terms that bordered on blackmail, irritated both the British and the Americans, and his less-than-subtle efforts at playing one ally off against the other fooled no one and only increased their suspicions. He particularly managed to anger General Patton by commenting, during a visit to the front during the fighting for Valence, that Patton's command post was too far to the rear. Patton, who, more than most army commanders believed in leading from the front, turned on Giraud and bluntly pointed out that, in the First World War, Giraud had been a battalion commander and had been taken prisoner when his headquarters was overrun, and in 1940 he had been a corps commander and had again been taken prisoner after the German breakthrough at Sedan. Patton added that he believed he could do more for the war effort outside of a prisoner of war camp than in one and would place himself where he saw fit.

Ultimately, it would be de Gaulle's winning over the French people themselves that would give him control of the levers of the French government, including the military, and it was Giraud who would gradually be marginalized. Giraud would retain his position as commander of the armed forces but would lack any significant control over the troops, while de Gaulle would make all of the key decisions and steadily mold the new French government in accordance with his *idée de la France.*

As it turned out, other than gaining formal or informal "recognition" from Churchill and Roosevelt for their respective factions, neither Giraud nor de Gaulle had much of an agenda for the Casablanca Conference. Their only priority, and one on which they agreed thoroughly, was to speed the rearming and modernization of the French Army and Air Force. As a secondary issue, they both pressed for the allocation to the French, once their forces had come up to strength, of the central sector of the front. It was the French view that the most direct route to Paris would lie through the Rhone Valley to Lyon and thence north to Paris. It was of the utmost importance to French prestige that French units actually liberate the capital, and Lyon as well, if possible.

In one of the separate sessions that Churchill and Roosevelt held with their staffs, without the participation of the French, Marshall explained that, while the route via Lyon was the shortest as the crow flies, it was also the most easily defended, wedged in between the Alps and the Massif Central, both of which were virtually impassable to mechanized forces. Consequently, a drive up the center would likely cost high casualties, and both the British and Americans were more than willing to let the French pay that particular butcher's bill if that was to their liking.

The Americans soon learned that British enthusiasm for the Allied victories thus far was due, at least in part, to a desire to set the stage for the pitch of their own pet project, one which was particularly dear to Montgomery's heart. Rather than join in the campaign in France as a junior partner, Montgomery's plan called for a separate amphibious invasion, this time of the Italian Peninsula. Churchill revealed that talks had been proceeding for some weeks between representatives of the British government and those of King Victor Emanuel in Madrid over a possible separate peace. At a stroke, such an agreement would eliminate over one million men from the Axis ranks, besides Italy's still considerable fleet and air force, and require Germany to pour tens of thousands more men into Italy if they were even to hope to hang onto the territory.

What this agreement required was, not unlike that with Vichy France the previous year, a commitment from the Allies to intervene in substantial force to protect the Italians from the vengeance of their former comrades-in-arms. Montgomery's presentation was well rehearsed, with the dapper field marshal stalking back and forth in front of his listeners, slapping at a large map of Italy with a pointer like a jockey hitting the flanks of a racehorse. With the allocation of most of the amphibious shipping capacity then on hand in Europe, Montgomery said that, within three weeks, he could launch his invasion with the XIII and XXX Corps of his 8th Army from North Africa, with two armored and four infantry divisions, supported by two airborne divisions, one British and one American, and with most of the air power coming from RAF elements already in Egypt, which would be shifted to Corsica until bases on the mainland could be seized. He said that no resistance from the Italians was expected, and that most regular army units might actually switch sides and fight against the Germans as they tried to confront the invasion.

Roosevelt raised the question about Italian reliability. He noted that everyone present had considered the move into Vichy territory a calculated risk, even though French hatred of the Germans was well known. The Italians, on the other hand, had been fighting alongside the Germans for over three years and had actually initiated invasions of their own, on Ethiopia, Greece, France, and Egypt. If there had been a chance for a trap at Marseille, wasn't there even more of one along the Italian Riviera?

Montgomery smiled patiently and admitted that those opposed to the French incursion had been mistaken, notably excepting himself from that number. But the situation in Italy would be different. While he did not expect organized resistance from the Italians, neither did he count on their active cooperation, at least at first. This would be a full-fledged amphibious operation, over the beaches, with naval gunfire support, air cover, the works. Leaflets would be dropped two hours before the start of the bombardment warning Italian soldiers and civilians to vacate the area, but there would be no sailing directly into Italian ports. If the Italians were as good as their word, the operation would be marvelously easy; if not, they would be swept out of the way.

This reply seemed to satisfy everyone, but then Marshall brought up the question of where, precisely, Montgomery had in mind to attack.

There was an inviting stretch of beach just north of Civitavecchia, Montgomery indicated on his map. It was barely fifty miles from Rome, along the coast, and what made the location particularly attractive was a ridge running parallel to the shore, about a dozen miles inland. The first wave would rush from the beach to the ridge and occupy it, providing a natural shield for the beachhead, while marshes along the coast to the north would limit any German attack from that direction to a narrow causeway, easily defended. With an airborne drop around Rome itself, to the south, Italy would certainly be knocked out of the war immediately, and the Allies would be free to build up their forces, first to push across the ridge through Italy's central valley to the Apennines, and then to drive north and south at will. With the collapse of the Italian Army, the Germans would undoubtedly be so disoriented that they would be unable to mount an effective defense for some time, probably not south of the Po, and any units cut off in southern Italy or Sicily would simply fall like ripe fruit.

The silence from the American delegation that followed this explanation indicated to all that they were not sold. Eisenhower joined in and commented that, in preparation for HAYMAKER, he had made at least a cursory study of most of the viable landing sites in the western Mediterranean. While virtually the entire French coast and that of North Africa was suitable for amphibious landings, and while there were numerous spots on Sardinia and Sicily, western Italy only had usable beaches at Salerno and Anzio bracketing Naples and the stretch just north and south of Rome itself. It seemed likely that this might have occurred to the Germans who might have deployed troops to cover these locations. He pointed out that, if the Germans managed to get to that coastal ridge first, instead of being a shield for the beachhead, it would be like a cork in a bottle, and the invaders would be trapped on the shore.

Montgomery countered that the Germans were likely to be fully occupied fighting off the Italians, apart from being taken by surprise by the invasion, and would hardly be in a position to devote enough troops to the ridge to stop an assault by six veteran divisions, with at least two more corps on tap from the British troops available m England. He was about to go into more detail, when Marshall called a brief recess.

In private, Marshall explained to Roosevelt, Eisenhower, and the other American commanders that, although he thought Montgomery was glossing over serious flaws in his plan, the Americans had no grounds to object after pushing through their own project the previous year. Perhaps Montgomery was right about the Italians, in which case the odds did seem to be stacked against the Germans, who were already reeling from defeats on every front. Moreover, since this was to be almost exclusively a British operation, even more than HAYMAKER had been American, it was only proper to defer to British judgment on the issue. Lastly, he noted that, if they dropped their objections to the plan, they would have a stronger hand for gleaning more troops for southern France as a *quid pro quo*. As a politician, Roosevelt could understand this reasoning, and, when the meeting reconvened that evening, Montgomery had no need to deploy the stacks of reference material he had amassed to support his case.

With this easy victory behind them, Churchill and Brooke readily agreed to Marshall's suggestion that the Polish Corps be immediately allocated to the French Front, to be followed by at least one British Corps within two months, as well as the newly arriving American 101st Airborne Division (which would be dropped from Montgomery's plan for Italy) and all new American units as they came into the field. The combined force would be designated as 1st Army Group, with Patton to assume command. The Italian invasion would consist of the bulk of the 8th Army, later reinforced by the 1st Army from England and the 2nd New Zealand Division, plus the British 1st and 6th Airborne Divisions, which would be responsible for the *coup de main* at Rome.

2200 Hours, 8 February 1943
Near Lyon, France

The Allies were wallowing. Rommel had seen this sort of thing before. They had had one outstanding strategic concept and had carried it through to a successful completion, but they had been taken aback by their own good fortune and were now at a loss as to what to do next. They had probably counted themselves so lucky that the raw American divisions had not cracked, one after the other, during his offensive at the end of December that they were reluctant to throw the dice again. For more than one month the Allies had done little other than shift units around and, of course, continue to build up their forces. There had been probes all along the line, but nothing serious other than the steady advance by the British and Canadians in the west which had resulted in the loss of Toulouse the previous week, but then they had appeared content to occupy the line of the Tarn and Garonne Rivers and go no farther.

This had been a godsend for Rommel. Every day for him was golden. His old Afrika Korps units had been refitted and formed into a strategic reserve, the nucleus of a force for which Rommel had great plans. The survivors of his original armored thrust, the 3rd Panzer Grenadier and 26th Panzer and the Hermann Göring Divisions had been pulled back and were also receiving reinforcements to make up their losses. He had strung a line of infantry divisions, of which he now had nearly twenty at various levels of strength, in a line across the valley of the Rhone, through the Massif Central and along the Tarn/Garonne River line down to the Spanish border. Behind this screen, which the Allies had chosen not to test seriously, teams of combat engineers and even conscripted French, Belgian, and German civilian contractors were working feverishly to construct a line of concrete emplacements, well-camouflaged strongpoints with interlocking fields of fire, built in some depth, along the main avenues of approach. He was even stripping the Channel defenses and the old Siegfried Line along the former Franco-German border of artillery and machine guns to equip the new positions. These preparations took time, and the Allies had graciously given him that gift.

His vision was to make maximum use of the difficult terrain along the north face of the Allied lodgment area to tum every passable road and pass into a death trap where the attackers would have to pay in blood for every inch of progress. In the open land to the southwest, he would use river lines where he could to enhance the defense, but his goal here would be to slow the enemy advance, keep it off the most rapid avenues, and bog them down on a front where he could eventually stop them completely.

Rommel realized that he had a window of opportunity coming, probably in the next month, that would not be repeated. The surrounded German Sixth Army at Stalingrad had finally surrendered the week before, costing over a quarter of a million men, not counting tens of thousands more in the Hungarian, Romanian, and Italian Armies that had also been shattered in the Soviet offensive. The good news for Rommel was that, now that the Caucasus had been evacuated, the German line in Russia had been shortened considerably, and the Russians had clearly spent themselves and would take weeks, if not months, to haul forward their supplies and fresh units across the devastated landscape to prepare for a new push.

This lull in the East gave Rommel top priority for new units, and he had made use of every ounce of influence he still possessed with the Führer and OKW to get new forces, particularly armor and air units, for France. His only competition was Kesselring, who was constantly screaming for reinforcements to deal with Italian duplicity, which Rommel could appreciate, given his own long experience with the Italians, but that was defensive and Rommel wanted to take the offensive. He had a concept that was audacious enough to appeal to Hitler's gambler's instinct, and to bring it off he needed not only tanks but fighters to keep the British and American air forces off their backs for a few crucial days. The traditional heavy overcast of March would be ideal for what he had in mind, and if his meteorologists were right, there would be a record low rainfall that year, which might not be good for the farmers, but it would give his armor added maneuverability.

Rommel was fairly confident by this time that he had already won the race with the Allies. Even if they suddenly regained the initiative, his defenses were in place and would channel them just where he wanted them to go. The only thing he could still pray for was that they would open a new front somewhere else, somewhere other than France, that would draw off their resources and prevent them from quickly making good the losses he planned to inflict on them. Most importantly, if they would commit the several corps' worth of British troops concentrated in England and their amphibious capacity, he would have a free hand to divert more of his own troops from Northern France to the south. Rommel was also aware, however, that he must act soon. As soon as the spring mud dried out sufficiently in Russia, he knew that Hitler was eager to mount a new offensive on the Eastern Front, and he would then not only lack for further reinforcement but would soon begin to lose units if he could not employ them aggressively. If he could just have a free hand for a few weeks, he could still conceivably turn the war around.

1500 HOURS, 24 FEBRUARY 1943
NORTH OF MONTAUBAN, FRANCE

Lieutenant Colonel Creighton W. Abrams, now commander of CCA of the 1st Armored Division, shook his head as he passed the smoking carcasses of two Shermans and several half-tracks. Charred bodies littered the frozen ground all about them, most of them hanging from the torn and crushed grapevines that marched in straight rows across the field. The Tarn River was only ten miles behind them, and yet this was the third such ambush site he had seen. The Germans would set up their deadly 88mm or 76mm anti-tank guns in a treeline or inside a barn covering *Route Nationale* 20, Abrams' avenue of advance. The infantry would be cleverly dug in and camouflaged, some-times right in the open fields in a kind of spider hole topped with a sheet of plywood covered with dirt and with shallow escape trenches dug to the rear. They would open an intense fire, knocking out several vehicles in a matter of minutes, and be on their way to their next fighting position before artillery or airstrikes could be called up. But the column would have to deploy and send out skirmishers to comb the woods and fields before the advance could resume. No wonder their progress was so slow.

There was no explaining this to General Patton, however. The Americans had been shifted to the left flank of the Allied lodgment after the Battle of Valence. VII Corps was now along the Spanish border, V Corp was in the center, and his own I Corps was pushing north along the western edge of the Massif Central. The two new French corps covered the Massif Central itself to the Rhone Valley, with the Canadians and British on the right facing the Italians. At least I Corps had the narrow arc of the American sweep around the German flank, with VII Corps units having to cover more than double the distance, but they also met with far less resistance as the Germans seemed to have written off everything south of Bordeaux. Patton had pressed them to get across the Tarn, which the Germans had heavily fortified, and it had taken two tries before they had established bridgeheads that would hold. Meanwhile, the 1st Division had been badly bloodied in the street fighting for Montauban the previous week.

Now they were across, but they were cutting across the grain of all of France's rivers, it seemed, with a major river crossing every thirty to forty miles. And in between, the Germans were employing these delaying tactics, inflicting casualties and buying time, then pulling back. The Americans were advancing too fast for their artillery support lo keep up with them effectively, and most of the 12th Air Force's planes were dedicated to protecting the Mediterranean ports and hitting Luftwaffe bases from which bomber raids on Allied shipping were launched. There was also scuttlebutt that air units were being pulled back to support some kind of offensive in Italy. So Abrams' tankers had to dig out the Germans themselves, treeline by treeline, stone farmhouse by stone farmhouse. This was going to be a very long war, he decided.

1200 Hours, 24 February 1943
Over Stuttgart, Germany

Lieutenant Heinrich Ladenberg slapped himself hard on both cheeks. Ordinarily, the prelude to combat might be expected to be the ultimate stimulant, but it had become all that he could do to avoid dozing off, even in the middle of a dogfight. He had flown and fought every day that weather permitted since the Allied landings in southern France, sometimes several sorties a day, and he found it amusing that even the aircraft he brought back with little or no battle damage were given more recuperation time than he was. It seemed that steel and titanium were not as durable as flesh and bone when it came to flying.

Not that Ladenberg's situation was different from that of any other pilot in the 3rd Fighter Division, or in any sector of the Luftwaffe now. For more than a year, it had only been the flyers on the Eastern Front who had really suffered the strains of an endless stream of high priority targets, although without much in the way of competition in air to-air combat. Here in the West, Ladenberg and his colleagues had been content to wait for the radar screen, which had been extended to cover most of the western border of the Reich, to advise them of a worthwhile enemy raid to attack, purposely avoiding fighter "sweeps" by the enemy in favor of pouncing on unprotected bombers once they ventured past the range of their fighter cover. There had still been losses, of course, especially when confronting the improved tactics of the massive American bombers, the well named "Flying Fortresses," but it had still been quite a gentleman's war.

But that had all changed in December. Now it was the Germans who had to escort lumbering bombers right into the jaws of the enemy fighters around Marseille, and, while the American planes had originally not been very good, there had been clouds of them. Now, there were more and more of the dreaded P-51s and the twin-tailed P-38s with considerably more speed, range, and firepower than the earlier models. Ladenberg, at only twenty years of age, had missed the Battle of Britain, so this kind of duty was new to him. And that was only the half of it. The same fighter squadrons that shepherded the bombers to attack Allied ports also had to scramble to beat off the waves of

American and British bombers that continued to pound the Fatherland.

The cost had been easy enough to measure. After six months of flying, Ladenberg was now squadron commander, the "old man," leading only six planes out of what should have been a full dozen. And not even all of these were real fighters. Ladenberg and three of his men flew top-of-the-line Focke-Wulf 190s armed with two machine guns and two 20mm cannon and with speed, climb rate, and maneuverability superior to any but the latest American fighters. The other two were older Me-110s, one equipped with stand-off rockets for firing at enemy bombers from outside of their machine-gun range, the other with a new prototype "fist" device. This was a set of half a dozen 30mm cannon mounted *vertically* in the fuselage that would be fired in a single devastating volley when triggered by a photo-electric cell sensing the shadow cast by the enemy bomber when the Me-110 dove under it at close range. Ladenberg had little faith in the new gizmo and had made certain that the co-pilot of that particular plane paid him the forty marks he owed before going on this mission.

And they no longer had the luxury of radar warning. With half of the enemy missions now coming out of southern France and Corsica, they simply bypassed the German radar network and most of the heaviest concentrations of flak as well, along the original routes across northern France and the Low Countries. Of course, new radar stations were cropping up, and there were still observers who could radio in reports of enemy bomber formations, which were far too large to sneak by in any case, but that left precious little time for the fighters to scramble and intercept.

The only good news for Ladenberg was that, now that the British and Americans were fighting on the ground again in Europe, their own air forces had other tasks than bombing the Reich. When the strategic bombing campaign had been the only game in town for them, they could devote every aircraft and all of their tremendous resources to it. Now they also had to fly close-support missions for the ground forces along the front, missions that were usually over with long before defensive fighters could intervene, and that was just fine with Ladenberg. Let the mud sloggers earn their pay, he believed.

That was where Ladenberg and his squadron were now. They had just reached 25,000 feet, well above the cloud cover, and he was scanning the sky to the southwest for the enemy, when his mouth dropped open and the first curses came over the radio. He had faced large enemy formations before, but now the sky was virtually tilled with the slowly growing forms of dozens upon dozens of enemy bombers, their tight Vs stacked up like pancakes, extending for miles to either side, and as far back as he could see. There would be other fighter squadrons coming in, of course, but Ladenberg knew only too well how heavy a toll his division had suffered in recent weeks, and there would never be enough to deal with this. He hauled back on his stick, and his squadron rose with him. Their only hope would be to gain altitude, launch a high-speed diving run and punch right through the enemy formation. Whether they could turn for another pass would depend upon how many of them survived to come out the other side.

He could make out the smaller specks of enemy fighters rising quickly to meet him, but his orders were to ignore them. It was the bombers he was after, and he rolled over for his dive. The forward firepower of the B-17 was too much for him, and he preferred an angle that cut across the target just behind the nose and forward of the wing, thus blocking the fire of the tail, belly and waist gunners, at least for a time. One pair of FWs and the rocket-firing Me-110 would circle around to hammer at the rear of the formation, while Ladenberg's wing man would follow him in high, and the "fist" plane would dive under the target.

He picked up speed as he dove, pressed back into the seat as the olive drab shape of the lead bomber grew in his windscreen. He could see tiny lights winking off to his left as a P-40 tried to cut him off, but it must have been a new pilot, and the man didn't lead him enough, his tracers passing harmlessly to his rear. At least that was what crossed Ladenberg's mind as his own finger tightened gradually on his trigger, but he felt his aircraft shudder and realized that his wingman had exploded behind him. Had the American gotten lucky, or had that been his target all along?

Yellow fingers of fire were reaching out toward Ladenberg from the target aircraft and from several others nearby, forming an intricate spider web that it seemed impossible he could pass through unscathed. He fired, and the joystick jerked in his hand as he walked his own tracers onto the fuselage of the target, sending chunks of debris flying. And in an instant, he was past. He kept diving down into the clouds to shake off any pursuit, checking his rear-view mirror, and seeing no signs of any, nor of the "fist" plane either.

He pulled back up into the sunlight and strove for more altitude. He could focus now on the radio chatter, listening for any of the familiar voices of his squadron mates, but they were not there. Another unit had joined the battle, pilots calling out directions and claiming kills, punctuated by an occasional frantic call for help or a scream. Contrails crisscrossed the sky, and he watched as one B-17 slowly banked, black smoke streaming from two of its engines and bright orange flames playing along the fuselage. That one would not make it home, he thought.

Then he looked southward again, and his blood ran cold. The formation he had first seen, the one he had felt so little hope of confronting, had only been the vanguard. There must have been a thousand of the huge bombers coming on, row after row, and he could see more enemy fighters turning toward him. That was enough for one day's work, Ladenberg thought, as he dove back into the clouds and headed for home.

0100 HOURS, 26 FEBRUARY 1943
MILAN, ITALY

Field Marshal Kesselring could hardly believe his good fortune. At first he assumed that the radio broadcasts that began early on the evening of the 19th had been some form of particularly ludicrous disinformation campaign by the Allies. It had almost immediately been confirmed by his radio intercept unit that the broadcasts were, in fact, originating with stations run by the Italian government. He had instantly informed OKH that the new Italian government had announced its withdrawal from the war, and was pleasantly surprised to receive an almost equally instantaneous authorization to launch Operation ALARIC. And the Allies had not come ashore yet. The enemy had tipped their hand before they were in a position to do anything about it, and Kesselring could deal with his two foes, one at a time.

Naturally, the defection of Italy hardly came as a total surprise, as preparations for ALARIC clearly showed. But Kesselring had been struggling for weeks between an increasing volume of intelligence information that negotiations were under way between Marshall Badoglio, King Victor Emmanuel, and other opponents of Mussolini and the Allies in Madrid, and the Führer's reluctance to take any overt action which might actually undermine Mussolini's waning influence in Rome. Then, Mussolini himself had been deposed and placed under house arrest, and Badoglio set up as a kind of provisional president under the king. Directives from Hitler suddenly became less conciliatory, even confrontational, demanding assurances from the Italians of their continued adherence to the Axis. The assurances had been forthcoming, but generally in such a lukewarm fashion that no one in Berlin was convinced.

This revelation had not made it any easier for Kesselring to pry reinforcements out of OKH, however. Naturally, there were other requirements at the front, in Russia and France, and provisions had to be made to replace the thirty Italian divisions stationed in Yugoslavia and Greece and others facing the Allies in the French Alps, but Kesselring's concern was securing all of mainland Italy and Sicily with reliable German troops, possibly in the face of open hostility with the Italians. Even those troops who had been released to him were finding it increasingly difficult to enter Italian territory without obstruction from the local military authorities. Although Kesselring had a very low opinion of the fighting qualities of the Italian Army, they did have over one million men under arms and possessed hundreds of guns, tanks, and planes. He had no doubt that, in a matter of one, or at most two weeks, with additional infantry divisions from Germany, he could overwhelm the Italians, but that was assuming they would stand alone. The Germans' greatest fear was that the Allies would launch a major invasion of Italy, somewhere along its hundreds of miles of coastline, in conjunction with a defection by the Italians. Kesselring could probably deal with each threat, but not both at once.

Given the limitations on the resources he was provided by OKH, and the sensitivity of the Italians to the arrival of more German troops on their territory, Kesselring had opted to concentrate on a relatively small number of elite troops. He had managed to obtain the 3rd Parachute Division, stationed at the Folgore Barracks near Rome, three panzer divisions, the 14th, 19th, and 24th, and two of panzer grenadiers, the 15th and the *Feldherrnhalle,* which he had spaced down the length of the peninsula, with his only two infantry divisions, the 305th and 334th, stiffening the Italian garrison on Sicily. Between these units and a host of independent tank, artillery, anti-aircraft, military police, and motorized infantry regiments, he could move quickly to shatter any nuclei of opposition the Italians might attempt to form, or move to counter any Allied landing. He could then leave it to the two or three infantry corps he had been promised from Germany in the event of an Italian defection to sweep down the peninsula over highways and bridges secured by his current forces.

The bases of his troops were carefully selected, astride the main routes of communication and near key political and strategic targets such as all of Italy's major cities, industrial centers, and military headquarters. They were well entrenched and oriented for all-around defense, with access by Italian military personnel strictly limited, while his own commanders had made a conscious effort at conducting "training exercises," maneuvers and troops rotations that sent columns rumbling back and forth all over the country, so that no future German troop movements would attract undue attention.

Lists had been made up by the Abwehr of the key leaders of the anti-fascist faction in the Italian government, and these would be rounded up to face the vengeance of Mussolini when the Germans had returned him to power. SS police companies were scattered around Rome for just this contingency. And, now that Badoglio had been foolish enough to make his announcement of dropping out of the war, with no Allied troops on hand to back his play, Kesselring's hands were free to deal with the Italians, but he would have to move fast. Aerial reconnaissance and intelligence reports had noted the departure from England of large numbers of landing craft heading for the Mediterranean, along with at least a full corps of troops, and sources in Egypt, notably from the Free Officers' Movement headed by an Egyptian Army Captain named Gamal Abdul Nasser, had reported that most of the British 8th Army had boarded ships in Alexandria for points unknown. For the moment, however, all Kesselring had to worry about was disarming about one million hostile Italians and conquering a country about seven hundred miles long.

0400 Hours, 26 February 1943
Rome, Italy

Colonel Gerhard Wolff watched from the cab of his half-track as troopers of the SS Police Brigade that bore his name kicked in the doors of several fashionable townhouses in the center of Rome. He could just see the dome of St. Peter's over the roofs of the houses to his right, and he crossed himself, as a good Bavarian Catholic, as he got on with his business in the deep blue of the night, indifferently lit by the few working street lamps.

It had been a frustrating morning thus far. He had been with the initial assault team that had stormed the palace where King Victor Emmanuel had reportedly spent the night. There had been a vicious firefight with the palace guard, leaving at least fifty Italians and nearly twenty of his own men dead, but the king had not been there. Although the staff had originally been unwilling to talk, a practiced interrogator like Wolff had taken less than five minutes to get a steward to admit that the king had been flown away in a small observation plane. Wolff truly believed that the man did not know the final destination, speculating either La Spezia, seeking the protection of the Italian fleet, or possibly all the way to Corsica. In either event, he had escaped. The same would prove true of Marshals Badoglio and Ambrosio, and most of the Italian High Command.

In fact, other than disarming over one thousand Italian soldiers, Wolff's "bag" for the night was thus far only a couple of minor ministers in the new government, one brigadier general, and a suspected organizer of the Communist underground, who had been summarily executed on the street. He could see now that his men were shoving prisoners out into the street, but they were only women in bathrobes and a few small children. What kind of men were these Italians who would run away and leave their families to suffer? Well, he would see how they enjoyed the accommodations at Ravensburg.

0730 HOURS, 26 FEBRUARY 1943
BOLZANO, ITALY

General Valentin Feurstein, commander of the LI Corps and of the Mittenwald Mountain Warfare School in Austria, waved from his open staff car as the mostly German population of the town crowded the sidewalks and waved Nazi flags, and even some old Imperial German flags as the troops of the 44th Infantry Division rolled southward. The ease of their *coup de main* had come as no surprise to Feurstein, who had been planning it for weeks. They had secured the vital Brenner Pass without a shot being fired, and more than three thousand Italian troops had been disarmed and herded aboard cattle cars for a quick trip to prison labor camps in Germany.

Feurstein had even recruited nearly two thousand Italian Alpini troopers who had been training with the Germans at Mittenwald. They had enjoyed the camaraderie of elite troops, and they tended to respect the German officers, who shared their hardships and training, much more than their own foppish officers who spent their time whoring and drinking, a practice that Feurstein had gone to some lengths to encourage lately. While they couldn't be trusted to take the German side in the current struggle, they would form the nucleus of a new Italian army once things got back to normal.

But it would not all go quite so smoothly, he knew. General Gloria, commander of the Italian 35th Corps, had pulled most of his units back intact to the south, probably planning to make a stand somewhere near Lake Garda north of Verona where the mountains crowded up against the Adige, with the lake on the west side, forming a narrow gap through which Highway 12 ran. But it was Feurstein's task only to secure the alpine passes and the border area. Other units would pass through his in a matter of hours and go on to crush any resistance they found. It had been a good night's work.

0800 HOURS, 26 FEBRUARY 1943
FLORENCE, ITALY

Giorgio Paglioni crouched behind a flimsy barricade made of old automobiles, furniture, and paving stones, and he could feel the earth tremble as the German tanks approached. He looked to his right and left and could count only about a dozen men still with him, alive. Most, like Paglioni, were civilians, armed only with old hunting rifles and shotguns or pistols, but there were also a couple of soldiers, all of them wearing bright red armbands to indicate their membership in the Communist Party.

Like most of the population of Florence, Paglioni, a machine tool operator at the Aero Macchi plant on the outskirts of the city, had been delirious at the previous evening's broadcast announcing Italy's withdrawal from the war. However, unlike most of the other patrons of the neighborhood bar on whose scratchy radio Paglioni had heard the news, he understood that this did not necessarily mean "peace" for Italy. What he and his comrades in his underground Communist Party cell understood was that this act merely unmasked the fascists and nazis for what they were, oppressors of the people, and opened the door to overt warfare between them and the working class, an unfortunate but inevitable step on the road to world revolution. He was heartened by the fact that, with the collapse of the puppet regime in Rome, most of the soldiers had seen clearly on which side their interests lay and had gone over to the resistance en masse. With the Soviet armies on the move westward, and the capitalist armies still locked in a mortal struggle with Nazi Germany, there would never be a better time for the workers of Europe to throw off the yoke of oppression and create a Communist utopia on the ashes of the old order.

But fighting had been raging in the streets of Florence for hours, and it was not going well. Paglioni had imagined that the Germans, scattered in isolated pockets up and down the length of the country, would quickly surrender, or even desert in a body to the side of the workers. At forty, he was old enough to remember how the Communist Spartacists under Karl Liebkneckt had come within a hair's breadth of victory in Germany in 1919, and would not many of these German soldiers be the sons of the workers who were herded back into their factories at the point of the bayonet? But it was not working out that way.

The 24th Panzer Division had been encamped just west of town, supposedly on the way to the front in France, although it had begun to be noted that they had lingered an unusually long time "refitting" their vehicles, more than ten days. Now it was clear that their presence had been no coincidence, and they had come roaring into the city, easily scattering the troops of the 103rd Piacenza Division, but they had been halted, not by the army, but by the workers. Most of the soldiers had simply turned and run, but the workers fought for every house, every factory workshop, every irrigation ditch, just as the Russian workers had done at Stalingrad. But it was beginning to appear that a just cause and boundless courage were simply not enough.

The long black snout of a tank gun poked around the comer of a building a hundred meters up the street, and Paglioni and his comrades froze as the bulk of the immense dark monster emerged. The barricade itself was shaking apart just at the approach of the tank, and Paglioni irrationally reached out a hand to steady the cross piece of a dining room table. The squealing of the tank's treads was almost unbearable, like a schoolchild scraping his nails across a blackboard. Then a shot rang out, which started a rattle of gunfire all along the line. Paglioni didn't bother. He could see bullets kick up sparks along the panzer's flanks, but it would do no good. He was waiting for some infantry, targets he could actually damage, but the enemy foot soldiers were holding back, firing from cover and only dodging forward a few meters at a time, using the vast armored bulk as a shield.

A man on the roof of a house just ahead of the barricade raised up and hurled a Molotov cocktail at the tank, its burning wick leaving smoky arcs in the air as it spun downward. But he was too far away, and the bottle smashed on the pavement, spreading burning liquid over the pavement. The fool had, however, attracted the crew's attention, and the turret whined as it swung in his direction, the gun elevating slightly. The man had ducked back down behind the low parapet around the roof, but the gunner merely blew apart the entire top floor of the building.

Paglioni suddenly heard the sound of pounding feet behind him and turned expectantly, hoping to see reinforcements coming up, but it was a squad of Germans, holding their rifles and submachineguns at the ready. Men along the barricade were throwing aside their weapons and raising their hands. Paglioni looked frantically from side to side, but there was no escape, and he, too, dropped his rifle and slowly came to his feet. A German officer jogged up, scanned up and down the line of ragged prisoners, and gave a little flick of his wrist, at which the soldiers opened fire and then turned at a trot to follow the officer down the street.

Paglioni was found an hour later by a team of medical students who risked their lives combing through the ravaged city in search of wounded men to succor. Although he would lose his left arm, he would be one of the few fighters to survive the day and the subsequent weeks of hiding in the basement of a convent, constantly hovering on the verge of death. He would later refer to his salvation as one of the few acts of sloppiness that he had witnessed on the part of the Germans in the war.

0930 Hours, 26 February 1943
Off "Blue" Beach, Near Grosseto, Italy

Major General Sidney C. Kirkman pounded his fist on the metal side of the LCI (Landing Craft, Infantry) as it plowed through the waves toward the beach. He craned his neck to peer over the sides, and the shore hardly seemed to be getting any closer.

What imbecile among the Italians had had the bright idea of announcing their surrender hours *before* the invasion? Now the Germans would have had ample time to seal off the Italian Army and get ready for the assault that they must know would be coming. They might have just as well sent them a printed schedule of the landings. Of course, Montgomery's penchant for overpreparation had not facilitated things and may have had to do with the foul-up, having delayed the landing for 24 hours while some additional artillery units arrived from England. Kirkman had a premonition that those 24 hours would cost his men dear.

Kirkman commanded the 50th Northumbrian Division, responsible for half of this northern of the two beaches designated for Montgomery's invasion. His beach straddled the mouth of the Ombrone River, and it was his responsibility to secure the left flank of the beachhead, driving inland at least to the Via Cassia and the high ground beyond it, perhaps twenty miles in depth. The 5th Division would be coming ashore to his right with the task of linking up with the XXX Corps, who would be landing at "Beach Red" to the south.

It was a fairly simple plan, if ambitious, but the plans had changed radically within the last few days. The projected drop of the British 1st Airborne Division near Rome had been cancelled when Marshall Ambrosio, commander of the Italian Army, had informed the Allies that the concentration of German units around the capital was just too strong, particularly in anti-aircraft units, and any landing there would probably end in a massacre, even with the support of the Italians. That, in itself, was not a major disaster, as the paras would at least be available to come ashore as infantry at need, and in a more concentrated deployment than air dropping, which Kirkman had never quite endorsed as a means of inserting troops into enemy territory. But the original plans had always assumed at least marginal combat support from the Italian Army, at least tying up the roads, and maybe helping clear the Luftwaffe from the skies. Now that the cat was out of the bag, Kirkman had no doubt that the Germans had moved quickly to neutralize the Italians, so the British would be on their own against an alerted enemy.

The only good news thus far had been that the maps of the coastal minefields that Ambrosio had provided to Montgomery had proven to be accurate, and there had been no losses to shipping from that threat. Also, the bulk of the Italian fleet, including several serviceable battleships and a number of dangerous destroyers and submarines, that might have played havoc with the invasion fleet if they had been willing to face the losses, had apparently escaped from La Spezia and Taranto unhindered by the Germans, although they had been attacked by the Luftwaffe on the way out, and there had been rumors of at least one battleship sunk. Still, the naval side of things had worked out better than one might have expected.

The catch was that, because of Italy's defection and the anticipation of little or no resistance at the point of entry, there had been no naval or aerial bombardment of the landing zones, and only a minimum of interdiction attacks along the highways, for fear of causing casualties among Italian civilians. Waves of fighters and bombers were now roaring overhead, and Kirkman could see destroyers racing back and forth just beyond the landing craft assembly area, their guns barking at invisible targets inland. But that would do little good for the initial assault.

The 69th Infantry Brigade from his division and the 13th from 5th Division had made up the first wave. The unskilled landing craft drivers had drifted south with the current, so all of the troops had landed south of the

Ombrone. This would not have been overly serious except that it concentrated the assault on a very narrow sector of the beach, allowing the defenders to concentrate their fire as well.

There would be little in the way of permanent, prepared fortifications, just some half-hearted efforts by the Italians from before the war, the odd pill box here and there, but the Germans had apparently moved in during the night and made use of the several peaceful hours before the landings to set up some daunting defenses. It was apparent that the enemy was well-provided with self-propelled artillery that would fire a few rounds from one position and then quickly displace to another, with all of the aiming points thoroughly registered. They were ignoring the boats and pummeling the beach itself, which had also been strewn with hundreds of mines, mostly not even concealed, but which greatly hindered the movement of the first tanks of the 44th Tank Regiment which were landing to support the infantry.

From the partial reports that had come in over the radio, Kirkman had learned that the handful of prisoners taken thus far were from an SS panzer grenadier battalion, among the best troops in the German Army. They were organized in platoon-sized strongpoints and would let the British advance in some areas into what they referred to as a "fire sack" in which they would be ambushed by fire from all sides. The few tanks that had thus far made it off the beach had been butchered at long range by the 88mm guns of the awesome new Tiger tanks, of which there appeared to be at least a company in the area, and by the squat, turretless assault guns of the panzer grenadiers. Still, initial progress had been made off the beach itself, but thus far neither brigade had been able to cross the open killing field of the Via Aurelia highway which ran parallel to the coast less than a mile inland.

It was Kirkman's plan to make sure that the Durham Light Infantry Brigade (DLI), that he was accompanying, would land north of the Ombrone and push inland to take the town of Grosseto and the high ground beyond it. It seemed that the Germans had blown a damn somewhere upriver, making the stream impassable, and destroying the only bridge as well, so he would be unable to mount a left hook against the defenses, but he should be able to pour a flanking fire into them to enable the 69th Brigade to continue its advance. Depending on the outcome of this move, they would then bring in his third brigade, the 168th, to reinforce whichever element had met with the most success.

Kirkman was lost in these thoughts when there was suddenly a lurch that nearly threw him off his feet, and would have except that the press of men in the cargo bay prevented him from falling. Then the bow ramp opened with a crash, and the tide of men carried him forward into water up to his hips. He strained to see as he sloshed through the surf, the sand and his wet clothing slowing him down as if in a dream, and he strained to see of the river was on his right where it belonged. He fought his way up to the top of a small dune tufted with grass and was relieved to see the muddy stream about three hundred meters to his right. Almost the instant his eyes had picked this up, he received a rough blow on the backs of his knees and was hurled forward into the sand.

"Sorry, sir," the booming voice of his sergeant major rolled out over the growling of the landing craft, the rush of the waves, and the rattle of machine guns. "Perching on the highest point of land in a firefight is strictly against regulations."

Kirkman grunted an apology, or his thanks, and hauled himself forward on his elbows for a few more yards until he could peer over the next rise with his binoculars. He could just make out the sand-colored houses of Grosseto in the distance, and the figures of a company of Tommies moving forward in rushes. There was resistance here, but scattered, and it appeared that the enemy had deployed most of his forces south of the river. Only an occasional geyser of earth spouted up from an artillery shell on the beach here, while farther to the right he could see a thick pall of smoke and hear the steady rumble of gunfire. Just then a tank, one of the older Valentine models that had been equipped with the new duplex-drive that enabled them to "swim" to shore along with the landing craft, burst into flame, its frontal plate, complete with its main gun, twisted halfway off.

Kirkman set up his command post in a small gully two hundred meters off the beach. He had been tempted to use the remains of a small villa, but as one of the few structures still standing in the area, he could see that it attracted an undue amount of artillery fire, and reports via radio and messenger finally started to come in. The 6th DLI Regiment had taken about half of Grosseto but had been brought to a halt by a company of Luftwaffe ground troops and a 20mm anti-aircraft battery holed up on the grounds of an old convent. The 8th DLI had tried to swing to the left through the marshes north of the town, but had been taken in the rear by a heavy fire of machine guns dug into the reverse slope of some hills hard up along the coast north of the landing beaches and impervious to naval gunfire. An effort by the remaining regiment of the brigade to slip men up the bank of the Ombrone to turn the enemy's left flank had likewise received heavy fire from the Germans still holding the line south of the river.

In the face of this stalemate, Kirkman was obliged to call for the 168th Brigade to land on the southern flank of the beachhead and to focus on making a link-up with the XXX Corps zone. They had apparently had a little more luck and had nearly cleared the port of Civitavecchia, although badly damaged by the Germans and unusable for the time being, and had advanced halfway to the town of Viterbo, several miles inland. They, too, were still far from reaching their first day's goal of the high ground near the Via Cassia highway, but they had at least carved out a respectable beachhead.

By late in the morning of the next day, the situation had hardly improved. The two landing zones had finally been securely joined, and the line had pushed out toward the brooding hills that paralleled the coast, completing the capture of Grosseto, but there had been no breakthrough. In fact, it was only now that the attackers had apparently reached the primary enemy defensive line, cleverly concealed strongpoints fronted by clear fields of fire and manned by veteran infantry. The first serious armored attack, by at least a battalion of the deadly Tigers, had only just been repulsed after inflicting devastating losses on the hopelessly undergunned Valentines of the 44th Tank Regiment, and then only by a massive concentration of naval gunfire. More troops were pouring ashore, but it was now clear that the enemy had every square inch of the landing zone registered for artillery, with the entire coast open to observation by enemy spotters along the ridge. The German guns were dug into the hills, safely out of range of all but the largest naval guns, and the ships were basically firing blind, scoring an occasional hit largely by luck.

Clearly this invasion was not going to be the walkover that everyone had anticipated. As the sun set on the first day, Kirkman could still distinctly hear the rattle of machine-gun fire not far from his command post on one side, and the murmur of the waves on the other. He received a report from 8th Army Headquarters just after dark that the 2nd New Zealand Division, a unit of nearly corps size with some 25,000 men, mostly veterans of the North African campaign, would be added to the invasion in XXX Corps sector the next day. While the reinforcements would be welcome enough, Kirkman could not help but be reminded of the Australian-New Zealand amphibious disaster at Gallipoli in the last war. That had not been the New Zealanders' fault, of course. It had been the fault of the high command, and notably a much younger Winston Churchill, disturbingly the same person who had masterminded this campaign.

1400 HOURS, 8 MARCH 1943
MANTUA, ITALY

As Kesselring sat in his new headquarters in northern Italy, he had some cause to be satisfied with his performance over the preceding two weeks. Despite the sudden defection of the Italians, he had managed to avert a mortal danger to the southern borders of the Third Reich. At the same time he had essentially added a new conquest to the empire, that of about two thirds of their former ally's territory, which was then being stripped of every moveable item of any value. He had overseen the disarmament of more than half a million Italian troops, many of whom had been shipped off to labor camps inside the Reich. He had even captured, intact, several hundred tanks, as many warplanes, 2,000 artillery pieces, and half a million rifles, the best of which would be incorporated into the Reich's armory, the remainder being used to equip the miniscule army of Blackshirts remaining loyal to Mussolini in the little puppet republic that had been set up in the foothills of the Alps, or to help arm the ragtag armies of Germany's other allies. He had even recovered 1.6 million gallons of fuel oil that the Italians had secreted in tunnels around La Spezia, and this after their navy had insisted that they could not escort supply convoys to Rommel's army in Africa the previous year due to a shortage of fuel!

Of greater importance, he had effectively bottled up more than two full British corps in a narrow strip of land on the western coast of Italy. Grabbing even that thin slice of territory had cost the British heavy casualties, although spirited counterattacks by the 14th and 24th Panzer Divisions had ultimately been beaten back through massive naval gunfire support and air attacks, just when it had appeared they would smash through to the sea. At least the British showed no sign of being able to crack the new German defenses any time soon. One regular infantry division and the 3rd Parachute Division now manned the complex of concrete fortifications that had been hastily constructed along the ridge hemming in the British landing zone, with the panzer and panzer grenadier divisions backing them up and conducting vigorous counterattacks whenever the British gained ground, all supported by an impressive concentration of artillery. In fact, Kesselring, a man not noted for his flights of wit, had casually referred during a conference at Berchtesgaden to the Italian beachhead as the largest POW camp run by the Germans, and one in which the prisoners at least fed themselves. Goebbels had picked up on this phrase and begun to use it in his propaganda broadcasts.

Kesselring had had to use all of his persuasive power to convince Hitler and his hand-wringing generals on the OKH that it would be necessary to abandon Sicily and Sardinia, which he had effected without the loss of a single German soldier. Even more difficult had been convincing them of the inevitability of the loss of southern Italy. Kesselring knew that Montgomery could pump enough forces into the lodgment that they would break out by sheer force of numbers—the only tactic that Montgomery apparently knew, right out of the pages of World War I—or he could launch another amphibious invasion that would turn the defenders' flanks. Consequently, Kesselring had lobbied for, and eventually won approval for devoting his limited resources to constructing an impressive line of fortifications across the peninsula farther north, running from the mouth of the Serchio River north of Pisa, southeast along the line of the Apennines to Rimini on the Adriatic coast. His primary combat units were concentrated north of that line or directly confronting the British north of Civitavecchia, with the rest of the territory sparsely garrisoned by infantry divisions supplied with commandeered Italian trucks for rapid movement to what Kesselring had dubbed his "Gustav" line if the British should break out. He knew that he could not hold on indefinitely, but he could hold onto northern Italy, where nearly all of Italy's substantial industrial complex was located, which was being retooled to produce tanks, guns, and planes according to German specifications and with German efficiency. This he could do for months, if not years, if only he were given even minimal support.

CHAPTER 7
THE BULGE

A BRAMS WAVED TO the combat engineers as his Sherman rolled off the Bailey Bridge over the Dordogne River, and they gave him a hearty thumbs-up in return. He had finally begun to think that they might really be home by Christmas 1943 after all.

After weeks of frustratingly slow progress, I Corps had finally broken through the last river line the Germans would be able to erect short of the Loire. Now the Americans could hook right around the end of the Massif Central and pocket half of German Army Group B that had been fending off the French in the Rhone Valley, and liberate half of France, if not all of it, in a matter of days. On the left flank, the newly arrived Polish Corps had mopped up German forces along the Spanish border to the sea and had even captured Bordeaux against surprisingly little resistance after only two days of fighting. The port had been made useless by German demolition, but engineers would soon set that aright and greatly facilitate the resupply of this wing of the army. More Allied troops were arriving too, with the Poles now on the far left, and a new American corps including the 90th Infantry and 6th Armored Divisions forming, while the French steadily built up their strength as did the Canadians and British.

Abrams had noticed for some days that the German resistance was beginning to crack. At the start of the offensive, after the Americans' transfer to the left flank of the Allied lodgment area, very few prisoners had been taken, and those mostly wounded. Recently, however, Germans had been surrendering as soon as it appeared that their position had been flanked or their retreat cut off—not exactly a flood, but a definite trend. As the advance picked up speed, the Germans had less and less time to organize their defenses in new positions, which made it even easier to overcome them, thus further speeding the advance. More and more enemy guns were being overrun before they could withdraw, which meant fewer guns to face at the next defense line.

The only thing that concerned Abrams a little was the lack of enemy armor. Not that he looked forward to facing any more Panthers or Tigers, to which the Shermans which now equipped almost all the American tank units were decidedly inferior. It was just that he would have liked to know where they were. The Germans had certainly taken some losses in the Rhone Valley fighting, but there had been no massive battles of annihilation or huge pockets like Stalingrad, so where was their armor? He would have liked to think that it was all going to face the Russians, but that didn't seem likely. They hadn't even seen the armored units they had faced during the German counterattack, like the Hermann Göring Division, just mobile nests of infantry backed up with anti-tank guns and artillery, and perhaps the occasional assault gun.

Still, the war was going well for the Allies. The Russians expected to resume their offensive as soon as the roads dried out, perhaps next month, and this time the Germans had already been bled white and were facing two fires now. The Axis had lost the whole of the Italian Army, and news reports had it that Sardinia and Sicily had simply declared for the Allies, as had the Italian Navy, bringing thousands of troops into the Allied camp. Germany was now cut off from Spain, from which they had obtained grain and a great deal of valuable resources, like wolfram, some kind of metal used in airplane construction, as Abrams understood it. And Montgomery was again promising his long awaited breakout drive, coupled with another amphibious assault south of Rome, although his campaign was looking more like the trench warfare of World War I than the lightning armored thrusts of the Germans and Russians in this war. Abrams thought it was a shame that all of the Allied landing craft were committed now in Italy, not only eliminating the chance of an end run on the Germans in northern France, but also freeing up those reserves for the Germans to use in the south; but wiser heads than his had made that decision.

Abrams had merely to focus on the task at hand. He braced himself in the turret of his Sherman, watching through his field glasses as best he could as the recon platoon of the lead battalion raced ahead along the highway toward a distant tree line. He no longer had one tank company pause to cover the advance from one cover to the next. It seemed secure enough just to leave a good interval between units now. He would probably have to pay for this at some point between here and Berlin, when the Germans decided to turn and fight, but for now speed was the best armor his command had, and he planned to make the most of it.

1500 HOURS, 25 MARCH 1943
WEST OF CHAMALIERES, FRANCE

Jean Pierre Belmont lay in a narrow depression in the earth, just behind a mossy log, trying not to shiver with the cold, and trying to make himself smaller. There were other members of his FFI guerrilla cell somewhere nearby in these woods, but he could not even risk turning his head to look for them. He was afraid to exhale lest the mist of his warm breath reveal his position to the dozens of German soldiers who had set up camp just on the other side of his log and who were noisily talking and eating as they waited for something to happen.

After sabotaging the vehicles of the 3rd Panzer Grenadier Division, Belmont had made it to the Vichy border, but the speed of the German advance had cut him off, and once more he had found himself in occupied territory. He had dreamed of still making his way south and joining one of the new regular divisions of the French Army that the nightly radio broadcasts on the BBC said were forming. But he had not shirked his duty when his FFI guides had incorporated him into this guerrilla unit. It had only seemed a temporary measure in any case. The Allies had come in force, and the Germans would soon be on the run. But that had been months ago, and here he still was.

The unit had been sent to monitor the transportation net around the important crossroads of Clermont-Ferrand, and they had set up an observation post with four men, including Belmont, on a lightly wooded ridge near the village of Chamalieres, just west of Clermont-Ferrand. The Germans would be using the highway that ran east and west here to shift troops along the front, and it was important to keep tabs on them.

They had been watching a column of tanks, new Tigers Belmont guessed, much newer than anything the old 3rd Panzer Grenadiers had possessed, as they moved west along the highway just before dawn, when the tanks suddenly swerved, all in unison, and plowed through the young trees along the road and up into the thicker woods. The Frenchmen had been well concealed where they were, but, while the evergreen trees provided a canopy against detection from above, the floor of the forest was almost bare of undergrowth. If they had attempted to run up the slope to get away, they would certainly have been seen and killed, so they had been forced to dive for the nearest cover and lay still, for over eight hours so far. Belmont was certain that none of them had been discovered, or there would have been shooting, but how much longer could that last? It had been pure luck that the crew of the nearest tank had stopped just a few feet short of his position, and any one of the other guerrillas could crack at any moment and make a break for it, and then the search would be on for the rest of them.

The minutes passed, although with agonizing slowness. Tears came to Belmont's eyes as he struggled to remain still while a battalion of ants explored his body for hidden treasure. He was certain he would be discovered, especially when one German strolled away from the camp to relieve himself, stepped directly over Belmont's log, but the drab brown clothing of the guerrillas and the dull half-light of the woods let them pass unnoticed once more.

Finally, mercifully, night came, and the drone of German conversation and the rattle of equipment died down to be replaced by a chorus of snores. Belmont carefully moved his cramped arms and legs and began to crawl, inch by inch, away from the camp. He paused to tap the heel of one of the guerrillas, and he could see the shadowy forms of the other two also beginning to make their way off into the woods. He could see the red tip of the cigarette of a sentry about twenty yards away, but he wondered if there were any other non-smokers nearer at hand. There was nothing for it now, however, but to keep going, and he clutched his Sten gun to his chest as he crept up the hillside.

The small group had hoped to make their way to a logging road less than a mile back where they had hidden bicycles under a pile of brush, and then to head south, sticking to the deep woods, but the forest was now alive with Germans. The main lines between the Germans and the Allies, with the French holding this sector, were some fifty miles to the south, and fairly sparsely held in the thick woods and rough terrain of the Massif Central. Although this was hardly the Alps, vehicular traffic was pretty much restricted to the roads, and there were few of those. A thin line of infantry posts had held this part of the front, on both sides, with the heavier armored forces being concentrated either in the Rhone Valley to the east or the open, rolling country which ran west to the sea. It should have posed no particular problem for this small band to drift through the lines, but things had definitely changed.

The hills and woods now seemed to be alive with the crumpled forms of sleeping men and the hulking dark shapes of tanks, guns, and trucks under camouflage netting. Mile after mile, paralleling the road south from Clermont-Ferrand, and tucked well back under the trees, were thousands of men and vehicles, and Belmont noticed that none of the German camps had a fire lit despite the crisp chill in the air. These Germans were definitely up to something.

The group of guerrillas plunged ever deeper into the woods and scrambled up the steeper slopes, preferring the more difficult terrain to the chance of stumbling on an enemy picket. During that first night they only made eight or ten miles and holed up for most of the next day. But a sense of urgency drove Belmont and his men on. They had never seen such a concentration of enemy forces, all of them armored, and they could see from the vehicle markings that they belonged to several divisions, including at least one from the elite Waffen SS. They were not in this area, so close to the front, just for rest and recuperation. They were preparing for an offensive, and the French Army needed to know as soon as possible. So, ignoring their own safety, the group moved on, even in daylight, with two men heading west toward Bort-les-Orgues, where a clandestine radio had been set up, although the Germans had been very effective with their radio direction finding equipment in locating and eliminating these posts if they did not move after every brief transmission. Belmont and the other man, a fellow named Maurice from a town that had been burned out by the SS weeks before, continued south toward the main lines.

They stayed west of the main highway, on which they could hear constant heavy traffic during the night, but which remained eerily silent during the daylight hours. Even though there had been a heavy, low blanket of clouds overhead for days, the Germans were clearly not taking any chances on being spotted by Allied aircraft. By the next morning they had reached the only major east-west road, heading toward the town of Aurillac on the western edge of the Massif Central, and they knew that the French lines lay just a few miles to the south. Now, instead of hidden tanks, they found the woods full of carefully dug in and camouflaged artillery, all pointed south, and jammed almost hub to hub in every fold of the ground, and this discovery spurred them on all the faster.

At the highway they faced a dilemma. If they tried crossing in daylight, there was a distinct chance that they would be seen by a hidden watcher in the woods. Yet, if they waited until night, the traffic along this road would certainly resume, making it just as likely that they might be discovered. Besides that, Belmont and Maurice agreed that they could not afford to waste another twelve hours in getting word to the French of the impending attack. The Allies would need every moment to shift units to meet the threat, and the lives of two men hardly mattered in that equation. So they picked a sharp bend in the road, limiting the view in either direction, and spent long minutes sitting in the underbrush, gathering their strength and their courage, and watching for any sign of German presence. When all appeared quiet, they simply made a dash for it.

Barely halfway across the macadamized road, a shout went up in the woods ahead and to their right. As they crashed through some holly bushes along the road, they could see that, in a slight depression off the road, a pair of trucks mounting anti-aircraft guns had been concealed, and one of the crewmen was raising the alarm. Belmont cursed himself as only now he noticed the marks of the truck tires in the mud at the edge of the road, but it was too late.

Both men shed their rucksacks and sprinted through the trees, still clutching the Sten guns the British had parachuted to the resistance weeks before. Bullets snapped twigs off the trees around them, and they could hear more shouting and vehicle engines starting up off to their left as well. Belmont half turned and could see the silhouettes of several German soldiers charging after them, less than fifty meters away. If it had not been for the trees, which suddenly seemed horribly thin and sparse to Belmont, they would have been cut down already.

"Keep going!" Maurice suddenly hissed as he spun about behind the bole of a tree and loosed a burst at the pursuing Germans.

Belmont instinctively stopped as well, but Maurice turned toward him, his face contorted with rage. "I said, keep going, you imbecile!" he shouted. "I have a personal score to settle, and this is as good a place as any to do it. Now, go!"

Belmont remembered what the others had told him of Maurice's village, although Maurice himself had never spoken of it, and he nodded, crouched low and ran on, tears filling his eyes. He slid down the steep bank of a little stream and dodged along its crooked bed. Short bursts of the Sten gun continued for awhile, punctuated by single shots of German Mausers. Then the throaty cough of a machine gun joined in, followed by one long rip from the Sten. A final flurry of machine-gun fire told him that it was over, but he ran on. He turned uphill now, at a right angle to his previous path, and dove in among some rocks, lying there panting. He peered back to the north, but could see nothing. He lay there a long while, but now only the birds could be heard, indifferently calling in the trees. He slowly pulled himself up and walked around the edge of the rock outcrop where he had taken shelter, and found himself staring into the barrel of a rifle.

Belmont braced himself for the flash, but then he realized that the soldier facing him had on, not the German coal scuttle helmet, but an old French one, the kind with the little ridge along the crest. Rough hands snatched away his Sten gun, but Belmont smiled as he raised his hands.

1800 HOURS, 27 MARCH 1943
VALENCE-SUR-RHONE, FRANCE

General Juin rubbed his jaw thoughtfully as he glanced back and forth between the intelligence report he held in one hand and the large map spread on the table in front of him. His headquarters was in the *Hotel de Ville* of Valence, and the press of staff officers who rushed about with stacks of papers gave the large conference room a crowded, stuffy feel, even though the tall windows had all been blown out during the fighting for the city in the German counteroffensive.

He had interviewed the breathless *maquisard* himself after receiving the first reports from the 10th Division headquarters, and it fit all too well with what little other information he had been able to gather. There was always the chance that the man was a plant, one of Laval's right-wing thugs in the pay of the Germans, even though he had been vouched for by the FFI liaison network, but there was some corroborating information. His was the only specific report of having seen large concentrations of armored vehicles and artillery, even identifying some of the divisions involved, since aerial reconnaissance had been grounded for days; but the Germans had many tanks, and they had definitely *not* been confirmed as being anywhere else along the line. And his forward units in the Massif Central had reported very heavy German combat patrols all along their front, preventing any scout units from penetrating across the line, a sure sign that something was being hidden. But why in the Massif Central? That was the part that didn't make any sense.

The roads in the Massif were few and far from the best in France, and the surrounding terrain would be virtually impassable for heavy vehicles, especially during the spring rains. *Just like the Ardennes!* Juin slapped his forehead with the palm of his hand. How could he have missed it? This was exactly the ploy the Germans had used to turn the flank of the Maginot Line in 1940. They didn't batter their way across the Franco-German border or attempt a von Schleiffen-like sweep along the coast. They drove through the lightly defended woods and hills of the Ardennes precisely because everyone assumed that it was impossible. That was why the lightly armed French had been given this sector, and even why he had concentrated his own strongest units in the Rhone Valley, because a German offensive couldn't possibly come through the Massif. What a fool he had been!

Juin began shouting orders at the top of his lungs while he scribbled a report to be transmitted up the chain of command to Giraud, and more importantly, to Patton and Marshall giving them his appreciation of the situation. He needed aerial reconnaissance, and he needed it immediately and at any cost. He knew that the British and Americans had some kind of window into Axis war plans, and he suspected that they had broken one or more of the German codes. If they were holding back vital information about a major offensive on his front in the interests of "security," there would be no forgiving them. Even some analysis on volumes of enemy radio traffic would be a help, since he didn't have the capability himself. And he needed Marshall to understand the absolute need to shift some of his reserves to this sector either from the American or Canadian sectors, as he had precious little in reserve himself.

Then Juin braced himself on the map table and studied his own dispositions. There was not much there to console him. The line from St. Etienne near the Rhone to Carmaux in the west at the edge of the Massif was nearly one hundred fifty miles long and was defended by a thin line of only six infantry divisions. And these divisions were substantially smaller than German ones, less than half the size of their American counterparts, and they were still woefully under-equipped in artillery, with no armor to speak of at all. For political reasons, which Juin understood perfectly well, it had been important for France to field as many divisions as possible, as nowadays these were the units of measure of a nation's strength. It had been easiest to give the soldiers of the old Armistice Army of Vichy a few days familiarization in

American small arms and machine guns, on the assumption that their previous military training would suffice for the rest. Troops who would be using the new American and British tanks and cannon, however, would require much more training, and only Leclerc's 2nd Armored Division had been formed with this equipment, being composed mainly of men from de Gaulle's Free French who had been using American and British equipment all along, and this was way over on the right grinding its way toward Lyon in the Rhone Valley. Even his two powerful North African divisions, the 3rd Algerian and 4th Moroccan, were on the right where the serious fighting had been expected to take place. It was true that a portion of this line was protected by rivers, mainly the Loire in the east, but the French units were actually well forward of the Lot River in the west and could be destroyed before they could withdraw behind it, and there still remained a gap twenty to thirty miles wide in the center with no river protection at all. And the Germans were more than capable of forcing a river crossing, as they had done at the Meuse in 1940 to unhinge the whole Allied line.

His only reserve force was a single regiment of the Foreign Legion, although this was arguably the best unit in the army. The remainder of his troops in the Massif were new recruits or former Vichy troops hastily formed into divisions under commanders who had not maneuvered a unit larger than a battalion since 1940. Some of these troops had already cracked once at the first German counterattack, and, while that had been a cobbled together affair with few troops of indifferent quality, Juin had every reason to believe that this new offensive would be Hitler's last gamble, one that he would back with every resource at his disposal.

Juin grabbed one staff officer after another, giving him concise verbal orders to rush to the appropriate troop commanders. Koenig was to halt the offensive by his corps and pull the 2nd Armored Division back for resupply and to be ready for a sudden change of front. Three artillery regiments then in training near Avignon were to curtail their courses and move north to Bessèges for possible deployment into the line. The same would go for several tank battalions, anti-tank, and anti-aircraft units that were in the process of being formed into the 1st Armored Division, and the 27th Alpine Division that was strung out along the Pyrenees, was to concentrate at Toulouse and entrain for the front. He dictated a telegram to North African Army headquarters in Algiers that the 2nd and 3rd Moroccan Tabors, the 7th Algerian Division, and the 1st Spahi Regiment were to be embarked immediately for

Marseille. The 1st *Choc* Para Commando Regiment and the 2nd *Choc* Marine Commandos on Corsica were both to be flown into Valence.

Just as he finished this message, a dull rumble could be discerned over the buzz of conversation and the static of the radios placed about the room. Juin put his hand to his throat. He was too late.

2000 HOURS, 27 MARCH 1943
SOUTH OF ST. FLOUR, FRANCE

General Jean de Lattre de Tassigny, commander of the French II Corps in the center of the Massif Central, remembered the terror of being on the receiving end of a massive artillery bombardment from his service in the First World War. What bothered him most about the experience, however, was not the ungovernable fear that welled up in every man's breast at being thrown to the ground and then having that ground heave beneath him; it was the sense of helplessness at a time when every second counted. There was so much that he needed desperately to do and he could hardly get to his feet. When the report of the *maquisard* had passed through his headquarters en route to Juin, de Lattre had taken the precaution of putting his corps on full alert, manning forward positions, and distributing extra ammunition. He had also ordered the commanders of his three divisions, the 10th, 29th, and 36th, to send out strong combat patrols to bring in prisoners for interrogation. Under the circumstances, that was about all he could have done.

Then, about half an hour ago, a series of frantic radio calls had come in from each of his divisions about a massive infantry assault all along the line. No tanks, just a solid wave of infantry that had rushed the forward French lines without artillery preparation, probably catching the combat patrols just as they entered no-man's-land and overwhelming them. Moments later, a rain of mortar rounds had engulfed the battalion headquarters just behind the front, well-directed fire that had obviously been laid out through a long program of clandestine scouting. And this had been followed by heavier artillery beginning to pound the divisional headquarters and his own command post.

This was blitzkrieg in the classic form. De Lattre needed to get information about where the enemy was penetrating, to shift his scanty reserves to meet them and to get on to the army command for reinforcements, but he could hardly get to his feet as the walls of the country chateau he was using as his headquarters shook, and a steady snowfall of plaster dusted him and his staff. The Germans were pinning his troops all along the line with infantry, drawing in local reserves, and pushing in the forward defenses. Then they would find their weak spot and pour in the armor that would rip open a hole and come streaming into the soft rear areas of the corps. De Lattre had a nauseating feeling of *deja vu,* as he suspected every man in the French Army was having at the moment. The only question now remained whether the Americans would cut and run for their boats the way the British did when the Germans made their breakthrough at Sedan three years before or whether they would stand and fight.

2300 HOURS, 27 MARCH 1943
LYON, FRANCE

Rommel paced back and forth across the floor of his command post, reading over the shoulders of his radio technicians as they scribbled down reports coming in from the front. Every now and then he would glance longingly at the door to the blast-proof cellar of the Post, Telephone, and Telegraph Building that led up to the courtyard where his "Mammut" armored car was parked, but then he would catch a disapproving stare from General Alfred Gause, his chief of staff, and Rommel merely sighed and continued his pacing. He paused in front of the large table map where staff officers were pushing wooden markers labeled with the designators of the various divisions that made up the offensive, and he nodded approvingly.

Initial reports were excellent. He had hand-picked two veteran infantry divisions from the Eastern Front, the 305th and the 352nd, and these had done a superb job of swarming over the thin French first line of defense, opening the route for the mailed fist he had so carefully amassed. This was divided into two key elements that he liked to think of as a rapier and a battering ram. The rapier was the two panzer and two mechanized divisions of his own beloved Afrika Korps under the command of General Hans Cramer, now fully rearmed with the latest Panther tanks. They would race south along *Route Nationale 9,* more or less along the seam between the American and French sectors, all the way to the sea near Montpelier. It would take finesse and flexibility to make at least two major river crossings and pick their way through nearly one hundred miles of difficult terrain over an indifferent road net, but he was confident that his men could do it.

The battering ram was comprised of the II SS Panzer Corps under Sepp

Dietrich, the three panzer divisions Liebstandarte Adolf Hitler, the Frunds-
berg, and the Hohenstaufen, plus the Lehr Sturm Panzer Grenadier Brigade,
and supported by the 2nd Parachute Division, which he had pulled away from
the battle for Lyon and mounted on trucks for the occasion. These troops
were the most lavishly equipped in the Reich and were totally indifferent to
casualties. They would smash their way through any resistance the Allies
might be able to mount, southeast along *Route Nationale 102* to the Rhone,
Avignon, and then on to Marseille.

Once these thrusts had developed themselves and the French had
stretched their line thin to try to cover the gaps, his original armored force
around Lyon, the Hermann Göring Division plus one panzer and two more
panzer grenadier divisions, would go over to the offensive and drive back
down the Rhone, catching the bulk of the French in a giant pincer movement
before cutting in behind the British and Canadians along the Italian border.
If all went according to plan, the entire center of the Allied lodgment would
be gutted and the two halves could be rolled up in tum, driving the enemy
back into the sea.

If the Allies would only delay their reaction for two, or at most three days,
the German spearheads would break out of the restricting terrain of the Massif and would be virtually impossible to stop in the open ground along the
coast, and it would be Dunkirk all over again. If this Allied front could be
annihilated, troops could be shifted to Italy to deal with Montgomery, who
Rommel viewed as being overly cautious and who might even embark his
troops of his own accord. If that could be accomplished, there would be no
new front in the West for months, if not years, and all the power of the Reich
could be focused on the Russians. Stalin would likely feel abandoned by the
West, and might even be in a mood to accept terms, thus putting an end to
the war. It all depended on gaining control of a few country roads and a few
bridges over the next seventy-two hours. *And* it depended on the weather
continuing to stay overcast to keep the Allied air forces off the backs of the
advancing troops.

0600 Hours, 28 March 1943
Avignon, France

Marshall virtually had to order his aides to drag General Giraud bodily from
his headquarters in the old abbey overlooking the old papal city tucked into

a sharp bend of the Rhone River. The first few minutes of the visit had been necessary, even productive, as they exchanged information about every possible resource the French could bring to bear on the looming crisis. But then Giraud had merely stayed on, instead of rushing off to lend his own command authority to the frantic efforts at shoring up the breach, and the very last thing that Marshall needed at the moment was the tall, dapper French general leaning over his shoulder providing sage advice, in the form of what sounded suspiciously like orders, on the deployment of the whole Allied army. Now Marshall tried to shut out the racket of the ringing telephones, chattering radios, and thudding feet of the staff officers and focus on the problem at hand.

During the night the German assault had shattered at least two French divisions, with at least two more being virtually useless as fighting units, and torn a gap thirty miles wide in the line. They had pored through this gap what appeared to be two armored corps, one each along the only two main highways through the Massif Central with an obvious intention of driving to the coast, cutting the lodgment in two and probably destroying the whole of the Allied Expeditionary Force. It was now Marshall's task to cram units into the breach and hold back the flood.

He cursed himself for becoming over-confident at the advances being made all along the front in the preceding weeks. He should have known that no major German unit had been destroyed in the battles of January and February, and that the enemy wouldn't simply roll over and accept the Allied presence in France. Now Patton was strung out halfway across France, and the only units in strategic reserve were currently the much-battered 82nd Airborne and the newly-arrived 101st Airborne Divisions, neither of which were ideally suited to stopping an armored juggernaut.

Well, the first priority was to shore up the shoulders of the German penetration. Juin appeared to be taking the appropriate first steps in that regard, concentrating his best units around St. Etienne and pulling his armor back from the front for a counter thrust. The Canadians could slide two divisions westward to screen Lyon and even free up an armored brigade, artillery, and other support units to back up the French. The American 29th Division had dug in around Aurillac on the western fringe of the Massif to serve as a rallying point for the survivors of the French III Corps, but that still left a huge gap in his center with virtually nothing to cover it. There were the 9th Infantry and 6th Armored Divisions that were hurriedly being assembled near Marseille as units arrived from the States, and a host of scattered French and

American units strewn all across southern France, but no cork of a size comparable to the mouth of the bottle. The only thing that even remotely fit the bill was the British XII Corps, with the Guards Armored Division and two infantry divisions, then aboard ship in the Western Mediterranean en route for Montgomery's front in Italy; but Marshall hated to go hat in hand to the British, especially to Montgomery, who had been taking tremendous heat for his failure to break out of his beachhead, and tell him that the British offensive would have to be postponed in order to pull the Americans' acorns out of the fire. But it would have to be done. Marshall knew only too well that too many young men were dying at that very moment for him to balk at eating a little crow.

What Marshall needed was time. He stared at the map at it screamed at him what needed to be done. It seemed at that moment that he had been studying terrain maps all his adult life, and the contours, splotches of color, and snaking river lines spoke to him as clearly as printed words on a page. There were locations that the Germans would absolutely have to occupy in order to break out of the Massif onto the open ground of the coastal plain. The town of Mende controlled the bridges over the Lot River on *Route Nationale 9* to the south, and Le Puy-en-Velay controlled the bridges over the upper Loire to the southeast and also the gap between the Loire and the Allier Rivers that the Germans could use to move south if the Loire were blocked to them. If those two points could be held, the Germans would be limited to picking their way through forty miles of the toughest terrain in the Massif. It would have been folly to think that they couldn't do it, just as it had been to assume that they wouldn't attack in the Massif in the first place, but it would take time, and Marshall would then have a chance to throw together another line ahead of them.

He turned to one staff officer after another, dictating orders. The 10 1st would go to Le Puy-en-Velay by truck immediately, but it would be the French who would have to hold Mende. Meanwhile, he sent a message to Patton to fly to Avignon to discuss what they might do on a more permanent basis to deal with the problem. Then he went to get a message to Montgomery. There was no point in appealing to the Prime Minister until he had first at least gone through the proper chain of command.

1800 HOURS, 28 MARCH 1943
NEAR MENDE, FRANCE

Colonel Franz Heussen had commanded the *Reece* Battalion of the Afrika Korps all across Libya and half of Egypt, right up to the gates of Alexandria, over hundreds of miles of daunting terrain with only one serviceable road, and that under constant harassment by enemy naval gunfire and air attack. He had not considered it a particularly difficult assignment to lead the corps less than one hundred fifty miles along RN 9 to the sea. But he was finding the Massif Central a rather different playing field than the Western Desert.

The initial French resistance had cracked like the shell of an egg, and there had been little behind it. His armored cars and half-tracks had raced through the streets of St. Flour even while the infantry shock troops had fought with the bayonet against artillerymen and clerks at the French corps headquarters there, and raced on southward. That had been the last thing that had gone right. Heussen felt like the engineer of an express train with a tight schedule who was constantly plagued by minor delays at every station or switching shack, and he could feel the traffic piling up behind him along the single two-lane road.

In the desert, whenever an army, either the Allies or the Axis, had been pushed out of a position, they would naturally retreat at full speed to their supply base, usually several hundreds of miles to the rear, lest they be cut off and starved quickly into submission. Here, every damned company of infantry, artillery battery, or section of tanks he encountered along the way had dug in, right across the road, and had to be blasted and maneuvered out of position. Every stone farmhouse turned into a fortress, and every bridge or culvert was blown. And, here, it wasn't like the desert where the only real problem with leaving the road was the chance of losing your way in the trackless, flat, emptiness. Here there were forests, gullies, and mountains that sometimes even his eight-wheeled vehicles could not negotiate, and the odd logging trail or farm track could start out in the right direction but then bend around and lead you back the way you had come. The reconnaissance done by the scouts had provided some useful hints, but Heussen was finding their maps to be less than accurate and sometimes downright misleading. The thin, cold rain that continued to fall was welcome in that it kept the enemy fighter-bombers away, but it also turned every stream into a torrent and every field into a bog, and limited his own vision so that his first indication of an enemy position was usually a flash of gunfire and the explosion of one of his vehicles.

His orders had called for him to be *in* the town of Mende by noon, already in possession of the bridge over the River Lot, and here he was, six hours later, still miles away and fighting a hot little action against what appeared to be a scratch force of French infantry, policemen, and farmers armed with shotguns, with nearly half of his vehicles already smoking wrecks dotting the road all the way back to St. Flour.

2000 HOURS, 28 MARCH 1943
LE PUY-EN-VELAY, FRANCE

Colonel William C. Bentley, commander of the 2nd Battalion, 509th Airborne Infantry, was getting thoroughly tired of this war. He was on the verge of his third major battle and he had yet to strap on a parachute. Once more, he and his men had been trucked, like a load of potatoes, to the front to fight like poor, bloody infantry rather than as the elite force of strategic envelopment that they were. To add insult to injury, he was now only a few miles from the site of his first battle, not much progress at all.

The 509th, along with about half of the 82nd Airborne had been added to the 101st, and told to dig in in a tight arc around Le Puy-en-Velay, denying the enemy the road, the bridge over the Loire, and also passage south along this side of the Loire. The G-2 officer of the 101st had informed them that their counterparts on the German side would be a full corps of SS panzer troops. Since Bentley remembered only too well how he had had his butt kicked by a mere brigade of the SS just three months before, he was not looking forward to this at all.

At least this time it wasn't just his own battalion hanging out on the line. There were at least 20,000 American paras, most of whom had seen some combat, plus two tank battalions, the 751st and 752nd, the 5th Artillery brigade, and the 333rd Field Artillery Battalion, the first unit of black soldiers Bentley had seen at the front, plus a host of motorized anti-tank, engineer, and other units. They were all frantically digging entrenchments around and inside the town, while the civilian population streamed south and the engineers wired the bridge with explosives. Even Bentley himself had pitched in, heaving sandbags as they built up a second wall behind the wall of the sacristy of the Church of St. Laurent, his command post, which gave him an excellent view of the little bridge over the narrow Borne River, a stream really, that ran along the northern edge of town. The bridge carried the *Route Nationale 102*, the main enemy avenue of advance from Clermont-Ferrand, straight to his door.

In the distance, Bentley could hear the rattle of gunfire, and the horizon to the north was occasionally lit by flashes reflected off the low clouds. In another setting he might have thought it could have been thunder and lightning, but not here. He knew that the French 14th Division had been encircled about ten miles to the north and had refused a German offer of surrender. It wouldn't take long for a panzer corps to deal with perhaps five thousand infantrymen, but the fighting had been going on for a couple of hours thus far and was obviously not over yet. He knew that, when the northern sky went quiet, he would have about an hour. He turned and grabbed another sandbag, moving a little faster.

0200 HOURS, 29 MARCH 1943
BRIVE-LA-GAILLARDE, FRANCE

Abrams did not like the idea of a night advance over a road that had not been reconned, but no one had asked him. The word from division, corps, and from Patton himself had been to "hang a right and keep going."

When word had first come through of the German offensive to the east, in what was now being referred to as "the Bulge," Abrams and everyone else in I Corps had assumed that they would be pulling back all along the line, then shifting units to meet the German spearheads face to face. But that had not been Patton's style. He had apparently not learned that a flank march in the face of an enemy is one of the most dangerous and difficult maneuvers in the military repertoire. That had been true enough in Napoleon's time, but with the immense logistical tail that modern mechanized forces had evolved over the years, it was almost an impossibility to change direction 90° at speed. But that was exactly what they were being ordered to do.

Allegedly, the Polish Corps would spread out, along with the American V Corps, to cover the current front, however thinly, while the rest of the American forces would form a compact mass to drive directly into the western flank of the German advance. On the map this looked logical, with the predominantly infantry VII Corps centered on Aurillac driving east through Murat to cut behind the right-wing German column, while I Corps, now just the 1st and 2nd Armored Divisions, farther to the north, would rush northeast along the upper edge of the Massif Central on *Route Nationale 89* to the headquarters of German Army Group B at Clermont-Ferrand and beyond. Supposedly, they would be met by a similar thrust westward from the Allied

Forces in the Rhone Valley, resulting in the "pocketing" of more than 100,000 Germans. That would be great, if it worked out. After the disaster of Stalingrad and the defection of Italy, it seemed to Abrams that Germany couldn't survive another such body blow. That was assuming, of course, that the Germans hadn't foreseen all of this and were simply sitting back, waiting to kill them all.

The key to everything would be the weather. If the skies cleared, Abrams was confident that the Allies could beat off the Luftwaffe and lay a carpet of bombs from here to Clermont, blasting any German foolish enough to stand in the way. At the same time, they could ravage the German armored columns now driving south, keeping them from turning to meet the new threat and also keeping reinforcements from arriving from Germany itself. But, as Abrams leaned back against the turret ring of his Sherman, which was crawling forward in a thick column of vehicles flanked by files of marching infantrymen, the sky above was absolutely black, no sign of the moon or even a single star.

0600 Hours, 29 March 1943
Mende, France

Special forces had fallen into a kind of disrepute in Germany after the fiasco in Vichy in which Otto Skorzeny had lost his life, but there would always be a place in modern warfare for troops who were willing to change out of their uniforms and cross into enemy territory to do a one-off job. Major Luther Markoff sat against the cold, sweating wall of the basement of a house in Mende, one of two adjacent structures owned by an Axis sympathizer that were now crammed with about forty nervous members of the Brandenberger Regiment. They wore French Army uniforms and had managed to join the fleeing columns heading south from St. Flour. They had then abandoned their captured vehicles and, avoiding the military policemen trying to round up stragglers, had drifted by ones and twos to this address over the previous day and a half. A technician had run a thin antenna up along the rainspout of the house, and Markoff now sat next to the radio operator, listening for the coded message from the German vanguard which would tell them that the time had come for them to join in the battle for the key river town.

Markoff was getting concerned, and he could tell from the murmuring of his men that they were as well. The lead elements of the 21st Panzer Division should have been storming the town's northern defenses by early the previous evening, and there was still not the least sound of fighting around the town. The previous afternoon, the French had blown two lesser bridges over the Lot, and his scouts had informed Markoff that the main highway bridge, the one less than a hundred meters from their hiding place, had been wired for demolition, but its destruction would cut off the French troops still resisting the German advance. There had been a steady flow of refugees, both civilian and military, across the bridge until a few hours before, and Markoff had noted the passage of a company of American-made tanks heading north, but things had been relatively quiet for some time.

The timing of his move would be everything. If he assaulted the bridge too soon, the French would be able to overcome his understrength company in short order. If he moved even a few minutes too late, they could blow the bridge in their faces, and the German advance would be stalled, perhaps fatally. A lookout was posted in the attic of the house, where he had carefully removed a few shingles, giving him a view of the bridge and the highway leading to it. If the codeword didn't come over the radio, and one could never be too sure of a radio signal getting through, the lookout at least should give them the word of an impending German assault. But no messages arrived, even now, as Markoff began to hear the thumping of heavy guns, still far off, but getting closer.

0700 HOURS, 29 MARCH 1943
NORTH OF MENDE, FRANCE

Heussen directed the fire of his own Puma armored car's 47mm gun at a dark patch on the slope ahead from which tracer rounds had been hammering a half-track stuck in a bog off the side of the highway while high explosive shells and smoke rounds peppered the hill and German infantry tried to pick their way forward. He had ceased to be leader of a recon element, and was just another part of an all-out assault on prepared enemy positions that spread half a mile on either side of the highway. A full panzer regiment and a battalion of grenadiers were also on line, backed up by several batteries of self-propelled guns, but their progress in the last two hours could be measured in tens of meters. A regiment of the French Foreign Legion had dug in across the highway and also had support from tanks and artillery, although not as much support as the attackers had. Twice now tanks had penetrated the trench lines, but all had been destroyed or disabled by point-blank fire from anti-tank guns hidden on the reverse slope of the slight ridge or by satchel charges hurled directly under their bellies by the Legionnaires in suicidal rushes. There remained only about three miles to go to the bridge at Mende, the last obstacle on the route to the sea, and the French obviously knew that and were holding on with their teeth. Heussen had seen the Legion fight at Bir Hakeim in the desert in similar circumstances, and he reminded himself that they had never actually been driven out of their positions.

The bridge was important, of course, but not vital. Two separate bridging units accompanied the 21st Panzer, and the rivers here in the Massif were just rising, still fairly narrow, if swift. The only problem was that every minute that passed gave the French that much longer to bring up reinforcements to man the far side of the river, making an assault that much more difficult. Only when a bridgehead had been established could the engineers begin to lay the steel sections and pontoons necessary to get the tanks across. And now Heussen scanned the sky nervously. It was full daylight, and he found the sky filled with a diffused white light, not the looming gray of even high noon yesterday. The cloud cover was higher and thinner, still too much, perhaps for flying weather, but it was clearing.

0800 HOURS, 29 MARCH 1943
MENDE, FRANCE

Colonel d'Ormesson nodded to the soldier dressed in a postman's uniform, and the man began to trudge along the street, a heavy leather sack over his shoulder. At the door of the house d'Ormesson had been observing, he knocked lightly and then left a large parcel on the doorstep before continuing down the street and around the next corner. No one had entered the building for hours, and d'Ormesson was confident that they had as many rats in the trap as they were likely to get. The enemy had been very cautious in infiltrating this far, but it had apparently not occurred to them that the owner of the property was a *known* Axis sympathizer, with a son in the *Legion des Voluntaires Fraincaises* with the Wehrmacht on the Russian Front. Mende was a small town, and everyone's business was known to all. The house had been under surveillance by the gendarmerie since the Allied intervention, and the arrival of several, then dozens of hardy-looking young men furtively during the night had raised the alarm. The fact that the house was so close to what was arguably the most important bridge in France at the moment was too much of a coincidence to ignore.

Still, d'Ormesson's stomach turned. He half expected some golden-haired child to open the door just as the explosive planted by the false postman went off, but he had no choice. He raised his gloved hand and brought it down with a chopping motion, and a dozen soldiers hidden with him behind the hedge in the garden across the street from the target house stepped back and hurled their smoke grenades into the street. At the same instant a sharp-shooter fired a round into the parcel, blowing the heavy double door off its hinges. Soldiers charged across the street and into the building while machine guns raked the upper story windows and a bazooka demolished the door of the adjoining building.

In an instant, d'Ormesson's straining ears could detect the snarling rip of the Schmeisser machine pistols carried by the enemy and he nodded. There had been no mistake. Blasts inside the building blew out whole rows of windows, and black smoke began to issue from the half-windows of the basement. He drew his own pistol and dodged across the street behind an armored car that he moved up to cover any possible escape routes with its machine guns.

In the few moments it had taken him to reach the doorway, the firing had died out, and panting soldiers had already begun filing back out of the building. Bodies were scattered in every hallway and in every room, a few French, but mostly German, and the stench of burning flesh wafted up from the basement stairway.

"No prisoners," grunted a sergeant who had an angry pink scar that ran diagonally across his forehead and left eyebrow. D'Ormesson was about to berate the man for denying him the chance of prisoners to interrogate, but the sergeant tossed the colonel a dented helmet. "They were wearing these." It belonged to the 92nd Infantry Regiment, d'Ormesson's old unit.

The colonel pouted his lips, tucked the helmet under his arm, and walked back out into the street. He had seen enough.

To the north, just on the horizon, several columns of smoke were rising, white smoke, the kind used to mask troop movements. The Germans would be here in less than an hour. He walked over to the small garage where the engineers had set up their demolitions station. General de Lattre de Tassigny was there, and d'Ormesson walked in just in time to see the general pat the nervous young sapper on the shoulder. The sapper twisted and pushed down on a plunger, and a series of sharp explosions rattled the windows of the building. D'Ormesson knew that, if he had not taken out the German commando unit, the men in this room would have probably been dead by now.

"And the men up there, sir?" d'Ormesson asked as he saluted, at the same time jerking his chin to the north.

"There are few of them left, colonel," the general replied. "There are a few boats left on the north bank to take off survivors, and the equipment we can always replace. We have a brigade from our own 1st Armored Division taking up position east of town and nearly a full infantry division digging in along the river bank, with three artillery regiments in position to cover the likely crossing spots. This is as far as the Germans will go for some time."

"Let's just hope that it's enough, sir."

1200 HOURS, 29 MARCH 1943
LE PUY-EN-VELAY, FRANCE

A battalion commander should not normally have to fire his personal weapon, but Bentley had already gone through five magazines of his Thompson submachine gun and was rummaging in his pockets for more.

The Germans had appeared just before dawn, and Bentley had had a front row view from the bell tower of the St. Laurent church. First, there had been a few scattered vehicles nosing their way down the highway from Clermont-Ferrand that were picked off at long range by anti-tank guns. Then the American artillery had plastered the woods farther up the highway, hoping to catch the Germans as they deployed. It had taken awhile for the German guns to respond, probably just coming into position off the march. Then came swarms of gray panzers, racing down the slope toward the narrow Borne River, and dozens of American tanks had emerged to challenge them. The Americans had fired a volley from cover, scoring only a few hits, and then dashed out to mix it up at close range, apparently hoping that this would compensate for their inferior armament.

The battle had raged for nearly two hours, with paras from another battalion of the 82nd rushing suicidally into the fray in the hope of getting a tail shot at one of the steel monsters with a bazooka and of preventing the German infantry from doing the same. The field had been littered with dozens of burning wrecks, but the Germans just kept coming. There had only been about sixty American tanks to start, and the Germans had over a hundred, and General Maxwell D. Taylor, commander of the 101st and the overall defense of Le Puy, ordered the bridges over the Borne blown. A few tanks had rattled back into the town just before then, some of them streaming smoke or with horrible gashes in their armor, their decks crowded with wounded paras, but any that survived after that were staying on the north side of the river, forever.

There had been hardly any respite before German parachute infantry in their mottled camouflage smocks had appeared at the river's edge with rubber boats and pushed off for the southern bank covered by a hail of fire from tanks and half-tracks while their artillery dropped a curtain of smoke rounds to mask their movement. Bentley had gone down to the shore, crawling through the zigzag of shallow communications trenches through the park to where his men were firing furiously with every weapon that could be brought to bear. An American half-track mounting a quad-50 anti-aircraft system backed out of a narrow street and swept the far shore with thousands of rounds, blowing away the first wave of German paras and their boats, but a 75mm round from one of the Panthers quickly eliminated the American gun. The Germans had occupied two small islands in mid-river and set up more machine guns there to take the Americans under a point-blank fire. Finally, word came down the line that the Germans were across the stream both above and below them, and Bentley and the survivors of one company had to break and run for their second line of defense at the church.

From the church, the Americans were able to keep the Germans from advancing more than a few meters beyond the riverbank, and, once the German engineers had laid a temporary pontoon bridge, every panzer that crossed and attempted to climb the steep southern bank received a fatal shot through its weak bottom armor from a platoon of tank destroyers hidden inside the buildings facing the river. Finally, as darkness fell, and the only light was provided by the burning houses and vehicles scattered in an arc around the northern and western edge of the town, the Germans dug in to consolidate their gains and bring up reinforcements. The Americans just slumped down in their positions, praying for clear weather.

1800 HOURS, 29 MARCH 1943
NEAR USSEL, FRANCE

Abrams guided the driver of his Sherman around another burning wreck. At least this one was German, a Marder self-propelled gun. He understood that they were built from obsolete tank chassis and armed with Soviet-made 76mm anti-tank guns captured in the thousands in Russia in 1941. The 1st Armored Division had been paired with a *tabor,* a regiment, of Moroccan mountain infantry that had been flown up from North Africa that morning and rushed to the front. Over the past dozen miles, whenever the tanks had been blocked on the highway, the Moroccans would fan out into the surrounding hills and take the German lines from flank or rear. From the prisoners taken thus far, it seemed that a single German infantry division, already understrength, was trying to cover the entire twenty-mile gap between the Dordogne and Vézère Rivers, and they could do little more than set up roadblocks on the highway itself with no defense in depth or any line to the flanks. VII Corps was finding the same to be true on its front to the south, where they had advanced parallel to I Corps almost to the town of Murat.

The resistance had begun to stiffen as the day ended, however. Abrams had trouble thinking of this as good news, but it was an indication that the maneuver was having its desired strategic effect. VII Corps had taken prisoners from the 90th Panzer Grenadiers, an Afrika Korps unit, implying that they had been pulled away from the main German advance on that front. Abrams own advance was now meeting more armor and artillery, also implying that Rommel was concerned about his flank, having drawn these units from the 3rd Panzer Grenadier Division that had been previously reported on the Lyon front. The bad news was that the weather had continued foul, enabling the Germans to make this switch of reserves across considerable distances with no interference from Allied air power.

There was little comfort for the American tankers in the town of Ussel, a burned out shell that had fallen only after two hours of street fighting, but Abrams would hold his men up here until dawn. Then the relatively fresh 2nd Armored would pass through their lines and continue the advance toward Clermont-Ferrand. Abrams gave hurried orders to his executive officer to head back down the column to bring up fuel and ammunition vehicles to replenish the tanks; then he laid down on the back deck of his Sherman, still comfortably warm from the day's driving, and fell instantly to sleep for the first time in nearly forty-eight hours.

0300 HOURS, 30 MARCH 1943
CLERMONT-FERRAND, FRANCE

Colonel Siegfried Westphal had long experience as Rommel's operations officer and had never known him willingly to take responsibility for any failure by his troops. He did not do so now. Rommel was just then screaming into a radio handset at General Cramer, commander of the Afrika Korps, for failing to press home his attack on Mende and then for detaching a division to cover his right flank against the American advance on Murat. Westphal noted the fact that the leading regiments of the corps had suffered over sixty per cent casualties, implying that they had indeed pressed home the attack. He also noted that if Cramer had not taken the initiative to block the American advance, Yankee troops could be on the outskirts of Clermont by now, although this did not impress Rommel in the slightest.

Westphal understood only too well the kind of pressure that Rommel was under from OKH, having received all the resources he had demanded, and then some, and not having delivered the stunning victory he had promised. But there remained the fact that, to get the most out of his men, a commander had to give them credit for their achievements. Cramer's men had battered their way forward nearly forty miles and were even now fighting to hold their third tenuous bridgehead over the Lot River, the previous two having been crushed by suicidal attacks by Algerian infantry and unexpectedly numerous French tanks.

Of course, Rommel did not spare Sepp Dietrich's SS troops either. They had advanced barely half as far as Cramer's men and had then been stopped cold by the Americans at Puy, a mere airborne division against a panzer corps. They too were seeking a way around, filtering units over back roads west of the town, but they had to take that important crossroads to be able to continue the offensive in any strength. It seemed that the Allies were using the tactic of blowing vital bridges as soon as the Germans threatened them, often abandoning their own blocking forces rather than holding them open until the last possible moment. It had been the tendency of both French and Russian commanders to save their bridges, either to rescue their own troops or in hope of using them in a future advance, that had worked so well for the Germans in 1940 and 1941. But they seemed to have learned their lesson.

Rommel's plans were beginning to collapse. Already he had had to abandon any hope of a new offensive along the Rhone, as the arrival of fresh Canadian troops had strengthened that sector, and he had been obliged to pull one division already from the area to meet the American threat to his right flank. Now reports were coming in that two new American divisions had come into existence from what had appeared to be replacements units around Avignon, and elements of at least two British divisions were now unloading at Marseille and Toulon. If the attackers did not break out of the Massif Central within the next twenty-four hours, in Westphal's estimation, the enemy defenses would be too strong to crack, and Rommel would find himself in possession of a thumb-shaped salient sixty miles deep, with strong enemy armored forces gnawing away at the base of the thumb.

Westphal was not surprised to see Rommel throw down the handset and storm out the door of the command post to his waiting Mammut, and this time not even General Gause dared try to stop him. If the battle were already lost, Rommel's presence here would make no difference, and there was always the chance that his appearance at the key point of the struggle might steel his men enough to bring victory.

0500 Hours, 30 March 1943
Avignon, France

All things considered, Marshall thought that the conference with Montgomery at Ajaccio the day before had gone much better than he had expected. Of course, Marshall, Juin, and Eisenhower, who had flown over for the occasion, had been obliged to listen to a long monologue of how Monty "could have told them" that they'd run into this kind of trouble, but both of the Americans had bitten their lips and taken his scolding in good part. Then suddenly, Monty had, with a flick of the wrist, offered them up the very corps they had come to beg of him. He would send the three divisions ashore at Marseille, and they could be landing within two hours, with arrival in the field by late on the 30th if they had priority in the use of the docking facilities, which they would.

Then the bill arrived. Monty added, almost as an afterthought, that he would naturally want to retain command of the British troops. Eisenhower spluttered momentarily, but the Americans had no choice but to cave in when Montgomery threw back in their faces the old American argument of not wanting his nation's troops being used as fillers in an army commanded by foreigners. He added that it seemed most expedient to him that the boundary between Patton's 1st Army Group and his own 21st now be placed at the Rhone River, with everything east of it going to Monty, continuing the line for planning purposes up through Dijon and then roughly northeast through the heart of Germany for the remainder of the campaign.

Even before the Americans could reply, Montgomery added that he had been talking with Marshal Badoglio, and it seemed that the Italians were very much interested in getting back into the fight. Nearly a quarter of a million of their best troops had been stationed on Sardinia and Sicily at the time of the surrender, and two full divisions of Alpini troops had turned themselves over, en masse, to the British V Corps in southern France. Monty proposed going ahead with his second amphibious assault, using the British 46th Infantry and 1st Armored Divisions still waiting in North Africa, plus the British 1st Airborne from Corsica and four Italian divisions from Sicily. He would land at Salerno, near Naples, timed to coincide with a breakout from his Civitavecchia lodgment that was already bursting at the seams with troops and guns. This would also coincide with a push by British V Corps at rearmed Italian mountain troops to break through the last few kilometers of the Alps into the North Italian plain.

Marshall just shook his head ruefully and agreed. He was not in a position to bargain. Juin opened his mouth to protest but Montgomery forestalled him with a raised hand, adding that, for political reasons, he realized that it was necessary for French troops to effect the liberation of Lyon, and he would exclude that city from his sector and facilitate the French occupation of it as soon as it became practicable. The arrival of the British troops at Marseille would enable him to release the American 8th Infantry and 6th Armored immediately, even before the British were completely ashore, to rush north and plug the gap between Le Puy and Mende. The British, in turn, would be replaced by the French units arriving from North Africa and could head north to take over the Canadian sector, freeing all of the French and Canadian troops, at least eight good divisions, to drive west from St. Etienne to meet Patton and pinch off the German salient.

Montgomery acknowledged that he thought the plan to be "top drawer" with the proviso that, of course, the Canadians would be "returned" to his command once the crisis was past. He explained that this was merely to simplify logistical arrangements, since the American and French forces used exclusively U.S.-made equipment and munitions, while the Canadians used British gear. Marshall smiled and patted his pockets with a worried expression on his face. When Montgomery asked him what was the matter, he replied that he merely wanted to make sure that his wallet was still there.

Now, as Marshall watched in the cold predawn darkness, thousands of British troops were pouring off transports under the harsh yellow arc lights along the Marseille docks. He had just shared a cup of tea with the arriving commander of the Guards Division and the departing commander of the American 6th Armored and, for the first time in nearly a week, he felt that he had the situation once more under control.

0700 HOURS, 30 MARCH 1943
TEN MILES SOUTHWEST OF LE PUY-EN-VELAY, FRANCE

Captain Hans Essen screamed at the troopers of his company of the SS Lehr Sturm Brigade to move faster. The sun was full up now, and, while the sky was still largely covered with clouds, they were quite high, and patches of pale blue could clearly be seen in spots. This was not weather that would keep the enemy *jabos,* fighter bombers, on the ground, and he had little faith in the power of Göring's Luftwaffe to keep them away. The men ran frantically from one vehicle to the next, pulling tattered camouflage netting over them, using tree branches to try to smooth away the deep ruts in the mud where they had pulled off the road into the trees, anything that would disguise their presence to the eyes of a pilot passing by at two hundred miles per hour.

As far as Essen was concerned, now was the time for Hitler to pull the rabbit out of his hat. Where were the secret weapons they had been hearing about for months, the super-fighters that would swat enemy bombers from the sky like flies, or the bombs that would hurl themselves across the Channel to punish the English and obliterate every enemy port? Because, if these weapons didn't appear soon, how could they win? He looked at the faces of the replacements his own company had received over the past couple of months, and most of them were mere boys, and ill-fed boys at that, while there seemed to be no end to the supply of big, burly Americans, to say nothing of the French, who had been justly beaten and now were back in the field against them.

For an instant, as Essen glanced nervously again at the sky, he felt a surge of hope. Well, the weather may have cleared up *here,* but it might still be completely socked in over the Allied airfields, either in England or southern France. And any bombers coming from England would be heavies that would go after rail lines or entire cities, not tactical columns, since they were notoriously inaccurate. If they could just survive the next ten hours or so, the darkness would provide their protection again, and they could continue the drive south. Just a few more miles, and they would be in the open, so mixed up with the retreating enemy that air attacks would not be practical.

Even as he thought this, the ground under his feet began to tremble, and he had to lean on the side of his armored car to remain upright. Shouts went up along the column but they were almost immediately drowned in a dull roar that increased in volume until Essen could feel his eardrums rupturing. He dove into a shallow depression in the earth, but kept his head up. He could see fountains of dirt sprout up in a barren field off to one side of the road, converging into a wall of flying earth and rock that rushed toward the road like a tidal wave, then swept across it and into the woods where the column was sheltering. As he lost consciousness, Essen casually recalled that he had not heard the aircraft at all. They must have been heavy bombers, flying high, and a contrary wind thousands of feet above must have carried away the sound of their engines.

When he came to, Essen could not at first remember where he was. The scene around him did not look familiar, and he thought for a moment that he must have been hurled some distance by the blast. Instead of a wood, he was now in the middle of a moonscape of endless craters, as if a troubled sea had suddenly been frozen and turned into land. Only here and there were the shattered trunks of trees visible, and the occasional scorched stump. Among them were the still-burning clumps of metal that might have been trucks or tanks, and what looked like piles of dirty laundry that must have been men. At first he was surprised at the silence, but then he felt the warm liquid draining from his ears and saw on his fingertips that it was blood. A bomb splinter had also gashed his left forearm, making his hand look like a red mitten.

He staggered to his feet, and he could see several other men doing likewise, but just a few. One of them had his mouth open, and Essen imagined that he was screaming, blood from a cut on his forehead covering half of his face. It was like that painting, what was the artist's name? But there was no sound, and for a moment that struck Essen as one of the funniest things he had ever seen in his life.

1200 HOURS, 31 MARCH 1943
LE PUY-EN-VELAY, FRANCE

Bentley and his men cheered as the American fighter-bombers swept in parallel to the Borne River, dropping bombs, firing rockets, or just raking the enemy with machine-gun fire. They had been doing this all morning and most of the day before, and their assistance had not come a moment too soon.

The defenders had been pushed back halfway through the city, with Bentley's battalion having given up the church just before dawn the previous day and falling back to the Rocher Corneille, a rock outcropping over one hundred feet high rising just north of the town center. It was an excellent defensive position and its height allowed the Americans to call in artillery fire almost anywhere on the perimeter. But there was less and less artillery to call in. The Germans had encompassed the three landward sides of the city, and even the crossings over the River Loire to their backs were under constant enemy fire. The guns had almost run out of ammunition, except for one shipment floated down the river on a barge, the only one that had not been quickly sunk by the Germans, and most of the artillerymen had been pressed into service as common infantry, holding the ever-shrinking perimeter.

Then the skies had cleared somewhat and the planes began to arrive. At first both the Germans and the Americans had let an unspoken truce take effect while the infantrymen watched dozens of planes circling and diving as Luftwaffe fighters tried to beat off the Americans and British. Every now and then the white contrails would be punctuated with a ball of black smoke, that would mark the end of one of the aircraft as it began its final spiral to the earth. Betting had been heavy, and Bentley had been too exhausted to try to curtail the ghoulish sport.

For a moment, the skies had been vacant, as the outnumbered Germans had broken off the engagement, and plumes of ack-ack fire had begun to blossom in the sky, even before the men on the ground could hear the rumble of the bombers' engines. The larger B-25s had begun hitting targets well north of the town, and then the new P-47s came roaring low over the city, dropping bombs on targets less than three hundred yards from the American positions. An Air Corps officer had swum the river several nights earlier and had been given one of the few functioning radio sets left in the city, and from a well-sandbagged position on Bentley's rock he was calling in flight after flight of aircraft.

At first the Germans had seemed stunned, and the Americans took advantage of the lull to replenish their ammunition pouches, often by stripping the dead now, and even retaking a couple of nearby points that had fallen to the enemy, but then the SS troopers came on again. They had realized that their best defense against air attack was to cozy up to the Americans, and, while they had been more than aggressive enough for Bentley's liking before, now they came on recklessly, often holding rooms in the same building half occupied by the defenders. Their armor, which had been reluctant to get into the street fighting, had come clattering down the narrow streets, preferring the odds against American mines and bazookas to those against dive-bombers on the outskirts of town.

Bentley had taken it as a good sign that the German paratroopers, who had made up most of the enemy's infantry during the initial assault, had been replaced by SS panzer grenadiers, as the few prisoners they had taken proved. He calculated that, since the enemy paras would be of little use in a running fight on the roads, the only reason they would have been replaced in the slugging match for the town by the more mobile mechanized troops was that the paras had been used up.

Of course, Bentley's own men had been pretty much used up as well. Out of nearly five hundred men available for duty at the start of the fighting in his battalion, there remained less than three hundred on the firing line, and most of those had one or more light wounds, wounds that would have seen them in a field hospital at any other time but now only rated a few minutes with a medic, a quick bandage, and a quick cup of coffee before returning to the fight. But there did seem to be fewer Germans now whenever they attacked, and almost no artillery support for them either, just their own mortars firing from close range. And, just before the first waves of bombers had come in after daybreak, Bentley had heard the distinct thud of artillery firing off to the south, not too far away. He couldn't tell whether they were German or American guns, but the cannonade implied a battle, and, when the Americans had arrived at Le Puy, General Maxwell Taylor had made sure that each soldier understood that there were no other Allied troops on hand between them and the coast. Well, there was someone out there now, so maybe help was on the way.

0600 Hours, 1 April 1943
North of St. Etienne, France

From the depths of despair, General Pierre Koenig had returned to the euphoria he had experienced when he first set foot on French soil in Corsica in December. For days, he had believed there to be a distinct possibility that the Allies would be hurled back into the sea, and he had vowed privately not to go with them. He would take to the hills with his men until the Germans were defeated or until he was hunted down and killed, but he would not endure exile again. He had long since grown accustomed to using a pseudonym to protect his family, still living, he hoped, somewhere in occupied France, but he resented the defeat that had made this necessary. Now, at last, he felt that he was within striking distance of ending the nightmare his country had lived through for nearly three long years.

The first of the British reinforcements had begun to arrive at the front, enabling the Canadian I Corps to take over the rest of the front east of the Rhone. Koenig had left a single division facing the half of Lyon that lay on the west bank of the Rhone, to take part in the liberation of France's second city if that should become possible, but he had concentrated the rest of his own corps, heavily reinforced, north of St. Etienne for the first major French offensive of the war. The Canadian 5th Armored Division, reinforced with two armored and two artillery brigades and an engineer brigade, would force a crossing of the Loire near St. Etienne and drive northwest toward Thiers to link up with Patton's forces that were already approaching Chamalières, about seventy miles to the west, cutting off the German salient. That had been the ultimate goal of the Allied counteroffensive, and French forces were to have played a key role in that maneuver until Koenig and Juin had "pitched" General Marshall with a new proposal just twenty-four hours ago.

The Allied air offensive had been so successful, both in crippling German front line units and in retarding the movement of their reinforcements, that there was no longer any threat to the lodgment. More precisely, all Rommel's efforts now appeared to be directed at the saving of his precious armored units, still strung out around the fringes of the "bulge," tens of miles into Allied territory and in imminent danger of being surrounded and destroyed. An achievement of that magnitude had originally been even more than the beleaguered Allied command might have hoped for in the early days of the German offensive, but it had occurred to Koenig that the moment for audacity had arrived.

He had made little effort to conceal from the Germans that he could, and soon would, put a bridge across the Loire well north of Le Puy, where the SS Panzer Corps was already trying to disentangle itself from the defenses. With the German 2nd Parachute Division firmly dug in at Lyon itself, most of the other available German reserves had been pulled into the area between the Loire and the American front line running between Ussel and Murat in the west, hoping to hold back both the American and French jaws that were expected to snap shut on the over-extended armored troops in the "bulge." Covering the thirty-mile gap between the Rhone and the Loire, however, Koenig's advance troops were only detecting the single Hermann Göring Division and the scraps of some decimated infantry units. And behind that line, between it and the outskirts of Paris, there was, *nothing!* There were no mountains and no major rivers to cross, and almost nothing by way of German units.

It was a good three hundred miles from the current lines to Paris by road, obviously too far to make in a single leap, and the Allies had too few units to secure the flanks of an advance that ambitious; but a determined thrust through that gap, paralleling the course of the Loire northward until the great river began its westward bend, would unhinge the entire German defense in France. From a position that advanced, the Allies would have the choice to turn east through Dijon toward Germany itself or continue toward the French capital. The German forces that survived their own failed offensive would be too weak to counterattack, and all of Germany's resources would have to be directed toward helping them escape, in the face of the relentless Allied air campaign that made every rail or road trip by Axis units an odyssey. They would have to abandon everything south of Dijon and west of Paris, if not all of France, or risk having their units cut up and defeated in detail.

Koenig did not have an innumerable host on hand for such an undertaking, but he believed that he had enough. The French 1st Armored Division had just joined the 2nd Armored, having been relieved of its role as a blocking force near Mende by the American 6th Armored. He also had the 3rd Algerian and 4th Moroccan Divisions, very experienced and fully motorized along American lines, nearly 80,000 men and over six hundred tanks, including various supporting units. He even had a Para Commando Regiment available to drop ahead of his columns as the Germans had been so handy at doing earlier in the war.

He kept reminding himself that he did not have, and did not need to have, the force necessary to reconquer the capital himself, not yet, but the vision burned itself into his mind. All he needed to do was make a breach in the dam, and the rest would take care of itself. They would call for a full uprising of the FFI throughout occupied France, and the British and Americans had been dropping thousands of weapons and tons of demolition gear for months, and the Germans would not be able to contain them. By the next day, he would have his men in position, and he would strike his blow. The Germans had made him take a false name, but it would be a name that would live forever in French history.

2000 Hours, 1 April 1943
Near Montbrison, France

Major Edward Bull-Francis, now commanding the 1st Canadian Reece Regiment attached to the 5th Armored Division, focused his attention on the shielded flashlights of the military policeman that guided the driver of his Greyhound armored car as it rolled down the steep embankment to the Bailey bridge over the Loire. It was full dark now, but the western horizon still glowed red from the fires in the town of Montbrison set by the Allied bombing late that afternoon, and he could still see the muzzle flashes of rifles and machine guns in a rough arc all around the landing site. The infantry had crossed over before nightfall behind a heavy artillery barrage and had only managed to push the Germans back a few hundred yards. They would need armor to make any more progress, and Bull-France's battalion was the first unit to be thrown into the breach.

They had to advance cautiously as the floating bridge swayed under the pressure of the stream, while engineer motor boats nosed up against its downstream side, straining their engines to keep it in place. A column of infantry trotted gingerly along one side of the bridge, stooped under heavy packs as more men were fed into the battle. Bull-France felt a little embarrassed as he hunched low in his armored turret, knowing that the poor infantrymen had no cover whatsoever, and several times during the crossing he heard the distinct ping of rounds caroming off the sides of his vehicle.

As soon as the front wheels touched solid ground, the driver gunned the engine and steered through a shallow cut in the far bank that had been cut by the engineers and marked with luminescent tape. He paused at a tree line beyond the bank just long enough for the other vehicles of his lead company to come up on line, and then they simply charged forward toward the burning town. Bull-France turned and saw a line of dark forms of infantrymen rise up and come pounding after them, at least hoping to get the benefit of the cover of the bodies of the armored cars for part of the run across the open field, even if a battery of 88s might knock them all out in a matter of seconds.

Every gun on every vehicle was firing wildly at the flashes coming from the edge of town and several stone farmhouses on either side of it. There was no hope for surprise, cover, or concealment. Only speed and the distraction that their own firing might provide could get them across the killing zone and, hopefully, buy time for the tank company following hard on their heels. Bull-France didn't much like the idea of being used as bait, but since the German guns could take apart a Sherman just as easily as an armored car, and since one hulking silhouette looked pretty much like another in the dark, the divisional commander had hoped that, if there were serious anti tank defenses before the town, they would "waste" their time blowing up Bull-France's force and give away their positions in the bargain, allowing the tanks to have a decent chance of breaking through. Bull-France had been a soldier long enough not to be able to argue with the logic.

But only two or three of his vehicles were stopped, and those apparently by mines scattered hurriedly by the enemy, mines they probably would have spotted easily in daylight, and the rest of the 1st Squadron bowled past a rickety barricade of loose railroad ties that blocked a dirt farm road leading into the town. Bull-France had not seen the flash of anything heavier than a few panzerfausts, and those had been fired too early, probably by nervous new recruits, causing little, if any, damage. Even buttoned up, he could see Germans dodging up the streets, trying to avoid both the onrushing Canadians and the bright orange flames that erupted from the windows of almost every building in town. He sprayed long bursts of machine-gun fire after them, sweeping his turret from side to side, and he wondered in passing whether there had been many civilians still in the town when the Allied bombers struck.

0600 Hours, 2 April 1943
Vichy, France

General Gause didn't care much for the town. It had an air of defeat about it, but Clermont-Ferrand had become untenable as a command center once Patton's artillery came within range the day before. Even after several Allied bomber raids, Gause had insisted on remaining in the old command post in the hope that Rommel would return soon. The last that had been heard from the Field Marshal had been late on the afternoon of 31 March after he had personally led a counterattack by the 15th Panzer and the remnants of the 90th Panzer Grenadier Divisions against the American 29th Division that had nearly resulted in the recapture of the town of Murat. At that time Rommel had been on the way back to Clermont, a trip that shouldn't have taken more than a few hours, once it had gotten dark. Gause only hoped that Rommel had waited until it had gotten dark before risking the road.

In the meanwhile, everything was coming undone, but in slow motion. Dietrich's panzers had done a masterful job pulling back from beyond the American bastion of Le Puy, although their columns had been badly mauled by enemy air attacks. The rest of the Afrika Korps had also broken contact with the French near Mende and were leap frogging back toward St. Flour at a good pace. But the 26th Panzer, which had been withdrawn from the Lyon front to launch a spoiling attack against the American armored thrust coming from Ussel, had spent two full days on what should have been a rail trip of just over one hundred miles, perhaps four hours, and only some fifty of an original force of two hundred tanks had survived to detrain at Chamalières, thirty miles farther to the east, since the Americans had long since overrun the original staging area.

Now the Canadians had crossed the Loire and taken Montbrison. Fortunately, Dietrich's troops were already almost that far north and had slipped across the Allier River to Brioude well to the west, leaving a screen of bedraggled infantry regiments to slow the Canadians' progress. But there still remained at least 100,000 of Germany's best armored troops west of the Allier and south of Clermont, with only a gap of perhaps twenty miles between Patton's spearhead near Chamalières and the river. A steady stream of men and vehicles had funneled through the gap during the night, but it was almost daylight, and the enemy bombers would be out in force. Or, if the Canadians put on a sudden burst of speed, they could close up on the east bank of the Allier and cover the gap with their artillery. In either event, the cream of Army Group B would be destroyed, and there would be little hope of forming a viable defensive line this side of the German border. Rommel would know what to do. Where was he?

Just as Gause thought this, an aide came rushing into the former casino where he had set up army headquarters because of the many phone lines running into the building. The young lieutenant's face was a pasty white, and his breath came in gasps.

"General," he panted, "Field Marshal Rommel has just been brought into the mobile field hospital."

"What happened?" Gause screamed, oblivious to the panic that had crept into his voice or the worried looks this caused among the staff.

"His command car was strafed by a *Jabo* this afternoon, sir. He was only just discovered. He is alive but has lost a great deal of blood and may lose his arm. The doctor sent me over to tell you and to say that the Field Marshal will not be fit for duty for weeks, if he lives at all."

Gause's shoulders slumped and he fell heavily into a gilded chair with frayed upholstery. Now what? he thought.

1200 HOURS, 3 APRIL 1943
CLERMONT-FERRAND, FRANCE

Patton strolled about the underground bunker that Rommel had used as his headquarters. The military intelligence people had already been through, gleaning every scrap of paper that might have some value for the analysts, but there were plenty of touches that helped give Patton a flavor of his opponent. He often felt that he could communicate across the field of battle with Rommel, like spirits thinking like thoughts. But it was cold comfort to be served wine from Rommel's own cellar with his lunch, knowing that most of Rommel's army had escaped his grasp.

The "Clermont Gap" debate raged for years after the war, but it was largely the product of a combination of fortuitous events, the tactical skill of the Germans, and one conscious, calculated risk taken by the Allied command. The clear skies that had bedeviled the Germans for days gave way to a heavy downpour on the morning of the 2nd of April. This served both to slow the Allied advance and, of course, to eliminate the advantage of airpower they had enjoyed. The Germans, taking full benefit of this respite, piled their units onto the roads, ignoring any pretense at march security or unit spacing and rushed them through the gap in their thousands. While both the Canadians and American armor had been criticized for not pressing home the attack, their progress to date had had a great deal to do with the availability of the Air Corps' "flying artillery" to blast the defenders out of each succeeding position. It should also be remembered that both arms of the pincers had advanced at a prodigious rate of 20-30 miles per day against stiff resistance. The troops were exhausted, the vehicles in bad need of maintenance, and supplies of fuel and ammunition had not been able to keep up with the spearheads.

The conscious decision was that of using the French for their own offensive to the north rather than for helping to close the trap on the Germans. However, had this not been the case, it is unlikely that the front east of the Rhone would have been left quite as bare as it was, and the French would probably have committed only marginally more troops to the drive west, with probably comparable results.

It should also be noted that, from a position where the defeat of the entire Allied effort in France had appeared in imminent jeopardy of destruction, the combined efforts of four Allied armies had procured a stunning victory. In the space of only a few months, the Americans had progressed from the status of untried rookies to a fearsome fighting force. Arguably, the individual German soldier never did meet his match in the war, and much of the German equipment was markedly superior to that of the Allies, but numbers will tell. Also, the Allies had made up in strategic concept what they may have lacked on the tactical level.

CHAPTER 8
TRIUMPHANT RETURN

E VEN BEFORE THE last of the German troops slipped north
through the Clermont Gap, Marshall had ordered a general
advance all along the Allied line. The German Army in the West
had been decimated by the previous weeks of combat, and no less than forty
thousand men taken prisoner and another twenty thousand killed in the
"bulge" alone, to say nothing of the massive losses in weapons and materiel.
The Polish and American troops in western France began a rapid advance
along a broad front, meeting only indifferent resistance from the thinly spread
German infantry divisions, starved of reinforcements and support by the
demands of the frantic German efforts to rescue their forces in the "bulge."
In Italy, Montgomery had finally begun his "big push" with simultaneous
thrusts from his lodgment at Civitavecchia and over the Alps from France
and with landings at Salerno by British troops and at the toe of Italy by over
60,000 newly allied Italian troops. The German high command obviously saw
their only chance of holding onto Kesselring's fortified line across the Apennines in north central Italy was to keep the British V Corps out of the North
Italian plain, and they quickly abandoned everything south of the British
lodgment and devoted their strained resources to holding onto the shoulders
of the Alps.

In short order, Allied troops in France were measuring their progress in
tens of miles per day. Even the battle-weary forces that had participated in
the reduction of the "bulge" had been given barely twenty-four hours to rest

and replenish their supplies before they too were turned northward by a Patton still hungry for his fleeing prey. Along the coast the Poles had liberated La Rochelle and the Americans had Bourges, and both armies had crossed the Loire, with the Poles turning west to clear the Brittany peninsula, and the Americans driving on Orleans. The Canadians, now under Montgomery's overall command per the agreement with Marshall, had taken Dijon and a British corps was sweeping along the Swiss border toward Germany itself. But it was in the French sector that the most dramatic advances had taken place.

Koenig's two North African divisions had broken through the thin crust of the Hermann Göring Division, and his two armored divisions then rushed northward, taking Roanne while the Germans were still evacuating the "bulge." Within three days they had overrun Autun, eighty miles to the northeast, and a week later they had reached Auxerre, then cut eastward to cross the upper Seine at Troyes. From this point there only remained barely one hundred miles to the outskirts of Paris, and no major rivers left to cross. They had outflanked any line the Germans might have intended to form along the Loire or Seine. In the last hundred miles Koenig's vanguard had not encountered resistance from the Germans on more than a company level, and then only when a bottleneck in the transportation system had caused a delay in their evacuation. Aerial reconnaissance showed that every German unit that could was moving by train, canal, or road back to Germany or Belgium with no indication of attempting to make a stand this side of the French frontier.

But now Koenig faced two intertwined problems. The first was that his little army had overextended itself. He had dropped off his infantry divisions haphazardly to cover his right flank, in case the Germans should be able to mount a counterstroke from their homeland. Even these troops were too spread out to be able to do more than act as a tripwire in the face of a serious assault, and now they were used up. To advance any farther, his two armored divisions would have to simply ignore their flanks and rear, and there were still tens of thousands of armed Germans swarming over northern France, still in organized units, still capable of doing considerable damage if the German command could get a handle on the situation. Moreover, the French had outrun their supplies, relying primarily on captured German fuel stocks for days, and all the heavily motorized Allied units were burning gasoline at a prodigious rate, all clamoring for supplies from a logistical system that was stretched to the breaking point.

That would not have made much difference if Koenig had been in a position to consolidate his position, to hold where he was and allow the Americans and Canadians to come up to his mark and let his men rest and his vehicles receive supplies and maintenance. But Koenig did not have that luxury. In response to the desperate call of General de Gaulle in the dark days of the German offensive in the Massif, thousands of Frenchmen in the occupied zone had taken up arms and attacked the Germans in any way they could. They had been as effective as the Allied bombing campaign in crippling the German efforts at reinforcing their front line, more so during the long stretch of bad weather, and they had paid a heavy price as frustrated German troops took brutal reprisals in dozens of towns and cities. That had been expected, but the speed of the Allied advance and the apparent dissolution of the Wehrmacht, at least in the eyes of the French citizenry, had prompted a full scale uprising in Paris itself. For two days the French command had been receiving reports that large sections of the city had actually been seized by armed partisans, that the police had gone over to the rebels, and that the freedom fighters were frantically calling for help.

The calls became more and more desperate because the German Army had not disintegrated. Paris, both for its political and strategic importance as the center of French communications and industry, was still garrisoned by two full infantry divisions, veterans of the Eastern Front, supported by SS police units, the Gestapo, and detachments of the pro-Nazi French *milice*. Because of its rail net, Paris was also the avenue of evacuation for most of the German combat units still working their way home from western France. The forces of the FFI, on the other hand, numbered no more than a few thousand men and women, armed with a hodge-podge of rifles, submachine guns, and pistols. In an open fight, it would only take the Germans a matter of a day or two to annihilate all resistance, and probably much of the civilian population in the process, to say nothing of the physical damage that would be done to the beautiful city.

Koenig would have been even more anxious had he known of the very specific orders that had been issued directly by Hitler to General Heinrich von Stulpnagel, commander of the Paris garrison. Hitler had ordered that, rather than let the city of light fall into the hands of the Allies, every bridge, every public building, every monument, should be wired for demolition and destroyed when the fall of the city appeared imminent. To make it more clear, he had explained that he wanted future archeologists to debate on which side of the Seine Paris had been located. Special engineer units had been dispatched, along with tons of explosives, to accomplish this task, and they had been hard at work since the collapse of Rommel's offensive in the south.

It was with this background that Koenig was obliged to make his decision. The Americans had offered all the logistical support available, even to denying it to their own units. The Germans had thoroughly sabotaged all of the ports along the Atlantic and Channel coasts, so, even though small amounts of supplies could now be landed over the beaches for the westernmost Allied units, the bulk of the fuel and ammunition needed by the advancing armies still came up from Marseille and the other Mediterranean ports over a road and rail system devastated by months of intense combat and the most concentrated air offensive in history. Funneling supplies to Koenig's vanguard would thus only exacerbate its exposed position as the other units fell behind. The Americans, therefore, urged caution.

Koenig was grateful that Giraud, who had largely been marginalized since the landings, had made the mistake of offering his resignation in a huff over some minor point of protocol, and de Gaulle had quickly accepted it. It was with some anticipation, therefore, that the general awaited the arrival of de Gaulle's aircraft at the former Luftwaffe field outside of Troyes.

The two men who had fought side by side in the wilderness greeted each other warmly, and Koenig could not help but feel a certain stiffness on the part of General Juin, the former Vichy commander. Still, they had all worked together well over these past months, and the euphoria brought by the liberation of more than half their homeland had gone a long way toward smoothing over old rifts. Colonel Henri Navarre, the representative of military intelligence and Julien Leclerc, commander of the 2nd Armored Division, were also present at the meeting, which, in the interest of time, was held in the hall of the tiny airfield control tower.

Koenig described the tactical situation using a large map of northern France, and Juin announced that the British had informed him that they were planning another landing, this time on the Belgian or Dutch coast, probably during May or early June. For the purposes of this meeting, however, that would be far too late to be of significance. Navarre provided the latest reports from the resistance movement in Paris of fighting in the industrial belt around the city, long a hotbed of Communist labor unions, but of relative calm throughout most of the city. He then launched into a bizarre story of the work of a minor diplomat, the Swedish *Chargé d'affaires,* Raoul Nordling, who was conducting a one-man peace offensive, strictly on his own authority as a long-time resident and lover of the city of Paris. He had been engaged in intensive negotiations between various resistance leaders—some of whom did not necessarily recognize de Gaulle's government as supreme authority in the land—and Navarre and General von Stulpnagel for a peaceful surrender of the city.

Nordling reported that he was convinced that von Stulpnagel, far from being a confirmed Nazi, was opposed to Hitler's regime and eager to seek a negotiated settlement of the war, at least with the Western Allies. Nordling had apparently convinced the German that the wanton destruction of this symbol of Western civilization would be an act of such magnitude that Germany would become a pariah, not just to the French, but to the entire world. He said that von Stulpnagel had darkly hinted that Hitler had committed acts, and planned others, that would make the demolition of a single city pale by comparison, but Nordling had assumed that this was some kind of hyperbole.

In any event, von Stulpnagel's only real concern, as a professional soldier, was the safe passage through Paris of thousands of escaping German troops. Since France's rail net was arranged like a giant spider's web radiating from Paris, it would be virtually impossible to evacuate those German forces still west of the city without the free use of that rail net. Secondly, von Stulpnagel had explained that, in the interests of his own personal safety and that of his family, he could only consider surrendering Paris to a major military force, not to the handful of partisans now in the streets, but to a ground combat unit conceivably capable of taking the city by assault. Nordling had added that it was his firm belief that von Stulpnagel had essentially promised to do just that, *if* such a force could present itself before the city.

Nordling had arranged a tenuous truce in which the rebels were left largely unchallenged in the buildings and *arrondissements* of the city that they controlled, as were the Germans, and clearly marked supply trucks were allowed to pass unmolested. The trains continued to run, with French railwaymen shuttling the fleeing German troops eastward through the city, and the hospitals were sanctuaries where the wounded of both sides were treated. Since neither Stulpnagel nor the leaders of the resistance had absolute control over their armed men, occasional firefights would break out, but they remained localized and of short duration. Both sides were gingerly maneuvering for advantageous positions, but generally doing so in such a way as to avoid open confrontation with their opponents.

That was the crux of the matter. Was Nordling indulging in wishful thinking? Was Stulpnagel, an enemy general, to be trusted? The only way to test their word would be to place a unit at the gates of Paris, probably cut off from all support. If either man turned out to be worth less than his word, that unit could easily be sacrificed to no purpose.

All eyes turned to Leclerc, and he straightened, raising his chin. "Another Henri of Navarre, Henri IV, once said that Paris was worth a Mass. I would say that it is worth a division." He shrugged, sticking out his lower lip and letting out a puff of air in the typical French expression of resignation.

0400 Hours, 23 April 1943
Over the Bois de Boulogne, France

Lieutenant Jean Marie Chaval leaned back against the ribbed fuselage of the heavy Horsa glider and raised his feet off the floor, although he doubted that this would help if the aircraft plowed directly into a tree or a bridge abutment. Only the dull red glow of the instrument panel of the pilots showed in the pitch darkness of the cargo bay, but he could sense the nervousness and tension among the thirty commandos of his platoon. He felt the nose of the aircraft dip, then rise slightly, then dip again, and he knew they were rushing earthward since the C-47 had loosed its tow line, and there was nothing for it now but to pray for a soft landing. There was no going back.

Not that Chaval wanted to go back. He and the other two thousand commandos of the 1st and 2nd *Choc* Brigades would be the first uniformed troops of a free France to enter the capital, and the honor was almost more than any of them could bear. Chaval was a *pied noir*, a Frenchman born in Algeria, who had been serving in the marines when the Allies had arrived and had readily volunteered for the new commando units that the British had offered to train. At only twenty, he had been too young to have been in the service in 1940, and this would be his first experience of combat. He was terrified, and the only thing that kept him focused was the firm conviction that, as one of the first warriors of the liberation of Paris, he would not be a virgin much longer, in any sense of the word.

There was a sudden jolt, and Chaval's forehead slammed forward painfully on his upraised knees. Then, still in the dark, there was a mad scramble of helmets, elbows, and flying feet as the men poured out of the rear of the aircraft. They were in one of the grassy fields of the Bois de Boulogne on the western fringe of Paris, and the area had been marked by huge bonfires around its perimeter. As he and his men dog trotted toward the trees, he could see a huge shadow detaching itself from the surrounding darkness and hear a hoarse roar as they were engulfed by a wave of cheering Parisians.

They were mostly women, children, and older men, and, while they had been yelling loudly enough to begin with, Chaval thought his eardrums would burst when they recognized the French flag on the shoulder patches of the commandos. Chaval made a feeble effort to call to his men to form up and look for the company commander, but it was useless. He actually began to fear being torn limb from limb as he and his men were carried bodily into the woods.

Chaval was concerned that his unit actually had a military mission to perform. The 2nd *Choc* was to capture the *mairie* of Neuilly, the western suburb of Paris, and then begin a drive straight down the *Champs Elysées* toward the *Arc de Triomphe,* the *Place de la Concorde,* the Tuilleries, and the *Hotel de Ville*. At the other end of town, the 1st *Choc* would be landing by glider in the Bois de Vincennes opening the way for the ground column that, hopefully, would be roaring up to the city gates at any moment. But, for the moment, that would have to wait. Chaval was put back on his feet, and a young woman immediately wrapped herself around him, arms, legs, and all, plastering her lips against his. Oh well, perhaps best to deal with the loss of one sort of virginity at a time.

0600 Hours, 23 April 1943
Melun, France

By any reckoning, the advance of Leclerc's 2nd Armored Division over the past sixty hours had been historic. They had covered over ninety miles and fought a more or less constant running battle against the scattered but still undefeated Germans. They had killed hundreds of the enemy, destroyed dozens of vehicles, and taken nearly three thousand prisoners, usually pausing only long enough to disarm them and turn them over to whatever handful of local residents they could find willing to stand guard. They had been given virtually all of the fuel available to the entire French Army at the front, and more had been airdropped to them yesterday, and now they were running on fumes still a good ten miles from the center of Paris. It seemed that Patton, while lending some support to the French drive, had harbored a fierce desire of his own for there to be an American hand in the liberation of Paris, and the 1st Armored Division from his own Fifth Army was also driving on the city from the southwest. Needless to say, it did not appear that the Americans were suffering from as acute a shortage of supplies as the French.

Leclerc was faced with the disagreeable possibility of having to leave part of his division behind in order to have enough fuel for the remainder to reach the city. The problem with that scenario was that even a single division might not be what the German von Stulpnagel considered "sufficient" force for him to be justified in evacuating Paris under *force majeur*. The arrival of a single tank regiment might merely provoke him into carrying out Hitler's plans for the destruction of the city without Leclerc having enough strength on hand to stop him. Even the insertion of two commando brigades ahead of his column, an idea suggested by de Gaulle at the last minute which cut a few hours off the French arrival time and added some much-needed infantry support, was really a minimal force for a city the size of Paris.

Leclerc was sitting on the hood of his jeep by the side of the road, pondering this dilemma when the captain of a recon company presented himself, saluted, and asked permission to consult with the general over a prisoner. Leclerc hardly had the time or patience now to discuss prisoners, an issue of no importance, but he raised his head and found an elderly German officer, a colonel by his insignia, under the guard of two troopers, standing at stiff attention. The German saluted and clicked his heels.

"He insists on surrendering only to the senior officer present, sir," the captain explained.

"Well, now he's done so," Leclerc growled. "Toss him in the schoolyard with the others. I've got other things on my mind."

"But he insists on your signature, sir," the captain persisted.

"My signature on what?" Leclerc snapped, losing patience.

"He seems to be custodian for a supply dump of 120,000 gallons of fuel, and he wants to make certain that he's not accused later of having sold it on the black market." The captain smiled.

0900 HOURS, 25 APRIL 1943
PARIS, FRANCE

By late morning on the 23rd the truce was breaking down fast. The Communist FTP units had only observed it grudgingly in any event. There was no central command for all the forces of the resistance for Paris, even though

Jean Moulin had arrived in the city several days before to attempt to coordinate the negotiations with Nordling and von Stulpnagel on de Gaulle's behalf. There was also a lack of command and control on the German side, with rabid SS units aggressively attacking positions held by the French and the even more rabid pro-Axis *milice*, knowing what their fate would be if and when the Germans departed, conducting a brutal extermination campaign while they still had the support of the Wehrmacht.

The Germans held most of the heart of the city, centered on the *Place de la Concorde* where Stulpnagel's headquarters were located, as well as *the Palais de Luxembourg* on the left bank and the large train stations, the *Gare du Nord, Orlean,* and *Lyon.* The French held most of the industrial suburbs, and the area immediately around the *Ile de la Cité* in the center of the city. The flow of retreating German troops had turned into a trickle now, and those few who remained west of the city were primarily being routed northward along the coast. But von Stulpnagel still had about 20,000 men under his command between two understrength infantry divisions, some Luftwaffe troops manning anti-aircraft defenses, SS police units, and headquarters troops. There were also upwards of 15,000 German wounded in Paris area hospitals that had yet to be evacuated to the Reich. The French had dismantled the demolitions equipment on many of the bridges, public buildings, and monuments throughout the city, but if the Germans were to detonate the devices they still controlled, the devastation would be tremendous.

Nordling, a comfortable, bourgeois sort of man, not fitted by physique or temperament for the frantic shuttling about an embattled city between resistance leaders, the Germans, and now the advance command posts of the Allies, was finally able to work out a simple, yet machiavellian formula for the surrender of the city. The German forces in von Stulpnagel's command were divided into three categories: the defenseless or harmless, such as the wounded or unarmed headquarters troops; the fanatics, like the SS; and the professionally competent regular troops. The first and second categories would be immediately evacuated from the city by all means available, along certain designated routes, and these evacuations would not be interfered with by the French. The final category, troops who still maintained their organizational discipline and could be relied upon to follow orders, of which there were relatively few left, would continue to fight for a few key points in the city, both to provide time for the evacuation and to give the illusion of greater resistance for the distant observers in OKH.

Against all hope, this arrangement worked reasonably well. With the assistance of French railwaymen, all of the German wounded who could be moved were entrained and sent off to the east, while the posting of the most zealous units to supposedly higher priority assignments closer to the German frontier avoided the creation of any diehard pockets that might have resisted to the last and destroyed part of the city along with themselves. All of this was accomplished by dawn on the 24th, with the equivalent of one German division making a series of timed withdrawals northward through the city as Leclerc's troops arrived, almost without bloodshed. The Germans, it turned out, had little problem with leaving Laval's collaborationist followers to their fate. There were some summary executions around the city, and the symbolic shaving of the heads of some women accused of "fraternization" with the occupying forces, but Leclerc's soldiers and the French commandos were able to avoid most excesses and establish order quickly. In fact, the only party wholly dissatisfied with the solution was Patton, whose vanguard only reached the neighborhood of Versailles, still some miles from the city, when the last of the German forces withdrew and the city was declared liberated.

A series of messages flew back and forth between Washington, London, and Lyon, where Marshall had established his new headquarters, about timing for the "formal" liberation of Paris and provisions for the new French government. However, these messages ended up having no basis in reality as the French occupation of the city had taken authority out of the hands of the other Allies. De Gaulle disembarked from a C-47 at Le Bourget airfield on the morning of the 25th, and, in a motorcade accompanied by Juin, Koenig, Leclerc, Moulin, and a host of pre-war French political leaders improvised a parade of victory. The column was obliged to circle the city from the north in order to enter from the west and have the procession advance along the length of the Champs Elysees, past the Hotel de Ville, to where a *te deum* would be sung at Notre Dame cathedral.

The parade formed up on the avenue just west of the Arc de Triomphe, and, along with some of Leclerc's tanks, companies of commandos, and small detachments of colorful Foreign Legionnaires and North African spahis, the French were gracious enough to invite Patton to participate along with a contingent of American troops. Virtually the entire population of the city turned out to line the avenue and crowd the *place* in front of the cathedral. Some of de Gaulle's advisors counseled against the ceremony, since collaborationist forces were still loose within the city, and snipers could be lurking anywhere along the miles-long parade route, but de Gaulle ignored them. In fact, small arms fire could occasionally be heard near at hand over the cheering of the crowd, but no overt acts of violence occurred to mar the day. De Gaulle had seen his visibly taking possession of the city, on his own, without the support of—even in defiance of—the other Allies as an important step in the reestablishment of the French state. In addition, the drama of his gesture virtually ensured his own dominance of the French political scene, although, by this time there were few serious competitors left in the field.

CHAPTER 9
COUP

I N THE MONTH or so following the liberation of Paris, something like a lull occurred on the Western Front. Allied armies continued to advance at a prodigious rate for some time in the north, up to the prepared German defenses of the Siegfried Line along the old Franco-German border and to a new line established by the Germans running from Antwerp southeast along the Belgian-Dutch border to join that line near the Ardennes. The meticulous sabotage of all French ports on the Atlantic and Channel coasts continued to hinder Allied logistical efforts, and bitter German resistance at Antwerp kept the largest port in northern Europe out of Allied hands, making it necessary for the Allies to pause for the reorganization, reinforcement, and resupply of their armies before plunging on into the Reich. In Italy, British troops had captured Turin, and a combined Anglo Italian army battered at Kesselring's line in the Appennines, but everything south of Florence was now in Allied hands. On the air front, no corner of the shrinking German empire was now out of range of Allied bombers with fighter escorts, and the Luftwaffe had been virtually swept from the sky. What air forces remained to the Germans were limited to defensive fighters, hopelessly outnumbered, and only marginally effective in blunting the hammer blows of the bomber fleets on German cities.

The fast pace of the war made it clear to all parties that another major political military conference was called for, and, with Allied armies now on the borders of the Reich in the west, it was increasingly evident that Stalin would need to be included in any such talks. It was obvious that a new summit meeting would not have as its primary agenda the strictly military issue of how to defeat the Germans, since their ultimate defeat was now virtually a foregone conclusion, but of the shape of the new Europe that would emerge from the ashes of the war. Although there was a certain desire among the Western Allies, notably Churchill, to exclude the Russians from such planning, especially since the Red Army was still well within its own borders, Roosevelt and de Gaulle convinced him that any agreement reached without Soviet participation would be moot when the Russians did come boiling into Eastern Europe, and the mere fact that talks had been held without them might sour East-West relations for years.

The Soviet leader's paranoid fear of travelling outside his own empire, however, complicated matters, while the alternative of travel to Moscow was still dangerous and time-consuming, to say nothing of uncomfortable, for a man in Roosevelt's condition. It was finally agreed that Teheran would be the meeting place since Iran had been jointly occupied by the British and Russians the previous year, giving Persia something of the air of neutral ground. It would still be an arduous journey for Roosevelt but would eliminate several days of travel from a Washington-to-Moscow trip. Facilities for meetings at this level were not exactly abundant in Teheran during this period, and the security officers of all of the delegations must have aged visibly as they attempted to ensure the safety of the participants in what was essentially a Wild West town, capital of a country that had been conquered by armed force only months before. With Axis agents known to be swarming throughout the region, the potential for a major disaster was always present.

The conference had originally been planned for late May, but a major German offensive on the Eastern Front, an attempt to destroy the Russian salient at Kursk through a pincer movement by Army Groups Center and South, had caused a postponement. This had been the largest German offensive in the East since Stalingrad, and Stalin had been leery of going into a conference when word of a significant defeat for his armies might arrive. The Red Army had had little trouble dealing a crushing blow to the Germans, however, since much of the German armor had been siphoned off for Rommel's ill-fated assault in France, and the concentration of Luftwaffe resources on protecting the Reich had given the Red Air Force superiority for the first time in the war. The German armies were now reeling back toward the 1939 borders, and Stalin felt he could deal from a position of strength.

Allied victories in the European Theatre had also benefited their efforts in the war against Japan. All of the Commonwealth's Australian and New Zealand troops had been shifted from the Mediterranean to the Pacific, and a substantial portion of the Indian Army as well. The addition of the French, and more recently the Italian, fleets to the Allied armory, along with their merchant marines, had freed more shipping for the Allied forces in the Indian Ocean and the Pacific as well. General MacArthur's campaign in New Guinea had been thoroughly successful, driving the Japanese back and eliminating the last serious threat to current Allied territory. Japan would remain on the strategic defensive for the remainder of the war, merely awaiting Allied pleasure to divert sufficient strength from the battle against Germany to crush the island empire once and for all.

Despite the Allies' favorable strategic position, or perhaps precisely because of it, the conference promised to present a political minefield for all parties. The preceding April the Germans had sprung a surprise on the West by inviting teams of the International Red Cross to investigate mass graves discovered near the town of Katyn in eastern Poland. While mass graves were hardly a novelty in either Germany or the Soviet Union in these days, the Germans called attention to these because the interred happened to be several thousand, possibly as many as ten thousand, Polish Army officers, most with their hands tied behind their backs and a single gunshot wound to the back of the head. The number roughly corresponded to the number of Polish officers captured by the Red Army during its seizure of eastern Poland in 1939.

At first the West gave this report no more credence than some of the other "big lies" generated by Goebbels' propaganda machine, but evidence from unimpeachable sources soon accumulated. It should be remembered that, at this time, names like Auschwitz, Treblinka, and Dachau had no meaning in the West, and even the extent of Stalin's own purges of the 1930s and his willful starvation of millions of Ukrainian peasants remained in the realm of vague and hardly creditable rumor. News of such a slaughter, therefore, landed like a bombshell in the West, particularly in London. Britain had entered the war originally in defense of Poland, and the Polish government-in-exile was housed there. A full corps of Polish troops, grown to three infantry divisions, an armored division, and a parachute brigade, were now in strategic reserve, having participated in clearing the Germans out of the western half of France. With Soviet armies now poised to invade the former territory of Poland, this evidence of Stalin's treatment of the Poles was highly significant.

Without getting into details of the Teheran Conference that would better be left for a history of the diplomatic aspects of the war, the discussions laid the groundwork for the subsequent military campaigns. Stalin was eager to create a sphere of influence for the Soviet Union in Eastern Europe, and there was little doubt that, under Soviet tutelage, only Communist-dominated governments would be allowed to survive there, providing Russia with a buffer of friendly states for protection against a West that Stalin had little cause to trust after Munich. However, despite the recent victories of the Red Army, the battle line was still well within Russia's 1939 boundaries, while those of the Western Allies were poised to carry the war into German territory. Roosevelt and Churchill were thus in a position to deny Stalin a specified "occupation zone" in Germany.

In fact, Stalin felt his political position deteriorating hourly as he attempted to take a hard stance against the West. Officials of both the Romanian and Hungarian governments had been known to have sent peace feelers, not to Moscow, but to the West. Even Tito, the diehard Communist partisan in Yugoslavia, was now receiving the bulk of his military support in arms shipments across the Adriatic from British-occupied Italy and even direct air support from British and American bombers, whereas Stalin could only offer political commissars skilled in purging Tito's own military of anyone suspected of harboring anti Russian sentiments. Tito, more a pragmatist than a Communist after all, was visibly drifting into the Western orbit.

Churchill thus discounted Stalin's unilateral offer to carve up Eastern Europe into spheres of influence on a kind of percentage basis. As much as the concept appealed to Churchill with his penchant for balance of power politics, the odds were simply too good that all of the minor Axis powers would desert the Reich en masse for the West as soon as any chance presented itself for slipping the German yoke.

Only on the subject of territorial aggrandizement did Stalin achieve any of his goals. Although the Atlantic Charter had specifically rejected the idea of territorial gain from the war, the Allies finally accepted the 1939 borders of the Soviet Union as valid. Previously they had consistently opposed Stalin's seizure of Finnish territory in 1940, the occupation of the Baltic States and Moldavia, and of the conquest of the eastern third of Poland in connivance with Germany in 1939. On a philosophical level, the Allies could not deny that much of this territory had formerly been Russian and had been lost to the victorious Germans in the First World War. On a more pragmatic level,

Russian troops were either already in possession of all of this territory, or soon would be, and it seemed better to marshal the West's resources to fight battles with more of a chance of success. However, Churchill stood fast, with Roosevelt's lukewarm support, on the issue of Polish independence, and Stalin quietly shelved plans to attempt to form a rival, Communist government-in-exile made up of the handful of Poles resident in the Soviet Union who had not already fallen in Stalin's relentless purges. The Poles, meanwhile, would be compensated with German territory to the west, and the rump state of East Prussia would disappear from the map, eliminating an anomaly that had been one of the prime causes of German revanchism after the last war. Hundreds of thousands of people would undoubtedly be displaced, but the Allies considered this a small price to pay for stability. Also, Stalin pointed out that the new borders would give the Soviet Union a common frontier with Czechoslovakia and Hungary as well, noting that, if the Soviets had had a means of putting troops into Czechoslovakia without crossing a third country's territory in 1938, there might never have been a Munich "sell out," and the war might never have taken place. Churchill took the slap at British policy in good part, mainly because he tended to agree.

What ultimately made Stalin more flexible in his dealings with the West than he had ever been in the past, was his appreciation, based on very accurate reporting from the extensive Soviet spy ring within Germany, that the Reich was on its last legs. Despite the propaganda, and the apparent vitality of the German military in the first three years of the war, the Nazis had only really begun to mobilize the economic and human resources of both Germany and its conquered territories during 1942. Too many concessions had been made to local party bosses throughout Greater Germany early in the war, trying to keep the cost of the war from seeming too high when an easy victory seemed within their grasp. But just as the fat was beginning to be trimmed and all efforts turned toward the war effort, the Reich had suddenly been deprived of the resources of half a continent. German occupation of France, Belgium, and most of Italy had ended, as well as of the rich Ukraine, and access to raw materials from the Iberian Peninsula and North Africa had been cut off. At the same time, virtually all German-controlled territory was now within reach of Allied bombers, with fighter escort and without a radar buffer, making defense almost hopeless. Just as Germany suffered its first major defeat on the Eastern Front, it had been handed another just as telling in the West, and there was no longer any "safe" sector from which reserves could be shifted.

The Wehrmacht was simply being stretched in too many directions at once.

The strategy agreed upon was hardly earthshaking in its originality. It was essentially to hit everywhere at once. The Allies had the resources to accomplish this, and the Germans could not long resist.

The Russians would continue to press the Germans all along the front with the goal of clearing their national territory. Once this was accomplished, the main thrust would be in the center, towards Berlin.

The British would carry the burden of the war in the Mediterranean, along with the newly allied Italians, and focus their efforts on driving the Germans out of northern Italy. At the same time, Montgomery had proposed landing a British mountain division and a parachute brigade in Yugoslavia to give Tito's partisans some tangible support. Stalin groused at this obvious political ploy, but he was in no position to offer any troops of his own.

On the central portion of the Western Front, there now existed two American armies, the 1st under Omar Bradley, facing northwest toward Holland, and Patton's 5th facing toward Germany itself, with a total of twelve infantry and six armored divisions and a strength of over half a million men. The French Army of the Rhine under Juin covered much of the old Franco-German border and had been reinforced to nearly a quarter of a million men, to discourage the temptation for another German offensive in that sector. The British 3rd Army included only the large Canadian I Corps, and much smaller British V Corps, completing the line down to the Swiss border, with another British corps plus two Italian corps occupying a line through Turin in northern Italy, all under Montgomery's overall command. The XVIII Airborne Corps and the Polish Corps were in strategic reserve, and between four and five divisions were still available from theater reserve in England.

The main offensive would come from Patton's 5th Army once more, as the most experienced and lavishly equipped of the Allied forces. The proposal by a junior staff officer to launch a series of airborne assaults to seize river crossings from the current Allied line through Nijmegen, Eindhoven, and ultimately Arnhem across the Rhine to open a route into Germany had been ridiculed as it justly deserved. Patton would drive across the Rhine north of the Ardennes, around Wesel, skirting the industrial zone of the Ruhr, although bringing it under close siege, even by artillery fire, and continue northeast toward Hamburg and the Kiel Canal. With any German forces remaining in Holland cut off and forced to surrender, Patton would be free to wheel to his right toward Berlin over the north German plain.

With a little luck, the war might really be over by Christmas this time.

The issue that would loom largest in the subsequent study of the Teheran Conference, however, was one that was not dealt with at all. The Atlantic Charter had laid a basic groundwork for the Western Allies in their pursuit of war aims, but there was no specific statement of goals for the Grand Alliance as a whole. During the course of 1942, there had been pressure on London and Washington to allay Stalin's fears that the West might seek a separate peace with Germany, fears that were enhanced by the absence of a major ground front in the West. Some circles in both capitals had advocated a declared policy of demanding "unconditional surrender" by the Axis as a confidence building gesture directed at the Soviets, but professional diplomats were appalled by this proposal which would have eliminated all flexibility in any future negotiations with the Germans. They feared a repeat of the disaster of the publication of Allied demands on Germany at Versailles in 1919 that had locked the Allies into a harsher position than they might have ultimately taken, and fed the revanchist feeling in Germany that Hitler had used in his own rise to power. Fortunately, the landings in southern France had demonstrated an Allied commitment to the war far better than any statement of policy might have done, and Churchill and Roosevelt were able to make do with general statements about war goals being aimed at "complete victory."

Stalin had come to Teheran with the intention of demanding a declaration of seeking "unconditional surrender" on a formal basis. Now, Stalin placed little credence in the significance of public statements and would certainly not have felt bound by any he might make himself, but he understood perfectly that the leaders of the democracies could not play so fast and loose with public opinion in their countries. His reason for seeking such a statement was the growing tide of reports that secret negotiations were taking place in Switzerland between Nazi officials and the West, and the old fear of some sort of agreement being reached which would leave the German Army free to turn its full force on Russia.

The rumors, of course, were quite true. Allen Dulles, the Geneva representative of the Office of Strategic Services (OSS), the predecessor of the CIA, had, in fact been conducting talks both with officials from Berlin and, unbeknownst to them, with officers from Kesselring's headquarters in Italy as well. Although the contacts had not resulted in anything substantive as yet, hope existed of some kind of arrangement as long as the Allies had the freedom to accept something less than the kind of total oppression that Germany had

dealt out to its victims in the war. It was significant that the various inter-
locutors for the Germans had made it clear that Hitler and his inner circle
had no knowledge of the talks and would never agree to a negotiated peace.

In any event, at Teheran the Western Allies now found themselves in a
position of considerable diplomatic leverage. Although, in terms of pure
numbers, the Red Army was still doing the majority of the fighting against
the Germans, it was still the British, Americans, and French who were now
poised to invade the Reich, with troops within a few miles of Germany's industrial heartland and less than one third the distance from Berlin than the
foremost Soviet units. Furthermore, after the brutality of the German occupation of much of European Russia, and the rising tide of Russian vengeance
as the Red Army pushed westward, it was highly unlikely that even Stalin's
battered and cowed people would have stood still for a sudden shift in policy
and peace with the hated enemy. Consequently, when Stalin raised the issue
of how Germany might be dealt with after the ultimate Allied victory, Churchill and Roosevelt were able to stonewall and limit themselves to mouthing
vague words about securing a lasting peace and permanently eliminating the
threat to world peace that Germany had posed over the past several generations. Only de Gaulle supported Stalin on this subject, proposing that Germany be "pastoralized" and possibly carved up into a number of minor states
as it had been during the 18th century, a formula that would have arguably
ended the German threat and would conveniently have left France as the
largest and most populous state in Western Europe. Again, Churchill and
Roosevelt were able to shelve the proposal as "premature" without causing a
major rift in the alliance, and this was to have considerable impact later in
the war.

1800 HOURS, 4 JULY 1943
BERLIN, GERMANY

It struck Admiral Canaris as somewhat ironic that the blow for the freedom
of the German people had been launched on American Independence Day,
and the events of that morning might well take on the aspect of a "shot heard
'round the world." The reports of the shot would be muffled for some time,
of course, by wartime censorship, but on the actions of a few determined men
rode the fate of huge armies and entire nations.

Among the plotters it had soon been agreed that the one target they ab-

solutely needed to eliminate, in fact the only target of any value in this struggle, was the person of the Führer himself. Even outside of the fanatical members of the SS and the inner circle of the National Socialist Party, Hitler had
too long been the very symbol of Germany in a war for the survival of the
Fatherland. There would never be a chance of recruiting sufficient force to
overcome the kind of resistance that would gather around the Führer. With
Hitler out of the way, however, it would become an issue of who would lead
the new government, party hacks like Himmler and Goebbels or sycophants
like Keitel, Göring, and Jodl, or the real leaders of the armed forces like Rommel, Rundstedt, Manstein, and Kesselring. It would then be a battle between
the Waffen SS and the Wehrmacht, and, for all the favoritism shown to the
SS in equipment and manpower, theirs was only a small fraction of the fighting strength of the Reich.

It had not been particularly hard to recruit and organize the conspiracy,
considering that they were operating in the ultimate evolution of the police
state, Canaris mused. As chief of the Abwehr, Canaris had considerable information at his disposal about the inclinations of many senior army officers
and had occasion to visit virtually any command in the Reich as well as every
justification for speaking confidentially to those he selected. He used his
deputy, General Hans Oster, as a stalking horse for this effort, and his network was now spread throughout Germany proper and now even included a
shadow government with officials named to take power once Hitler had been
dethroned. The field marshals had largely been bought off by Hitler with huge
cash awards, extensive estates, and piles of medals, but Hitler's habit of issuing
impossible orders and then berating officers for failing to comply with them
had alienated virtually the entire remainder of the officer corps.

Germany was defeated. The officers knew this, since they had access to
the facts, unadulterated by Goebbels' propaganda, and there was a natural
tendency to place the blame for this defeat on Hitler. Canaris had to recognize
that Germany would never have come to this pass without the support of the
armed forces, and all must share some responsibility for the war itself, a
doomed venture pitting a few tens of millions of industrious and dedicated
people against virtually the entire world. But Hitler had become less and less
rational as events had turned against the Reich. In the early days, some of
Hitler's ravings had turned out surprisingly well, but it could now be seen
that these had been flukes. The only idea Hitler seemed to have anymore was
to issue orders to defend to the death, not to surrender an inch of ground, no

matter what. Those orders had cost the lives of thousands of good troops, both in the East and West, when the ability to maneuver might have not only saved the men but brought victory in the bargain. It was true that no foreign soldier had set foot on historically German territory as yet, but that had been true at the end of the last war as well. Now was the time to make a negotiated peace, Canaris and his colleagues were saying, very quietly but more and more insistently, not when American paratroopers were dropping on Tempelhof Airfield in Berlin or Russian tanks driving under the Brandenburg Gate.

A serious plot to replace Hitler organized by Wehrmacht officers had actually been afoot in 1938, but his bloodless victory at Munich had robbed this of steam and the Führer's unbroken string of successes in the following three years forced such plans into abeyance. Murmuring had resumed in 1942 as victory eluded Hitler's grasp in Russia and North Africa, and became all the more serious after the Allied landings in France. By 1943 the defection of Italy, the loss of France and Belgium and further defeats in the East had reinforced this movement. Surprisingly, it was the failure of the Germans to secure the person of the Pope when they evacuated Rome that proved the decisive blow. Without the pressure of the German military presence and with Mussolini sitting sullenly in his little republic in northern Italy, the Pontiff had become an outspoken critic of the Nazi regime, and this had a profound effect on Catholics in Germany. Canaris had long believed that, while one often thought of Spain or Ireland as the most Catholic countries in Europe, in those places only old women and children regularly attended church, while Bavaria was a land alive with fervor for the One Church. It was among these disaffected zealots that the most dedicated of the new converts had been found.

No fewer than six attempts had been made on the Führer's life thus far in 1943, and the counterintelligence arm of the SS had proven so inept that they had not even noticed several of them. But they had all failed. Security around the Führer had become extremely tight, with even the most senior generals having to surrender their sidearms and submit to degrading personal searches before entering the august presence. But Canaris had to recognize that the early efforts had been rather amateurish, and it was only recently that he had been able to obtain the services of an expert in demolitions, an ardent Catholic and a veteran off the Eastern Front, to undertake the next attempt.

The vehicle for this operation was to be Claus Schenk Graf von Stauffenberg, an aristocratic Catholic from southern Germany who had lost an eye, his right hand, and two fingers of his left in North Africa. He was now a colonel, chief of operations for the *Ersatzheer,* the Replacement Army, and frequently gave briefings to the Führer on the state of recruitment and training for the Wehrmacht. The plan was fairly simple, calling for von Stauffenberg to carry a briefcase of papers concealing a powerful explosive into the bunker used by Hitler in his East Prussian refuge, the Wolfschanze, from which the war in Russia was being directed. With a ten-minute delay fuse on the bomb, von Stauffenberg would have time to activate the device and then excuse himself to make a telephone call to Berlin from the communications room outside the bunker. On the morning of July 4th, von Stauffenberg accomplished this.

Hitler survived the explosion, apparently shielded by the heavy map table over which he was leaning and the supporting table leg against which the briefcase had been inadvertently kicked. A number of staff officers had been killed and still more wounded, but Hitler, his right arm shattered and his face blackened with smoke, was helped out of the ruined conference room by Jodl as SS guards swarmed over the grounds. The second explosion, timed to go off fifteen minutes after the first, was even more powerful. The staff car von Stauffenberg had used to reach the meeting had been parked some fifty feet from the bunker, and every cavity in the body, inside the doors, under the seats, even the spare tire, had been filled with explosives, and a layer of carpenter's nails had been embedded all around it. The force of the blast collapsed the roof of the bunker, but the real mayhem was caused by the nails and shrapnel from the body of the vehicle itself that sliced through the converging guards, and the emerging survivors from the first bomb who were then just staggering away from the site. If Hitler had managed to cover just another ten meters, he would have been shielded by a concrete retaining wall, but the fragments scythed through his body, killing him instantly along with nearly fifty of his guards and staff officers. The second bomb had been the suggestion of the unnamed demolitions expert who had counseled against ever trusting to a single mechanical device. He had calculated that, if the first bomb caused enough damage to require more than fifteen minutes to extract the Führer from the bunker, Hitler would certainly be dead, but that it would take some minutes to move a wounded Hitler to the door of the bunker, leaving him within the killing radius of the second explosion for a good five minutes more. Meanwhile, von Stauffenberg had been able, in the confusion of the first explosion, to bluff his way through three guard posts and to board a small plane for the flight to Berlin.

Now the work of the other conspirators came into play. Von Stauffenberg's immediate superior, General Friedrich Olbricht, had envisioned the *Ersatzheer* as the ideal tool for a coup d'etat. Besides having units scattered throughout the Reich, mostly the skeletons of battle-scarred regiments who were to form the cadres for incorporating new recruits into the Wehrmacht, the Replacement Army had the task of being always on the alert to counter any rising by the millions of slave laborers from the conquered lands who had been transported to Germany to work in the fields and factories. Olbricht had earned commendations from his superiors for his energetic program of lightning mobilization and deployment of these *ersatz* units to meet domestic threats to national security. He was thus able to conduct considerable coup training right under the noses of the Gestapo.

Since von Stauffenberg had no independent means of communicating with the plotters, Olbricht, Canaris, and the others were obliged to sit by their radios, waiting for reports from East Prussia. An hour after the bombs went off, initial word arrived of some kind of assassination attempt, but it was unclear whether Hitler had survived, with some sources reporting one thing and others the contrary. The failure of the plotters to place one of their number at the Wolfschanze, safe from the bombs but with access to communications to make a timely report, could have proven a fatal flaw in the plan as the senior officers in Berlin and throughout the Reich, even those amenable to ousting the Nazis, were understandably reluctant to move while Hitler might still be alive. It seems, on the other hand, that Goebbels and Himmler got first word that Hitler was, in fact, dead, and they took immediate steps to attempt to secure the succession. Their handicap was that, unlike the conspirators, they were starting virtually from scratch. Himmler correctly felt that he could count on the unwavering support of the SS, but these units were not on alert and, in some cases, had been intentionally positioned by the plotters to delay their intervention.

In the event, Canaris was able to convince Admiral Dönitz—who had begun to be discussed as a possible heir apparent to Hitler due to Goring's gradual eclipse with the continued failures of the Luftwaffe and the fact that the Kriegsmarine had remained unconnected to the nature of the war in the East—that the Führer had been killed and that swift action was necessary to prevent a coup by Himmler. The relations between the SS and the Wehrmacht had never been good, with open warfare only being avoided by Hitler's overshadowing presence. Actually, the very fact that Himmler had begun to move his troops first gave Canaris the "proof" he needed for Dönitz that a coup was underway by the SS. The plotters now had the green light to make their own deployments.

While Himmler had only been able to reach SS units in and around Berlin itself, the extensive conspiratorial network had only to issue coded messages to commanders throughout the Reich, and thousands of SS officers and key Nazi officials were arrested and those SS units not actually at the combat front were disarmed and placed under guard. Only in Berlin itself did any fighting take place, as the Grossdeutschland Regiment battered its way into the city from its barracks in Potsdam supported by Luftwaffe ground troops against desperate resistance by scattered SS units. But since Hitler spent so little time in the capital anymore, most SS strength was concentrated at his favorite haunts or at the front, and the Wehrmacht eventually prevailed after twenty-four hours of street fighting. Goebbels was arrested, but Himmler was killed, either leading his men in one final charge, by suicide when resistance seemed futile, or by summary execution by a special squad of paratroopers assigned to the task, depending on the version one prefers.

The next few days were extremely tense for all Germans. Dönitz announced that "partisans" had probably been responsible for Hitler's death and that Himmler had made an unsuccessful bid for power in the chaotic aftermath, leaving the implication that Himmler may have had a hand in the assassination as well. He vowed to continue the war to a "just peace" but deferred any further discussion of this subject for the time being. Hundreds of thousands of SS troops on both fronts remained under arms, but as displeased as they might have been with the murder of Himmler and the arrest of most of their senior officers, they were hardly in a position to go over to the enemy, certainly not the Russians, so they held their places in line amid assurances from Berlin that they would be reincorporated directly into the Wehrmacht with all ranks and privileges and with their valuable combat formations intact. Rommel, now recovered from his wounds, was named as the new chief of OKH, a move popular with the troops. Ulrich von Hassell, a former ambassador to Rome and a longtime member of the conspiracy, was named in Ribbentrop's place as Foreign Minister.

One of the first acts of the new government was the dismantlement of the Nazi death camp system. This is not to say that the generals, who certainly had knowledge of the systematic genocide being practiced against Jews, gypsies, the handicapped, Slavs, and political opponents of the Nazis, were suddenly overcome with warm feelings for any of these groups. It was a calculated decision to make eventual peace talks, especially with the West, easier. The camps remained in existence. Slave labor continued to provide a major source of manpower for the German war machine, although now directly under the government instead of as Himmler's private fiefdom, and the regime in the camps hardly improved in terms of diet, sanitation, or comfort, but the organized, mechanical killing stopped.

The war continued, of course, with the Russians pressing westward and now beginning a broad sweep through the Baltic states and entering what had been pre-1939 Poland at several points. The Allied bombing campaign went on unabated, and pressure was kept up all along the front. It only remained to see when and where the line would crack first.

1200 HOURS, 19 JULY 1943
BOCHOLT, GERMANY

Patton did not like the new attitude of his troops. Caution was a quality that he did not respect very much, particularly in fighting men. It was just as likely to result in higher casualties as in lower ones, and he could sense that his troops had become decidedly cautions.

He understood perfectly why they would be so. It looked to everyone, including himself, that the war would soon be over. In Italy, Montgomery had finally cracked the line of the Appennines, or more likely Patton figured, the Germans had abandoned it and pulled back to the line of the Adige River, vastly shortening their front and gleaning troops to send elsewhere. The British had been out of contact with the enemy for several days and were only now coming up to the Adige after a leisurely advance against no resistance. The Germans had also chosen to abandon Greece and southern Yugoslavia after the governments of Hungary, Romania, and Bulgaria had almost simultaneously declared their neutrality. The Germans had let the Bulgarians and Romanians go, but they had seized Admiral Horthy in Budapest and disarmed the Hungarian Army, or what remained of it after Stalingrad. Again the Germans had shortened their line to one running along the Carpathians along the western Romanian border, and west through Bosnia to the Adriatic, keeping hold of Hungary's oil production facilities and agricultural production and the mines of Croatia for the present.

The Russians had balked at the Romanians' condition for withdrawing from the war, that no Russian troops enter their territory. The Soviets had argued that Romanian troops had participated in the invasion of the USSR alongside the Germans and deserved to be punished, but Churchill and Roosevelt had convinced Stalin that the loss to the Germans of the Balkans, the Ploesti oilfields, and tens of thousands of Romanian and Bulgarian troops more than justified this exception, adding assurances that any Romanian government officials found guilty of war crimes would be brought to justice along with their German overlords. Stalin had finally relented, although radio intercepts indicated that suspiciously large concentrations of Soviet troops remained poised along Romania's eastern border. While these events would normally have been very good news, Patton could not help but worry where the Germans would deploy the numerous divisions thus freed by the drastic shortening of their lines elsewhere.

Meanwhile, here in the West, the Rhine had at last been forced. Patton's army had crashed through the Siegfried Line in a week of fighting that reminded Patton all too much of the carnage of the First World War. Hundreds of large guns and heavy bombers had pounded the German defenses around the clock and carpeted the German rear areas preventing the arrival of reinforcements or supplies. The Germans had built elaborate and ingenious networks of pillboxes, trenches, and tank traps, but technology had given a definite edge to the offensive, and his tanks, some equipped with flamethrowers or mine-clearing plows, had bulled their way through. But the effort had told on his men, now used to measuring a day's progress in miles, who had been lucky to advance a few hundred meters, and this at tremendous cost. The crossing of the Rhine had been the same, with a curtain of fire and steel covering the defenders on the far shore until pontoon bridges could be laid and a bridgehead secured.

Now that they were through the thick belt of fortifications, the pace of the advance had certainly picked up, as Patton rotated exhausted units out of the line and replaced them with fresh ones. But he felt he was hearing too many calls from armored spearheads claiming to be "pinned down" by enemy fire and waiting until artillery or airstrikes could clear the way before they would resume the advance. It was Patton's view that this was symptomatic of men who did not want to run risks, particularly the risk of being one of the last casualties in a war that was ending. He feared, however, that, if the enemy were not kept on the run, the reserves released from other fronts would turn up facing the Americans and result in having to pay dearly in blood for terrain that could be scooped up almost for free with a little audacity now.

Consequently, he was leading from the front, driving his division commanders relentlessly, perhaps too much so. Patton had just received a reprimand from Marshall and had been forced to go through the humiliating experience of "apologizing" to his troops for having slapped several shirkers in a field hospital some days before. The men had complained of "combat fatigue," a malady of whose existence Patton seriously doubted, and the men had been abetted in this by overly sensitive doctors who had no understanding of war or the military, even though they now wore army uniforms. Had it not been for the fact that Patton was commanding a consistently victorious army plunging deep into the enemy's territory, he very likely would have been removed from his post. At least being up front, standing in his open jeep and shouting encouragement to his men as they rolled past kept him from thinking too much about it.

Perhaps the British landing on the German North Sea coast would crack the front open. They would come ashore at the mouth of the Weser River north of Bremerhaven. He would drive northeast toward them, through Munster and Osnabrock to link up east of Bremen, cutting off Holland and a large slice of northwest Germany. The French would be busy rolling up the Siegfried line from north to south from the breach he had made and investing the Ruhr. Bradley's army would mop up along the coast and send reinforcements east to join him in a drive on Berlin itself Even if the Germans did bring in troops from Italy or the Balkans, they would be weary and combat-worn, if the Air Force let them through at all, and in the open plains of northern Germany, they would have to stand up and fight in the open, with the Russians breathing down their backs all the while. In two months, perhaps three, the war could be over, and Patton would have achieved his lifelong dream.

1800 HOURS, 22 JULY 1943
BERLIN, GERMANY

For some reason, even though evidence of inevitable defeat was piling up all around them, Admiral Canaris found the meetings of the new OKH much less depressing than he had the interminable sessions with Hitler, enduring pointless monologues late into the night only to have the best advice of the greatest military minds of the century discarded on the whim of a mere Austrian corporal. Now there was no collection of placemen in uniform, just fighting generals looking for solutions, not excuses. Dönitz presided, having been nominated to head the new junta along with Field Marshal Ludwig Beck, his chief of staff. Kesselring was there, and Rommel, von Rundstedt, and von Kluge, while Manstein was closely consulted in regard to pragmatically shortening the front in the East through withdrawals from the Kuban and other pointless salients. There was no longer Goebbels nor any of the other Nazi Party hacks. The only civilian in the bunker, which they still had to use because of the Allied bombing, was Foreign Minister Ulrich von Hassel, since there was nothing in the Reich these days that did not have to do with the country's current and future relations with the enemy.

Kesselring was just completing a report on the state of Wehrmacht reserves. After the recent pullbacks in the south, there were now a full twenty infantry and four mechanized divisions, in addition to eight new *Volksgrenadier* divisions of militia, a home defense program Hitler had just begun before his death. All Luftwaffe production had been turned over to fighters, including some new jet-powered aircraft whose development Hitler had delayed, preferring panzers to planes, but there were no illusions that these could prove any more than a nuisance to the Allied air fleets. Even Russian bombers were beginning to appear in the skies over Budapest and Warsaw lately. The Navy had given up attempting to construct new warships, since the dockyards were too easy a target for enemy bombers. Those U-boats that still existed were now concentrated in the North Sea, now that the French and Belgian ports had been lost, and there was no chance of making a significant dent in the delivery of Allied troops and supplies across the Atlantic. Their primary role would now be coastal defense.

Dönitz thanked Kesselring for the overview and then announced, "I suggest that we give Rundstedt the *volksgrenadiers* and perhaps two infantry divisions, plus some replacements for his armor to defend in the West. The remainder of the troops should be moved into Poland and Hungary against the Russians."

"But that won't even make good my losses over the past two weeks," von Rundstedt protested. His command now included everything from Norway to Switzerland on the Western Front.

"It's not meant to," Rommel responded. "We are at the point where victory is not an option, not even the defense of the Fatherland, only the question of which set of enemies we would prefer to deal with and whom we would prefer to have in occupation of our territory."

"I agree," Manstein joined in. "If the Russians set foot on German soil, they will raze every building to the ground and then salt the ground. The British and Americans will only occupy it, and they will eventually go home."

"And the French?" Rundstedt insisted. "They may consider that they have a score to settle as well."

"The French can do nothing without the support of London and Washington," von Hassel replied. "They may wish to do more, but they won't. And, besides, there is a qualitative difference between the two."

"But we must make the West pay for every inch of ground," Beck interjected. "You must instill this spirit in your commanders. In the East we must hang onto real estate, but in the West the British and Americans are very sensitive to casualties, and they love to calculate. We need to give them some figures to work with. Let them think, 'It cost fifty thousand men to advance fifty miles into Germany, and it's still 200 miles to Berlin, ergo . . .'"

It seemed as though the meeting were about to adjourn when a short, swarthy man who had been sitting quietly at the far comer of the conference table cleared his throat and leaned forward in order to be heard.

"Of course, that still leaves us with the question of the Jews." The sliding of chairs and the rustling of papers stopped, and all eyes turned toward him.

General Ernst Kaltenbrunner had taken over command of the *Sicherheitsdienst* (SD), sometimes still known as the Gestapo, upon the assassination of Reinhard Heydrich by Czech partisans in Prague in May of 1942. Since the SD had come under the jurisdiction of Himmler's SS, one might have expected Kaltenbrunner to have supported his former boss in the brief power struggle following Hitler's death, but he had instead offered his services to the conspirators even before official word of the Führer's demise had reached Berlin. With control over thousands of security troops and an extensive network of spies and counterspies, and having conducted a largely successful war against enemy intelligence agents and partisans over the past year, Kaltenbrunner possessed skills that the new government could not do without, and he had kept his position. Now he raised a question they had all been avoiding.

"I'm sure you are aware that we have closed down 'operations' at our principle 'processing facilities' in Poland, Chelmno, Treblinka, Sobibor, and Belzec, over the past couple of weeks," the man went on in a dull monotone. "I understood the logic of that decision, at the time, but I fear we now stand at a crossroads regarding future Jewish policy."

"Hasn't there been enough killing?" Kesselring snapped.

"Exactly my point," Kaltenbrunner continued. "According to our files, nearly four million Jews and other individuals considered 'undesirable' have been eliminated from Europe to date, either at the facilities or in the field by our *einsatzgruppen* on the Eastern Front. This was in compliance with orders from the Führer himself and Herr Himmler. There still remain some two to three million Jews either in those camps, in the labor camps like Auschwitz, and gathered from across Europe in the ghettos of the major Polish cities. The question we face is whether it would be wise to leave these two million *witnesses* alive to eventually fall into Allied hands."

"But couldn't we, with some justification, blame the entire Jewish question on Hitler and Himmler," Kesselring asked, "especially since they're both conveniently dead?"

Kaltenbrunner cocked his head and raised a bushy eyebrow. "That would be nice, but it's not very likely. You all know as well as I that the SS did not in fact act alone in killing the Jews. Not that it would matter to the Allies. With the testimony of so many survivors, they will be looking for vengeance, particularly the United States with its large and influential Jewish population, and they will want *live* victims, not dead ones."

"There is no way in which we could ever hide the fact of the elimination of the Jews," Rommel joined in.

"We might not be able to hide the evidence of the killing and the disposal of the bodies," Kaltenbrunner agreed. "The question is whether it would be well to have two million living, breathing people clamoring for German blood, which is what they will be doing, of course, or whether we would prefer to face condemnation for what would then just be a historical event. You must remember that someone will have to be pushing the prosecution. Will it be the Poles or the French, the Hungarians or Romanians? I doubt it. Their governments cooperated to an embarrassing degree with the rounding up of the Jews and claiming pressure from Berlin will not relieve them of all responsibility. Will it be the Soviets? Hardly. Stalin has just as many skeletons in his closet, literally, as we do in ours, and he has no more love for the Jews. Trotsky was a Jew, after all. And the Americans and the British? To some extent, but none of the victims were their citizens, while the countries to which the Jews did belong will be much less vociferous, and this will rob their offensive of impetus."

"*If* the Jews are dead," Dönitz concluded.

"Precisely, Admiral. We have weeks, perhaps months, before the Allied armies begin to overrun the areas where these activities have been taking place. I strongly suggest that we make use of this time to ensure that the only evidence they find will be of a forensic nature."

"That will mean diverting resources from the war," Rommel noted.

"As little as possible," Kaltenbrunner said. "Even while the Führer was alive, our schedule was delayed by rail requirements for the armies. I would not bother trying to root out the Jews we know must be hiding throughout the Reich, just finishing with those who are already conveniently collected."

The generals sat in silence for a moment, avoiding each other's eyes.

"Do whatever you think is best," Dönitz finally said.

CHAPTER 10
WARSAW RISING

0600 Hours, 24 July 1943
Warsaw, Poland

G ENERAL Tadeusz Bor-Komorowski, commander of the Polish underground *Armija Krajowa* (Home Army), huddled with his brigade commanders in the basement of a small house in the working class suburbs on the south side of Warsaw. This kind of conference was extremely rare as it took the commanders away from their units for days at a time, travelling clandestinely over hundreds of miles of German-occupied country and posing the risk of the decapitation of the entire resistance movement. But this time it was necessary. A crisis was at hand.

Even before the leading Soviet Army spearheads had crossed into what had been Polish territory prior to 1939, Soviet-led partisan units, some of which included numbers of Poles, had migrated ahead of them to continue their battle against rear area German support troops. That in itself would have been a welcome addition to Bor-Komorowski's battle against the Germans. He commanded nearly two hundred thousand men and women throughout Poland, but barely one in eight of that number was armed, and the Poles had hoped that the Soviet partisans would bring with them a conduit for receiving airdrops of Russian arms and ammunition, but this had not been the case. Far from supporting the Home Army, the Soviet partisans had taken advantage of their superior organization and logistical support to dominate the regions they entered and then to eliminate any Home Army cadres that had been foolhardy enough to present themselves to the new arrivals. While the world may still have been withholding judgment on the Soviets over the

Katyn massacre of Polish Army officers after the partition in 1939, the Poles themselves had no such doubts. If Poland were ever to be free again, it would have to be by her own hand. She could expect no help from the Russians.

To reinforce this view, word had reached Bor-Komorowski by shortwave from the Polish government-in-exile in London that some kind of deal had apparently been struck between the Soviets and the Western Allies that would leave the Russians in possession of the territory they had seized by stabbing Poland in the back during the German invasion. Bor-Komorowski had not been the only hardened Polish officer who had cried at the thought of the perfidy of the British, who had supposedly entered the war to defend Polish independence years before. The British had done precious little to help the Poles in their struggle at the time, but a professional military man could recognize that there had been little either the British or the French could have done to reach Poland across the breadth of Germany. But now, without a shot being fired, it seemed that the Allies were ready to sell the Poles out once more, and that he could not stomach.

There was only one thing left to do, and it appealed to the Polish sense of the dramatic. Not unlike the crew of a sinking ship that might set the vessel on fire in order to attract the attention of potential rescuers, Bor-Komorowski and his valiant freedom fighters would hurl themselves on the bonfire in the hope that the flames would bring help to their nation.

Suddenly, he had been presented with a situation that, while forcing the pace of his rising and cutting the time available to the Allies to react, also fortuitously increased the chances that the Allies, especially the Americans, might help. For that reason he had invited Moredechai Anielewicz, commander of the Jewish Fighting Organization (*Zydowska Organizacja Bojowa*, ZOB), from the Warsaw Ghetto to this meeting. Relations between the ZOB and the Home Army had never been very close as the Home Army had more than its share of anti-Semites, and the ZOB had more than its share of Communists, and open fighting had occurred between Jews and Poles on occasion over the past two years. But now, the two groups had a chance, by joining together, to save each other.

Poland had long been the center of European Jewry and had thus been convenient for the Nazis as the center for their campaign to exterminate them. Hundreds of thousands of Polish Jews were first concentrated in the narrow confines of the ghettos formed in major cities such as Warsaw, Krakow, and Lodz, and then periodically culled for shipment to the death camps of Chelmno, Treblinka, Sobibor, and Belzec. Later, Jews gathered from the rest of Europe—those not designated for other camps in Germany, such as Dachau and Buchenwald—were also funneled into the much more efficient death factories in Poland when the more primitive expedients of starvation, overwork, or simple shooting proved inadequate to the task.

At one point the Warsaw Ghetto had held as many as 380,000 men, women, and children, but by the end of 1942, the total was down to less than 70,000, and there had been indications that the SS planned to clean the ghetto out once and for all to create a clear holding area for new shipments of Jews from Hungary, Romania, and elsewhere. But two events had disrupted Himmler's plans. The first was the unexpected resistance of the ZOB, whose handful of poorly armed fighters had met the death squads with gunfire and grenades, causing them to pull back in confusion. The second was the Allied landings in France combined with the Russian offensive at Stalingrad that obligated all rail transport to the movement of reinforcements to both the East and the West.

In the intervening months an uneasy truce had reigned in Warsaw, with German run factories in the ghetto continuing to produce uniforms and other items for the Wehrmacht while the Jews slowly starved on a diet of barely 300 calories per day. Only the frantic cultivation of small gardens and an ingenious network of smugglers managed to obtain enough food to keep the inhabitants alive, trading their last few treasures for miserable quantities of potatoes and bread.

By late June, however, it appeared that Himmler had reasserted his authority, and plans were afoot to renew the *aktions,* the lightning raids by heavily armed SS squads that would round up the remaining Jews and "select" them for deportation to the death camps. This plan had once more been derailed by the deaths of Hitler and Himmler in July, and there had been a brief moment of hope in the ghetto that the new regime would demonstrate a complete break with the Nazi past. But this was not to be. The walls had remained in place, the guards just as surly and vigilant, and now informers inside the Polish police reported that the "final solution" was at last to be put into practice.

If that had been the only consideration, Bor-Komorowsky and the Home Army would probably not have taken much of an interest. They might have provided some weapons to the ZOB, whose leaders had made it clear that they would rather die fighting than in the gas chambers, but only to the extent that the Jews would be fighting the Poles' battle. With the crushing of the Polish state by the Soviets a distinct possibility, however, it had occurred to Bor-Komorowsky that the best way to ensure a favorable response to the Polish plea for help from the West would be to tie their fate to that of the Jews. At the very least, the ZOB in Warsaw alone would add another 1,500 fighters to the struggle, although with even a smaller percentage of armed men than the Home Army possessed. Since Anielewicz and his men were determined to fight, with or without outside help, it only remained to attempt to coordinate their efforts with the Home Army and, hopefully, with the Allies.

It was quickly agreed by the men crowded around a small card table with a map of Poland scrounged from an elementary school that the Home Army could never hope to seize and hold all of Poland. One colonel argued that what they needed to do was take the capital, Warsaw, and possibly the city of Lodz as well, a pocket of resistance in the middle of Poland, and hope for relief from the West. Bor-Komorowski, however, pointed to the map and asked how the British or Americans, save for through air power, could get to Warsaw in time. Their armies were still fighting on the far side of Germany and would have to march right through Berlin to get there, by which time the war would be over. He agreed that a rising must take place in Warsaw as a symbol of Polish independence and to save the principle target of the German *aktion,* the Warsaw ghetto, but he added that any serious help must come by sea. Hopefully, the Allies would quickly begin flying in more supplies, and perhaps even troops by air, but the Americans and British had just captured the length of the Kiel Canal, and it was possible—highly risky but possible— that they could send forces by sea through the Baltic. The Luftwaffe no longer posed a serious threat, and the German Navy had almost been eliminated as well. Therefore, the main Polish effort had to be made to the north, nearer the coast, possibly in the hilly country south of Danzig, where the Allies at least had a chance of reaching them.

2100 HOURS, 25 JULY 1943
LONDON, ENGLAND

Stanislaw Mikolajczyk, Prime Minister of the Polish government-in-exile frankly did not enjoy his meetings with the urbane and ever-so-discreet British Foreign Secretary Anthony Eden, but the fate of his country was at stake, and men were already dying for the cause. The least he could do would be to make his arguments as cogently as possible and try to get the British to support them.

Eden had already made it clear that both Churchill and Roosevelt had agreed to the Curzon Line as the new Polish-Russian border, moving the line westward approximately to include the area seized by the Russians in 1939, allowing them to profit from their disgraceful deal with the Nazis. Poland was to be compensated with a "gift" of nearly all of East Prussia and another slice of German territory up to the Oder-Neisse River line in the west. Mikolajczyk had pointed out that, while the land the Allies were giving up to the Soviets was populated almost exclusively by ethnic Poles, that which they were giving to Poland was populated almost entirely by Germans. Eden had only concurred with this assessment, adding casually that certain "demographic adjustments" would certainly have to be made, but that there was no point in belaboring the matter as the Soviets were in occupation of much of this territory and were not likely to relinquish it short of war.

Mikolajczyk had known that this would be the British position before the meeting had occurred. The Polish Ambassador in Washington had received the same response from Secretary of State Stimson earlier that day, and the Poles' best chance of support always came from the Americans, with their millions of Polish-American voters to consider. But Mikolajczyk's purpose at this meeting was not really to argue about Poland's future borders. That was an issue beyond his control. What he was to spend the next few hours fighting for was Poland's very existence. General Marshall sat uneasily in a corner of the tastefully furnished office in Whitehall, along with General Kazimierz Sosnkowski, the Commander-in-Chief of the Polish Armed Forces, probably wondering why two military men had been called to attend an essentially diplomatic meeting. He would not have long to wonder.

"Without endorsing this agreement, to which the government of Poland was not a party," Mikolajczyk continued, "I can see that we have been presented with a fait accompli." Eden nodded. "Another matter that I would like to raise, and which General Sosnkowski will be able to address in more detail, is the issue of a Polish national rising against the Germans."

Eden raised his eyebrows and Marshall leaned forward. "What rising?" the latter asked.

"It hasn't begun yet, but it will within one week," Sosnkowski joined in. "Two hundred thousand men and women will fight with whatever arms they have or can take from the enemy. The Russians are about to enter Poland,

and we have no illusions that the Red Army will recognize the Curzon Line either. There is already reporting from our intelligence service that Polish Communists have been gathered up within the Soviet Union in an effort to form a puppet government, just as the Soviets did with the Finnish Communists during the Winter War in 1939. Soviet partisan brigades have also begun killing Home Army men in the areas they control."

"It is interesting that the Soviets have made similar charges that the Home Army has been exterminating Communists among the partisans," Eden sniffed. "One expects that both stories contain at least a grain of truth."

"One would have hoped that we would have learned about the tactic of the 'big lie' from dealing with Goebbels all these years," Mikolajczyk countered. "The dictators commit the most heinous acts and then accuse their opponents of doing the same, causing reasonable men, used to more civilized behavior, to assume that the truth is 'somewhere in the middle.' That is not the case, and you know very well that the only mass graves we know of are those at Katyn."

"Which is still under investigation," Eden pointed out.

Sosnkowski snorted in disgust and ignored the comment. "Be that as it may, the Polish government intends to commit all of its armed forces to support our countrymen." "Including the forces under Allied command?" Marshall asked.

"Obviously. We currently have an armored division and three infantry divisions, plus another armored brigade and several artillery regiments and support units. There are also two Polish bomber, three fighter, and one transport squadrons, two destroyers and several merchantmen, all crewed by Poles."

"All of them armed and supplied by the Allies," Marshall pointed out.

"And who have fought long and well against the common enemy from the Battle of Britain to North Africa to France. Now we want them to fight in Poland."

"And how do you propose to get them to Poland?" Marshall asked drily.

"Through the Kiel Canal and into the Baltic for a landing on the Polish coast. Our aircraft will fly over, and our ships will carry every man and gun that they can." "That's suicide," Marshall said.

"It seems that every road open to Poland is suicidal," Sosnokowski shrugged. "The only question is the form we choose and whether we can do what needs to be done with honor." He paused and raised his hands. "Of course, if the Allies choose to help us, perhaps the effort might not be quite so hopeless."

"There is another reason for the timing of the rising, besides the advance of the Russians," Mikolajczyk added in a low voice. "The Germans are planning to complete their massacre of Europe's Jews, starting with those held in the ghettos and concentration camps in Poland."

"The Germans have been killing Jews very enthusiastically for some time," Eden commented. "This is the first time I can recall the Polish government taking a particular interest in the matter."

"We have stood by too long, as has everyone else," Mikolajczyk sighed. "I will not pretend that our concern is totally disinterested now, but we Poles and the Jews are like two drowning men, holding onto each other for dear life. If either of us goes under, the other certainly will. So we have decided to join our fate to theirs. When the Germans attack the ghettos, the Jews will fight, and we will be with them."

Eden began to object, but Marshall leaned closer to the general. "What, exactly, do you have in mind?"

The muscles around Mikolajczyk's mouth tightened to hide a smile. Sosnokowski had told him before the meeting that if Marshall, the great strategic planner of the war, could be lured into a discussion of planning for the operation, he was already halfway convinced of its viability.

"We have over one hundred thousand men under arms in General Anders' Polish Army, and shipping exists to lift all of them to the Baltic in one movement. The RAF and the American 8th Air Force routinely run thousand-plane raids into Germany. If a thousand bombers carried canisters of weapons and ammunition instead of bombs, we could arm virtually all of the Home Army overnight. The only real threat on the seas would be mines, and our intelligence service has good information on their location in the areas we would be concerned with. With an airdrop of our paratroop brigade near Danzig timed to coincide with our rising, the amphibious troops should be able to walk ashore, as the coastal defenses in the Baltic have never been strong. At the very least, this would draw considerable German resources away from both the Western and Eastern fronts and possibly provide the one last decisive blow needed to bring the Germans down."

Marshall shook his head and Mikolajczyk held his breath. "The airdrop should be much larger, and not at Danzig, farther west, in the old Polish Corridor. Every mile we can save by both sea and air to the landing site will be important. We have the British 6th Airborne and the American 101st ready to go and the lift to carry them and the Poles in two waves. We do have the shipping, even landing craft, in the area since the British landing in Friesland met with very light losses. It would give Patton a choice between driving east along the coast to link up with your men or turning south toward Berlin, and the Germans would either have to cover both avenues or leave one too weak. What about the Russians?"

'We can't expect any support from them," Mikolajczyk added, his voice a little too loud as relief flooded over him. "I doubt if they would even allow our aircraft to land and refuel in their territory. We would have to inform them that, while joint operations against any German forces caught between us would be welcome, the Red Army must not enter any territory that we have liberated. They still have plenty to do in the Baltic republics, and they would still have southern Poland, Czechoslovakia, and Hungary to move through."

"They will never agree to that," Eden said categorically. "They'll never accept being cut off from the most direct route to Berlin, over largely flat terrain, to a long, roundabout route through the mountains of Slovakia."

"We're hoping that the Germans will collapse before this becomes a major issue," Mikolajczyk answered. 'We won't be able to stop the Red Army if they do break through the Germans and reach our territory, so we would let them pass, if pass they will. At least the very fact of such a problem would mean that our men would have to be alive and in possession of some real estate, and that is a problem we would love to have."

"The presence of British and American troops should also help prevent things from coming to a head," Marshall suggested, and Eden cocked his head noncommittally.

"I have to note that you did not ask that any representative from the Imperial General Staff be present," Eden commented.

"We didn't ask for representatives from any of the *national* contingents," Mikolajczyk countered. "Just the commander of the Allied forces, and General Sosnokowski, whose plan this is."

"It will have to be staffed out, as they say," Eden said.

"But very, very quickly," Marshall noted as he zipped closed his leather briefcase. "General," he said, turning to Sosnokowski, "if you will accompany me, we will do precisely what Mr. Eden has suggested and see if this dog will hunt."

"What dog?" Sosnokowski asked as they hurried out the door.

1200 HOURS, 28 JULY 1943
BERLIN, GERMANY

Even after the elimination of Hitler and most of his clique, Dönitz had found his strategy extremely hard to sell to the fervent patriots in the officer corps. The idea that the Wehrmacht would fight to the death in eastern Poland and the Carpathians while giving ground in Germany itself was appalling to most of them, Dönitz included. The German Army had been following a scorched earth policy in all the conquered lands through which it had retreated in the preceding months: Russia, Italy, France, and the Low Countries. Whenever time allowed, mines were flooded, bridges blown, ports blockaded with sunken ships and clogged with anti-shipping mines, and factories demolished. And the army on the Eastern Front continued to leave a barren moonscape behind as it withdrew through the Ukraine and Belorussia into eastern Poland. But now Dönitz was changing all that.

Although the Wehrmacht had fought bitterly west of the Rhine to delay the advancing Americans, once Patton had bulled his way across the river, the only battles were fought in the countryside. There was no house-to-house fighting in the larger cities, and the Americans had been amazed to find entire factories, in perfect running order, falling into their hands, with half-completed trucks or planes still sitting on the assembly lines. Even the ports of Bremerhaven and Wilhelmshaven had been taken by British amphibious troops the week before, with those cranes and piers spared by the Allied bombers still functioning, although the approaches had been heavily mined. Now, the remnants of a dozen infantry divisions formed an arc shielding Hamburg from the British, who had bypassed the city to the north and driven across the Jutland peninsula to Kiel on the Baltic, and the Americans to the south. But these troops had orders that, if pressed back into the suburbs of the city, they were to break contact with the enemy and evacuate to the east, leaving untouched whatever had not already been destroyed by the waves of Allied bombers over the past three years.

Some of the officers present considered this foolhardy, even treasonous behavior, but Dönitz's opinion had won out. He had argued that whatever fell to the Soviets would be lost to the German people forever, either territory, industry, or people; but everything captured by the Allies would be available to rebuild Germany after the war. And he had emphasized that the end was all too close and completely inevitable. Nearly one hundred thousand German troops were cut off in Holland and would probably surrender in the next few days, and the skeleton garrisons in Denmark and Norway, while still in contact by sea over the Baltic, could not hold out for long if the Allies took any interest in that direction. Kesselring's forces had been pushed back into the Alps on the Italian front, while Tito's partisans, now heavily armed by the British, were gleefully massacring the pro-Axis Chetniks in Croatia and nibbling at the Hungarian border, and Romania had now declared for the Allies and had also attacked into Hungary. The Russians were pounding Konigsberg, the citadel of East Prussia, and the French and Canadians were clawing their way toward the Rhine through the Siegfried Line. In fact, the only good news Dönitz had received since assuming the Chancellorship had been delivered by Admiral Canaris just moments before.

"And what analysis does the Abwehr make of the loading of Polish troops on board ships in the French Channel ports?" Dönitz asked, loosening his collar in the oppressive heat of the bunker under the Berlin Zoo. The smell from the animal cages, most long empty but apparently not cleaned, hardly helped.

"Well," Canaris sighed, "they could be on the way to reinforce the British for an attack on upper Jutland or on Norway."

"But why the Poles?" Rommel asked skeptically. "The Poles are already on the continent, and there's plenty of fighting for them to do just by driving across Belgium and into Germany. If they've got more ships than they know what to do with, there are still new British and American divisions forming in England that would have to take ship to get into the battle."

"Exactly," Canaris went on. "We do have some preliminary reporting that they're going to Poland."

The eyebrows of several of the generals seated around the conference table rose noticeably.

"Impossible!" Chief of Staff Kluge snorted. "They can't have that low an opinion of either the Luftwaffe or our navy to try to thread their way through the Danish archipelago. The Baltic is still a German lake! Our E-boats would cut them up, and our submarines would finish the job."

Admiral Raeder, now commander of the navy, joined in. "We have only six seaworthy U-boats left in the Baltic, and perhaps a dozen E-boats. We also have some experimental piloted torpedoes that suicide commandos could ride into the side of enemy ships in restricted waters like those. We could certainly make them pay their passage."

"We could, but we won't," Dönitz announced, slapping the conference table with the flat of his hand.

There was a confused hum of conversation around the table, but Canaris nodded and smiled. Kluge attempted to argue, but Dönitz held up his hand to silence him.

"The only thing I regret is that the Poles only have a handful of divisions. I wish they had twenty."

Kluge had turned red in the face and could only sputter.

Dönitz laughed. "The war is over, my dear general, and the Russians are coming. There is nothing that I would rather see at this time than a strong, independent, well armed Poland sitting astride the road from Moscow to Berlin. If there is anyone who has more cause to hate the Russians more than we do, it's the Poles. They may even hate them more than they hate us at the moment."

Canaris rolled his eyes, and Dönitz coughed slightly.

"Well, perhaps not," he corrected himself. "But I propose that we allow the Poles through. Maybe harass them a bit, and make them fight their way ashore, but put them in the same category as the Americans or British. We will make them pay for their victory, in order to make them all the more ready to negotiate a peace, but still concentrate our main effort at holding off and punishing the Russians. We will test the viability of a new Polish state in the crucible of war, then leave them to their godforsaken country. We will pull our eastern forces back into East Prussia and down into Czechoslovakia and Hungary, and of course along our own eastern border, and let the Poles serve as a shield for us against Stalin. If they can establish themselves, that will be the time for us to seek final peace terms from the West. And our men must fight hard every day, against all our enemies, for at any moment they could reach their breaking point and ease their terms for peace, and we must be in as strong a position as possible whenever that happens. With luck, perhaps half of Germany proper can be spared the pain of the war passing over it, and hundreds of thousands of our men will live to help rebuild Germany after the war."

Kluge just shook his large head and hid his face with his hands.

"It's the only way, my friends," Dönitz concluded. "Some of our brothers had the duty of giving their lives in defense of the Fatherland. It is our unpleasant duty to supervise the dismantling of the Reich while safeguarding as many of the building blocks as possible with which to construct our nation anew."

Allen Dulles had wanted to play a significant part in the Allied war effort, and as the chief representative of the Office of Strategic Services on the continent during the heyday of the Reich, he had been at the vortex of the storm that was breaking over Europe. He had assumed that, while neutral Switzerland would undoubtedly continue to be a hotbed of espionage activity by all parties, German, American, British, French, and Soviet, the relative importance of his own role would diminish as the Allied armies rolled over Western Europe and the end of the Reich came visibly closer. He had badly miscalculated.

Since the assassination of Hitler, and it was now his firm belief that Hitler's own generals had done the deed, he had served as the most direct contact between Berlin and the Allies for the first tentative feelers for an ultimate peace. There had been other approaches, in Sweden, Argentina, and Turkey, but in Geneva senior German officials could actually conduct meetings, face-to-face, with him or other Allied representatives, who could now travel freely to Geneva via liberated France, and both sides could get prompt answers from their respective governments.

Now, as he sat in his office in the American consulate, Dulles had just completed a lengthy session with General Hans Oster, a fellow intelligence officer and deputy to Admiral Canaris, head of the Abwehr. Oster had delivered the most concrete proposal yet received from the Germans related to a possible surrender. It had just been an opening bid, of course, and would not be acceptable to any of the Allied governments, but it was a serious offer, nothing like Hitler's ultimatums from early in the war in which the Allies would have to accept a German victory and hegemony over Europe if they wanted any hope of peace. Now the Germans only seemed interested in salvaging something like a sovereign German state, and to keep the Russians out.

Oster had made some startling concessions for this early in the game, Dulles thought. The Germans would accept responsibility for the war and, in theory, the obligation to pay reparations to the victims of her aggression. They would return to their pre-1938 borders, without the Anschluss with

Austria or the Sudetenland, much less any of their later conquests. They would even accept limitations on the size and composition of their armed forces and military-related industry, only asking that enough remain to provide for "territorial security," presumably against the Russians, although that would entail quite a force. Even more striking was the suggestion that some senior Nazi officials would be surrendered to the Allies for trial for "crimes against humanity," something that Dulles knew the Allies would insist upon but that he never expected the Germans to offer up unilaterally. The one sticking point was that Oster insisted that Germany must be allowed to police herself and that foreign occupation must be ruled out, claiming that popular disgust with the presence of foreign troops on German soil would result in a complete breakdown of society, the collapse of the current government, and probable civil war, in which he hinted heavily that the Communists would likely emerge victorious.

Dulles prided himself on having a pretty good poker face, and it had taken all of his skill to remain noncommittal with the German, limiting himself to pointing out some of the obvious flaws in the German position, but otherwise only promising to pass the proposal along to his superiors. He had sensed a certain desperation in Oster, a need to get something moving, but against a very tight deadline. Dulles knew that they were all at a dangerous crossroads right now. If the Allies wanted, they could almost certainly obtain a very favorable peace settlement with the Germans by freezing out the Russians, but Stalin, as paranoid as he was reputed to be, would undoubtedly see that as a betrayal by the West, and feelings in Russia against Germany were justifiably fervent enough that the price of an easy peace now would be another war in the near future. And this time the enemy bent on revenge wouldn't be a crushed and partitioned enemy, as Germany had been after World War I, but an immensely powerful, victorious nation, just really coming into its own and with a worldwide network of ideological converts at its beck and call. Both Churchill and Roosevelt had made it clear that any agreement with Germany had to be arrived at by all the major allies, including the Soviet Union and now France, or there would be none at all. It might make things difficult in the short run, but Dulles recognized that this was the only viable solution.

0500 HOURS, 1 AUGUST 1943
WARSAW, POLAND

At only twenty-four years of age, Mordechai Anielewicz was rather young to command what amounted to a brigade-size force, the entire combat strength of the ZOB in the ghetto, and he had no military experience; but he did know the streets and alleys of Warsaw better than the rooms of his parents' apartment from before the war. He may not have been in the army, but he had been fighting all his young life, one way or another, though he had never felt the rush of emotion he did now.

For two years he had watched in rage and frustration as trainload after trainload of Jews had been shipped out of Warsaw, stripped of their possessions and every scrap of human dignity, never to return. His decision in January, taken with other young Jews, to fight rather than submit had just been their way of dying with dignity, not in any hope of actually succeeding. But now things had changed. During the night hundreds of Allied bombers had droned over Poland dropping thousands of canisters filled with rifles, Sten guns, grenades, mortars, and ammunition. While most of this bounty had gone to the Home Army units scattered in a corridor from Warsaw north toward the coast, in anticipation of the delivery, the Home Army had transferred to the ZOB nearly 500 captured German Mauser rifles, with which his fighters were already familiar, along with some machine guns, panzerfaust anti-tank rockets, and plenty of ammunition for all, every gun and every bullet of which was dragged through sewers or over unguarded stretches of the ghetto wall by teams of experienced "smugglers," some of whom were barely ten years old. This more than trebled the firepower with which he had expected to face down the more than 2,000 SS troops known to be encircling the ghetto and preparing their assault.

Even more important, the Home Army would be launching an attack of their own throughout the capital and all across Poland while the attention of the Germans was focused on the Jewish ghettos. Some of Anielewicz's subordinates had howled that the Poles would betray them and that the Allies would never come, mostly diehard Communists, but the very real evidence of the arms deliveries had quieted their protest almost immediately.

He could hear the growl of truck engines and the high pitched squeal of tank treads as the German forces moved into position for what they hoped would be a surprise assault on a largely defenseless people. The attacking units were actually mostly composed of Ukrainian and Lithuanian fascists in SS uniform, very brutal and quite adequate for bludgeoning unarmed men and women in the streets, but not exactly elite combat troops.

The ghetto was an irregular sector of northwest Warsaw some fifteen blocks from north to south and from three to five longer blocks east to west. The southern third of this area, known as the "small ghetto," was nearly cut off by a corridor of German occupied land, and so was left out of Anielewicz's defense strategy, which would concentrate on the "productive ghetto," where the factories were located manufacturing goods for the Wehrmacht; the "wild ghetto," a now largely uninhabited stretch slightly to the north around Powiok Prison; and the "central ghetto" north of that, since this was where most of the ghetto's remaining tenants lived. From the sounds of mobilization beyond the wall, and reports coming to Anielewicz over a field phone line laid by the Poles from the Aryan side, it seemed that the Germans, under the command of SS General Jurgen Stroop, planned to carve off sections of the ghetto and annihilate resistance in each before moving on. They were now poised at the southern end of Nalewki Boulevard to drive north to Muranewski Square, thus slicing away four blocks of the old "brushmakers' district," but the Jews were ready for them.

In the pale predawn light, from each end of Nalewki Boulevard, a squad of Jewish policemen now appeared, nervously filing past the barricades and into the ghetto, but the defenders could see the shadowy forms of German infantry dodging from cover to cover along either side of the street behind them. One part of Anielewicz felt sorry for these traitors, whose families were held hostage and who cooperated with the Germans in their searches for "selected" Jews for shipment to Treblinka under the threat of being sent themselves in the place of any shortfall. There were others who risked their lives by working with the ZOB, passing information about planned sweeps or even stealing weapons for the resistance. But there were some who seemed to relish their power and authority, and there was, in any event, no means of separating one from the other now. When they had advanced about one hundred meters, the first armored cars appeared rolling quickly forward, two with each column, and each followed by a densely packed mob of infantrymen. This was the moment they had been waiting for.

Anielewicz nodded to a young red-haired fighter hunching next to him in the second floor apartment he was using as his command post at the corner of Nalewki and Gensia, and the man shouldered his MG42 machine gun, letting a long burst rip into the advancing Germans. This was answered by a virtual storm of fire from both sides of the street and a hail of grenades, German potato mashers, and homemade Molotov cocktails that burst all around the armored cars, turning them both into bonfires. A few of the Germans, most actually shouting in Ukrainian, returned fire until they were cut down, but most turned and fled, despite the lashes of the leather whips carried by their SS sergeants. Over the roar of battle, Anielewicz could hear the sweetest words he had ever heard uttered in German, *"Juden haben Waffen!"* You bet your ass, Anielewicz thought grimly, the Jews *do* have weapons! A German ambulance attempted to drive up to recover the wounded, but it too was met with a murderous fire, since the young men and women who had seen their parents and younger siblings dragged off to death no longer subscribed to the chivalrous rules of war.

As the firing died down, dozens of dark forms crept out from the basements of the houses along the street, quietly knifing the wounded, and stripping all of weapons and ammunition. Anielewicz was told later that a mortally wounded Jewish policeman had been heard thanking God that he had lived long enough to be killed by a bullet fired from a Jewish rifle.

The Germans had been expecting some kind of resistance after the violence of January—perhaps pistols, knives, and pipe bombs—but they had obviously not been expecting anything on this scale. Now they pulled back both of their columns, and there was a long pause as reinforcements were brought up. Fortunately, the defenders knew that the Germans had very little armor in and around Warsaw, as most of it had been sucked into the offensive at Kursk and the subsequent withdrawals. But now came the sound that Anielewicz had been expecting, something like a freight train rattling by overhead followed by a dull crash as an artillery shell hit somewhere within the ghetto. The Germans would have no compunction about smashing the entire ghetto with high explosives, since there was nothing in it they needed and the only residents were men and women they wanted dead in any event. Besides, any "overs" would just land in some other part of Warsaw, and Poles stood very little higher on the German scale of humanity than Jews.

The first shot was followed by another, and another, and the redhead with his machine gun looked toward Anielewicz, raising one eyebrow. Then the explosions stopped, and the sound was replaced by the muffled, staccato tapping of small arms fire and the crump of grenades. It was the Poles! The Home Army had promised to wait until German attention was focused on the ghetto and then hit the German support units throughout the city, including their artillery. Anielewicz smiled and raised the telephone receiver.

"Cross over Jordan," he said into the mouthpiece and hung up.

He listened carefully and could distinctly pick out the thud of new explosions as gaps were blown in the wall at several points around the ghetto
perimeter, permitting teams of Jewish fighters to move out into the city to
link up with the Home Army and take the battle to the Germans.

0500 HOURS, 2 AUGUST 1943
CHLEMNO, POLAND

At least he was out of France. *And* he had just made his first combat jump in
the war, just as he had been trained to do. But never satisfied, Bentley could
not help thinking that he would have liked to have jumped just a few miles
behind enemy lines like the boys from the 101st and the British 6th Airborne,
not nearly two hundred miles from the coast where Allied troops would hopefully be landing in a couple of hours, *if* they survived the trip by sea, weaving
between islands controlled by the Germans, and a good eighty miles even
from the main center of the Polish rising in Warsaw. He supposed that he
would have to wait for the next war to get to do things by the book, just once.

Word had come down that someone had talked very convincingly to
President Roosevelt and Vice President Truman about the need to support
the rising in central Poland to prevent the Germans from annihilating the
freedom fighters before the main forces from the landings on the Baltic coast
could come to the rescue. That had seemed logical enough, so General Marshall and the other Allied planners had diverted some of their precious C-
47s to drop the Polish airborne brigade near the capital, apart from the main
drop by the British and Americans. But then, one of these Washington lob-
byists had also provided considerable detail about a story that, even now,
Bentley had trouble believing in its full scope. Rumors had been coming out
of the Reich for some time of Hitler's campaign to destroy the Jews, which he
had said all along that he would do, but everyone had more or less assumed
that this meant treating them just a little worse than the other people he had
enslaved, which was bad enough. Now, however, they were talking about
some kind of "death factories," concentration camps designed, not just for in-
carceration and slave labor, but the actual, mechanical destruction of people,
like the big slaughterhouses around Chicago, but with trainloads of people
being fed into them instead of cattle or hogs.

Consequently it was decided that, if such camps existed, and there was a
growing body of evidence that they did, the Germans would crank them up

to maximum "production" as the Allied armies closed in. If this were the case, it behooved the Allies to do everything in their power to throw a monkey wrench into the German plans and to save as many innocent people as possible. Bentley, and the men of the 505th Airborne Regiment, which he now commanded, along with his old 509th Airborne Battalion, were to be that monkey wrench. He could not argue with the concept, it just seemed to him that the tool they had chosen was rather small for the job.

The problem was the lack of air transport. The Allies were already dropping two full divisions closer to the coast, plus the Polish brigade at Warsaw, and the flight from forward airfields in Belgium and France was already near the limits of the C-47's endurance, especially since they were taking a long dog leg to the north over German territory occupied by the Allies in order to avoid the flak. Presumably, those C-47s that survived the flight would be turned around and, tomorrow night, would bring in the rest of the 82nd Airborne to support Bentley, as well as a French airborne regiment to support the Poles in Warsaw, assuming that there was anyone left alive to support.

The camp at Chelmno had been chosen by the planners because the other three "death camps," as they were called, were well east of Warsaw, even farther from the Allied bases and relatively close to the advancing Russian lines, whereas Chelmno was almost due west of the capital. The plan was quite simple. Bentley's men, supported by Polish partisans, would overcome the camp guards and secure a perimeter, then just try to keep the inmates alive until reinforced by air the next night and then relieved by the ground offensive in three or four days.

The problem Bentley saw immediately when studying a large-scale map of central Poland was that it was a damn long way from either Warsaw or the beaches, and he suspected that the planners were being unduly optimistic about how fast German resistance would crumble. Furthermore, Chelmno had apparently been selected as a site for this "death camp" precisely because it was handy to a number of major rail lines running in from Germany and other points in Poland, so the Germans would have little trouble bringing in their own reinforcements. Of course, as had become the pattern for the war in the West, the Allied air forces would be prowling almost at will, making any movement for German forces a hell on earth. But, again, they would be operating at extreme range here, and most of the terribly efficient fighter bombers could not reach targets in Poland, only the heavy Fortresses and Wellingtons, which were much less effective in hitting tactical troop movements.

But there was no point in worrying about that now. The landings had gone off reasonably well. The weather had held, and very few aircraft had been lost or forced to turn back on the run in. Neither had there been an appreciable German presence in the drop area, apart from scattered patrols that had been dealt with by the Polish partisans. However, Bentley began to appreciate just how fortunate he was never to have had to conduct an airborne assault into a well-defended enemy position since, nearly two hours after the drop, he had only been able to collect about one company's worth of paratroopers, and those from no less than three battalions of the 505th as well as a few men from the 509th. Time was of the essence, however, and Bentley soon had his meager force moving out in a skirmish line over the rolling hills in the direction of the Chelmno camp.

As the sky grew brighter and the march progressed, Bentley began to notice a distinct odor in the air, a sickly sweet smell that he at first attributed to his imagination, but then he saw others of his men wrinkling their noses and looking around dubiously. When he asked one of his Polish guides, through an interpreter provided by the OSS, what the smell was, the man just frowned and pointed over the next ridge.

From the crest, the camp appeared through Bentley's field glasses much as it had in the aerial photographs he had studied, with rows of drab barracks-like sheds and several large buildings with tall smokestacks, all surrounded by double barbed wire fences with tall watch towers spaced around the perimeter. In the photographs the chimneys had been spewing thick, gray smoke, but now they stood inert, and there seemed to be no activity in the open areas of the camp. Only a large pile of yellowish lumber in one corner of a camp yard had not been present in the photos, and Bentley ordered his men, now grown to a battalion, to rush the nearest gate.

The gates stood open, and bursts of fire from the paratroopers brought no response from the towers. Bentley trotted into the camp just behind the lead squads, and he could hear men calling out in German, Polish, and Yiddish to anyone present to come out with their hands up. He watched as one squad deployed around the closed door of one of the sheds, and a tall trooper kicked it in with one blow, diving into the room followed by his comrades. There was no shooting, but the Americans suddenly reappeared, backing out the door with looks of horror on their faces, and one man doubled over, retching in the dust.

The Americans were followed by a ghost-like figure in striped pajamas, who shuffled to the door, blinking in the light, his dark eyes bulging out of a skull covered with almost translucent skin, tight against the bone. One of the OSS men, a Yiddish speaker, walked forward and talked to the man in a low voice for several minutes before a look of comprehension came over the dazed face, and the man pointed vaguely off to the West. Then the inmate took the American's face in both his gnarled hands and began to pat his shoulders and arms until he found the American flag shoulder patch. The man touched the patch and brought his fingers to his lips and kissed them before collapsing in the soldier's arms.

"The guards all went away this morning," the OSS man told Bentley as tears streamed down his own face.

Bentley strode past them and peered through the doorway. Inside were rows of bunks, more like shelves, six or eight high, barely a foot apart, and from each shelf peered out several shaved heads with huge, dark eyes, indistinguishable from that of the man outside. He stared at them wordlessly for a moment, when someone tapped him on the shoulder.

"Sir, I think you'd better see this," a captain from the 509th said softly, pulling him by the arm.

Bentley followed at a trot down one row of sheds and around the comer. There he stopped cold.

Knots of paratroopers stood gawking at the pile of lumber Bentley had seen from the ridge. It was as tall as the sheds and nearly fifty feet long, but it wasn't lumber.

"I guess the incinerators got backed up," the captain said in a flat tone.

Bentley had heard the expression "bodies stacked like cordwood," but he had never imagined such a sight. One row of skeletal corpses had its feet pointed toward him, the next was heads, then feet again, all very orderly. There was no way to tell whether they were men or women, and the children were only identifiable by their size, all looking as old and worn as the oldest grandfather. He now realized what the white dust was that covered the ground, the grass, everything for the past kilometer or more, and now his own uniform, and he felt his stomach lurch. Half the men in the yard were now vomiting copiously, and it took Bentley a moment before he could even focus his vision.

"To think that human beings actually did this," the captain growled.

"Get the interpreters together and have them go from hut to hut," Bentley hissed as he wiped his mouth. "Have them announce that the Americans are here, and that no one will harm them again. Then get all the medics together to start looking at these people and doing what they can. Every man has five days' K-rations in his pack. I want three of those deposited with the XO and make a search of the guards' quarters for more food, but have it distributed very carefully. A full meal will probably kill these poor souls off faster than a bullet."

The captain saluted and jogged off. Bentley took a pull of water from his canteen and spat it out, but the bitter taste remained. He no longer had any doubts about the need for this mission.

1400 HOURS, 2 AUGUST 1943
USTKA, POLAND

Colonel Leon Mitkiewicz strode up the broad, pebbly beach a few yards, then knelt to cross himself and to kiss the soil of Poland. Up and down the strand thousands of other Polish soldiers had done or were doing the same as they poured out of the landing craft and rushed inland. Four years of exile was a long time.

There had been very little trouble on the voyage in from France. Twice U-boats had attacked, but only one transport had been hit and the Polish destroyer *Burza* had sunk one of the attackers. From about 0200 hours that morning on, the American battleship *Texas* and the British *Nelson*, and the cruisers *Tuscaloosa*, *Quincy*, and *Frobisher*, and a swarm of destroyers had pounded the shore and every suspected enemy position within fifteen miles of the beach with guns from five inches up to sixteen. Then LCTs crammed with row upon row of rockets had added their banshee howl to the din. When the first wave had finally hit the beach shortly before sunrise, not a shot had been fired against them.

Now, leading mechanized elements had raced over twenty miles inland and linked up with the American and British airborne, and the beachhead was secure with a width of over thirty miles and spearheads driving on the town of Bytów on the highway toward Warsaw. Several thousand dazed Germans had been rounded up as prisoners, and the roads were littered with the burned out hulks of trucks and tanks that had been caught in the open by Allied planes flying off the American aircraft carrier *Ranger* and several of their "jeep" escort carriers. The plan now was for two Polish infantry divisions, the 3rd and 4th, to dig in along parallel lines on each flank of the beachhead. The American and British airborne divisions would extend those lines farther inland, and the 1st Polish Armored Division, the 2nd Armored Brigade, and the 7th Light Infantry Division would drive down this corridor toward Warsaw.

Obviously the flanking infantry divisions could only cover, perhaps, thirty or forty miles, and thinly held at that, beyond which the mechanized forces would be flying solo for some one hundred fifty miles, dropping off occasional units to garrison key crossroads. But achieving speed was worth the risk, and a measure of flank security could still be provided by airstrikes by Allied bombers and the bands of Polish partisans who infested the entire sector. Of these last, thousands had already turned up at the beachhead to receive weapons brought ashore for the purpose. Somewhere around Wloclawek, about two thirds of the way to Warsaw, the 2nd Armored Brigade would veer to the southwest to relieve the American paratroopers at Chelmno.

Mitkiewicz was proud to be taking part in this glorious battle for his nation's honor and survival, and he had pulled every string within reach to be released from the staff position he had held in London as liaison to the OSS and British intelligence to take up command of a battalion in the 2nd Armored. He retained the fatalistic sense, however, that it was useless to worry about what they would be doing a week from now, a hundred and fifty miles away. The bulk of the German Army was still just to the east, fighting for its life against the Russians, and the German homeland was just to the west, still probably filled with reserves ready to be thrust into the battle, and now the Poles were stuck in the middle, the position they had been fated to by history. It was reassuring to have some Allied troops with them this time, on Polish soil, but Mitkiewicz was still certain that they would all be consumed by the fires of this terrible war. And he thanked God for the chance to play his part in it. Poland loves its dead heroes best of all.

1700 Hours, 4 August 1943
Warsaw, Poland

General Bor-Komorowsky rubbed the stubble on his chin as he stood in the control tower of the Piastowa airfield southwest of Warsaw. The wrecks of a few Luftwaffe planes had been shoved onto the grass verge away from the runway, and now American transports were landing and taking off every few minutes, disgorging piles of supplies or files of troops, and a full squadron of

Spitfires, piloted by Poles, was now stationed at the field. He had to shake his head in disbelief.

The first twenty-four hours of the battle had been desperate, with the SS troops of the city garrison fighting to the death as they were assailed from front and rear. That had been expected. But other than small security detachments that drifted into the fighting from the immediate vicinity, no major German reinforcements had arrived, either from east or west. Naturally, he had hoped that Allied airpower and the attacks by the Home Army guerrilla units would slow them up, but he had never expected them simply not to appear.

But that was exactly what was happening. Intelligence reports from Home Army units in eastern Poland indicated that the old regular Wehrmacht units, especially the armor, were slipping away from the front and racing westward, some of them shooting the gap between Warsaw and the Allied troops advancing to the south from the coast, but most swerving south of the capital, where the attentions of Allied bombers was less and the rail lines in better condition, but all of them heading for Germany, save for those troops now trapped in East Prussia. Their infantry was following as best it could. Only the SS units had been abandoned in the front lines, and the frantic radio transmissions, many of them now in the clear, revealed that the surrounded SS men had simply been left to the tender mercies of the Russians by their colleagues, who probably knew that the SS had no option to surrender to them.

Now, the French paratroopers had arrived safely, and Bor-Komorowsky, who had retained command of what was now referred to as the Army of Warsaw, had nearly one hundred thousand men, not too well armed but certainly determined, in and around the city, counting French, American, and Polish paras, the Jewish ZOB fighters, and his own Home Army men. Another quarter of a million Poles were under arms in central and northern Poland, and half that many more in the well-equipped corps under General Anders pushing in from the coast. In the east, the Russians had taken Brest and Bialystok, and in the west, Patton had taken Rostock and his forces were approaching Neubrandenburg, almost due north of Berlin itself Even the American enclave at Chelmno had been reinforced with the bulk of an airborne division and ten thousand Polish partisans. The war would soon be over.

1800 HOURS, 7 AUGUST 1943
NEUBRANDENBURG, GERMANY

Patton was not normally a nervous type, but now he was pacing back and forth in front of the portico of the ornately decorated town hall as a thin rain fell. The other officers present huddled in small groups, mostly by nationality, or stood alone, smoking, lost in their own thoughts. There had been a flurry of radio and telephone messages flying back and forth from Patton's headquarters to SHAEF headquarters in Paris and thence to London, Washington, and Moscow since late the night before when a German general had been brought in under a flag of truce to announce calmly that a delegation would arrive this evening from OKH in Berlin to negotiate a full armistice for all German armed forces. There had been a lot of hemming and hawing from the professional diplomats and politicians about whether anything could be done without a full political settlement in place, but the Germans had broadcast their intentions via shortwave, and this had been picked up by sets all around the world. Roosevelt, Churchill, and de Gaulle had immediately realized that they would face the unbridled fury of their own people if it became known that they had allowed the fighting to go on for one more day when the Germans had offered to lay down their arms.

Consequently, very few of those officers present, despite the weight of gold braid and medals they wore, had gotten much sleep in the past twenty-four hours as they flew in from all points of the compass. Marshall and Juin had arrived in short order from Paris, as had Montgomery from the southern front, along with Colonel General I.S. Koniev, commander of the Soviet Steppe Front. An invitation to the Italians had been considered, but Churchill had suggested that the presence for Germany's former allies might unnecessarily create additional tension at the meeting. The Poles were represented, at Churchill's insistence, by General Sosnkowski, and there were token delegations from the Dutch, Belgians, Greeks, and Yugoslavs as well. Only the Russians had chosen to send a civilian envoy, Foreign Minister V.M. Molotov, to oversee Koniev's behavior, although the Western Allies were insistent that only military officers actually participate in the talks at this point.

It was still quite light, despite the overcast, when a column of American military policemen riding motorcycles and jeeps rolled into the small square lined with armed troops, just in case the entire episode were some elaborate plot to decapitate the Allied commands. But only three officers disembarked from the German staff car at the center of the procession, two colonels and Field Marshal Erwin Rommel.

Rommel marched somewhat stiffly to the foot of the steps where Patton awaited, and executed a salute which Patton returned smartly. Both men recognized the other and opened their mouths as if to say something, but neither could apparently find the words. Patton turned to introduce Rommel to the other officers present.

What followed over the next two hours was something of an anti-climax. The Germans simply offered a cease-fire to begin at 0600 hours the next morning. German units would hold their positions and surrender their weapons to the first Allied unit to request them. They made no demands other than that their men be treated as prisoners of war.

The Russians had spluttered about demanding an occupation zone in Germany, since their troops would not be able to reach German soil, except for East Prussia, before the Western Allies had occupied the rest of the country. They also insisted that all Soviet citizens found wearing German uniforms, and there were hundreds of thousands of Balts, Ukrainians, and Russians in General Vlasov's renegade anti-Communist army and in various SS units, be repatriated immediately to the Soviet Union. Marshall pointed out that, since the Russians would occupy East Prussia, that should be their zone for the moment and that, on his own authority, he would gladly accept Russian troops to mount guard in Berlin, but that agreements on all other subjects could await a fuller meeting of their respective civilian chiefs in the near future. And it was over.

CHAPTER 11

CURTAIN

1200 Hours, 28 September 1943
Potsdam, Germany

N THE WEEKS that followed the armistice, the shape of the post-war world rapidly congealed. The German armies still beyond the frontiers raced back home as fast as they could go or dropped their weapons at the first sight of an Allied unit. Dönitz and the government had hit upon the unique formula of surrendering the army and specifically *not* making any political agreement with the victors. It thus remained to the Western Allies, or at least to the British and Americans, to act as representatives of German interests in the hope of reintegrating Germany into the family of nations, while freeing the government of the opprobrium of agreeing to a humiliating peace as had occurred after the First World War. Russian troops rushed westward and occupied Hungary, Slovakia, East Prussia, and Poland to the east of the Curzon Line. The Italians and British occupied Austria, southern Bavaria and the Czech Republic, which declared its separation from Slovakia under President Benes, and the French occupied northern Bavaria, with the Americans taking everything north of Frankfurt. A four-nation commission was set up to administer Berlin among the primary Allies.

The conference held at Potsdam in September 1943 was a stormy affair in light of the Communist regimes that were being set up in Romania, Bulgaria, Hungary, and Slovakia, but Churchill and a still relatively healthy Roosevelt were able to stave off Stalin's demands for further advances in Central Europe. While the governments of Western Europe had been concerned about the possible influence their local Communist parties might have fol-

lowing the armistice, it resulted that the rapid end of the war and the domi-
nant role of the Western Allies in liberating the region had deprived the Left
of some of the popularity it had gained during late 1941 and 1942 when only
the Soviet Union seemed to be actively resisting the Nazis, and these parties
soon dropped down into the single digits in terms of voter support.

The map of Europe was significantly redrawn at the conference, with
Poland being bodily dragged westward to the Oder-Neisse line and Germany
losing all of East Prussia to both Poland and the Soviet Union. Except for
minor nibbling at the borders, Finland was left in a neutral status, and Stalin's
other territorial gains were recognized. One major surprise was the old-line
Communist Tito, frightened by Soviet encroachments in the Balkans and
encouraged by generous Western financial support, who declared himself to
be much more of a socialist in nature and who held remarkably free elections,
resulting in an overwhelming victory for himself as president. Tito's conciliatory policies toward the various ethnic groups in the patchwork nation
quickly bound up the country's wounds and set it on the road to economic
and political recovery.

Talk soon shifted to plans for dealing with the one remaining Axis partner, Japan. Soviet troops were already being diverted to the Far East for an
offensive into Manchuria, and Roosevelt finally derailed General MacArthur's
plans for the liberation of the Philippines as a useless sideshow, focusing all
of America's immense resources on a drive across the Central Pacific toward
the Japanese home islands. As is well known, the rapid collapse of Germany
and the Soviet invasion of Manchuria, coupled with American advances to
Guam, Okinawa, and Iwo Jima in late 1943 and early 1944, thoroughly dis-
heartened the Japanese high command and government, already staggering
under the intense bombing campaign and the destruction of the Japanese merchant fleet by American submarines. Then, on the eve of the planned American invasion of Kyushu, timed to coincide with the Russian conquest of
southern Sakhalin Island and the destruction of the Japanese army in Manchuria, a palace coup in Tokyo resulted in a peace offer not unlike that given
by the Germans, with no preconditions required other than the continuation
of the Emperor as titular head of the nation. Thus the Second World War
ended.

As a footnote, it has often been speculated whether the Americans would
have dropped the atomic bomb on which they had been frantically working
at the time of the Japanese surrender. The most credible version is that some

kind of demonstration would have been arranged to convince the Japanese of their utter defenselessness in the face of this new weapon, but the contrary argument is that the dropping of one, or even two atomic weapons would not have been more horrific than the fire bombing already taking place on a regular basis of Japanese cities and that this would not have affected the decision-making process in Tokyo one way or the other. Since the bomb, which was only finally developed in 1949 after funding was decreased, has never been used in combat, we may hopefully never find out.

After the initial euphoria of the Allied victory wore off, and this was not long in coming, inevitable tensions arose between East and West, due to the incompatibility of the two political systems, but several factors served to minimize this effect. First of all, while the Western powers were displeased with the puppet regimes set up by the Soviets in Eastern Europe, the fact that these nations had all been active allies of the Germans in the invasion of the USSR, a certain amount of leeway was allowed. Secondly, with an extensive buffer zone established both by the Soviet Union's own extension westward and the creation of a number of viable and violently anti-German states across the width of Europe, even Stalin could rest easier and thus decreased the size of his own army almost on the same scale as did the British, French, and Americans. The victory of the Chinese Communists over Chiang Kai Shek in their civil war in 1947 reinforced this sense of security in Moscow without needlessly adding to the apprehensions of the West. Lastly, with security issues on the margin, attention could be focused on the economic recovery of the continent and the institution of the plan that bears Eisenhower's name, one in which America's vast wealth could be shared with all of the belligerents, including the former enemy. While the Soviet Union's participation was grudging at first, the rapid recovery of Germany and Poland in particular made a parallel effort on Russia's part a necessity.

The war crimes trials at Nuremberg were a traumatic experience for Germany, but a cathartic one as well. Hitler and Himmler were already gone, and a number of other prominent architects of the hellish Nazi world vision had cheated the victors by committing suicide before the armistice; but enough leaders remained, headed by Kaltenbrunner and a host of lesser Nazi officials to at least slake the thirst for vengeance of the victims of the terror. With no imminent threat to the West now being posed by the Soviet Union, Germany was disarmed and left with a simple force of gendarmes while token Allied forces continued the occupation for some years. It has been argued that one reason for the near-miraculous economic recovery of Germany, despite substantial reparations payments, was the advantage of not having to sustain a defense budget.

In short, the Allies, both East and West, had managed to construct a peace that did honor to the victory of their armies on the battlefield rather than merely to create a new scenario for world conflict.

SELECT BIBLIOGRAPHY

Ambrose, Stephen E., *Citizen Soldiers: The U.S. Army from the Normandy Beaches to the Bulge to the Surrender of Germany*, New York: Simon & Schuster, 1997.
——-. *D-Day: June 6, 1944*. New York: Simon & Schuster, 1994.
Amouroux, Henri, *La Grande Histoire des Français sous I 'Occupation: Les Passions et les Haines*, Paris: Robert Laffont, 1981.
Aron, Robert, *Histoire de Ia Liberation de Ia France, Juin 1944–Mai 1945*, Paris: Marabout Universite, 1959.
Auphan, Amiral and Mordal, Jacques, *La Marine Française dans Ia Seconde Guerre Mondiale*, Paris: Editions France-empire, 1976.
Barnett, Correlli, *Engage the Enemy More Closely: The Royal Navy in the Second World War*, New York: W.W. Norton & Co., 1991.
——-ed., *Hitler's Generals*, New York: William Morrow, 1989.
Bergamini, David, *Japan's Imperial Conspiracy*, New York: William Morrow, 1971.
Bialer, Seweryn, ed., *Stalin and his Generals: Soviet Military Memoirs of World War II*, New York: Pegasus, 1969.
Bland, Larry I., ed., *The Papers of George Catlett Marshall*, vol. 2–3, Baltimore: Johns Hopkins University Press, 1986.
Blumenson, Martin, *Patton: The Man Behind the Legend*, New York: William Morrow, 1985.
Berries, Vance von, "Breakthrough to the Coast: The U.S. II Corps in the Battle of el Guettar and Maknassy," *Command Magazine*, no. 112, June, 1987.
Bourderon, Roger and Willard, Germaine, *La France dans la Tourmente*, Paris: Editions Sociales, 1980.
Breuer, William B., *Geronimo! American Paratroopers in World War II*, New York: St. Martin's Press, 1989
——-, *Operation Dragoon: The Allied Invasion of the South of France*, Novato: Presidio Press, 1987.
Bullock, Alan. *Hitler and Stalin: Parallel Lives*. New York: Alfred A Knopf, 1992.
Bykofsky, Joseph and Larson, Harold, *United States Army in World War II: The Technical Services, The Transportation Corps: Operations Overseas*, Washington,

D.C., Office of the Chief of Military History, Department of the Army, 1957.

Carell, Paul, *Hitler Moves East 1941–1943,* New York: Bantam Books, 1965.

———-, *Scorched Earth,* New York: Bantam Books, 1965.

Churchill, Winston S., *The Hinge of Fate,* Boston: Houghton Mifflin Company, 1950.

———, *Closing the Ring,* Boston, Houghton Mifflin Company, 1950.

Craven, Wesley Frank and Cate, James Lea, eds., *The Army Air Forces in World War II: Services Around the World,* vol. 7, Chicago: University of Chicago Press, 1958.

Cummins, Christopher, "Pas de Calais: Historical Alternatives 1943 vs. 1944, Calais vs. Normandy," *Command Magazine,* no. 6, May–June 1988.

DeGaulle, Charles, *The Complete War Memoirs,* New York: Da Capo, 1967.

D'Este, Carlo, *Bitter Victory: The Battle for Sicily 1943.* New York: E.P. Dutton, 1988.

———-, *Fatal Decision: Anzio and the Battle for Rome,* New York: Harper-Collins, Publishers, 1988.

Eisenhower, David, *Eisenhower: At War 1943–1945,* New York: Vintage Books, 1987. Eisenhower, Dwight D., *Crusade in Europe,* New York: Doubleday & Co., 1948.

Erickson, John, *The Road to Stalingrad,* London: Panther Books, 1975.

———, *The Road to Berlin,* London: Panther Books, 1975.

Farago, Ladislas, *The Game of Foxes,* New York: David McKay Company, Inc., 1971.

Greenfield, Kent Roberts, ed., *The United States Army in World War I: European Theater of Operations, Logistical Support of the Armies,* 2 vols., Washington, D.C.: Office of the Chief of Military History, 1953.

—-, *United States Army in World War II: Pictorial Record, The War Against Germany: Europe and Adjacent Areas,* Washington: Office of the Chief of Military History, 1951.

Harries, Meirion and Susie, *Soldiers of the Sun: The Rise and Fall of the Imperial Japanese Army,* New York: Random House, 1991.

Higgins, Trumbull, *Soft Underbelly: The Anglo-American Controversy over the Italian Campaign 1939–1945.* London: The Macmillan Company, 1968.

Howe, George F., *United States Army in World War II: The Mediterranean Theater of Operations, Northwest Africa: Seizing the Initiative in the West,* Washington, D.C.: Office of the Chief of Military History, 1957.

Huston, James A., *Out of the Blue: US. Army Airborne Operations in World War II,* West Lafayette: Purdue University Studies, 1972.

Irving, David, *The Trail of the Fox,* New York: Avon Books, 1977.

Jane's, *Fighting Ships of World War II* New York: Crescent Books, 1996.

Kurzman, Dan. *The Bravest Battle: The Twenty-eight Days of the Warsaw Ghetto Uprising.* New York: G.P. Putnam's Sons, 1976.

Lacouture, Jean, *De Gaulle: Le Rebelle,* Paris: Editions du Seuil, 1984.

Leighton, Richard M., *United States Army in World War II The War Department: Global Logistics and Strategy 1940–1943,* Washington, D. C., Office of the Chief of Military History, Department of the Army, 1955.

Lottman, Herbert R, *Petain,* Paris: Editions du Seuil, 1984.

McMullocgh, David. *Truman.* New York: Simon & Schuster, 1992.

Macksey, Kenneth, *Tank versus Tank,* New York: Crescent Books, 1991.

Mayer, Arno J. *Why Did the Heavens Not Darken? The "Final Solution" in History.* New York: Pantheon Books, 1988.

Miller, Merle, *Ike the Soldier: As They Knew Him,* New York: Putnam Publishing Group, 1987.

Morison, Samuel Eliot, *History of United States Naval Operations in World War II: Operations in North African Waters,* Boston: Little, Brown & Co., 1947.

———-, *History of United States Naval Operations in World War II: The Liberation of France,* Boston: Little, Brown & Co., 1947.

———-, *History of the United States Naval Operations in World War II: Sicily- Salerno Anzio,* Boston: Little, Brown & Co., 1954.

Mosley, Leonard, *Marshall: Hero for Our Times,* New York: Harvest Books, 1982.

Nofi, Albert A., "Sicily: The Race to Messina 10 July–17 August 1943," *Strategy & Tactics Magazine,* June 1985.

Payne, Robert, *The Marhsall Story: A Biography of General George C. Marshall,* New York: Prentice-Hall, Inc., 1951.

Pogue, Forrest C., *The United States Anny in World War II: European Theater of Operations, The Supreme Command,* Washington, D.C.: Office of the Chief of Military History, 1954.

———-, *George C. Marshall: Ordeal and Hope,* New York: The Viking Press, 1965.

Robertson, Terence, *Dieppe: The Shame and the Glory,* London: Hutchinson & Co., 1963.

Robichon, Jacques, *Jour J en Afrique,* Paris: Robert Laffont, 1964.

Schoenbrun, David, *Soldiers of the Night: The Story of the French Resistance,* New York: E.P. Dutton, 1980.

Sereau, Raymond, *L'Armee de l'Armistice,* Paris: Nouvelles Editions Latines, 1961.

Spector, Ronald H., *Eagle Against the Sun: The American War with Japan,* New York: The Free Press, 1985.

Tompkins, Peter, *The Murder of Admiral Dar/an,* New York: Simon and Schuster, 1965.

Vigneras, Marcel, *United States Army in World War II: Special Studies, Rearming the French,* Washington, D.C.: Office of the Chief of Military History, Department of the Army, 1957.

Walters, Vernon, *Secret Missions,* New York: Doubleday & Company, 1978.

Warner, Geoffrey, *Iraq and Syria 1941*, Newark: University of Delaware Press, 1974.

Weigley, Russel F., *Eisenhower's Lieutenants: The Campaigns of France and Germany, 1944–1945*, Bloomington: Indiana University Press, 1981.

In addition to the preceding books, the author has also made extensive use of a number of war games in order to test his hypotheses on the probable course of events following a given strategic decision and also as a rich source of order of battle information. The following are those most frequently consulted.

Astell, John, *Torch: Europa XI*, Game Designers' Workshop, 1985.

——-, *Second Front: Europa XII*, Game Research/Design, 1994.

Astell, John and Chadwick, Alan, *Western Desert: Europa VI*, Game Designers' Workshop, 1983.

Berg, Richard, "The Trail of the Fox," *Strategy & Tactics Magazine*, no. 97, July–August 1984.

Cochran, Laurel, "Anvil-Dragoon: Southwall 1944," *Wargamer Magazine*, no. 60, December 1986.

Simulations Publications, Inc., *War in the East/War in the West*, New York: 1976.